QUESTING FOR A DREAM

QUESTING FOR A DREAM

P.D. WORKMAN

ISBN: 9781989080092 (IS Hardcover)

ISBN: 9781989080085 (IS Paperback)

ISBN: 9781989080078 (KDP Paperback)

ISBN: 9781926500539 (Kindle)

ISBN: 9781926500553 (ePub)

pdworkman

ALSO BY P.D. WORKMAN

YOUNG ADULT FICTION:

Tamara's Teardrops:

Tattooed Teardrops

Two Teardrops

Tortured Teardrops

Vanishing Teardrops

Between the Cracks:

Ruby

June and Justin

Michelle

Chloe

Ronnie

June, Into the Light

Medical Kidnap Files:

Mito

EDS

Proxy

Toxo

Pain

Breaking the Pattern:

Deviation

Diversion

By-Pass

Stand Alone YA novels

Stand Alone

Don't Forget Steven

Those Who Believe

Cynthia has a Secret

Questing for a Dream

Darkness before the Dream (prequel story)

Intersexion

Making Her Mark

Endless Change

Gem, Himself, Alone

MYSTERY/SUSPENSE:

Series

Auntie Clem's Bakery Gluten-Free Murder

Reg Rawlins, Psychic Detective What the Cat Knew

Zachary Goldman Mysteries She Wore Mourning

Kenzie Kirsch Medical Thrillers Unlawful Harvest

Parks Pat Mysteries Out with the Sunset (Coming Soon)

High-Tech Crime Solvers Series Virtually Harmless

Stand Alone Suspense Novels

Looking Over Your Shoulder

Lion Within

Pursued by the Past

In the Tick of Time

Loose the Dogs

AND MORE AT PDWORKMAN.COM

*For brothers and sisters
who dream of a better life.*

*G*randfather!" Nadie shook him hard, trying to rouse him. She tried their native Nehiyaw—what the white man called Cree. "Nimosôm! Willie Laplante!" She shouted in his ear and shook him so hard she nearly pulled him off of the couch, but to no avail. He wasn't waking up. Nadie made a noise of disgust and let go of his arm. "Have a nice sleep!" she muttered.

She didn't have a lot of time before school started. She knew everybody would be late getting there anyway, including the teacher, and they wouldn't start until all were there who were expected to come. What was the point in being on time? But Nadie still wanted to get there to say that she, at least, was on time every day.

Nadie went to the baby room, a tiny room barely bigger than a closet, and found the door locked. She rattled the handle as if she might have been mistaken, or it might have just been stuck, but it was no use. She went back to Grandfather and went through his pockets. Nadie knew it was disrespectful. But what other choice did she have?

"If you were awake, you would give it to me," she reasoned aloud.

Grandfather just snored in response. His breath was powerfully strong. He must have a new batch of home brew ready, on top of the medicine he usually took to sleep. Nadie's fingers touched the key, and she pulled it out with a flourish. She hurried over to the baby room and unlocked the door.

Luyu sat on the floor, cross-legged, leaning down to study something on the floor. There was little light coming through the dirty window; Nadie wondered how Luyu could see anything at all. Luyu didn't look up when Nadie opened the door.

"Tân'si, Luyu," Nadie greeted softly, letting Luyu know she was there before she tried to pick her up. She had startled Luyu enough times, touching her without speaking first when she was intently focused on something.

Luyu's head went up slightly, like a bird listening. She still didn't look at Nadie, but she knew Nadie was there. Nadie stepped into the room and stooped to pick tiny Luyu up.

"Hello, baby." She cuddled Luyu against her and kissed her head. Luyu grasped Nadie's long black hair and wound it around her fingers.

"Say 'Hello, sister,' " Nadie prompted.

Luyu didn't respond. Nadie took Luyu to the living room where she had room to move. She laid Luyu down on the floor and stripped off the sopping wet diaper.

"Hello," Luyu said suddenly. "Hello, sister." Her lisp made it sound more like 'thith-ter', which always made Nadie laugh. She loved Luyu's lisp.

"Hi. Did you rest well?"

Luyu squirmed to get up before Nadie had a clean diaper on her. Nadie held her still and sang in a low voice to keep Luyu calm while she finished. Luyu stilled, her eyes intent on Nadie's face. Once Nadie had the new diaper on, she released Luyu and let her get up. While Luyu pattered around, Nadie threw the wet diaper in the kitchen garbage and splashed water from the water bottle on the counter over her fingers to wash up. Drying them on her pants, she went back to the baby room and picked up the discarded shirt and pants from the floor. Luyu had already disappeared when Nadie came back out. Nadie found her in the kitchen cupboard, rifling through the meager contents.

"Come on, mischief maker."

Nadie pulled Luyu out of the cupboard and stood her up. She pulled Luyu's t-shirt on over her head before Luyu anticipated what was happening, and threaded Luyu's arms through the sleeves despite the girl's angry squawk of protest. Luyu tried to twist free, but Nadie was expert at this job and had the shirt on Luyu before she could squirm away. Luyu stopped struggling and just plucked at the shirt in irritation. Nadie sat Luyu in her lap and pulled on the pants. The elastic waist meant she didn't have to pin Luyu down for long enough to zip and button them, so the procedure was quickly over. She released Luyu.

"Now you keep those on," she told Luyu. "It's cold, and you can't just go around in your diaper and your pony undershirt. You will get sick."

But Luyu rarely got sick, and Nadie knew that when she got out of school, Luyu would be stripped back down to her underwear, even if it was cold enough to see her breath.

"Pony?" Luyu repeated. She pulled her t-shirt up to look at and show off the dingy pink pony undershirt.

"Yes, there is your pony." Nadie pulled the t-shirt back down and took Luyu by the hand. "Let's find something to eat."

Luyu pulled her to the cupboard and they looked at the options. Grandfather had not been back to the grocery in town for a few weeks and the cupboard would be bare before long. Nadie grabbed a plastic box of cereal and put it on the counter. The plastic container was supposed to keep out the mice, but Nadie could see they had been chewing on the corners. Before long, there would be a hole large enough for them to squeeze in through. Luyu was tapping Nadie on the leg, eager for her breakfast.

"Eat!"

"One minute, Luyu."

Nadie grabbed a bowl from the sink and wiped it out. She

poured cereal into it. Luyu's tapping became more insistent. Nadie was going to use some powdered milk and the water bottle to mix Luyu up some milk for the cereal, but Luyu started to pinch her, and Nadie changed her mind. Luyu would just make a mess with milk. It was tidier if she ate the dry cereal with her fingers.

"Okay, okay. Here you go." Nadie walked over to the table with difficulty, Luyu hanging onto her legs and tripping her up. She put the cereal down in front of the one unbroken chair. Luyu climbed up into the chair as quick as a squirrel and thrust both hands into the bowl.

Nadie's stomach growled loudly enough for Luyu to hear it. Luyu laughed and looked at Nadie. She reached out her hand, offering Nadie a handful of her cereal.

"Thank you, no," Nadie said, not taking it. Luyu was too skinny; she needed all the food she could get. Last year, Mona's baby boy had died and the social worker and policeman who had come to talk to them said it was because he had not gotten enough to eat. Nadie lived in fear that Luyu would suffer the same fate.

As Luyu ate, Nadie grabbed the rag beside the sink and moistened it with water from the water bottle. While Luyu sat chewing the cereal she had packed into her mouth, Nadie held her head still and cleaned her the best she could. Luyu would only get dirty again the minute she went back to her room to play on the dusty floor.

It only took Luyu a couple of minutes to finish the cereal.

"All gone," she announced. 'Gone' sounded like 'don.' Nadie wasn't sure why Mouse had such a hard time understanding Luyu. She couldn't form the words properly, but Nadie didn't have any trouble understanding what she meant.

Luyu climbed down from the chair to make a break for it. Nadie grabbed her and swung her up in the air. Luyu shrieked, a sound partly of protest at being caught and partly delight at being swung around. Nadie twirled around to keep her occupied and danced her way back to the baby room. She put Luyu in the crib and Luyu started to wail.

"Where's your ball?" Nadie asked, looking around at the floor and under the crib. It wasn't there. She went back out to the living room and found it beside the couch. Nadie went back to the baby room and offered it to Luyu. "Here you go. Something to play with."

Luyu just fired the ball back at Nadie. Her face was getting red. Nadie backed out of the room. "Goodbye, Luyu. See you later."

She pulled the door shut. Nadie hesitated, trying to decide whether to lock it or not. Grandfather said it needed to be locked, or Luyu would get out and get into mischief, but Nadie hadn't seen her open the door and wasn't sure she believed it. Probably Grandfather had forgotten he left it open, or the catch hadn't clicked into place and Luyu only had to push the door to get out.

With a sigh, Nadie turned the key in the lock. She wouldn't want Luyu to get into something that might harm her if she could get out of the room by herself.

She went back to the living room to put the key back in Grandfather's pocket. She shook him in one last attempt to wake him up. But she still couldn't rouse him. Leaving the house, Nadie glanced up at the position of the sun. She was pretty sure she could still make it on time, but she needed to hurry.

"Nadie!"

Nadie turned around at the call and saw Mouse trying to catch up to her. Her heart warmed at the sight of him. He had a doo-rag around his head, a dark blue, patterned cloth. His braids, starting just behind his ears, hung in front of his shoulders. His eyes, slanted slightly down, always looked pensive, belying his natural good humor. He was munching on what appeared to be freshly-made bread. Nadie eyed the flat piece of bread, her mouth watering. When he caught up with her, Mouse delved into his pocket and pulled out another and offered it to Nadie.

"Thank you!" Nadie brought it up to her nose and inhaled the sweet smell. It was still warm in her hand. "And thank your mother."

Mouse nodded. "She told me to bring extra for you."

Nadie smiled and took a big bite.

"I would have brought you one anyway," Mouse advised.

"I know you would." Nadie gave him a one-armed hug as they walked side-by-side.

"It's a nice day. I hope we spend time outside today," Mouse said.

The air was cool and crisp. The sky was clear and it looked like it would warm up to a summer-like day. "I want to spend time on my blanket today."

"Is it almost done? You've been working on it for a long time."

"Good workmanship takes time."

Mouse cleared his throat. "Especially when you make a mistake and have to go back to take it out," he teased.

Nadie smacked his arm. "You be nice! I don't see you attempting any big projects."

"Exactly. Running Deer doesn't demand big school projects. She's just as happy with small demonstrations of our skills."

It was true. Running Deer would accept and praise any attempt to demonstrate what they had learned or mastered. Nadie could have chosen to do a small, doll-sized weaving without any special pattern or knots, something she could have produced in a single afternoon, and their teacher would have been satisfied.

"But don't you want to learn more? Don't you want to get really good at something? I never would have learned so much and gotten good at it if I had just spent a couple of hours on it."

Mouse stretched out his arms, embracing all of nature. "Mother Earth does not ask me to be good at everything. She provides food for the hunt, beauty for the eye, sleep to refresh myself at night… It is better we work with the earth, not to try to control everything, like the white man."

Nadie snorted. "And how much sleep do you think Mother Earth would give you without a blanket?"

"I'm a man. I'll bring home the food. My wife can make blankets. Or… I will buy one at the store in town."

"Nobody's going to marry a good-for-nothing who just wants to sleep all day."

"Who said I would sleep all day? I will sleep at night and hunt during the day. My wife won't even need to make blankets, with all of the furs and skins I will bring home."

"Oh, great hunter," Nadie mocked. "A challenge: you bring in sufficient skins and furs to keep your manly body warm for the winter by the time I finish my blanket."

"But you're almost done!" Mouse protested. "You started long before me. And the animals haven't finished putting on their winter coats yet."

"Weasel words."

"I'm not a weasel! It's not a fair challenge!"

They reached the school house. A small trailer had been pressed into use for the band's school. Nadie and Mouse were the oldest students. No one else was there yet and Nadie knew it would be too cold to concentrate on the school work. Sweltering hot in the summer, freezing in the winter. At least in the winter, they could keep the wood stove stoked all day. During the summer, they let out once it got too hot to use. On fall days like today if the temperature rose above normal, they would go outside for the hottest part of the day. Without a word, Nadie loaded up her arms with firewood and went into the school building to light the fire. Mouse stripped off his jacket and started chopping more wood, wearing only a thin muscle-shirt. Nadie shook her head at this display, but when she got the fire going and went out for a second load, sweat was already glistening on Mouse's slim arms. He stopped chopping for a moment while she loaded up.

"In the spring," he said.

Nadie squinted her eyes at him. "What?"

"I will bring you enough furs to keep you warm before the first flowers bloom. Except crocuses. Crocuses don't count."

Nadie paused before going back into the school. "Okay, deal. You do that, and I won't bug you any more about being lazy."

"And you make me a blanket."

"What? I'm already making a blanket."

"You'll be done before the snow flies. You'll be sitting around all winter watching me work; hunting, trapping, cleaning, curing... If I don't make it, you keep the blanket for yourself. Because you won't have any furs to keep you warm. But if I do it, you give me the blanket. That's fair."

Nadie stomped the dirt off her shoes before re-entering the school. She stacked the wood and warmed her cold fingers near the stove. When she went back outside, Mouse was putting away the newly split wood.

"You see?" he pointed out. "I'm not lazy. I work as hard as you do."

His tone was injured and Nadie realized her words had wounded him. "I'm sorry. I know you work too." She couldn't bring herself to say 'work hard,' because he was always lounging around, shirking whatever duties he could get away with not doing. Nadie felt like she worked from sunup to sundown. It wasn't the same.

"So is it a deal?" Mouse asked.

Nadie sighed. Mouse spending time hunting and preparing furs all winter? Even if he won the challenge, she would have secretly won too, making him actually work and learn a skill properly. One that was important to his future family and to the band.

"Fine," she said. "But I think you're getting the easy part of the deal. Weaving a blanket properly takes a lot more time than shooting a couple of animals."

"Shooting a couple of animals? You make it sound like I can go out and do that in an afternoon. It takes time to track and kill an animal or to set a trapline. And you need a lot more than two animals to make a blanket!"

Nadie laughed. At least he had an idea of what he was getting into. Mouse put his jacket back on and pulled out another piece of bread. Nadie thought he was going to break it in half and offer her a piece, but he shredded a few crumbs off the edge and started tossing them to the birds. Nadie's mouth dropped open.

"Don't do that!"

Mouse looked at her and raised his eyebrows. "Just feeding the birds. What's wrong with that?"

"Somebody… somebody might be hungry. One of the other students. You shouldn't waste it on the birds! It's not even stale!"

"Oh…" Mouse scratched the back of his head. "Sorry. Do you want it?"

"I wasn't asking for it," Nadie clarified, a bit embarrassed by her own reaction. "Maybe one of the other children…"

"They're not here yet." Mouse held the bread out toward Nadie. "Here. You have it while it's still warm."

Nadie took it from him without further protest. "You're very generous. Even with the birds."

He gave a modest shrug and looked away while she ate the bread. "I'd better go stand by the fire before I cool off too much." Mouse went into the schoolhouse while Nadie stood outside, trying to force herself to eat slowly while watching for the smaller children.

*S*chool let out mid-afternoon and Nadie headed straight for the house. Mouse had been rough-housing with some of the younger students, but chased after her when he realized she was leaving without him.

"Come to my place," he suggested. "You can have some more baking. My mother has probably baked all day."

Nadie's stomach growled and her mouth watered at the suggestion, but she shook her head. "I have to look after Luyu. Make sure she gets dinner. Maybe I can come over later after I put her down for bed."

Mouse sighed dramatically. "Yeah. Sure. Whenever is good for you."

"I need to look after Luyu," Nadie said firmly, giving him a glare. "She depends on me."

"Somebody else can look after her today. Your grandfather will be up by now."

"No. I need to make sure she's okay. Grandfather... even when he's there, I can't be sure she'll be fed..."

"Fine. Maybe I'll see you later," Mouse grumbled. He gave her a wave and broke off toward his house.

Nadie returned to Grandfather's house. A lot of the houses in the band were trailers or other prefabricated homes, especially since the flooding had wiped out a lot of the older homes, forcing them to relocate. But Grandfather's had been built by his grandfather with his own two hands, up above the flood plain. So even though it was further from the school than most of the others, it was sturdy and didn't rattle and sway in the wind. Grandfather complained about the trailers being firetraps and not being able to hold the heat in the winter. Not that his house stayed warm, but at least the water bottles didn't freeze indoors.

She touched the wind chimes hanging beside the door and went in.

"Hello, Nadie!" There was a woman in the kitchen who gave Nadie a big smile of welcome when she came in, but it took a few seconds for Nadie to recognize her. She had dyed her hair blond and had put on weight. There were heavy bags under her eyes that her makeup could not disguise. One of Grandfather's daughters, Melinda.

Nadie nodded at her. "Hi, Mel. When did you get here?"

Mel laughed. "I've been in and out for a couple of days. Just kept missing you."

"Oh. Well, it's nice to see you."

"Melinda, are you getting drinks?" Her tall, lean husband walked into the room and frowned when he saw Nadie standing there. He had a big, crooked nose and Nadie didn't know if he was Nehiyaw or some other nation. Maybe Apache. She didn't know anyone else with his features. "What are you doing here?" he asked Nadie, scowling.

Melinda made a noise of protest.

"I live here," Nadie said. "You don't."

"Well, we're staying here for a few days."

People who came to stay with Grandfather for a few days seldom stayed for a few days. Sometimes they were there for months. Nadie at least had her bedroom to herself, mostly, unless girls came to stay, and then she had to put up with other children camping out in her room as well. She wasn't sure where Melinda and the Nose were staying. They had to be in Cam's old room, along with the four Foxes who had come for 'a few days' and had been living there for almost a month now.

"This is a dry reservation," Nadie told the Nose. "You aren't allowed to bring alcohol in."

He snorted. "We're not bringing any booze in." He and Melinda exchanged a sly look, as though they were pulling one over on Nadie, and she was too naive to know how many house-holds made their own mash.

Nadie rolled her eyes. "Don't leave any cups out where little ones can reach them," she warned. "Lu is really quick at getting into things. She could get sick."

She knew most of the members of the band didn't worry much about whether their kids drank out of their glasses. Some even gave them a taste when they begged at the table or were fussy going to bed. It was no wonder all of the teens in the band drank.

Luyu didn't need all of the problems alcohol would bring.

Neither adult bothered to answer Nadie. They would leave their drinks wherever they pleased. Nadie couldn't force them, and Grandfather wouldn't enforce any rules. Nadie shook her head and went to the baby room. She tried the handle and found it unlocked.

"Tân'si, Luyu."

Luyu was lying on her side on the floor like she'd fallen asleep, but her eyes were open. She didn't look at Nadie.

"Luyu? Are you okay?"

Nadie crouched down and put her hands around the girl, expecting her to sit up and squirm away. But Luyu didn't resist. Nadie picked her up and held Luyu against her body.

"Lu? What's wrong, little sister? Are you sick?"

Luyu made a little noise of protest. Nadie tried to analyze it. Sick? Hurt? Was she weak from hunger? Scared? She could be tired, but Luyu was never tired unless she was sick. She would play for half the night and still be awake before anyone in the house the next morning. Nadie studied Luyu's face. Under the dirt, she might have a bruise under her eye. Nadie touched it with gentle fingers and thought it was a little puffy. But Luyu didn't flinch or pull away.

Nadie sat down on the floor. She was too uncomfortable in a crouching position and there was no furniture for her to sit on. She started with Luyu's feet, gently feeling and squeezing the limbs every couple of inches, feeling for anything out of the ordinary. Luyu had broken her arm once and no one had realized for several days. Nadie moved up the legs to the hips and felt Luyu's soft belly, ribs, and arms. It wasn't until she got to Luyu's head that she realized she had started at the wrong end.

There was a big bump on the front of Luyu's head, just above her brow, hidden under her tangled, uncombed black locks. Nadie prodded it gently and Luyu pulled away, making another sound.

"That's it," Nadie murmured.

She went back to the kitchen. Mel and the Nose were already gone, either back to Cam's room or out to meet with another couple or group of friends. Trying to hang onto Luyu, Nadie wet the rag beside the sink with the water bottle and held it to the bump on Luyu's head. Ice would work better, but that would require electricity, and the nearest freezer that actually worked was probably Grandmother Dora's ancient propane-powered one. Nadie didn't feel like going all that way, either having to carry Luyu with her or leaving her behind again.

"School out already?"

Nadie turned at Grandfather's rumbling grumble. He was vertical. While he looked like a grumpy old man—not that old, Nadie realized, but still a lot older than she—Nadie knew he was really a softie.

Usually.

Lately, Nadie had worried about how tough he was on Luyu. She didn't know whether it was his pills, Luyu's incessant activity, or just his advancing years. But he wasn't quite the same Grandfather with Luyu that he had been when Nadie was a young child.

"How did Luyu bump her head?" Nadie asked, holding the wet cloth in place despite Luyu's moans of protest.

"Did she bump her head?" He looked away and didn't answer the question.

"Did she fall?" Nadie suggested. "I know she climbs on things…"

"Maybe she fell down," Grandfather agreed.

"You don't know?"

"Did school let out early today? Running Deer needs to make sure she is keeping you for long enough. You need to be taught."

"Outdoor education," Nadie said. "We are supposed to be outside communing with Mother Earth."

Grandfather didn't like her irreverence. "You treat your teacher with respect. And Mother Earth too. You would do well to learn some lessons from our earth mother."

"I did Running Deer's meditations all the way home. I'm enlightened. I saw lots of birds and trees on the way home."

"What did they say to you?"

"The birds said cheep cheep cheep. And the wind rustled the leaves in the trees. Just like always."

"Cheep," Luyu echoed faintly.

Nadie smiled and stroked her cheek. "Cheep cheep cheep," she repeated.

"Cheep."

"Are you okay, little one?"

"She is fine," Grandfather assured her.

"She's got a big bump on her head and she's not acting like herself. Do you think we should take her to the doctor?"

"In town?" Grandfather objected. "I'm not driving for hours just because she has a little bump on her head. She's fine."

"Have you given her anything to eat today?" Nadie nudged open the cupboard. "You need to go to town anyway to get food. When are you going to get some?"

"Harrumph. Maybe next week."

"Maybe?" Nadie repeated. "What is she supposed to eat until

then? You have a dozen people living in the house; can't anyone help put food in the cupboards?"

"People stay here when they don't have anywhere to go," Grandfather said. "They don't have money for food; they are trying to get on their feet." He gazed into the cupboard himself. "There's cereal. Canned beans. Mac and cheese. If she's hungry, she'll eat anything."

Nadie bent down to pick up a box of macaroni and cheese. The generic stuff that cost less than a dollar per box, if he got them by the case on sale.

"The little ones need their fruits and vegetables. All of this white man's food…"

"Fruits and vegetables don't keep. I'll get us some venison. That will hold us over until I go to town."

The stove was already stoked and radiating heat into the kitchen. Hitching Luyu up further on her hip, Nadie filled a pot halfway with water and put it on the stove. Luyu was leaning back, pressing against Nadie's arm and making the muscles ache. As light as she was, she was difficult to hold when she refused to cuddle up. Nadie took Luyu over to the chair and set her down. She kept her hands close for a minute. Luyu seemed wobbly and Nadie wanted to make sure she was going to stay there and not topple over and bang her head again. Luyu leaned forward and laid her head on the table, blinking sleepily. Nadie didn't like it.

"Don't you think—" She turned to talk to Grandfather and realized he was gone again. She couldn't pursue him with a pot on the stove and a sick child who might fall off the chair or else decide to climb up on the stove or pull the pot down. Nadie sighed loudly, hoping he heard her frustration.

❧

Luyu didn't want to eat, which was a big red flag. Luyu was always hungry, and as far as Nadie knew, she had not eaten since breakfast. Nadie managed to get a few spoonfuls of macaroni down her, but Luyu kept pushing the spoon away and trying to put her head down.

"Poor baby," Nadie murmured. "You want to go to bed?"

When she picked Luyu back up again, the girl leaned her head into the hollow of Nadie's neck and snuggled in. Nadie kissed her head and carried her to her crib. Luyu whined as Nadie lay her down. She moved restlessly. Nadie stroked her hair until her eyes closed and she was still.

Nadie headed toward the door. Luyu coughed. Nadie whirled around, realizing Luyu was throwing up. She returned to the crib and rolled her onto her side. She patted Luyu on the back, waiting for her to stop retching.

"Grandfather!"

Grandfather appeared in the doorway a few minutes later and looked questioning.

"She's throwing up. I think we should take her to a doctor."

"She is getting the evil out of her system. She'll be okay."

"She is hurt and she's throwing up. She should see a doctor."

"We can talk to the medicine woman tomorrow and get some herbs and medicine for her."

"Can you go get her tonight?"

Grandfather walked over to the crib and looked down at Luyu. He touched her cheek. "She doesn't have a fever. She'll be okay. She'll sleep tonight and probably be fine in the morning."

Luyu had stopped vomiting and Nadie picked her up again. "My poor baby. I'm going to bring her to my bed."

"She'll get into mischief," Grandfather warned.

"She's too sick right now." Nadie put steel into her voice. If no one else was going to take care of Luyu, then Nadie needed to be her mother. And when a mother put steel in her voice and in her eyes, then the rest of the band better listen. Best not to get between a mother bear and her cub.

Grandfather recognized this and didn't argue any further. He turned to go.

"Who is going to clean this up?" Nadie gestured to the vomit in the crib.

"I will do it in the morning." Grandfather waved a hand, dismissing it.

Grandfather wouldn't be doing anything in the morning. He would be passed out, like any other morning in recent memory. But Nadie wasn't going to put Luyu down to clean it up. She was too worried about the little girl. She returned to her own room and lay down on the bed with Luyu in her arms.

"Poor baby," she murmured again.

She sang a lullaby to Luyu in a low voice and prayed to the Great Spirit that all of the evil had gone out of Luyu with the vomit so she would be okay. Luyu was still. After a long time, Nadie fell asleep as well.

CHAPTER THREE

She slept in the next morning. Nadie didn't want to wake Luyu up. Luyu needed whatever sleep she could get to heal her body. So Nadie lay there, with one of her arms numb from Luyu lying on it, and didn't move. She dozed on and off, having weird dreams and thoughts. She hadn't realized she had fallen asleep yet again when she awoke to Mouse shaking her.

"Nadie! You're late for school. Aren't you coming?"

Nadie tried not to disturb Luyu, keeping her voice low. "Shh. Luyu is sick, I have to take care of her today."

Luyu stirred anyway. She opened her eyes and saw Mouse there. She reached out her arms for him to pick her up.

"Tân'si," she lisped to Mouse. "Hello."

"Tân'si," he responded, and kissed her on the cheek. "She looks okay, Nadie." He wiped his mouth and nose with the back of his arm. "She smells like puke, though."

"Are you feeling better this morning?" Nadie asked, gazing at Luyu.

While she didn't appear to have her usual energy, the sparkle was back in Luyu's eyes. She started to play with one of Mouse's braids and used it to poke him in the face.

"So are you coming to school?" Mouse asked. "Running Deer sent me to find out."

"Is it that late?" Nadie had a knot in her stomach. She looked at her window, but the blind was drawn and she couldn't tell how high the sun was. "Please tell her I'm sorry. I think… I'd better stay with Luyu today. Just to make sure…"

Mouse rolled his eyes. "I suppose that's why you didn't come over last night, too."

"Yeah. She was really bad. She has a bump on her head, and she was drowsy and throwing up, and… just not like Luyu. I held her all night."

"She looks fine now."

"I'll stay. I have to feed her and make sure she's not going to throw up anymore." Nadie yawned. "I didn't sleep very well, either. I was so worried every time she moved."

"I'll tell Running Deer."

He didn't leave immediately. Nadie thought he wanted to say something more, so she waited. But he didn't say anything else. He just put Luyu down on the floor and waved goodbye. Then he was gone.

Luyu seemed more like herself and was begging for breakfast, so Nadie got her a bowl of cereal. But less than usual, in case Luyu's stomach couldn't handle it. She popped a couple of pieces of cereal in her own mouth, thinking longingly of the baking she had missed in not going to Mouse's house the night before. And Mouse hadn't thought to bring her anything when he came to see why she was late for school. He was probably mad at her for not going.

Luyu gobbled down the cereal and didn't ask for more. She didn't throw up again, which Nadie took as a good sign. When Nadie tried to put a cold cloth on the bump on Luyu's head again, Luyu pushed her away grumpily and squirmed to be put down.

There was a sharp knock on the front door. Nadie and Luyu both startled. No one bothered to knock on doors on the reservation. No one but outsiders. Her heart beating rapidly, Nadie looked around the kitchen for anything that shouldn't be there, then went to the door.

She was obviously a social worker. If the skirt and blazer didn't give it away, slightly rumpled after sitting in the car for hours, she couldn't mistake the plasticized picture ID hanging around the woman's neck.

"Jacky James," the petite white woman announced, without so much as a hello. She rattled off the social services agency she was with and stepped into the house without an invitation. "Just here for a routine inspection."

There were so many different agencies, Nadie didn't even try to keep track of them. They were lucky if they ever saw the same social worker twice in a row. It was always someone different. Even when it was the same agency, it would be a new worker. Nobody wanted to make the trip from the city to the reservation more than once. Nadie had never been further than the nearest town herself. That was long enough to have to sit in the car. And all the way to the city was twice as far.

Jacky James looked around the living room. She was startled to see Grandfather asleep on the couch.

"Luyu was sick last night," Nadie whispered, as if she was afraid that speaking louder would wake Grandfather up. "So he's very tired. We should let him sleep."

Jacky's lips pressed together, forming a thin, straight line and she wrote a word or two in the small notebook she held in one hand. She didn't object, though, and walked into the kitchen.

"This is Luyu?" she asked, looking at the little girl in Nadie's arms.

"Yes. Say hello, Luyu."

Luyu didn't look at the woman. She squirmed to be put down, but Nadie didn't comply. If she put Luyu down, there was no telling what she would get into. And it would go into the social worker's report.

"Say hello," Nadie prompted again.

"Hello," Luyu echoed in a flat voice, still refusing to look at Jacky.

Jacky looked at the bottled water next to the sink. "You still don't have a potable water source?"

"No. Chief Frank says the government won't clean the water. It's too expensive. Cheaper to truck in water. There is talk of relocating the band, but…" She waved her hands in a wide shrug. "This is our ancestral land. This house was built by my grandfather's grandfather."

Jacky nodded. She walked over to the sink and turned on one of the taps. Nothing happened. "No plumbing at all?"

"Well… no."

"How do you bathe? Wash your clothes?" The woman looked at Luyu, filthy as usual.

"I haven't had a chance to clean her up yet this morning. She was sick last night… we just got up."

Another note went into the notebook. Jacky looked in the bare cupboard. She glanced at the ancient, doorless fridge in the alcove opposite the sink and raised a questioning eyebrow.

"We took the door off for safety," Nadie explained. "Children can get stuck in fridges. Suffocate in them."

"That's right," Jacky agreed. "They can. You wouldn't want that to happen to Lulu."

"Luyu."

"Luyu. It doesn't work?"

"No electricity."

"You have wiring." Jacky pointed to a plug-in.

"The flooding messed up the wiring. Even before that… gasoline to run the generators is expensive. And hard to truck in."

"No plumbing. No electricity. Heating?"

Nadie realized she still had a blanket tied around her shoulders. Luyu was, as usual, stripped down to her undershirt and diaper. "Yes, we have the fireplace and a wood stove. I was just going to fill the stove…"

Jacky nodded and made a note, giving Nadie a small, tight smile. "Why don't you show me Lulu's room and get some clothes on her? I assume you have changed her diaper?"

"Luyu," Nadie corrected again. "This way."

She led the way. Jacky glanced around the tiny room. "Well, this is cute." She walked in to look around. Nadie's heart sank when Jacky looked in the crib, her nostril's flaring at the vomit drying on the sheets.

"She was sick last night. I haven't had a chance to clean up yet."

"She slept in this?"

"No! She slept in my bed. I held her. All night. I wanted to know if she threw up any more…"

"You cannot have a baby sleep in your bed. She could smother or you could roll over on her."

"She's not a baby," Nadie said. "She's two. Nearly three."

Jacky looked at the diminutive toddler and flipped through the pages of her notebook, looking for some kind of confirmation. "She's very small. What does she weigh?"

"I don't know. The last social worker had a scale. She weighed her."

"And what was it?"

"I don't remember. I wasn't home, Grandfather was looking after her. She said Luyu was too small. But lots of our babies are small. She'll get bigger."

"She's not potty trained?"

"Potty?"

"Toilet. She still wears diapers."

"Well… yes. Luyu… is special. She's not ready yet."

"Special. She has FAS. Is she getting therapy? Any special teaching programs?"

Nadie looked at her blankly. "FAS?"

"Fetal Alcohol Spectrum." Jacky spoke quickly, impatient. "Her mother drank while she was pregnant."

"Oh."

"You're not her mother, are you?" Jacky was flipping pages again, looking for details.

"No. She's my…" Nadie almost said 'sister' before she remembered what the outsiders said. "She's a cousin to me."

"Where is her mother? Has she been to see Luyu at all?"

"No." Nadie shifted. "I think she's in Saskatchewan, last I heard."

"Does she call? Does she have any contact at all?"

Nadie shook her head helplessly. "No."

"And she's not getting any therapy. Lulu. Nobody comes in to help with her."

"Grandfather helps. Others in the band help sometimes. We're all her kin. We work together."

"But no one comes from the city to work with her."

"No."

Jacky scribbled down some more notes. She cast her eyes around the bare room. "Why don't we get her dressed? She'll be much more comfortable then. I'll hold her while you get some clean clothes."

Nadie was bending over to pick up Luyu's discarded pants and shirt when Jacky emphasized clean clothes. She straightened up. Jacky tucked away her pen and notepad and held her hands out for Luyu. Nadie felt uncomfortable giving Luyu to the social worker but didn't know what else to do. What if she didn't get Luyu back again? What if the social worker just took her away? Sometimes they did. Usually the little ones went into kinship care with someone else in the band. But sometimes they took them away from the band completely, putting them into foster care with white families in the city, hours away. Jacky waited, hands held out insistently. Nadie passed Luyu over. Luyu protested, pushing on the social worker and complaining, "No, no, no!" Nadie hurried to get her clothes so she could get the little girl back again.

"It's okay, Lu. Nadie will be right back."

She walked quickly to her own room and rifled through the laundry basket on her floor, eventually finding a pair of pants and long-sleeved t-shirt for Luyu. She returned to the baby room, where Jacky was trying to calm a squirming, furious Luyu. Nadie pulled Luyu from Jacky without asking.

"I'll just take a quick look around while you're getting her dressed," Jacky said.

"Uh—there's probably still people sleeping in the other bedrooms. Don't go anywhere the door is shut."

"I'll be careful."

Nadie put Luyu on the floor and wrestled with her to get the clothes on. Luyu shrieked and kicked like someone was beating her. Nadie's face got hot. Luyu wouldn't likely wake up anyone who was still sleeping, but Nadie was embarrassed at what the social worker would think.

"Shh," she told Luyu. "It's just a shirt and pants. You can take them off once she leaves." She hummed softly, a traditional beat that helped to calm Luyu at bedtime. "It's okay, Luyu. Shh."

Luyu quieted enough that Nadie recognized the squeak and thump of the bathroom door being closed. Her observation was confirmed by the social worker's choking cough and drag of fresh air. With no working plumbing, the bathroom was occupied by a camp toilet, a simple bucket with a seat that had to be emptied down the outhouse frequently, and wasn't emptied nearly frequently enough. Maybe that would teach Jacky not to go opening doors after Nadie told her not to.

The woman was standing in the living room when Nadie picked Luyu back up and went to find her. Jacky looked at Luyu, miserable and pulling in irritation on the long sleeves of her t-shirt.

"There, that's better, isn't it?"

Luyu's face was wet with tears and bubbles of snot blew out her nose. Nadie wasn't sure how much better it was.

"Are you done?" she demanded.

"Who is Luyu's primary caregiver?"

Nadie nodded to Grandfather, snoring on the couch. "Grandfather."

Jacky looked at him, frowning. "Is he Luyu's grandfather as well?"

Nadie had to stop to think about that.

"Are your mother and Luyu's mother sisters?" Jacky prompted.

"No… Grandfather helped raise Luyu's mother. She is… eight years older than me. Luyu is her fourth baby. Ronnie couldn't handle her. The social worker put her into kinship a year ago."

"Is she an actual relation?"

"We're all related," Nadie said with a shrug. "I just don't know how."

"Is your grandfather your mother's father?"

"Yes."

"How long have you been living with him?"

"As long as I can remember. I don't know how old I was when I came here. Just a baby."

"And when he is asleep, who takes care of Luyu?"

"I do. And others help. Everyone is working or sleeping right now, but there's always someone around. We have to keep a close eye on Luyu; she gets into things. But everyone knows. We all make sure she is safe."

"And when you're at school? You do go to school, don't you?"

Luyu had had enough of the interview with the strange woman and started hitting and pinching Nadie when kicking and squirming weren't enough to convince Nadie to put her down. Nadie winced and pulled Luyu's hand away from the soft skin of Nadie's throat, where Luyu had just left long, burning scratches.

"Ouch, Luyu. That hurts. Sit down here." She put Luyu on the floor and nudged her legs into a crossed position, a signal she was supposed to sit still and listen. Luyu unbent her legs and attempted to get up. Nadie sat down cross-legged in front of her, pushing her legs back into position. "That's a girl. Sit still. It's time to be quiet."

"No!" Luyu shouted, folding her arms and pouting, her bottom lip sticking way out. "No sit!"

"Are we done?" Nadie asked Jacky with a sigh.

"Does Lulu have any toys? Books? I don't see much for her to occupy her time here."

"Her books are in my room. She tears them so she can't have them except when I'm reading to her. She has a few toys... mostly our children copy what adults do... learning to do chores, hunt, fish, cook, make useful things. We don't have a lot of toys."

"She's too young to do any of those things."

"Not little things. She helps to sweep and clean. When I wash the laundry, she has her own little bar of soap..."

"I see." The social worker's glance around the room clearly indicated she didn't believe much cleaning went on. She dragged out her notebook one last time and made her final notes. "I will file my report when I get back to the office today. It's my belief that this is not a safe environment for Lulu. I'm sure you do everything you're able to take care of her, but you're not equipped to do it on your own. And without water or power..." Jacky shook her head. "I think you want the best for your cousin. Your grandfather doesn't appear to have the stamina to take care of such a high-needs child. She should be somewhere she can get therapy and specialized teaching, and proper food and clothing. I'm sure you agree."

Nadie swallowed. She didn't know what to say.

"I'll let myself out," Jacky said.

CHAPTER FOUR

For a long time, Nadie just stood there, her brain trying to process what the social worker had said. They were going to take Luyu away. And it didn't sound like she wanted to place Luyu with someone else in the band. She wanted to put Luyu in a white family in the city, where she could get therapy and lots of food and wear clothes washed in the washing machine every day. Somewhere there would be fresh fruits and vegetables, and she could grow into a big, strong girl.

A crash in the kitchen brought Nadie back to herself. Nadie wiped tears from her cheeks and glanced swiftly around the room and saw that Luyu was gone. She went into the kitchen to find one of the chairs tipped over and Luyu trying to drag another over to the counter to climb up. The chair was broken, and if she tried to climb up on it, she would get hurt for sure.

"Namôya, Luyu! No, no. You will get hurt. What do you want? You already had breakfast."

Luyu hit Nadie when she pulled the chair away. "Namôya!" She slapped Nadie's hands. "Dat mean no!"

"Shh. Be still. What do you want up here? I will get it for you."

"No!"

Nadie grabbed Luyu around the waist and picked her up, so she could see the counter from above. "What do you want?"

"Wasser." Luyu gestured at the water bottle.

"Good. I'll get you water." She put Luyu down. "Sit down."

Luyu looked over at the table, where she had already knocked down the one unbroken chair. She sat on the floor and put her legs into a perfect cross-legged position. Nadie smiled while she filled a cup of water for Luyu.

"Good girl. Here's water."

In an effort to make up for missing her agreed visit with Mouse the night before, Nadie went to his house to wait for him to get home from school. His mother, who insisted Nadie call her Beth, was full of smiles and clucked and fussed over Nadie while they waited for Mouse to get home.

"You are so thin and pale," she observed. "You need to eat! What can I get you?"

Nadie shrugged. "Mouse said you were baking yesterday. I don't know what you made."

"Let me get you some bread and stew first. You shouldn't have dessert until after dinner."

"You don't need to feed me dinner," Nadie protested. "I'll eat at home. I thought I'd just have a little snack."

"No, no. Not with you looking so thin. Grandfather Willie is not feeding you enough!"

Nadie made no further protest while Beth warmed up stew on the burner of the stove and several generous pieces of bannock on the back. Before long, the hearty smell of pea soup was filling the kitchen. Nadie's stomach growled repeatedly. She tried to focus on something else while she waited.

"Where did you learn to bake?" she asked. "Most of the women only know how to make bannock."

While they sometimes bought cookies or crackers or other

commercially baked goods at the store in town, few of the band cooked such things. Their supplies were basic. They didn't get into town often enough to get any specialty ingredients.

"I went to college before I got married. Home economics."

"Is that baking?"

"Baking, cooking, cleaning, sewing, household organization, lots of different things. I liked baking, though." Beth smiled and put a hand on her ample belly. "Really liked it!"

Nadie laughed. "I would like that too."

Beth got out a bowl and ladled stew into it until it was almost full to the brim. She set it in front of Nadie and stacked the warm bannock beside it.

"Enjoy!"

"I will," Nadie agreed. She made no further effort at conversation but dug into the hearty food.

By the time Mouse got home, Nadie had moved on to dessert. She was full to bursting, but there were cookies and brownies, and she couldn't turn them down.

"Nadie! I didn't know you were coming!" Mouse swooped down to kiss her on the cheek and snagged two cookies from her plate.

"Don't you steal her cookies, Mouse Running in Dust!" Beth objected, her tone stern.

"Oh, full name!" Nadie laughed. "You're in real trouble."

"Sit down," Beth told Mouse, putting a plate of cookies and brownies in front of him, and adding two more to Nadie's plate.

Mouse sat, his cheeks full of cookies. "Luyu okay?" he asked, his words muffled by the food.

Nadie didn't answer right away. She nibbled at the edge of a brownie. She was too full to eat anything more, but it was too good to turn down. Mouse looked questioning, waiting for her to answer.

"She's better than last night. But a social worker came today."

"You take good care of Luyu!"

"She didn't think so. And I'm not the one who is supposed to be taking care of Luyu. Grandfather is."

"And he was… asleep?" Mouse suggested.

Nadie nodded. "She said she's going to file a report and get Luyu moved." Her eyes and throat were hot. She looked down at the brownie, but she couldn't taste it anymore. "I don't want them to take her away, Mouse."

She sniffled and struggled to keep the tears from escaping her eyes. Beth massaged Nadie's shoulders to comfort her.

"Maybe it is better," Beth said. "You can't look after her while you're at school and Grandfather Willie wouldn't want you to drop out."

Nadie thumped the table in frustration. "Why won't he take better care of her? He was a good parent to me! He always fed me and was waiting for me when I got home from school. I always had clothes and the stove was stoked." One tear escaped her eye and slid down her cheek. "Why won't he take care of Luyu?"

Beth took a chair beside Nadie. She gazed at Nadie. Nadie looked back, studying the fine wrinkles around Beth's dark eyes. She was younger than Grandfather, but no longer a young woman. Mouse was her youngest child and he would soon be man-grown. Beth folded her hands and sighed.

"Your Grandfather Willie has his troubles. His demons."

Nadie nodded.

"Lots of Nehiyaw have problems with alcohol," Beth said.

"Why won't he stop? He knows he has to take care of Luyu."

"Because he is sick."

"Somebody needs to fix this." Nadie jabbed her finger on the table, thumping it down. "Why won't someone fix it? If he wasn't on a reservation, they would fix it. They would take him to the hospital and make Grandfather better!"

"It isn't that easy, Nadie."

"Why not?"

"We will talk to the Elders," Beth suggested. "Ask them for guidance."

She walked out of the room. Nadie looked across the table to Mouse, who was still working his way through the plate of baking. He looked embarrassed and swallowed a big mouthful, his Adam's apple straining.

"Can the Elders help?" Mouse asked, though he knew the answer already.

"The Elders are a bunch of fifty-year-old drunks." Nadie's voice was flat and hopeless. "They can't change anything. They can't fix Grandfather." Nadie looked down and wiped away two more tears that traced down her cheeks.

"Don't cry. If they take Luyu away... it will be better for her. They'll take care of her."

"No, they won't. I want her to be okay. I want them to help her. But... you know what happens when they take children away from the band."

"They never come back."

"They never come back... and they take their culture away... and sometimes..." More tears fell. Nadie gave up trying to wipe them all away. "They disappear, or they die."

"No—" Mouse tried to argue the point.

"Don't tell me they don't!"

"How would you know that? They don't come back to the band. We don't hear what happens to the children who leave."

"Never?"

He cast his eyes down. "Not usually." He couldn't say never because he knew it wasn't true. Sometimes they did hear of a child who had died. Rarely, a body was returned to the band for burial.

"At the library in town, the librarian showed me how to read news stories on the computers. I read about what happens to the children who are put in white foster care. They die. They're abused and neglected and they die, even worse than when they stay on the reservation. If they take Luyu away, they're not putting her in a better place. That's not how it works. No one can love her like we do."

"Is Luyu feeling better today?" Running Deer asked at school the next morning. "Mouse said she was sick."

"She's doing better. She got a bump on her head and I think that made her sick."

"Well, I'm glad she's feeling better. She's such a sweet girl."

Nadie nodded and looked for a change in conversation. "Can we start with free reading this morning?"

Running Deer considered.

"It's too cold to start with outside work," one of the younger students piped up. "Can we read? Please?"

Most of the students remained silent. Few of them enjoyed reading like Nadie and Little Bird did. None of them suggested math or another subject, and none was eager to go outside when it was still cold out. They all waited for their teacher's answer.

"I have a better idea," Running Deer said. "Why don't we start with Nadie reading to the class?"

"Yes!" Dean shouted out, pumping his fist in the air.

Everyone laughed. Dean, one of the littles, only seven years old, was not much of a scholar, but he loved listening to Nadie read stories. Nadie nodded her consent and all of the children put their heads down on their desks to listen to her. The school's library consisted of only one shelf of books; a few Cree stories and some popular children's books. Nadie picked one of them out and sat at the front of the room to read.

When Nadie finished reading, Running Deer started to make assignments for the younger children, breaking them up into groups she could supervise. Nadie picked up her heavy correspondence books. Mouse had a matching set and she grabbed them too. They put their desks together. Nadie opened up her books to start on her next lesson. Mouse didn't. Nadie worked for a few minutes and looked up at him.

"School work," she said. "Remember?"

"I don't feel like doing this white man's work."

"Well, what else are you going to do? Running Deer said she couldn't teach us anymore. If we want to stay in school, we have to study the correspondence work ourselves."

"She can teach us other things. Or we can learn them from the band. Nehiyaw stuff. Not white man's books. I should be out with the men. Outside doing something. Not inside reading this."

Nadie frowned at him. "You want to drop out? You can't drop out, Mouse, you're the only one left my age! I'll be all alone."

"You wouldn't be alone. There's still the younger children."

"That's not the same. You're my only classmate."

"And there's Running Deer."

"She's the teacher! You can't drop out, Mouse."

"I didn't say I was dropping out," he sighed. "I just said I don't feel like doing this work. This doesn't mean anything to us."

"It could still be useful."

"Drawing triangles? Reading about the people who oppressed the Nehiyaw and stole our land and way of life? How is any of this helping us?"

"We need an education... to get work... to be able to teach the younger kids... to learn about our people..."

"But that's not what we're doing," Mouse pointed out. "How is learning white man's curriculum doing any of that? It will only help you with work if you work outside the band. Go to town or the city. If you want to work here, you should be learning from the women. And I should be hunting with the men," Mouse gazed out the window. "Not sitting around here with the little kids."

"Learning is learning. It all enriches us."

"You spend all your time studying this," Mouse thumped his finger down on the pile of books in front of him, "and you just become more white. To be a whole woman, you need to balance your body, mind, spirit, and feelings. Like the medicine wheel. Just studying books… you become unbalanced."

Nadie rolled her eyes. "How many people in the band are balanced? Everybody fights sickness and evil. Our babies die. Children go hungry. Houses burn down and the people passed out inside never even know they are dying. Roaming around outside all day isn't going to solve anything. If I learn from these books, I can help us. Find solutions. We can learn to be a strong people again."

"That's in there?" Mouse asked skeptically.

"Yes! The white man is strong, isn't he?"

"Not spiritually. Spiritually, they are dead. You can't be a whole person without your soul. They are just walking bodies."

CHAPTER FIVE

adie was out of sorts when she got home. All of her worry over Luyu, and now she was worried Mouse was going to drop out and she would be the only older student in the school. She couldn't understand why he didn't see that education was the only way for them to improve things for their people. He just wanted to sit around being lazy or to tromp around outside hunting. He wouldn't even cure his own meat, but would pass it on to Beth or one of the other women in the tribe to prepare for him. That was if he even killed anything.

She didn't know exactly how learning the white high school curriculum would help her either. But everything she read and studied helped her grow and who knew which things she would need to know in the future?

Nadie tried Luyu's door and found it locked. "Grandfather!"

It was a few minutes before she heard him coming up the stairs from the root cellar.

"Grandfather!"

"You're home. Is it that late?"

"I need the key for the baby room."

He patted his pockets absently, as if he didn't know where the key might be hiding. He found it in the breast pocket of his flannel shirt. "You didn't lock it this morning and she was out and into mischief. You can't let her wander the house. She could get hurt."

"She can't just be locked in her room all day," Nadie countered, going back and unlocking it. "She needs to play and learn. She needs to be around people and not by herself. You didn't lock me in when I was a little girl. You played with me and took me with you everywhere."

"You were not like Luyu. You did not get into trouble like she does."

"She gets into trouble because you do not watch her." Nadie opened the door. Luyu scampered toward the door and Nadie scooped her up. "Look, she's like a puppy that's been kenneled all day. She needs to play."

Nadie pushed back Luyu's messy hair to look at the bump on her head. The swelling had gone down some more.

Luyu pushed Nadie's hand away and squirmed to be put down. "Hungry. Firsty." Once on the floor, she grabbed Nadie's hand and pulled her toward the kitchen.

"She gets plenty of time to play," Grandfather said. "She's not locked up the whole time you're at school. Only when I need a break from watching her every second."

Nadie didn't argue the point any further. She knew she wasn't going to get anywhere. "The social worker is going to take her away."

"I told you, they always say that. They think it will scare you into raising children their way. Even if she tries to take Luyu away, her bosses won't let it happen. Luyu will be fine."

Nadie got food out for Luyu, her hands on auto-pilot. "You said you would get venison," she nagged.

"And I will. You can't expect me to be home playing with Luyu and out hunting at the same time."

"We are going to be out of food. I will have to go to the neighbors to ask them for scraps."

He glared at her. "You will not. We are planning a trip into town on Friday. Our food will hold until then."

"Friday?" Nadie's dark mood lifted a little. She still got as excited as a child about trips into town. Food. Books from the library. Maybe a few new clothes for Luyu. More thread for the blanket. "Is everybody going?"

He nodded. "Most of us."

Luyu tapped on Nadie's hand as Nadie spooned cold canned beans into Luyu's bowl. "Town?" she repeated. "Town? Me?"

"Yes, Luyu too." She ignored Grandfather's glower. "We wouldn't leave you here by yourself all day while we went into town."

"You will have to watch her."

"Yes. I will."

Luyu ignored the spoon Nadie gave her, diving into the beans with both hands.

"Oh, you are a messy girl!" Nadie shook her head. "We need to do laundry. Especially once she is done. Would you put the clothes on her floor into the basket?"

He nodded and retreated. Nadie expected him to just retrieve the clothes and put them in the dirty laundry basket, but he came back to the kitchen.

"What...?" Nadie started.

He held up the shirt Nadie had put on Luyu when the social worker was there. Luyu hated any shirt other than her pony undershirt, but long sleeves were the worst. The shirt hung from Grandfather's hand in long, ragged strips. Nadie went over for a closer look. It was torn to shreds. Nadie had no idea how Luyu could have torn the tough, stretchy material like that. She must have used her teeth.

"I guess I don't need to wash that one! Add it to the rag box."

Grandfather agreed.

"Father?"

Nadie turned at the unfamiliar voice from the direction of the bedrooms. They were already filled to overflowing; who else had Grandfather invited to stay?

"We're in the kitchen," Grandfather called back. "Come in here." He looked at Nadie, a conspiratorial glint in his eye. "We have a special visitor today," he told Nadie.

Special? With all of the people who came and went through the house, Nadie didn't know what would make anyone special. Anyone who was important in the governing of the band had houses of their own. She hadn't heard of anyone of importance visiting from a neighboring band. The nearest Indigenous settlement was hours away.

A woman came into the kitchen. She was older than Nadie, younger than Grandfather. Her face was vaguely familiar, but Nadie couldn't put a name to her. She had obviously come from the city; she wore skinny red pants, a fresh, brightly colored shirt, and she was dripping with jewelry. Bangles on both wrists and ankles, big hoop earrings, a couple of necklaces, rings on her finger and toes, which Nadie could see because she wore sandals. Not sandals like old Eb would make, but white sandals from a women's clothing store. Other than her face and hair, the woman looked completely non-Indigenous. A dark-skinned woman living a white woman's life.

The woman stared at Nadie. Nadie looked away and focused on Luyu, trying to convince her to use a spoon instead of making a mess with her hands.

"Are you Nadie?" the woman asked.

Nadie nodded.

"This is Nicole," Grandfather said.

Nadie nodded, and then something tickled in the back of her brain. She looked at Grandfather rather than at Nicole, waiting to be told.

"Your mother."

Nadie looked searchingly at the woman's face. Her memory had faded over the years. She remembered Nicole visiting once when Nadie was about five. But she couldn't recall the face. It was completely foreign to her.

"Nadie, it's so good to see you again," Nicole gushed. She walked around the table to grab Nadie and give her a big hug. "Oh, my little girl! I can't believe it. You're taller than me."

"That happens," Grandfather agreed, with a low, rumbling laugh.

Nicole released Nadie from the hug, beaming. "It's so good to see you again, Nadie. You've grown into a beautiful young woman."

Nadie said nothing.

"Show your mother respect," Grandfather prompted. "She came a long way to see you."

"You are my mother," Nadie told Grandfather. "You are the one who fed and clothed me and who took care of me. Not her."

"I couldn't," Nicole protested. "Things were really messed up and I couldn't take care of you. So Father did."

"She's still your mother," Grandfather said. "She carried you inside her. She brought you into the world."

"Anyone could do that."

"Nadie!"

Nadie wet the rag beside the sink and started to wipe Luyu down. "Raising a child takes work. You have to be there."

Nicole stood watching Nadie, her face sad.

"Grandfather can welcome whoever he likes into his home," Nadie said. "I just hope you'll give me a little space. Because you're not my parent."

"Nicole is in your room," Grandfather announced. "Or actually, you've been living in hers."

Nadie swallowed. "Fine. Of course she can sleep in her own room or whatever room you want to put her in. I'll move in with Luyu."

Luyu didn't sleep well. She would be climbing over Nadie half the night. But Nadie didn't want to be forced to sleep in the same room as the woman who had abandoned her. Nicole had never been a part of Nadie's life. Nadie didn't see the need to start a relationship now. They could be sisters, like the other women in the band and the nation were her sisters. But Nicole was not going to be Nadie's mother.

CHAPTER SIX

Sleeping on the floor was not easy. Neither was trying to sleep with Luyu still awake and wanting to play. Add on top of that Nadie's excitement over going into town the next day, and she barely got a wink of sleep. She knew she was being a wimp about sleeping on the floor. Her people had slept outside on the ground for millennia. But her whole body was sore. Her joints ached and her back felt like it would never be unkinked again.

Nadie sat up, rubbing her eyes and groaning. Luyu crowed in delight and jumped on top of Nadie.

"Hello, sister," she announced, burying her face in the smooth skin of Nadie's neck and giving it a wet kiss. "Tân'si."

The sounds were awkward in her mouth, but Luyu rarely attempted the words in her own traditional language.

"Good job!" Nadie told her, kissing her on the cheek. "Are you excited about going to town today? I am."

"Town? Me?"

"Yes."

Luyu plucked at the waist of her diaper. "Change." It sounded more like 'tane,' but Nadie understood well enough.

"You going to lay still for me?"

Luyu shook her head.

Nadie laughed. "You won't lay still while I change it?"

Luyu again shook her head in response.

Nadie went and got a fresh diaper and laid Luyu on the floor. Luyu squirmed while Nadie took off the soaked diaper but didn't try to get up. She tapped Nadie's hand and made a humming sound.

"Hmm? What?" Nadie asked.

Luyu kicked and tried to roll over. Nadie held her still. "Shh. Be still." She hummed softly, and Luyu stilled, watching her face and making a little hum of her own.

"Good girl."

Nadie dressed Luyu, reminding her she would have to keep her clothes on in town. It was always a challenge keeping her fully dressed outside of the house.

Nadie avoided Nicole and Grandfather and the others, focusing on getting Luyu fed and ready to go. It was unusual for everybody to be up first thing in the morning. Luyu's head went back and forth continually, distracted by so many people. She barely even ate.

❧

They assembled near Mouse's house, everyone milling around and determining who was going to ride with whom. Not everyone had vehicles and the band didn't want to have to use more gas than necessary to make the trip. Nadie managed to get in the same truck as Mouse, away from Grandfather and Nicole. Mouse's eyes popped when she told him about Nicole showing up.

"Your mother?" he repeated. "I don't think I've ever met your mother."

Nadie nodded. "Exactly. If she thinks she can just show up and act like a parent to me..."

"Wow. What is she like?"

"I don't know. Citified. Looks like a white woman. I don't know what she's doing here."

"What did she say?"

Nadie thought about it for a minute, then shrugged. "I don't know. I never asked. I didn't really want to know anything. I just want her to go away again."

"Why? Why don't you get to know her?"

Nadie glared at him.

"What?" Mouse protested. "You might find you like her. I don't know."

"What if your father showed up? Would you want to get to know him?"

Mouse's eyebrows went up, almost all the way under his doo-rag. "I don't even know who that is."

Nadie waited for him to think it through and answer her.

"I don't know," he finally admitted. "I never really thought about him." He looked out the window at the scenery passing by. "I wonder what he's like," he mused.

Little Bird, one of the little boys, had a bad toothache. That was one of the reasons they needed to go into town. His mother and the medicine woman couldn't do anything for him. He needed to see the dentist.

But when they got into town, Little Bird was crying. He shook his head and refused. "No, no, I don't want to go!" he shouted. "I'm not going to the dentist!"

"But you have a toothache," his mother said. "The dentist can make it feel better."

Little Bird put his hand over his mouth. "No! I don't want to see the dentist!"

His mother looked at the others for help, unsure what to do.

"Are you afraid he's going to pull out your teeth?" asked Ben Fermet, an old man with big gaps between his remaining teeth.

"They won't do that unless they have to, and if they do, it will stop it from hurting."

Little Bird squealed, apparently not comforted by this. "I'm not going," he said frantically. "I'm not going to the dentist. I want to go back home. Let's get in the car."

"Shh." Nadie comforted. She crouched down and tried to stay on Little Bird's level, even with Luyu yanking and pulling on Nadie's arm, trying to get her to move on to something more interesting.

"Little Bird. You don't need to be scared." Mouse said to the little boy. "Little Bird, come here. I will tell you a story about when I went to the dentist. Once when I was little, just about your age, I had a bad toothache."

Little Bird nodded, his eyes big. He hung on Mouse's words.

"It hurt day and night. I couldn't eat, because it hurt when I chewed, or when I had anything hot, or cold, or sweet." Little Bird nodded along, agreeing. "At night, I held my face and moaned. It hurt so much. I curled up in a little ball and wished someone could make the toothache go away."

"Who made it go away?" Little Bird demanded.

"My mother said I needed to go to the dentist. The tooth had a hole in it the dentist needed to fix. The dentist has good medicine for teeth. He is a special kind of doctor who only works on teeth, and he makes them feel better."

"Did you go to the dentist?" Little Bird was breathing hard.

"I told my mother no. I told her it didn't hurt much, even though it made me moan all night and she knew how much it was hurting. She said I was going to waste away to nothing if I couldn't eat and couldn't sleep."

"Did she make you?"

"She didn't make me. She said I was a big boy and old enough to decide whether I should go to the dentist or not myself."

"Me too. I'm big. And I don't want to go."

"But that didn't make it any better. Finally, I went to my mother and begged her to take me to the dentist."

"And she did!"

"No. It was winter and the roads were impassable. We couldn't go into town yet. We had to wait until the roads were clear, and it seemed like a very, very long time."

Little Bird's hand was clamped over his mouth as if to keep anyone from looking at it or trying to fix it.

"While we were waiting, I got very sick. The infection in my tooth gave me a fever and made me feel very bad. I couldn't even touch my face myself, it hurt so much."

"Then what?"

"The roads were finally clear and we could go into town to see the dentist. When I sat in his big chair, he used a needle to put medicine into my mouth."

Little Bird squawked at this, his eyes wild.

"When he put the medicine in my face, it felt better for the first time. It was so good not to have any more pain. It had been hurting for so long I almost forgot what it was like to feel good. The dentist fixed up the tooth that had a hole in it and hurt so bad. When he looked at the pictures he took, he said the infection from my tooth had spread to the bone in my jaw." Mouse touched his jaw. "They had to send me to another doctor who gave me very strong medicine to get rid of the infection in the bone. It made me feel very sick. But it didn't make the infection go away and they had to send me to another doctor to take out the infected piece of bone so the rest of my body could heal."

In spite of himself, Little Bird's mouth hung open as he listened to the story.

"They said if I hadn't waited so long, I wouldn't have gotten so sick. The infection would not have gotten into my bone. When the dentist was done, I would have been able to go home and feel better. Instead, I had to suffer through more sickness and medicine and surgery at the hospital."

They looked at Little Bird. He swallowed hard and spoke to his mother. "I think I should go to the dentist."

"I do too," she agreed.

Little Bird took a long look at Mouse. "I will go."

"Good man," Mouse approved. "You are being brave and being wise about taking care of yourself. You will feel much better when the dentist fills your tooth."

"Will the needle hurt a lot?"

"No. Just a little. And then he will make your whole face numb and you won't be in pain anymore."

Little Bird's eyes turned to Nadie. "Will you go with me, Nadie?"

"You want me to?"

He nodded. Nadie looked at Mouse. "Would you take Luyu for a few minutes?"

"Sure."

Nadie released Luyu from her grip directly into Mouse's. "Hold onto her. Don't let her wander."

"I will."

Nadie joined Little Bird and his mother as they walked to the dentist. In the waiting room, Nadie held Little Bird in her lap and recounted stories to keep his mind occupied. When it was time for him to go in, Little Bird went with his mother, looking over his shoulder once at Nadie as he went down the hall to the procedure room.

Nadie opened up a paperback to read as she waited. She didn't get nearly as much reading time as she would like to, between school and chores and looking after Luyu's needs. Quiet, unoccupied moments were rare and precious. She heard a man talking to the receptionist and glanced up to look at him. It was the dentist, one Nadie had seen several times herself. He hadn't yet had time to work on Little Bird's tooth. Nadie suspected he had put the freezing in and was just waiting for it to take effect before he started drilling.

He shook his head at the receptionist, giving a little grimace. "Stupid Indians," he commented. "Don't teach their kids anything about oral hygiene. Never bother to see a dentist until their teeth are practically falling out of their heads. It's time to put an end to all this special treatment."

The receptionist gave him a little shush, glancing at the people in the waiting room. He shook his head again and went back into his office.

CHAPTER SEVEN

*N*adie had been working on her blanket during almost all of her school hours the past few days. The nights were getting colder and she wanted the special blanket to keep Luyu warm. It was soft and thick, painstakingly hand woven over a period of months. She had thought it would be done in early fall, not anticipating how many hours the careful hand work would take.

Mouse was glad to see her working on traditional craft work instead of her correspondence classes, and he sat with her, carving or doing other traditional men's crafts while she worked on it. He never had much patience for a project and was rarely working on the same one from one day to the next, jumping from one to another like a frog.

Nadie had thought Running Deer would be worried about her abandoning her correspondence work temporarily to finish up the blanket, but she wasn't. "I know you'll pick it back up again," she said. "You need a break. You work so hard. This will help you to get refreshed and refocused. You need to work on spiritual development too. This is good balance."

Nadie did find the weaving helpful. In spite of her worries about Luyu's care and the possibility of the social worker taking her away, Nadie was able to relax with the careful, repetitive work of weaving, finding a sort of quiet meditation even in the busy schoolroom.

The blanket had a red background, with a pattern of triangles and an owl in the middle, all of Nadie's own design. Running Deer said it all counted toward her math—counting, patterns, triangle construction, and so on. It was a good thing it counted, because Nadie struggled with the complex math in her textbooks, floundering her way through the examples and copying the answer key when she couldn't sort it out herself. But the blanket, that was good math. That she could understand.

Then finally, it was done. Nadie finished the edges and carefully folded the blanket into a compact rectangle, smoothing it with her hands.

"I can't believe it's done. It took so long to do!"

"You did a really good job," Mouse said. "You are a lot more patient than I am. I could never do that."

"You could if you worked on it."

"Never," Mouse repeated. "Not my kind of thing."

"How are those furs coming along?" Nadie teased.

Mouse drew himself up, his neck stiffening. "I am working on it," he insisted. "We had an agreement. I haven't forgotten."

"Really? What have you been doing?"

"I have been talking with the men, learning about where the animals go in the winter. Where the traplines are best. I have to make a frame and tools for working the hides, and I have been doing that. I have been practicing snares that will hold tight."

"You have?" Nadie had seen him engaged in some of these activities, but had never put it all together to realize he was, in fact, working toward a bigger goal.

Mouse nodded, his chin lifted proudly. "I did not forget our agreement."

"Well, it's a good thing we made it for spring and not for when I was done my blanket."

"Now you can start your second blanket. The one that is for me when I give you the furs."

Nadie had forgotten about that part of the agreement. But she pretended not to have. "I'll have the blanket done before the spring flowers bloom."

She hoped it would be a long winter.

&

Nadie was excited to get home to give Luyu her gift. She tried to stay calm about it, reminding herself Luyu was only a little girl and couldn't understand all of the work and love that had gone into the blanket. Luyu hated clothes and tended to kick off her blankets in bed, so she might not even like it. But Nadie pictured herself waiting until Luyu finally settled in to sleep and gently placing the blanket over her to keep her warm through the night. Even if Luyu didn't like it, Nadie would still use it to keep her little sister from being cold.

She hurried home, arriving out of breath. The door was locked and she had to go looking for Grandfather. He was down in the cellar but came up at her call.

"Here I am, with the key," he announced. "She was a little devil today. Getting into everything."

"Maybe she's coming down with something. She always seems to get sort of wild when she's fighting a cold."

He handed her the key. "Your blanket is done?" He was looking down at it.

Nadie's face got warm and she couldn't hold back a smile. "All done," she confirmed. She took the edge and let it unfold, holding it up off of the floor so he could see the whole thing at once.

"Oh, Nadie… I've never seen such a beautiful blanket."

Nadie almost teared up. She smiled more widely. "You like it?"

"It reminds me of your grandmother. She had the most wonderful gift in making blankets and beautiful things." He touched the edge of the blanket with reverence. "You have put a piece of your spirit into this blanket. It is a thing of great value."

Nadie couldn't stop smiling. She tried to answer modestly. "It was a lot of work and I am still just learning. But I'm very pleased with the way it turned out."

"You should be. I am very proud of you."

Nadie nodded.

"Ôhô, the owl, has a very powerful spirit. It is a good symbol."

"I want to give it to Luyu now."

His smile faded. "She will not know to respect it, Nadie. She won't know what value it has."

"Its value is in keeping her warm. She can appreciate that until she gets old enough to understand."

"Give her another blanket. Put this one on your bed. Or mine!"

"I made it for Luyu. That's who it is meant for," Nadie said firmly.

Grandfather made no further protest. Nadie draped the blanket back over her arm and went to get Luyu.

When the door opened, Luyu looked up from the floor where she was prodding a dustball that looked suspiciously like a spider. She got up and stared at the blanket. She lifted up her arms for it.

"Lu see?"

Nadie crouched down to put it into Luyu's hands and stretched it out for her to see.

"Oh!" Luyu crawled across the blanket to the owl and put her hand over it. She lay down on the blanket, resting her cheek on the owl's face. "Luyu," she said. "Mine."

"Yes," Nadie laughed. "Luyu's blanket. This is ôhô, the owl. He will watch over you while you sleep. An owl stays awake at night. Like you think you should!"

Luyu reached behind her and grabbed the blanket, pulling it over herself so she was cocooned inside like a sleeping bag.

"Ay-hay," Nadie heard Luyu say softly.

"You're welcome, baby. But it's not time for sleep. Do you want to come out and have some supper?"

Luyu crept out from between the folds, her eyes sparkling. "Eat?"

"That's right. Time to eat."

Luyu ran to Nadie and gave her a hug, then ran into the kitchen. Nadie followed her. There was more food now, including fresh produce. It wouldn't last, but for a few days, there were crisp, fragrant fruits and vegetables that made Nadie's mouth water every time she walked into the kitchen. Used to her limited fare of canned beans, macaroni, and cold cereal, Luyu tended to turn her nose up at the healthier food. But Nadie kept offering it to her for as long as it lasted. She worried about getting enough vitamins into Luyu's diet.

Nadie cut up an apple and arranged the small pieces into a smile on Luyu's plate. Luyu poked at it for a few minutes before picking up a piece with her left hand. Nadie's forehead creased. She looked down at Luyu's other hand. Two of her fingers were dusky and purple.

"What happened to your hand, Luyu?"

Luyu looked down at it, nibbling at the apple piece. She put the swollen fingers in her mouth and sucked on them.

"Did you shut them in the door, Lu? What happened?"

Luyu shook her head.

"Grandfather?"

He didn't come into the room. "What, Nadie?"

"How did Luyu's hand get hurt? Did something happen?"

"She's been in all kinds of mischief today. It could have happened any time."

"You don't know? You didn't see?" Nadie went to the kitchen doorway so she would be closer and hear Grandfather better.

"I told you it could have happened any time."

Nadie bit her lip and went back to the table. Luyu pushed the pieces of fruit around. "Mmm, dinner?" Luyu asked.

"Have your apple, I'll make something else while you're eating it."

She started a pot of water boiling and turned back around to face Luyu.

"How did you hurt your fingers?"

Luyu looked at her.

"You have an owie on your fingers?"

Luyu held them up.

"How did Lu get the owie?"

Luyu looked toward the doorway as if waiting for Grandfather to answer.

"You tell me, Luyu. How did you get the owie on your fingers?"

Luyu didn't respond.

"Do you remember getting the bump on your head? How did you bump your head?"

Luyu again looked toward the doorway. Nadie sighed and continued to get her dinner ready.

CHAPTER EIGHT

Nadie had a feeling something was wrong when she walked into the house. It felt too quiet. Empty. It didn't make any sense and she shook off the feeling of unease.

It had been a long day at school. She had spent several days trying to get caught back up on her correspondence work at school, now she was done Luyu's blanket, but she was floundering. She was good at the reading portions of the English Language Arts work, but the math and history sections boggled her mind. She attempted to do the math, copying out one line of the answer key at a time, trying to solve each step on her own before copying out the next line.

The history and government work was almost as incomprehensible. Even though she understood the words used to describe parliamentary procedures and passing of bills, she had no idea what any of it meant. The history work mostly chronicled wars overseas, in faraway places Nadie would never see. They were dry facts with dates and maps, as if the wars had been fought on paper and never touched human lives. When she did come across chapters on Canadian history, particularly those that touched on contact with her people, she felt a little sick.

She had once heard 'history is written by the victors,' and that seemed particularly apt. Battles where hundreds of Nehiyaw and other aboriginal nations were killed were glossed over. The settlement of the country by the French and English, rolling out east to west was related as if those lands had been vacant, free for the taking. Treaties were related as if the First Nations were full partners, voluntarily giving up their rights and freedoms.

As Nadie penned answers that echoed the reading sections in the text, she felt like she was betraying her people. She wanted to get full points for her answers, so she said what the white men and women who sat at their desks in the city wanted to hear. She wanted to write about the poverty and oppression. About the her peoples' generosity repaid with smallpox-infected blankets. About children ripped from their homes and sent to residential schools where they were starved and abused, punished if caught speaking their own language.

But she didn't.

Nadie walked into the kitchen to get herself a drink of cool water before going to get Luyu. It was a surprisingly warm day for the end of the fall. She'd have to make sure Luyu had enough to drink and didn't get dehydrated after being shut in a stifling warm room all day. Or however long Grandfather had left her there.

Grandfather wasn't in his bedroom or the living room. Nadie tried the door handle of the baby room. Not only was it not locked, but the catch hadn't engaged, and the door swung open at her touch. Nadie's breath caught in her throat.

"Luyu?"

She scanned the tiny room, but Luyu wasn't there. Nadie went through the motions of looking behind the door she had just opened, and of checking the blankets, both her own and the owl blanket, spread out on the floor. Her mind was whirring.

Grandfather had taken Luyu out with him fishing or to play in the neglected garden in the warm sunshine. That was a good thing. It was good he was taking her out to play somewhere.

She looked in Grandfather's room, even though she knew they weren't there. The kitchen. The living room.

"Grandfather? Luyu?"

She quietly checked the other bedrooms. Nicole was not home, Nadie's old room left in messy chaos. Mel and the Nose were sleeping in Cam's room. No one was in Grandfather's room.

Not only was there no sign of Luyu, but there were also no messes to indicate where she had been. If she had been out of her bedroom without supervision, there would be some sign of it.

"Grandfather?" Nadie poked her head out the back door, looking around for them. "Nimosôm? Where are you?"

There was no answer. His truck was not behind the house. He was out somewhere. Visiting a friend.

Nadie went back to the kitchen and made a sandwich for Luyu. She'd be hungry when she got home. She'd be crabby and would want something to eat.

Time passed and Nadie got more anxious. She couldn't see Grandfather taking Luyu out for so long. Unless Luyu had been hurt and he had to take her into town to see the doctor. If that had happened, then surely Grandfather would have sent word to Nadie at the school.

Restless, Nadie paced through the house once more. She paused at the closed bathroom door. The big buckets of grain they got in town had warnings on the side about small children being able to drown in a few inches of water in the bottom of a bucket. Holding her breath, Nadie cracked the door open just enough to reassure herself Luyu wasn't in there. She pulled it shut again and released her breath.

As Nadie walked back to the baby room to wait, she saw the cellar door was cracked open an inch.

"Grandfather? Are you down there?"

She hesitated at the top of the stairs. She never went down into the cellar. It had been off limits from the time she was as little as Luyu. And besides that, it was creepy. She had no reason to go down there. She should just pull the door shut so Luyu wouldn't fall down the stairs by accident.

Nadie pushed the door open.

"Grandfather? Luyu? Are you down there?"

Nadie started down the steps, a tight knot of anxiety in her stomach. She whispered a prayer to the Great Spirit. A bargain. If Luyu were okay, then Nadie would drop out of school to look after her properly. No more letting Grandfather lock Luyu up half the day. Nadie would parent her full-time. She'd be a good mother like Grandfather had been when Nadie was little. Just as long as Luyu was okay.

She got to the bottom of the stairs and looked around. There was no sign of Luyu. She breathed a sigh of relief. The room was warm, with the sour and yeasty smell of mash emanating from the big bucket in the corner.

It wasn't until then that she saw Luyu's feet, bare and dirty, protruding from the bucket. With a wordless cry, Nadie flew across the dirt floor. She hauled Luyu out of the half-filled bucket.

A few inches of liquid.

A child could drown in a few inches of water.

Luyu was cold and lifeless. Her wet hair was pasted to her scalp, the bump on her head visible and still not fully healed. Her eyes were closed like she was asleep. Nadie wiped the liquid from her nose and blew air into her mouth. Her lips burned from the mash. The air came out Luyu's nose, bubbling.

"No!" The air was supposed to go into her lungs. She'd studied the pictures on the wall at the public pool when they went into town to splash around in the summer heat. Nadie pinched Luyu's nose to seal it off and blew again. Luyu's chest rose. Nadie waited. She blew in another breath. Still, nothing happened.

"Oh, please, baby. Please, Luyu. No…"

She picked Luyu up and cuddled her close.

"Come on, baby. Wake up, Lu. Please, sweetie, open your eyes. Breathe."

She held Luyu's face against her, feeling for any hint of breath.

She put her ear to Luyu's chest, listening for the beating of her heart. She let out a howl of anguish.

The room was dark and though it had previously felt warm, Nadie's body had lost all of its heat. There were goosebumps on her skin, numbing cold right down to her bones. Luyu got colder and colder in her arms. Nadie held her cuddled up close, trying to keep her warm. She had no strength in her legs to get back up. No desire to move from this place. Time was suspended. All she knew was her loss and her grief, the impossibility of what had happened.

She had seen mothers lose their children. She had felt sorrow and pity for them in their loss. But this was something she could never have comprehended. A gaping hole ripped in her heart, torn from her very soul.

"Come back to me, Luyu," she begged. "Great Spirit, Mother Earth, bring her back to me. I'm sorry. Oh, Luyu, I'm so sorry."

There was no movement or breath from the tiny child in her arms.

An eternity later, she could hear movements and voices from upstairs. She didn't move. They seemed to be on the other side of the world from her.

She heard Grandfather's voice. "Nadie? Are you home? Where are you?"

"Nimosôm!" The cry was ripped out of her. "Nimosôm! Grandfather, help me!"

There was a shadow when his body blocked the doorway at the top of the stairs.

"Nadie? What happened?"

She was afraid he was going to fall down the stairs, he came down so fast. He tried to take Luyu from her arms, but she refused to release the small body. Grandfather touched Luyu's face, now dry, though her hair was still damp. He listened for sounds of life in her body. His face looked like Nadie felt, a reflection of her grief.

"Nadie… Nadie, I'm sorry! I don't know what happened. She was safe. I left her safe…"

Nadie tried to swallow the lump in her throat. She couldn't find any more words. Grandfather put his arms around her.

"My child, you're like ice. Come. Come upstairs."

He lifted her to her feet. Nadie was numb. He had to guide her up the steep wooden stairs. Nadie didn't know what to do when she got to the top. Others were there. Other household members, maybe even her mother, crowding around, asking questions, trying to take Luyu out of her arms.

Nadie refused to let go. Her arms and shoulders ached, but Luyu was hers and Nadie was never going to let her go again.

Grandfather tried to guide her into her old bedroom, but Nadie shook her head. She found her way into the baby room. Grandfather lowered her to sit on the blankets. He draped the red owl blanket around Nadie's shoulders, then wrapped it around her, Luyu hidden beneath.

"It's okay," Grandfather assured her. "It will be okay, Nadie. Everything will be okay."

"No," Nadie moaned. "Nothing will ever be okay again."

CHAPTER NINE

People came and went. Nadie didn't want anything to do with them. The medicine woman tried to pull Luyu out of her grasp, but Nadie wouldn't allow her to. The woman put herbs in the room. Sage, tied into braids. Other sacred plants.

Nadie thought Beth was there too, and maybe Mouse himself.

❦

She awoke in the morning to strangers, still sitting holding the stiff body, her own body feeling stiff and cold.

There was a man with a uniform and a face like a sad hound dog. He was white, not Indigenous, and spoke to her in a language that bore a strong resemblance to English, but with strange intonations she had never heard before.

"You must give me the little girl now," he told Nadie firmly. "I will take good care of her. I will not let anything bad happen to her."

Nadie didn't relinquish the body. Her chest ached. Her heart hurt when she breathed. She thought—hoped—her heart was so hurt she would die. She had no desire to live, with Luyu dead in her arms.

"Can you tell me her name?" the stranger asked.

Nadie swallowed hard and cleared her throat. "Luyu," she whispered.

"Luyu. That is a beautiful name. Is it Cree? What does it mean?"

"I don't know."

"Can I take the blanket off?" he unwound it and laid it aside with respectful hands. "Now I can see her sweet face. She looks peaceful, like she's sleeping, doesn't she?" His voice was hoarse and gentle. "You love her very much."

Nadie nodded.

"What's your name?"

It was hard to speak. But he was so kind to her that she felt like she had to show him respect. "Nadie."

"That is another beautiful name. You are going to want to lay Luyu to rest. You know her spirit can't rest until you send it on its way."

Nadie didn't want to talk about laying Luyu to rest. She bit her lip.

"You can't do that until my people have had a chance to look at her. Please. You need a rest. I won't let anything else bad happen to her."

Nadie shook her head. But he had big, strong, capable hands and she was weak and sore from holding Luyu all night. With gentle care, he took the body from her.

Her arms now as empty as her heart, Nadie looked around, at a loss. She picked up the blanket and hugged it to her.

"Nadie." The whisper came from behind her and arms enveloped her. She turned her head far enough to see it was Mouse. "Oh, Nadie. I'm so sorry about Luyu."

There were no tears. Through it all, there had been no tears. Nadie didn't know what had happened to them. She needed to cry, to announce her grief and pain, but she couldn't. She held the blanket and Mouse held her. The policeman quietly took Luyu's body away.

♨

Nadie moved like a sleepwalker. She didn't eat and didn't sleep, even though everyone kept saying she should. There were people gathered together in the living room, lightly scented with sage, talking about Luyu and laughing about her many exploits. Nadie couldn't understand the laughter. Her heart hurt so badly she thought she would never laugh again. Certainly not about Luyu.

"It's okay," one of the women told her. "Luyu's spirit is happy now. We want to celebrate her life. She needs to know it is okay for her to be happy. Laughing is part of healing."

Nadie shook her head and buried her face in her hands.

♨

Nadie wasn't sure how long it had been since she had last slept. It might have been two days, or it might have been three. Or if she counted passing out sitting up when it all became too much for her body to handle, then maybe it hadn't even been a day.

Her thinking was too muddy and fogged in to sort out the passing hours, or what people said to her, or what she should do next. People told her what to do and she ignored them.

Grandfather and Chief Frank came to her together. A united front. Two grown men to confront one stubborn teenage girl. They both looked worried and sheepish, like little boys caught with their hands in the cookie jar.

"Nadie. I know you won't want to, but we need to go into town," Grandfather said, his voice taking on a stern parenting tone that said he would not take no for an answer.

Nadie looked back and forth at the men's faces. "Why?"

"The police want to talk to you. And to me. They are trying to understand how this happened. We need to explain to them that it was an accident."

"I don't want—"

"I told you we need to. We have to do this for Luyu."

"It's not for Luyu. Luyu knows what happened."

"Well, yes. But they won't release her body until we answer their questions. And we have to lay her to rest for her spirit to move on."

"You go talk to them." Nadie looked him in the eye for the first time since she had found Luyu dead. Maybe for the first time in years. "You're the one who knows what happened. I was at school."

"You must not have locked her door. She could only get out if it was unlocked." He said the words softly. Not in an accusatory way. But they cut Nadie to the quick. She had left Luyu's door unlocked other days.

"When did you check on her last?" she demanded. "When did you play with her? If I left it unlocked in the morning, you would have locked it later. After you checked on her. Or after you played with her. Or gave her lunch."

"Nobody is to be blamed for this," Chief Frank told both of them. "Let us not accuse each other and hurt each other's feelings over something that was an accident. Something that could not have been prevented. We all miss Luyu."

"It could have been prevented," Nadie protested.

Chief Frank waved her protests into silence. "We all loved Luyu. No one would have wished for this to happen to her. But it did happen and she is happy where she is now. We miss her, but we will let her spirit move on."

"We need to go into town to talk to the police," Grandfather repeated. "They won't give her body back until we do."

"Where is the policeman who took her?" Nadie demanded. "He said they would give her back. He said nothing bad would happen."

"He will give her back," Chief Frank reassured her. "After their questions have been answered. You know how it is when the white man investigates a death on the reservation. They want to know why everything. They cannot accept death is simply a part of life. It has always been so. Man's spirit comes into his body, and he learns and grows, and when he dies, it leaves him. Investigating why a death happened and how it happened is pointless. It was because the Great Spirit willed it so. We do not let death come between us, as the white man does."

"I also want to know why and how," Nadie argued. "I want to know why my sister is dead," she told Grandfather. "I want to know why you didn't love her and care for her like you did others. Why couldn't you love her like you loved me? Why did you lock her up, and hurt her, and let her die?"

"Your Grandfather didn't hurt Luyu." Chief Frank's voice was pitched to soothe Nadie, but she wasn't a horse or a hurt dog. She was an angry mama bear. And bears didn't care how softly you talked. "Your Grandfather loved Luyu just like the rest of his children, all the children he raised."

"He did hurt her," Nadie insisted. "He didn't feed her or dress her. And when I came home, she would be hurt. He was the only one with the key, so who else could have hurt her?"

"Children get bruises playing," Chief Frank spoke over Grandfather's choked response, so she couldn't make out what Grandfather said. "They fall, they drop things, they get their fingers caught in drawers. A happy, active child always has bruises."

Nadie glared at her grandfather in silence. He knew the truth, no matter how much Chief Frank tried to protect him. "I will go talk to the police," she decided. "I want to talk to them."

"We will have a talking circle when you get back," Chief Frank said. "So you and your grandfather can be reconciled and the band will be in harmony."

❧

The policeman with funny speech welcomed Nadie when she got to the little police station in town.

"I don't know if I told you my name at the house," he said in an apologetic tone. "But you weren't much in the mood for talking at the time. I'm Mac Bolewicz."

It was on his name badge too. She'd never seen such a name before. He pronounced it bowl-a-wish, but Nadie decided she would just call him 'Mac' in her mind. It was a lot simpler and matched his hound-dog face. She held out her hand tentatively.

"I am pleased to meet you."

They shook hands.

"How are you doing? Can I get you any coffee? Tea? A glass of water?"

Nadie drew herself up. She wasn't going to let him think she was a weak, helpless child. She needed to show she was strong. She was an adult who knew the difference between right and wrong. Otherwise, he wouldn't believe her or take her word for what had happened.

"No, thank you. I'm just fine."

He nodded. "Come on into my office then," he invited with a sweep of his hand, and he escorted her in. It was a small room, mostly taken up by a big wooden desk covered with papers. There was one big chair behind the desk, and three smaller chairs in front of it. One of them was already occupied by Jacky James, the social worker who had come out to the house. Nadie swallowed, looking at her. Jacky's mouth was a thin, angry line. Her eyes blazed. She looked like a wolf ready to consume Nadie.

"I believe you've met Ms. James," Mac said casually, with a motion in Jacky's direction. "Please. Have a seat."

Nadie sat down, leaving the middle guest chair unoccupied as a buffer between them.

"Nadie, we're so very sorry about this tragic accident and are mindful of your loss. My job is to make a determination as to what led up to Luyu's accident. We can't move on until I do. You and your Grandfather seem to be the ones with the most knowledge about what happened. So if you can fill me in, we can lay Luyu to rest."

Nadie nodded. There was a big, hot lump in her throat and the pain in her chest was getting so bad she wondered if she would drop dead before she was able to relate her story to Mac. She wished she had asked for a glass of water and wondered if it were now too late.

"Rather than me asking you a lot of questions and maybe pointing this investigation in the wrong direction, I'd like you to just give me your story, if you please could. Start to finish; I won't interrupt you with questions. Then at the end, we'll discuss it further. Do you think you can do that?"

"What do you want me to say? Just what happened that day, when I got home from school?"

"That would be a good start. But if there's something else you want to tell me, feel free."

Nadie took a deep breath. It all came out in a jumble, out of sequence, stream of consciousness. She was afraid it wouldn't make sense. But Mac was as good as his word and did not interrupt her to try to clarify. He just sat back and listened, his eyes on his desk most of the time, a frown line between his eyebrows.

Nadie didn't look at Jacky, but could feel the anger and discontent coming off of her like waves of heat. What was she so angry about? It wasn't her child, her little cousin. Luyu was a stranger to Jacky, who couldn't even get her name right. Jacky had threatened to take Luyu away, but then had left her there to be killed.

When Nadie was finished her story, she didn't look at Mac. She looked at Jacky, expecting a tirade.

Jacky didn't disappoint.

"That child was in your care. You knew the dangers she faced. You knew she needed to be constantly supervised. How could you let a thing like this happen?"

"Ms. James," Mac started warningly.

"It's true," Nadie said. "I know. I should have dropped out of school, so someone was watching her properly. I just thought… I thought Grandfather could do it. He raised me. He knew how to take care of children. But…"

"But he didn't take care of Lulu. You knew that. You knew he was not feeding her or taking care of her. It was obvious to me when I came all the way out there to visit. What did you think was going to happen?"

Nadie gazed at her, schooling her own anger. She had been taught anger was destructive. It wouldn't help her here. "I thought… you were going to help."

It stopped Jacky cold. Her eyes widened. She made several sputtering sounds, like an old car that was trying to start, but couldn't spark.

Mac was nodding. "This child was on Child Services' radar from the time she was born," he pointed out. "Many different agencies were in touch and promised to do something to help her. Child Services has to bear some of the responsibility if they put her in a home where the caregivers were unable to provide the level of supervision needed. Especially if Child Services was aware of that fact."

"I did my part," Jacky snapped. "I did report it to my supervisors. I tried to get a decision made to take her out of the home. I knew something like this was going to happen. I told them. And I was right."

"Not something you want to be right about," Mac observed.

"No. Of course not."

"Who was the child's legal guardian?" Mac asked.

Jacky didn't answer immediately, her eyes wary of a trap.

"Was it Nadie Laplante?" Mac persisted.

"No. It was Willie Laplante. The grandfather."

"And we will be speaking with him soon. In the meantime… it would be best if you don't put the responsibility on the wrong person. Nadie was a schoolgirl, unrelated to Luyu, not her guardian. A child trying to help out with household duties. She isn't responsible."

"She took responsibility. When I asked her who was taking care of the baby, she made it clear she was. And she's old enough to be held legally responsible."

"I'm not sure that is true."

"Other teen parents have been held responsible."

"She's not the parent." Mac's gaze shifted to Nadie. "Unless you are Luyu's biological mother...?"

"No!" Nadie shook her head. "I'm going to get off the reservation! I'm not going to have babies I can't take care of and leave them for someone else to look after. I'm not like that. I do good at school. I'm going to graduate and I'm going to go to college."

"Good for you. Sorry, I had to ask. Sometimes the relationships on the reservation can get a little bit... complicated."

"Luyu's not my baby. I've never had a baby and I don't plan to anytime soon."

"So Nadie... why don't you tell me what you think happened? The last time you saw Luyu alive was before school?"

"I told you, I fed her and got her dressed like usual."

"And then? What did you do when it was time to go to school?"

"I put her back in her room. I shut the door so she couldn't get into any trouble. I... tried to wake Grandfather up and told him I was going to school."

"You tried to wake him up."

"Yes."

"Which implies you weren't successful in getting him up?"

Nadie frowned. "He was moving around a bit. I thought he'd wake up the rest of the way once I was on my way. It takes him a while to get his motor running, sometimes."

"And you told him you were going to school?"

"Yes."

"Why would you bother to tell him that if he wasn't awake?"

"I just did. So he'd know it was time to wake up. I always told him."

"And did he ever get up?"

"Yes."

"Before you walked out the door?"

"Yes… I… think so. Sometimes. But usually after I left."

"But you didn't see that."

"I know he got up. He wasn't still asleep when I got home from school."

"But you don't know what time he got up. Whether it was right when you left for school or not."

"He got up," Nadie repeated.

"Right. So you imagine he got up pretty soon after you left for school. Then what would he do? Let Luyu out again?"

"Yes. To play with her. Or she would go with him and learn by watching him."

"What would she learn?"

Nadie shrugged. "Everything. That's how we learn. We go with the adults and we watch, and we practice."

"And you go to school."

"Yes, but Luyu wasn't old enough for school yet. She just learned by going with him."

"Did she go with him?"

"When he went out."

"He never left the house and left her locked in her room?"

Even though Nadie had come to the police station with the intention of telling them all about her Grandfather's shortcomings and his responsibility for Luyu's death, she was finding it difficult to do. The policeman was trying to back her into a corner, and even though it was where she had planned to be anyway, she didn't like to be trapped like an animal.

"I wasn't there. I was at school."

"Yes. Now I want you to think about something, Nadie. When you went home after school and went to get Luyu out of her room most days, do you think she had been out during the day with your Grandfather? Or do you think she was locked in the room the whole day?"

Nadie thought about it, trying to quantify 'most' days.

"Was she still in the same clothes?" Jacky suggested. "Or had she been changed into a different shirt because she had gotten dirty during the day?"

"She didn't keep her shirt on," Nadie reminded her. "She wouldn't wear anything but her diaper and the pony undershirt."

In a flash, she remembered pulling Luyu out of the mash bucket. In her diaper and the pony shirt. She had drowned in the pony shirt. Nadie closed her eyes, trying to block it out.

"Was her diaper wet or dry when you came home from school?" Jacky persisted.

"Wet."

"Always?"

Nadie concentrated. Always? Had Luyu ever had a dry diaper on Nadie's return?

"I don't know."

"Ninety percent of the time? Fifty? What?" Jacky leaned forward in her chair, eyes hard.

"I... I can't tell. I don't know."

"Was she always hungry when you got home?"

"She was usually hungry," Nadie agreed.

"How hungry?"

Nadie looked at Mac for help. She had no idea how to answer Jacky's questions. Mac's were easier. Nadie needed Mac to be the one asking questions.

"Do you think your Grandfather fed her lunch most days?" Mac asked, his voice soft and uninflected.

"No... not most."

Nadie heard Jacky's intake of breath to ask another question, but Mac shook his head at her and just sat in silence for a few minutes.

"Did you ever have any indication your Grandfather had taken Luyu out of her room during the day?" Mac asked.

Nadie nodded. "Yes. Yes, sometimes."

"What made you think that?"

"She got into things during the day. Grandfather said if the door wasn't locked, she would get out, and she would get into things. And I saw the messes; things she had broken or gotten into. So I knew she'd been out during the day."

"How often did that kind of thing happen?"

"He kept the door locked most of the time. He didn't want her to get into trouble. So... not a lot."

"What other clues did you have he was taking care of her during the day? That she had been out of her room?"

Nadie bit her lip. "She... sometimes she had bruises..."

Mac bent over and flipped through one of the stacks of paper on his desk. He looked down at one page for a minute, pressing his lips together in concentration.

"She had a pretty big bump on her head. They said that wasn't from the day of the accident."

"No. It was from a little while ago. A few days. She was very sick..."

"Did she have a concussion?"

"I don't know."

"Did a doctor look at her?"

"No."

"When you say she was sick, do you mean she was throwing up?"

"She threw up once. And she was... tired and dozy... not like Luyu usually is. She didn't want to eat. Just cuddled and slept."

"How do you think she got that bump?"

"I don't know. She couldn't have just gotten it in her room. She must have fallen down."

"She could have fallen down in her room."

"From what? She climbed out of the crib without hurting herself all the time. There was nowhere else to fall from."

"So you think she fell off of something and that's how she got the goose-egg."

"Goose egg?"

"The bump on her head. You think she fell."

"Yes..." Nadie drew the word out. She didn't actually think Luyu had fallen down, but she didn't know how to approach it.

"And the black eye, too?"

"I don't know. She must have fallen."

"Or someone hit her. Maybe because she was getting into mischief again."

"I don't know. I wasn't home."

"And she had a recent injury to her hand. A couple of fingers." Mac wiggled his index and middle finger for her as he read the report.

"I don't know what happened. Maybe they got shut in the door. But it was while I was at school. So she had been out. Grandfather had been looking after her."

"More or less," Mac commented.

Nadie frowned. "I don't know what that means."

"Maybe he took her out of her room, but he wasn't watching her well enough to prevent her from getting injured."

"Oh. No... but she's pretty quick. You can't stop kids from getting bruises." She knew she was echoing Chief Frank's excuses. All normal, active kids got bruises.

Mac sighed, looking further at the notes on his desk. "She had a number of other bone breaks that had healed. Breaks not treated by any doctor."

"Bones?" Nadie repeated. "She broke her arm once."

"She had quite a number."

"I... don't know how she got them. It must have been before she came to us."

She endured the looks of the social worker and policeman. Mac dropped his gaze first.

"The day Luyu died, did you lock her door?"

"Yes."

"Was the door at the top of the stairs locked or latched?"

"No... I don't think so."

"It does have a latch on it."

"Back when I was a little girl… I wasn't allowed to go down there, and the latch was out of my reach."

"But your grandfather never used it to keep Luyu out of the cellar."

"No… she was already locked up."

"Unless you didn't lock the door."

"I'm certain I did."

"If you locked it, then your grandfather unlocked it. And failed to lock it again."

"I… I don't know. I wasn't there. Maybe it didn't latch. You have to pull it tight, or it doesn't latch properly. You can't turn the handle, but you can just push—or pull—it open."

"So you think you locked it but didn't pull it shut tight?"

"Or Grandfather didn't."

"Just an accident."

Nadie looked down, nodding.

"That child was horribly neglected," Jacky jumped in, unable to hold back any longer. "Locked in an empty room all day long, with no interaction, nothing to play with. Like a prison. That's criminal negligence. A child's brain can't develop properly in an environment like that! She was dirty, starved, and abused. Somebody should have done something about it!"

"Yes," Mac agreed, looking at her.

Jacky flushed red. "I was only out there one time. I asked her to be moved after my visit. It isn't my fault she was placed in that home, or that she remained there. I was doing what I could to get her out."

"We are aware of that. Nevertheless, Child Services has had their hand in this from the start. Not you. But others."

"It wasn't like that," Nadie said.

Her heart broke at the image they painted. Luyu wasn't neglected. She was dearly loved. Nadie did everything she could to make Luyu's life happy and to take care of her. And if she was abused… Nadie had never seen Grandfather hit her. Ever.

Nadie and Grandfather were both silent all the way back to the reservation. It was an uncomfortable car ride. Nadie wondered what Mac and Jacky had said when they talked to Grandfather. Had they accused him of hitting her? Had they said they thought he was neglecting and abusing her, and that had led to her death? Did they say that was what Nadie said?

It was rare for Grandfather to be so solemn for so long. Normally, he was making wry jokes, trying to cheer her up, chatting away about gossip among the band or things that had happened while they were in town. It was always an adventure. A car trip back from the town was never quiet.

on't you come back to your own room?" Nicole asked Nadie when she got home. "There's plenty of space. I can sleep on the floor; I don't mind. It's your room and I hate kicking you out."

Nadie shook her head.

"Don't you know I love you, just like you loved Luyu?"

Nadie just looked at her, unable to find the words.

Nicole looked away. "Well, I do," she said with a pout. "You're my baby."

"I'm not yours and I'm not a baby. If you loved me, you would have taken care of me."

Nadie turned her back on Nicole before she could argue the point. She went back to the baby room and pulled the door shut behind her. She picked up the red blanket and wrapped it around herself. Lying down on her other blankets, she closed her eyes and tried to shut it all out.

❧

Nadie awoke at the voices and movements throughout the house. She had expected everyone to go home and to leave them alone.

The normal routines would resume, other than the loss of Luyu. But it was obvious something was going on.

She got up and, tying the blanket around her shoulders, shuffled out to the living room. Various elders of the band, men and women, were gathered in the living room and kitchen, speaking in low voices. Nadie didn't hear their words or understand what they said to her as she entered the room. She looked into the kitchen, not understanding what the noise and activity was all about.

Luyu's body had been returned and was stretched out on the table. Nadie felt sick to her stomach, seeing the small naked body lying there. One of the women grasped Nadie's arm and pulled her into the room, speaking to her softly in the traditional tongue. One of the other women pressed a wet cloth into Nadie's hand. Like a sleepwalker, Nadie joined them in washing the body. It was so tiny and frail, the flesh mottled with what looked like bruises.

The white man had desecrated it with a Y incision down the front of her chest and belly, stitched up with small, neat black stitches. Had they taken anything from her that they had kept? Was she whole? Nadie tried to push all thoughts aside, losing herself in the task at hand. She had washed Luyu many times before, but never had she been so cold and unresponsive.

She helped the women to dress Luyu again. Or they helped her. Gone was Luyu's pony undershirt. She would have hated the clothes they pulled onto her still body. Beth gave Nadie a small pair of moccasins that she slipped onto Luyu's feet. Beth had tears in her eyes. Most of the women, like Nadie, were dry-eyed and gave no sign of grief.

The medicine woman put a bundle of sweetgrass into Luyu's right hand and folded both hands across her chest. The men arrived with a tiny coffin. Nadie's throat constricted as she watched them pick Luyu up and lay her inside. Someone put Luyu's red ball into Nadie's hand and she nestled it beside the child's head. The medicine woman put tobacco in the casket as well and started to sing.

They sang and they told stories about Luyu. And they

laughed. Nadie stood, staring at the small coffin and didn't know what to do. She couldn't speak. She couldn't cry. She felt nothing but Luyu's absence. She had known as soon as she walked into the house that day that something was missing. She hadn't realized how big the little girl's spirit really was. How she had filled the whole house with her presence. And now it was gone.

Someone guided Nadie into the one unbroken chair. She sat there, not singing or laughing. She had seen other women mourn their children and had never realized the immensity of the loss they felt.

On the third day, they took the casket to the burial grounds where the men had dug a hole. It was so big for such a tiny girl. Nadie thought Luyu would have been frightened of it if she had been alive. The thought of laying Luyu in the cold, hard ground, burying her and leaving her there forever increased the pain in Nadie's chest. She thought she would faint from it. Maybe she would die from it. They could lay her beside Luyu and Nadie could keep her baby company there for the rest of eternity.

Chief Frank handed Nadie a blanket to put over the casket. Nadie ran the fabric between her fingers, looking at it. Luyu should be covered with the red owl blanket. She had only had it for a short while, but Nadie had made it especially for her. The owl would keep her safe. The owl would take her spirit to the afterlife.

She mumbled an explanation to Chief Frank and the others and hurried back to the house for the owl blanket. It was not in the baby room. It was not in Nadie's old room. She couldn't find it anywhere. Eventually, she was forced to return to the graveside. She laid the other blanket over the casket and it was lowered into the ground.

They sang a song for Luyu as they threw dirt over the coffin until Nadie could barely make out any of the blanket beneath it.

Everyone said goodbye to Luyu, speeding her on her way to the world of spirits. Beth put a plastic shopping bag into Nadie's hands. It was filled with Luyu's clothes. The clothes she couldn't stand to wear. Most of them still looked brand new. Swallowing a lump in her throat, Nadie gave a few items of clothing to each of the women who had children around Luyu's size or smaller, until the bag was empty. Nadie let go of it, letting it blow away in the wind. Everything that belonged to Luyu had now been passed on to others.

They took Nadie back to the house. Grandfather hugged her and spoke words of comfort. Nadie pushed him away and closed herself up in the baby room. She curled up on the blankets and waited for tears or sleep to come.

Grandfather and the medicine woman came into the baby room. Nadie sat up. She wanted to shout at them to get out and leave her in peace, but it was Grandfather's house and not Nadie's. She only lived there because he had taken her in, back when she was a baby even younger than Luyu.

They sat on the floor near her. The room was very crowded with three people there.

For a long time, they all just sat in silence. Grandfather looked old and grave. His eyes didn't sparkle. His mouth turned down with deep wrinkles around it.

The medicine woman began to chant. Nadie closed her eyes and listened to the beat, letting it carry her away. After some time had passed, the woman stopped chanting. Nadie opened her eyes.

"It is time to let Luyu go," the medicine woman said solemnly. "You are preventing her from her journey on to the spirit world. You must make peace with her death so she can move on in her journey."

Nadie cleared her throat. It felt like she had not spoken in days. Maybe she hadn't. She couldn't remember saying a word since the meeting with the policeman and social worker in town.

"I don't want Luyu's spirit to move on. I want it to stay here with me."

"She has a place to go to with the Great Spirit. She will be happy there. She is not happy if she has to stay here, where she does not belong."

Nadie shook her head. "I am not ready. She is my baby, I want her here."

"She is gone, Nadie," Grandfather said. "She does not belong in this house or with you anymore. Her body has been buried and her spirit needs to move on."

"She will always be in you," the medicine woman comforted. "She is a part of your heart and soul, and that will never leave. But you must let her spirit be free."

"No," Nadie said flatly. "I can't do that."

Mouse came into the baby room. He knelt down to give Nadie and tight hug and a kiss on the cheek.

"Come with me. Let's get you out of here."

Nadie shook her head. But Mouse grasped her hand and pulled her to her feet, not taking 'no' for an answer.

"Come. This place is bad medicine for you. Come to my house."

"No. I can't leave Luyu."

"Luyu isn't here. Come on, Nadie. I mean it. You have to come."

He pulled her and Nadie didn't have the strength to resist. He stopped at the door to let her put on her sneakers and then pulled her outside. Once they were walking on their way, he let go of her. There was no reason he had to keep holding onto her. She was out of the house. Her feet seemed to have a will of their own and they kept walking, following the path down to the road, and the road down to the other houses, and then the path up to Mouse's house.

He didn't talk to her. Maybe he understood that words didn't mean anything anymore. Nadie had always loved words. She loved to read everything she could get her hands on and knew more words than anyone else in the band. She had never anticipated that words would fail her. She had never thought they could be inadequate to express what she was feeling so utterly.

Mouse had never been so enamored with words. He understood the value of silence.

Usually, when she went to Mouse's house, they went to the kitchen. When Beth had been baking, or they had promised to work on their schoolwork together, that was the logical place to be. But Nadie wasn't hungry. She had no use for food. And there was no point in doing schoolwork. Even if she could focus, what value did it have for her? Schoolwork and book learning hadn't saved Luyu. Maybe if she had dropped out like the other teenagers, and stayed home to look after Luyu, the girl would still be alive now. School had taken Luyu away from her. Nadie always tried to do the right thing, and she had thought school work was what she was supposed to spend her time and energy on. But that had been a trap laid by the white man. White man's textbooks had no value for her. Mouse was right.

Nadie stood there, in the doorway, not sure where to go or what to do. Mouse took her hand again and led her into the bathroom. Nadie stopped again, not understanding. What did Mouse want? She hadn't bathed in days; she probably stank. Mouse slid past her and turned on the hot water tap in the tub. Mouse's house had running water and a working hot-water heater, propane powered. Nadie waited for Mouse to leave, so she could wash herself. He didn't leave. He just stood there, while the room started to fill up with steam. He didn't say anything to her.

After a while, Nadie looked at him, shaking her head slightly. "If you want me to bathe, you should go."

Mouse gave a short laugh. "No. Don't you get it? It's a sweat lodge." He motioned to the toilet. "Sit down. You look like you're going to pass out. Just breathe the steam. Let the sweat take the evil out of your body."

Nadie sat down. She breathed the steam. It wasn't long before she was sweating, her clothes clammy. She felt even more faint. Mouse pulled out a bundle of sage, tied together at one end. He used a cigarette lighter to get the end burning, and he moved it around, spreading the smoke through the small room. He brought it closer to Nadie and she waved the smoke toward her face and her heart. While she didn't really believe in Nehiyaw medicine, the smoke soothed her, taking her back to happier times, to better memories.

Mouse started to sing in a low voice. His words were uncertain. She wasn't sure she had ever heard him sing before. She didn't look at him or comment on it. He was hesitant enough as it was.

He blew the sage out. He shut the hot water off. Eventually, he took Nadie by the hand again and led her to his bedroom. Nadie resisted. She wasn't in the mood for intimacy. She didn't want anything to interrupt her grief. But Mouse tugged insistently.

"No, it's okay. Come."

Nadie went in. He shut the door and nudged her toward the bed, but didn't sit or lie down himself. Nadie sat on the edge of the bed watching him. There was a bottle on his dresser, and he retrieved it, taking a swig and then handing it to her. Nadie took it by the neck and looked down at it.

"You need sleep," Mouse said. "This is good medicine for sleep. It will help you relax. It will help you forget so your mind can be easy. You need it, Nadie."

Nadie tipped the bottle up for a small sip. It was home brew, not the commercial alcohol on the label. The sour taste reminded her of Luyu's lips when Nadie had tried to blow breath into her. It made her feel sick and lost.

"Have some more. You need enough for it to work."

Nadie took another drink. She was afraid she would throw up, drinking brew on an empty stomach. Her head spun. Even though the memories made her anxious and nauseated, the drink stayed down. Mouse had another drink and passed it back.

It wasn't long before she knew the medicine had taken hold of her. She started to feel warm instead of cold and clammy from the sweat. Her mind started to ease. She felt incredibly tired.

Mouse's hands laid her down on the bed and pulled a blanket around her. He lay down beside her and held her in his arms. She felt comforted and protected. Safe and at ease for the first time in days. Mouse hummed. He didn't have much musical talent, but the humming vibrated in her head, making her more drowsy. Before long she was asleep.

CHAPTER ELEVEN

When Nadie awoke, she knew she had been asleep for a long time. Her head felt heavy and thick, but the incredible fatigue was gone. She was comfortable and warm in Mouse's bed. Mouse was not there with her anymore.

Nadie sat up, rubbing her eyes. She pulled one of the blankets around her like a robe and went to find Mouse. He was sitting in the living room carving something that might have been a tool. It didn't look like a work of art. There was a sprinkling of shavings in his lap and on the couch and carpet. Nadie didn't think Beth was going to be too happy about that. The alcohol bottle was close to Mouse like he might have been drinking it while he'd been whittling. He looked up as she walked in and gave her a smile.

"Hey. Feeling any better?"

Nadie nodded. "A little. Thanks." Her chest was starting to hurt again, and she picked up the bottle and took a little sip to numb the pain. She winced at the burn of the alcohol. "Where did you get that?"

Mouse shrugged. "Lots of people make their own brew."

It was a non-answer, but Nadie didn't pursue it. She rubbed her aching forehead.

"You need to eat now," Mouse said. "Come into the kitchen."

"I'm not hungry."

"Doesn't matter. Come on."

Again he caught her hand and pulled her into the other room. Nadie sat down in one of the chairs without further protest. Mouse zipped around the kitchen, pulling something together for her. There was venison with bannock, some fresh vegetables starting to go limp, and a couple of cookies for dessert. Nadie chewed on the bannock. It was getting dry and stale.

"Where's Beth?"

Mouse bit his lip. He looked out the window for a minute, then poured her a glass of water from the water bottle beside the sink. "She's not here. You need to drink. Lots of water."

She opened her mouth to protest that she didn't want anything, then realized how dry and cracked her lips were. However much she didn't want life to go on without Luyu, her body still needed food and water, and she couldn't keep refusing. The medicine woman would come around with bitter herbs to cure her sickness, even if the sickness was in her spirit and not her body. Nadie took a long drink of water. Mouse watched her and nodded.

"Have a cookie," Nadie suggested, nudging one toward him. She felt awkward with him just staring at her and not doing anything.

Mouse eventually picked it up and nibbled at the edge. "Only if you eat," he bargained.

"I am eating."

She couldn't manage much. Eventually, she had eaten all she could.

"I should go home. Grandfather will be wondering where I am."

"He knows where you are. You can stay here as long as you need to."

It was tempting. On one hand, she wanted to get away from the house of mourning. The house that was empty of Luyu's lisp and mischief. But on the other hand, she needed to be there. She needed to be where Luyu's spirit still resided. Needed to feel her close by. She couldn't stay away and lose that connection. It would be like losing Luyu all over again.

She stood up.

"I'll walk you back," Mouse said.

He didn't try to converse along the way. Nadie was content to walk in silence and not to have to talk about Luyu or to tell him her thoughts. Mouse put his arm around her once to give her a comforting squeeze, but Nadie pulled away and he didn't pursue her any further.

She paused for a minute at the door before going in. Again feeling the loss of Luyu's presence from the house.

She whispered. "My poor baby. I'm sorry."

"What?" Mouse asked.

"Nothing."

They went in. Nadie wanted to be alone but didn't have the heart to tell him to leave. Not after he had tried so hard to help her. Mel and the Nose were in the kitchen again. Mel turned to look at Nadie, her big black eyes sorrowful.

"Tân'si, Nadie." She reached out to touch Nadie. "How are you? Are you okay?"

"How could I be okay?"

"It's part of the circle of life," Mel said. "Without death, there is no life. Without an end, life would have no sweetness."

"Tell me that after you've lost a baby," Nadie countered.

"We've all lost people, Nadie. Brothers and sisters, parents, friends…"

"It's not the same. I don't know how anyone goes on after losing a child."

"She wasn't even yours," the Nose said. His voice wasn't intentionally mean. Just stating a fact.

Nadie looked at him, trying to decide how to respond. Or whether to even bother. It wasn't until then she noticed the blanket he was wearing around his shoulders. Luyu's blanket. The red owl blanket Nadie had spent so many hours on.

"That's Luyu's blanket! What are you doing with that?" Nadie demanded.

"Luyu is gone. Her earthly possessions have been distributed amongst the band. It is our way."

"You are not part of the band! I didn't give that to you!"

"Luyu had no more need for it."

"You stole it! I have been looking for it, ever since the burial."

"It isn't yours," the Nose maintained.

"It is! I made it. Hundreds of hours! You know it is mine! You took it from my room!"

"I took it from the baby room. There are no more babies in the house. Luyu had no further need of it."

"I want it back!"

The Nose gave her a little bow, ignoring her words. "I thank you for your generosity in sharing with the band. Your many hours of work and your talent are of great benefit to us all. I am honored to have it."

Mel said something to her husband under her breath, motioning him out of the room, and they walked out together. Mel looked back over her shoulder at Nadie, the skin around her eyes pale. Mouse put his hand on Nadie's back, directing her back to the baby room.

"Don't worry about it," he advised. "Our possessions are not our own, but should benefit whoever has the greatest need."

"He doesn't have a great need! There are many blankets he could choose from. I'll give him another one. That one is mine!"

"You put a part of your soul into that blanket," Mouse said. "That will always be there."

"It's mine!"

"You gave it to Luyu. And Luyu has no more need of it." His voice was compassionate. He was trying hard not to hurt her feelings. But it cut her to the quick that her best friend wouldn't support her in this.

She turned away from him, furious tears filling her eyes.

"I'm sorry," Mouse apologized quickly. "Please don't worry

about it, Nadie. The blanket will always be a part of you and a part of Luyu. It doesn't take away your memories of her." He tried to hug her, but Nadie pushed Mouse away.

"I want to be alone," she snapped. "I don't want to be with you."

"I'm sorry, Nadie…"

She turned her back on him. He stayed there, watching, waiting for her to change her mind. Then he finally left the room. Nadie waited until she heard him leave the house and then shut the door to the room.

❧

Grandfather opened the door, hoping to coax Nadie out for dinner or to visit with others, showing her face so they would know all was well and that Luyu's spirit was at rest. Nadie wiped her eyes and look up at him. She explained to him about the Nose stealing away Luyu's blanket.

Grandfather scratched his nose, frowning over the story.

"You will tell him that he has to give it back," Nadie prompted.

He shook his head slowly. "The blanket was not yours, Nadie. It wasn't yours to keep or to give away. It was Luyu's, and Luyu is gone. We don't want her spirit to stay because it is attached to an object. We want her to be free to continue her journey in the next life."

"Luyu would want me to have it. I was the one who made it and gave it to her, it should come back to me."

"It is not yours to decide, Nadie."

"He took it from my room. He didn't even ask."

"I'm sure if he had asked, you would have shown a generous spirit," Grandfather said. "Just like when you gave away Luyu's clothing."

"I would not. He doesn't understand how much that blanket means to me. You don't understand."

87

"You are showing pride for something you created." Grandfather's voice was firm. "You are showing selfishness. That is not our way."

"I'll go to the Elders. I will go to Chief Frank. They'll give it back to me."

Grandfather held up his hands in a shrug. "We are not in the habit of taking away another's blanket. I hope the Elders will help you to understand."

Nadie had observed talking circles many times as a child, but she had not participated directly in one before. She was nervous about her participation. Would the Elders take her concerns into account? Would they decide she was too young, only a child, and should not have any say in the outcome?

She sat on the floor on one side of the circle and the Nose sat on the floor on the other side. There were several Elders and other participants in the circle. Grandfather was there too. Chief Frank sat down and lit a small bowl of sweetgrass, waving it back and forth and letting the smoke waft over all of them.

"We are here to reconcile Nadie and Willie Laplante and Horatio Long," Chief Frank announced. "The talking circle is a sacred place and a safe place. Those with angry feelings should focus on the harmony of the band, and thinking of what is best for all. The talking circle is not a court of judgment. That is a white man's idea. The talking circle is a place to make peace with your brothers and sisters."

Nadie swallowed and nodded. She wasn't sure she wanted to make peace with Horatio. She'd never heard his first name before; it was certainly a strange one. But the circle was the one place she would be allowed to vent her feelings about Luyu's death and explain how the Nose had wronged her. She hoped for some sort of resolution would see her getting the blanket back.

Chief Frank spoke about the problems in their community

and about grieving over the loss of Luyu and other children the band had lost in the past few months. There were nods and echoes of his words around the circle. The eagle feather was passed to Grandfather. He was sitting close enough to Nadie that she could see his pupils were widely dilated. He spoke slowly, some of his words slurred. He talked at length about Luyu's death and his partial responsibility for her death since she was supposed to be in his care. He apologized to Nadie for not being there when Luyu needed him, and for not being there when Nadie had discovered her and needed his support. Nadie nodded, but she wanted to talk about the blanket.

The feather passed on to the Nose. Horatio. She had better show him the respect of using his name if she was going to get any kind of respect from the rest of the circle. Horatio talked about meeting Mel and how she had helped him to get on his feet and rediscover himself. About how Grandfather had invited them into his home and generously offered them whatever they needed to be comfortable until they were able to move into a place of their own. He talked about the band's plan to bring in another trailer that he and Mel could call their own. Just something small, as it was only the two of them. Nadie wondered absently how long it would be before there were more. Surely they were planning on bringing children into their home. What home would be complete without any children?

Nadie was feeling a little lightheaded. Her body still wasn't feeling well and the sweetgrass smoke was affecting her. The eagle feather continued to be passed around the circle. Nadie closed her eyes and drifted a little. She was still listening to what they had to say, but her mind wandered in many other directions and briefly into and out of dreams.

"Nadie."

The medicine woman sat beside her and handed her the eagle feather. Nadie looked down at it and stroked her finger down the delicate fibers. How did Mother Earth form such beautiful colors and patterns? Nadie swallowed and started to speak. It was too hard to talk about losing Luyu. Instead, she told about the Nose going into her room to take the blanket. She remembered to call him Horatio. She felt small and selfish as she explained she needed that blanket, not any other, because she had put so many hours into weaving it and had given it to Luyu.

When she passed the feather on again, no one said anything about her being proud or not letting Luyu go on her spirit journey. As others talked, Nadie again closed her eyes, feeling for the dream she had been experiencing when the medicine woman had interrupted to give her the feather. She had felt calm and at peace there, instead of anxious and upset. Like she had gone to the spirit world where they said Luyu was, and that it had been everything they said it was.

Eventually, everyone had said all they had to say. Chief Frank was lighting the peace pipe, with its sweet tobacco smell. Nadie wasn't ready for the peace pipe. She still wanted to say more. She still wanted them to fix it and give the blanket to her. But what else was there to say? She had already explained. And this wasn't a court of justice; it was a talking circle. They did not assign blame or set reparations or punishments. Nadie had more to say and she had nothing to say. She realized as she watched the pipe make its slow way around the circle that she wasn't ever going to get the blanket back. The Nose had taken an unclaimed blanket from a dead child's room. There was no fault. Not that the circle would ever assign.

Horatio smoked the peace pipe, blowing smoke out his generous nose. He was looking across the circle at Nadie, making sure she saw him. Nadie closed her eyes again until the pipe made its way around the circle to her. She had seen many circles and none of them had ever assigned blame. There had been painful circles between husbands and wives who fought. With children who had to face their abusers in the community. When she was young, there had been an angry teen who had intentionally burned down one house after another, eventually causing the deaths of two children.

There had been no blame, no punishments. No turning them over to the white authorities.

The disputed ownership of a child's blanket was such an inconsequential matter. She was ashamed to have brought it to the circle.

Nadie took the pipe in her hands and brought it up to her mouth, pulling in the smoke and blowing it out again.

It was hopeless. She had lost Luyu and there was no way to get a measure of that peace and happiness back again. What was the point in fighting over discarded possessions?

CHAPTER TWELVE

Grandfather touched Nadie tentatively on the shoulder, his fingers light and quick like he was afraid he might burn himself. He patted it a couple of times.

"You feel better now?" he asked, his smile of concern like a grimace.

"Yes," Nadie said tonelessly. "Everything is fine now."

His black brows went down.

"I'm going for a walk," Nadie told him. "I need some time to clear my head."

His hand closed around her arm. "Nadie..."

"What, Grandfather?"

"You'll... you won't go too far, will you? You haven't regained your strength yet."

"I won't go too far."

"Okay." He released her slowly. "You be careful. You need to take care of yourself, Nadie."

"I just need some fresh air."

He nodded, his brows still drawn down in a scowl. But there was nothing else for him to say to her, so he went into the house and allowed her to go off on her own. Nadie didn't walk down to the other houses, but into the bush.

Nadie wasn't big on the outdoors. It might be unusual for a member of the band, but she'd always been more of a bookworm than an explorer. Mouse loved to be outside, always begging for more outdoor education at school and dragging her out on hikes when she just wanted to stay home and read. She could get along just fine outdoors and knew all of the terrain within a few hours of their houses. She wouldn't easily get lost.

Grandfather was right about her strength, though. Within twenty minutes, Nadie's legs were exhausted and she looked for somewhere comfortable to sit down. There was a sandy area beside a fallen log and she brushed aside some sticks and debris and sat down cross-legged. After a few minutes of sitting to catch her breath, she cleared the area in front of her. She got up and foraged in the bush of the surrounding area, finding plenty of wild sage, which she brought back to the little clearing. The frost had already killed it, so it was drying, not entirely green. She laid the sage down to begin with, spreading it out in a layer, winding a few stalks together into a braid. With the pocket knife she always carried in her jeans, she sawed off chunks of her hair and spread it over the sage.

She didn't have a lighter like Mouse, but she did have a paper book of matches, and after a couple of failed strikes, she managed to get the slightly damp sage to light. The smoke was sweet and pungent, but quickly turned acrid as the hair started to burn. Nadie coughed and choked, and had to back away a few feet to get clear of the smell. She ran her fingers through her shortened hair, a sick feeling in her stomach. She returned to her fire in spite of the smell.

"It's an offering for you, baby girl," she whispered. "I would give my life in exchange for yours if I could. I'd do anything, give anything to have you back, alive and well."

She swallowed and wiped at her running nose. The smoke was stinging her eyes and throat.

"My life for yours," Nadie whispered.

Mouse was chopping wood. He stopped to rest when he saw Nadie approaching. He raised an eyebrow as he took in her altered appearance. He didn't ask her what had happened. He knew she was in mourning.

"How are you doing?" he asked. Not just a greeting, but an honest question.

Nadie shrugged. There was no point in telling him how she was doing. He could already guess. Mouse sighed.

"Let me just split a few more," he said, gesturing to the logs. "Then we can go in."

Nadie started to load up the wood he had already split to take into the house. She'd spent plenty of time at his house. She knew where everything was supposed to go. The house was quiet. The only sound was Mouse's woodchopping outside. Nadie looked around the kitchen as she stacked wood beside the wood stove. There was an electrical stove as well, but it didn't heat the house like a wood stove. Beth used the electrical stove for her baking, which helped to produce a nice, quality product.

There were a lot of dirty dishes in the sink. There was no sign Beth had done any baking lately. No sign she had made any family meals. Snooping for a moment in the fridge, Nadie found it nearly empty. There were still boxes and cans in the cupboard, but no homemade food stored in plastic in the fridge.

Mouse's chopping had ceased and she heard him gathering the rest of the wood to bring in. She quickly closed the fridge door and turned around so he wouldn't catch her snooping. Mouse entered and stacked the rest of the wood in silence, then turned to her.

"You want to hang out?"

Nadie shrugged. She couldn't stand spending any more time shut up in the baby room. Even with a book, the house was too quiet and empty without Luyu. Nadie couldn't focus on anything.

"Where's your mom?"

Mouse scratched his jaw. "She's laying down," he said eventually. "She's not feeling well."

"Oh. Anything I can do?" Nadie already knew there was nothing she could do. Though she did have extra food at her house from after Luyu's burial, and could bring that over if Mouse needed meals. She offered, even knowing he would say no.

"She just needs some sleep," Mouse said. "She'll be fine…"

"Are you sure? Has she seen the medicine woman?"

Mouse shook his head. "She doesn't want to see anyone."

"Okay."

Mouse made a motion for her to follow him and led the way to his bedroom. Nadie lay down on the bed crossways, closing her eyes and making a tired sound. "Oh. That feels good."

He sat beside her, leaning against the wall and bending his knees up in front of his chest. "Are you coming back to school?"

"I don't know."

"I don't know why I'm staying if you're not coming back."

"I don't know what to do anymore. I can't focus on schoolwork. But I don't know what else to do. I don't have the energy to do anything but lay around."

"You were always the one who did everything. You were so focused and driven."

"I know."

"Do you think… after you feel better, you'll go back again?"

"I don't think I'm ever going to feel better." She looked around his room for any sign of the liquor bottle, but there didn't seem to be anything around. Nadie knew there was plenty of brew back at the house, but she needed company today. Someone to join her.

"After you get used to Luyu not being around… you'll start to feel better."

Nadie shook her head. Mouse leaned his head back against the wall with a bang. Neither one said anything for a while.

"Do you remember… back when we were little kids?" Mouse asked. "And you told me you were going to go on a vision quest when you got older?"

Nadie remembered. "You told me only boys go on vision quests."

"And you said you didn't care, you were going to go anyway."

Nadie didn't say anything. She remembered, but wondered why he had brought it up.

"I think you should," Mouse said.

"I should go on a vision quest?"

He nodded. "Yeah."

Nadie thought about that.

"It's like you've lost your way," Mouse contributed. "You could ask the spirits to help you to find it."

"Yeah… but only boys go on vision quests."

"Do you know what the Lakota call it? Crying for a dream."

"Yeah?" Nadie thought about the dreamy feeling she had had during the talking circle. She had felt very close to figuring something out. Like remembering a dream that was just at the edges of your consciousness. Something had made perfect sense, and then she woke up and couldn't quite remember it anymore.

"Cool, huh?" Mouse said. "Crying for a dream. I bet you would get one. A vision. A dream. You have…" he hesitated, searching for words, "…sort of a talent for seeing things."

"Do you think so?"

"Yeah. I don't think it matters if you're a girl. The Elders wouldn't stop you from going on a quest. Not that they could stop you, if they wanted to."

"No," Nadie agreed. "I'll think about it. Maybe I will."

"Good." He took her hand and interlocked their fingers together. "I don't like seeing you so sad."

Nadie was getting herself a small bowl of oatmeal when Nicole came into the kitchen. Nadie looked for a way to leave gracefully, to get out without it looking like she was just trying to avoid her mother, which she was.

"Hi, Nadie," Nicole greeted brightly. "I'm sure glad to see you eating again."

Nadie still didn't have much appetite, but she forced herself to eat a little, to keep from being taken to the medicine woman, or into town to see a doctor. She didn't need anyone to tell her what was wrong with her. She said nothing to Nicole.

"Did you hear about your friend Running Mouse's mother?" Nicole asked.

"Mouse Running in Dust," Nadie corrected. "But we just call him Mouse. What about his mother?"

"They took her to the city. To the hospital."

Nadie looked at her. "To the hospital? Why?"

"She has an evil spirit. The medicine woman couldn't help her, said she needs medicine from the doctor in the city. She has to stay there for a while."

Nadie nodded. "She has to do that sometimes. She has a spirit of sadness... she can't get out of bed or do anything... it has happened before."

"You should go see Mouse. Make sure he is okay."

"Yes. I will. I wondered the other day... he said she was sick."

Nadie finished eating her oatmeal, then headed over to Mouse's house. He wasn't outside when she arrived. Usually, he found things to do outdoors, especially if he was upset. Nadie noticed a red gas can that hadn't been put back in the shed. Probably they had needed to run their generator and Mouse had refilled the fuel tank. He was good about things like that. He'd been the man of the house for several years.

It was odd for him to leave the gas can out, though. Nadie picked it up along with the screw-on lid lying on the ground nearby. She screwed it back on and got gasoline on her fingers in the process. She popped it into the shed and looked for a rag to wipe off her fingers.

Nadie went into the house. "Mouse? Is everything okay? Where are you?"

There was no answer. Nadie went down the hall to his bedroom.

"Mouse?"

She was relieved to find him in bed asleep. There was a rag on his dresser that smelled of gasoline that Mouse had obviously already wiped his hands on after handling the gas can outside. Nadie wiped off her fingers as well.

"Mouse. Wake up, lazy."

She shook him. He stirred a little but didn't open his eyes.

"Don't play possum with me," Nadie warned. She shook him harder. "Mouse!"

His lips were a dusky color. The gasoline smell was stronger; he must have spilled it on his clothing. Nadie's chest was tight.

"Mouse. Wake up. You're okay, right?"

She leaned in close to watch and listen for his breath. The gasoline fumes were overwhelming. Nadie picked up a second rag, soaked with gas, and flung it to the floor. She was getting frantic now. She felt for the pulse in his throat. She could feel it beating away. She pried open one eye and his eyeball moved around as he dreamed, the pupil widely dilated, not getting smaller when exposed to the light of the room.

Nadie climbed onto the bed and shook him and pinched him. He made a noise of protest and opened his eyes a slit.

"Nadie." Her name was indistinct on his lips.

Nadie swore. "You scared the hell out of me, Mouse! I thought you were dead!"

"Namôya. Not dead."

She jerked him up forcefully, propping him into a sitting position, hoping that would help to wake him up. "What do you think you're doing?"

"Where's my cloth?"

"On the floor. It was giving me a headache."

"Yeah. It starts that way." He moved like a sleepwalker, trying to find and retrieve the discarded rag. "But after that... isss better."

"What's better?"

"Everything."

He fished the rag up with one finger, then held it over his mouth and nose and inhaled. Nadie snatched it away from him in alarm. Mouse sighed.

"Try," he said. "Ignore the smell. Just breathe in."

"You're getting stoned!" Nadie was angry. "You could kill yourself."

"No. Dunnit before. Don't worry."

His expression was slack. She could see his eye moving through the tiny slits of his eyelids. He held the drenched rag toward her, unseeing.

"Come with me."

"No, Mouse. It's dangerous."

"Who cares 'bout dangerous? Don't you want…" He struggled to finish the thought. "Don't you want… the pain to go away?"

Nadie paused. She did want the pain to go away. More than anything. She even considered ending her own existence but wasn't sure enough that it would end the pain. She didn't want to end up journeying through the world of spirits for eternity in just as much pain as she was in—or even more.

She gulped. "What do you mean? How can it take away the pain?"

"I was sad. And now… I'm not. One big sniff and it all goes away. Try it."

Nadie looked down at the cloth in her hand. She was already going home smelling like gasoline. There was no way it would all wash off. She already had a headache from it.

Just one sniff; that wasn't enough to do any permanent damage. If it could truly take away the pain for a time…

Nadie brought the choking fumes closer to her face, gagging at the smell. Just once, and then she would know. She couldn't breathe through her nose anymore, the smell was too overwhelming. She put the cloth over her open mouth. She could taste the sharp tang of the gasoline even though she was holding her breath. She took a deep intake of breath through the rag.

It was totally unlike drinking, where the warm feeling took time to develop and wash away her cares. It was like an explosion in her brain. Her heart gave a painful throb like she was going to have a heart attack and then she was floating, flying.

She couldn't even remember the pain and the worry anymore. She thought she might have laughed aloud.

It was like she was up in heaven and none of the earthly crap mattered anymore. She was happy. Wildly, crazily happy, like she'd never been before.

Nothing would ever take that away from her again.

Nadie awoke to Mouse moving around. She could feel him leaning over her and tried to open her eyes, but the light was too bright. It hurt.

"Go away," she murmured.

Mouse made a noise like a laugh, but one that was faint and far away. "Go away?" he repeated in a hoarse voice. "You're in my bed."

"What?"

She felt the mattress and blankets beneath her. He was right; it wasn't her pile of blankets on the floor. She was in a warm, comfortable cocoon and she didn't want to leave it.

"Are you okay, Nadie?"

"Yeah."

She was too tired to get up or even to stay awake while Mouse moved around the room and to the bathroom next door. She heard him running water and retching over the toilet. She was glad she didn't feel nauseated. Just numb. And tired. It wasn't like a hangover. She imagined she was still high, since the feeling of well-being hadn't entirely left. It was a relief to feel calm and peaceful after all of the anguish of the recent past.

Mouse was back in the room with her. He crawled into bed beside her. Nadie felt her chest and the bed beside her, looking for the rag she had dropped while unconscious.

"Where is it?"

"I put it away."

His arms went around her. Nadie pushed at him irritably. "Why? I want another sniff."

"Don't want you getting sick."

"Mouse…!"

"Shh." His light fingers traced a circle on Nadie's forehead. He smelled like soap. "Just sleep it off."

"I wanted another hit! Come on…"

"You're not used to it. Just go back to sleep for a while. I'll get you a Tylenol when you wake up."

The sleepiness was almost overwhelming and Nadie soon drifted off again.

❧

She was more aware the next time. More aware of her surroundings and more aware of the pain. The effects of the inhalant were, after all, only temporary. Nadie lay there on Mouse's bed with him breathing evenly beside her and thought about what had happened.

She'd always considered Mouse privileged. With both plumbing and a working generator, he was better off than most of the other families on the reservation. He had a mother who loved and doted on him and made fantastic food. When they had been younger and his older siblings lived at home, he had never lacked for entertainment or physical care. It wasn't really until his brothers and sisters started to move out that she saw the dark side. The mother consumed by a depressive spirit. Mouse's sisters had always fed and clothed him and seen him off to school if their mother was 'under the weather.' His brothers had taught him how to care for things around the house, like the generator. He had a knack for keeping it running. It was one of the only generators in the settlement that worked more often than it was broken.

But now they were gone, not only from the house but from the reservation. Leaving Mouse to look after himself whenever Beth went down the tunnel of despair. Mouse was usually so cheerful, teasing Nadie and making her laugh. He covered up his pain and didn't burden Nadie with it.

Nadie punched him in the chest. Mouse startled comically, his arms thrown wide in surprise, eyes open and wild. He took a deep breath.

"What was that for?" he demanded.

"Why didn't you come see me when your mom was having trouble again? You could stay with me."

"In the baby room? I prefer my bed."

"You don't want to be here all by yourself. Sniffing gas. Come and stay with me while Beth is in hospital."

He shook his head. "I'm a man, Nadie. I can live by myself. I don't need a babysitter."

"But you're lonely."

"How do you know?" His voice was defensive.

Nadie was confused. It was all wrong. Why was he getting angry when she wanted to help him? She hadn't challenged his manhood. Just offered him a place to stay.

"Because I would be… because you're sniffing gasoline…"

"That's my business, not yours. And how could I come to you? You're so wrapped up in yourself you don't even know I exist!"

Nadie stared at him, mouth open, unable to find the words. Wrapped up in herself? Was that how he saw her? She was suffering through the worst trauma of her life and he thought she was being selfish with her pain?

"I'm… I'm…"

He plucked at her hair, ragged from being cut with a knife. "You're in mourning. I know. But there's no room left for anybody else. Not even me."

His voice was bleak. Nadie suddenly had to leave. She pushed the bedding away from her, trying to untangle herself and get out of the bed. She got up too fast, staggering with a head rush.

"Nadie!" Mouse protested. He grabbed for her, catching hold of the back of her shirt and jerking her back.

Already dizzy, Nadie overbalanced backward and was not able to catch herself. She toppled over backward, smashing the back of her head on the metal frame of the bed. She saw bright lights and black splotches. The pain was excruciating. Mouse swore, jumping off the bed and crouching beside her.

"Nadie, I'm sorry, I didn't mean to pull you over! Are you okay? You hit your head."

He pulled her forward and turned her head to look at the back where she had hit it.

"Oh, crap!" She felt his hands begin to shake. "Stay right there. Don't move."

Her vision still hazy, Nadie gingerly felt the back of her head. It was swelling up, the skin split, and she drew her fingers back sticky with blood. It was dripping down her neck. Nadie felt nauseated.

Mouse returned with a wet cloth and an ice pack. Nadie tried to hold her head still while he cleaned off the blood. He switched to the ice pack and Nadie just about passed out when he pressed it against the bump.

"We need the medicine woman," Mouse said. "Can you get to the car?"

"I don't know."

He swore again. "Come on, we gotta try." He stood up and pulled on her arm, heaving her to her feet. He put her arm around his neck and his arm around her waist. Nadie's legs wobbled. She managed a few steps, but the dizziness was overwhelming, and she felt herself sliding away from him. Mouse clutched at her and bent over. She thought he was going to help set her down gently, but he scooped up her legs and carried her the rest of the way.

CHAPTER THIRTEEN

An hour later, Nadie was lying on her stomach and the medicine woman was peeling back the compress she had made of herbs.

"That's a nasty cut," she observed again. "And a really good bump. But it looks like the bleeding has stopped."

"So I can go home now?"

"Hah. Now we need to stitch it up."

Nadie moaned. "I don't want stitches."

"I didn't ask you what you wanted. Mouse Running in Dust, you come over here and hold her hand."

Mouse did what he was told. He grasped Nadie's hand. "Are you going to give her something to numb the pain?" he asked.

There was no answer from the medicine woman and Nadie lifted her woozy head to look at her. The medicine woman had Mouse fixed with a glare. "Sometimes it is better to feel the pain."

Mouse swallowed and looked down at Nadie, his eyes wide. Nadie laid her head back down again. Just how much did the medicine woman know? Did she know or guess they had been sniffing? She gritted her teeth and waited for the piercing pain of the needle.

"Now can I go home?"

"You just rest, Nadie. Your grandfather is coming to pick you up."

"Grandfather? He doesn't have to come! Mouse can drive me home."

"Mouse is not supposed to drive."

Mouse looked back and forth between the medicine woman and Nadie. "I had to drive her here! She couldn't walk and I couldn't leave her alone."

The medicine woman did not concede the point.

"I can drive," Mouse said sullenly.

"You have not learned your lesson."

"I had one accident. Anybody could have an accident."

"Accidents can often be prevented." She was again giving Mouse that fixed stare, making him squirm uncomfortably. "I took a bottle of home brew from your house this morning when I saw to your mother."

Mouse looked steadily down at his feet, refusing to meet her gaze.

"And that didn't make any difference, did it?" the medicine woman said.

Nadie closed her eyes, pretending she was faint or tired. The old woman did know. They couldn't hide what they had been doing from her.

"So you had another accident. Nadie got hurt. I thank your spirit guide you did not have another accident on the way here." Emphasizing her words, she lit a pipe of tobacco to thank the spirits and wafted the smoke toward Mouse and Nadie.

Mouse sat down on the bed next to Nadie and lightly stroked her hacked-short hair, keeping well away from the newly-sewn injury.

"Children always think they have discovered something new," the medicine woman went on. "They think they are the first ones to try. But it is the same foolishness. You will only hurt the ones you love."

Mouse shifted. "I'd better go before Willie gets here," he muttered. "I'm sorry, Nadie. I didn't mean to hurt you."

"Stay here. Grandfather won't hurt you. If he's angry at anyone, it will be me. Stay and… come to the house. Stay with me while Beth's away."

"I told you no," Mouse growled. "I am a man, not a baby. I will live in my own house."

With that, he got to his feet and headed toward the door.

"You will walk home, Mouse Running in Dust," the medicine woman called after him. "I will bring the car back to your house later."

Mouse slammed the door and was gone.

Nadie had said Grandfather wouldn't be angry at Mouse for his part in the accident, but she was wrong. He came barreling into the medicine woman's house, puffed up with fury, his normally quiet feet stomping into the house.

"Where is that boy?" he demanded, before even looking at Nadie or acknowledging her presence. He looked around the room as if Mouse might be hiding in a corner. "Where is he? I saw his car outside!"

"He is not here," the medicine woman said calmly. "His car is here because I told him he was not allowed to drive. He is walking home."

"He left her here? Alone?"

"She was not alone. I am with Nadie, looking after her. Mouse Running in Dust was right to leave before you got here. We don't need a fight."

"Oh, we're going to have a fight. As soon as I get my hands on him, I'm going to beat the tar out of him! He can't hurt my grand-daughter and get away with it."

"He didn't hurt me, Nimosôm," Nadie said. "I fell down. That's all. It wasn't Mouse's fault."

The medicine woman indicated the door with her gaze, and she and Grandfather walked out. There was no yelling. Whatever she decided to tell him, it didn't cause an explosion. Nadie was relieved and worried at the same time. If he exploded, it would be over quickly. She might get a smack or be grounded from seeing Mouse for a week, but then it would be over and done. Without a release of his anger, she worried he might brood for days or weeks. Not speaking to her or telling her what was on his mind. Not disciplining her. Just getting further into his own dark place. The calm was more than she could stand.

They were gone from the room for a long time. Nadie closed her eyes, hoping it would stop the spinning, but it didn't. Her head throbbed liked it was going to explode. When Grandfather came back into the room by himself, he didn't say anything to her. He just stood there, waiting for her to get up. Nadie pushed herself up into a sitting position, balancing herself on her hands. That was as much as she could handle to start with. She was seeing double and her stomach lurched with her movements. Grandfather eventually moved to her side and put his arm around her waist to lift her to her feet. Nadie leaned on him. He was stronger than Mouse, his arm around her as hard and unyielding as steel. He guided her slowly out through the house to his truck, stopping whenever she got off-balance or started to sag. He boosted her up into the cab of the truck.

Nadie steadied her swimming head with her hand. She couldn't put her head on the headrest because that was right where her injury was. She tried to hold herself together, feeling every bump and jolt all the way back to the house. When they came to a stop, Nadie climbed out of the truck without waiting for Grandfather, holding onto the side of the vehicle for support while she bent over, throwing up in the gravel of the driveway. Grandfather waited until she was done, then took her by the arm and guided her into the house without a word of either rebuke or sympathy.

"Nimosôm…" Nadie tried.

He ignored her.

"I'm sorry. It was just an accident."

He said nothing, guiding her into her room. Not the baby room, but her old room.

"No—" Nadie protested.

"Get your daughter changed and put her to bed," Grandfather told Nicole, seating Nadie firmly on the side of the bed. He walked back out of the room. Nadie felt abandoned. He'd never left her to be taken care of by her mother. Grandfather had always provided whatever she needed. She felt like he was writing her off, disowning her by throwing her back at her mother. Tears prickled in Nadie's eyes.

"What happened?" Nicole asked, approaching Nadie's side.

"I can… I don't need help," Nadie said. She didn't want Nicole to take care of her. Nicole needed to know Nadie was tough and independent. She was her own woman, nearly an adult, and she could take care of herself.

"Whew, you stink!" Nicole exclaimed. "What were you guys doing? Siphoning gas tanks?"

Nadie tried to pull her t-shirt off, but it was impossible. She couldn't even get her arms out, and when it came time to pull it off over her head, she didn't know how she was going to get it past the goose-egg. Nicole moved in and helped Nadie get out of first one sleeve, then the other. Looking at Nadie's injury for a moment, Nicole stretched the neck of the t-shirt as far as she could, nearly throttling Nadie. With one quick movement, it was up past the bump and over Nadie's head.

"Do you have a button-up shirt?" Nicole asked, leaving Nadie sitting shirtless on the bed as she went to the closet for a look. She came back with a soft flannel shirt and helped Nadie put it on.

"Okay, lie down now." Nicole moved things around on Nadie's bed to make room for her to stretch out and Nadie rested her face in the pillow. Nicole sat there for a minute. She started rubbing Nadie's back in small, soothing circles. Nadie squirmed under her touch.

"No, don't."

Nicole stopped. She continued to sit on the edge of the bed beside Nadie. "Do you want to tell me what happened?" she asked. "I don't know when was the last time I saw your Grandfather so mad. Probably when they first brought you here."

Nadie's heart gave a throb. She was surprised she could even feel it with the way her head hurt. "Because he didn't want me?" she asked.

"What? No, baby," Nicole rubbed her back again. "No, of course he wanted you. He wasn't mad he had to take care of you. He was mad at me. Because..." She stopped, choked up. Nicole stopped rubbing Nadie's back and just sat there with her hand on Nadie, reaching for the words. "I wasn't a good mom," she said. "That's why they gave you to your Grandfather."

Nadie nodded into the pillow. "I figured," she mumbled.

"It was more than that... more than just not being good at it."

Nadie swallowed.

"I got frustrated," Nicole said. "I didn't know how to take care of a baby and I was messed up... on some pretty bad junk... I was with a guy and he didn't like competing for my attention." She looped back around again, away from the excuses and back to the explanation. "I hurt you. I hurt you bad, and they took you away. They should have. It was the right thing to do. They gave you to Grandfather to take care of. He raised me. Other babies. He was the one they trusted."

Nicole sniffled for some time. Nadie didn't look at her. She didn't know why Nicole was crying. Because she had hurt Nadie long ago? Because Nadie had been taken away from her? Because she felt sorry for herself? She hadn't lost a child the way Nadie had lost Luyu. She hadn't ever loved Nadie. She hadn't been the one to care for her every day and watch her grow. That was Grandfather. And now Grandfather was angry with Nadie.

"That's why he was angry," Nicole said finally. "Not because he didn't want you. He did. He loved you from the moment you were born. He was mad because I had hurt you. Because I didn't care for my own flesh and blood. They told me I couldn't be around you, even when Grandfather was taking care of you. So I left. Went back to the city, where I'd got into trouble in the first place. Went back to my boyfriend, or another one, I don't remember anymore. I was so messed up."

Nadie just breathed for a while. "Why did you come back?" she asked at last.

"I had to see how my baby was doing!" She sighed. "I know you're not a baby anymore. I keep calling you that because I don't know what else to call you. When I left, you were a baby. I'm sort of stuck there; I can't believe how grown-up you are now. I came back because… I'm better now… and I knew you were too big for me to hurt anymore. That it would be okay if I came and saw you."

She rubbed and kneaded Nadie's back. Nadie stopped resisting her. Her thoughts drifted. She thought about Nicole abandoning her. And about Luyu's mother. She hadn't even come back for the burial. Did she know Luyu was dead? Did she even care? If Nadie had died when she was still a toddler, would Nicole have come back to see her buried? It was easy for Nicole to act like she cared now. She could say the words and rub Nadie's back and pretend to love Nadie. But she couldn't really love Nadie the way Nadie had loved Luyu. The way Nadie still loved Luyu.

"Will you see… if he'll come talk to me?" Nadie asked.

Nicole considered it. "I think you'd better give him some time to cool down first," she advised. "He's not ready."

❧

Nadie had a restless night, not able to sleep soundly with her head hurting so much, but unable to stay awake either. Dreams and nightmares chased each other around in her head and she wondered if she had a fever, with how wild and colorful the images were.

There was a bitter taste in her mouth. Nadie didn't know whether it was from the gasoline, or throwing up, or the herbs the medicine woman had used on her wound. She called for water, but no one brought it to her. Nadie's eyes watered from the throbbing pain of the head wound. It felt like a knife being plunged into her brain, over and over again.

In her dreams, she heard Nicole's excuses and explanations. Too messed up. Frustration. Jealousy. Too hard. She heard Nicole moving around the room, whirling around like a spirit, first on one side of the room, then on the other. Nadie tried to sleep, but Nicole kept waking her up.

In the morning, it was Grandfather who woke her up. It was strange for him to be up before she was. She was always up early to take care of Luyu and to go to school; and he had to sleep off his pills and his brew, sometimes not getting up until noon.

"Nimosôm… water…?" Nadie whispered.

He felt her forehead. Without a word, he went to the kitchen and returned with a bottle of water. He held it to Nadie's lips and she drank deep. She cleared her throat.

"Please don't be angry, Grandfather. I'm sorry…"

He sighed. A sad, frustrated sound. "I don't know what to do for you, Nadie. I can't give you a bottle and rock you to sleep anymore. Teenage troubles… I always lose them as teenagers."

"You haven't lost me. I know you love me…"

"You're a big girl and you're old enough to make your own decisions without me. I can't be responsible for the consequences."

"I'm just… I'm just so sad… it hurts so much."

He touched her head. On the side, not on the back where it was injured. "Your head hurts?"

"No… my heart." Nadie's voice broke.

Grandfather gave her a hug around the shoulders. The best he could do with her still lying face-down on the bed. He kissed her hair. He was silent for a long time.

"She's gone," he said. Nadie thought he meant Luyu. That desolate voice echoed the way she felt about losing Luyu. But Nadie saw Grandfather looking around Nadie's room and she frowned, slowly recognizing what he was looking at.

All of Nicole's things, previously spread around the room like it had been hit by a tornado, were gone. No clothes or jewelry. No suitcases. No electronics gradually losing their charges.

"Nicole left? Where did she go?"

That was what Nadie had heard in the night. Nicole chattering away, giving excuses while she flitted here and there gathering up all of her possessions. Had Nadie's rejection prompted her to leave? Was it the painful memories of what had happened when Nadie was a baby? Remembering the anger and disapproval of her father?

"Back to her home," Grandfather said. "In the city."

She heard the sadness in his voice. He had hoped she would come back; make the reservation her home again. But she couldn't. Like so many others, she had left and no longer belonged there.

❦

After reassuring himself Nadie was okay, Grandfather retreated to his room and shut and locked the door. Nadie spent most of the day sleeping. Late in the day, the activity in the house started to get louder and Nadie got up. Grandfather was still locked in his room. Nadie was still hurting and unsteady on her feet, but she could get around without help. She made it to the outhouse and back and washed up in the kitchen, trying to avoid the rest of her housemates.

She knocked on the door to Grandfather's room. "Grandfather? Are you okay? Can I come in?"

There was no answer. Nadie knocked again.

"Please, Grandfather? Nimosôm?"

He still didn't answer.

"The old man is sleeping," said a male voice. One of the Foxes. Nadie couldn't keep their names straight. "Why don't you just leave him alone?"

"I want to talk to him," Nadie said. She pushed past the man and went back to her room.

The pain was growing again. Both physical and mental. Grandfather could have given her some of his pain pills. He should have. She was injured; she needed them just as badly as he did.

Whatever herbs the medicine woman had used to stop the bleeding and reduce the swelling had infused Nadie's hair with an earthy, bitter green smell. It clung to her and was making her crazy. She needed to wash her hair, but she didn't think she could without hurting the cut. Especially not with the cheap, harsh shampoo they bought in town. Even if she just used water, it was cold and there were too many people around. She didn't want to deal with anybody just then, and the house was waking up, getting rowdy. Things had been quiet since Luyu had died. Or maybe Nadie had just been too wrapped up in herself to notice what was going on around her. But she could tell tonight was going to be a loud, wild night. Not a good time for her to be worrying about personal hygiene.

She thought about the warm running water at Mouse's house. She could wash it there. But Mouse didn't want her around. She had screwed that up too. First ignoring him in the midst of her mourning and then pitying him, undermining his manhood. She couldn't go back there.

She lay down in her bed, but she had slept all day and was hurting too much to go to sleep. She wanted to lie on her back, but she couldn't. She wanted to cry, but the tears would not come.

Her thoughts went back to Mouse again. He wasn't stuck in a house full of people and unwanted clamor like she was. He was all alone, drifting around his house like a leaf blown in the breeze. So lonely. Would he be sniffing again? Killing his pain by drugging it out? And how was that any different from the pain pills she had just been wishing for?

"Oh, Mouse."

Nadie got out of bed and started to clean up. She put all of the clothes from the floor into the laundry basket. As much as she would like to blame Nicole for the mess, plenty of it was her own doing. She was no better than any other teenager on the reservation, lazy and messy and making more work for the adults, who were already overwhelmed with their own chores and problems. After the clothing had been picked up, she started clearing off her desk. So many keepsakes gathering dust. Little treasures she'd been given as birthday presents. Special rocks or pine cones she or Mouse had found, collecting them or gifting them to each other. Little crafts they had made for each other, school projects various teachers had taught them. Nadie threw them all into the garbage, one or two at a time. She didn't have any need for all of that junk. It was just cluttering up her room and her spirit. She needed to start fresh, with a clean surface.

Nicole had left a bottle of nail polish remover behind. Nadie didn't have any need for that. She hadn't painted her nails since she was a little girl and actually had peers at school other than Mouse. They had all dropped out now. Some had left the reserve. Some had died. Some were still there, hanging around like they were waiting for something to happen. And nothing ever would. They were just going to keep dying. Death was the one constant. Then one day, they would all be dead, and there would be no reservation. No more Nehiyaw. The white man could then do whatever he wanted with the land. Nadie glanced at her dirty window. But what did the white man want with their land, other than another place to dump garbage? They didn't want the wilderness. They weren't tied to the earth like Nadie's people. To them, it was just empty space.

Nadie sat down on her bed again, still holding onto the nail polish remover. Ten minutes of tidying up and she was out of breath and exhausted. What had happened to her strong spirit?

She was weak now. Not strong enough to take care of anyone else. Not strong enough to take care of herself.

She closed her eyes and swayed, having a hard time keeping her balance without the visual cues. Nadie opened them again and looked down at the bottle of nail polish remover. She eyed the garbage can. Could she hit it from across the room? Normally, she could. But nothing was normal now.

There were warning symbols on the label. Flammable. Use in a ventilated room. She wasn't sure what all of the symbols meant. The label said it was peach scented. She opened it up, wondering if the peach-scented polish remover smelled any better than the stuff she remembered from when she was a little girl. As soon as she removed the cap, the perfume filled the air. Heady, cloying, sweet; but it couldn't cover up the acrid chemical smell underneath. Anyone who thought that stuff smelled nice or tasty had to be crazy. Or so old they had no sense of smell. Nadie raised it to her nose and took another sniff. Like the gasoline of the day before, it gave her an instant headache. She had thought she already had a headache, but the smell added a whole new depth to the pain.

It always starts that way, Mouse had told her. Just take a big sniff and it is better. Everything is better. Nadie took another sniff, breathing it in deeper this time. It didn't hit her as hard as the gasoline. Maybe because she wasn't getting as much. Maybe they had tried to reduce how much of the chemicals got into the air while you were using it. Use in a ventilated room. That meant there was still enough to affect you if you were in an enclosed space. If you were breathing enough of it in. Nadie looked at the rag bag inside of her closet. Grandfather had cut the shirt Luyu had destroyed into smaller, more regular shapes that could be used for cleaning jobs. Nadie went to the closet and picked a couple of them up. Luyu had worn it before she died. She held it up to her face, feeling the texture against her skin. Nadie put her nose into it. Either Luyu had not worn it long enough for her body's smell to get into it or Nadie's smell receptors were already clogged by the cloying scent of the nail polish remover.

Operating on autopilot, trying not to think about what she was doing, Nadie put the rags over the top of the nail polish remover bottle and inverted it, letting half of the bottle soak into the fabric. She put the lid back on the bottle and set it on her desk.

Lying down on her side, she put the rags of Luyu's shirt over her mouth and nose and breathed the scent of peaches.

adie awoke in the morning with a headache. But also with a new sense of purpose. There was nothing left for her there. Not in Grandfather's house, and not in the community. She had never felt fully a part of them. Even though she'd been born into them, the Nehiyaw ways felt foreign. Foreign and old and dying. She had lost her friends and her family and her sense of purpose. The most important thing had always been to go to school, to learn everything there was to know, to graduate with a high school diploma. Then she would leave and find work and be a strong, independent woman.

But in the face of Luyu's death, none of that mattered. She wasn't strong anymore. That had been an illusion; her strength had just never been challenged.

Nadie found a backpack she had used for hiking and put a change of clothing into it. She added a water bottle and a few other necessities and left the house.

She didn't say goodbye. Grandfather's door was shut. The partiers of the night before had all gone to bed, or at least to sleep. There were a few unconscious forms still in the living room.

She didn't go to see Mouse or Running Deer or Chief Frank or the medicine woman.

She just left.

Knowing she was still weak from her mourning period and the head injury, Nadie started off slowly. She forced herself to walk more slowly than she normally would have. A brisk pace and she would be wiped out within an hour. That wouldn't get her anywhere. She didn't head for the road, but for the river. The brush was thicker, but it was a shorter route.

She thought about all of the times she and Mouse had tromped through the woods together. They had spent hours exploring, building forts, and finding treasures. It had always been more Mouse's thing than Nadie's, but she had always enjoyed it once she got out there. Pulling her away from her books was the difficult part.

But she and Mouse had grown up. They were too old for building forts now.

Nadie took breaks, pretending to herself that it was to take in the old sights and remember the old times. But her body was tired and she couldn't walk for more than a few minutes without stopping. Her drinking water was gone by the time she reached the river, which was a problem. She couldn't refill at the river, which was contaminated upstream. Even though the water was fast-moving, it was not safe. It was too late in the year for berries, too early for snow. That meant she was going to have to go thirsty.

Nadie walked downstream. It had been a long time since she had come so far, and she wasn't sure of the landmarks. She wasn't sure she would find what she was looking for. It could be long gone.

But a few minutes later, she was clearing fallen leaves from the raft. It had taken her and Mouse a whole summer to make when they were… how old? Twelve? Nadie inspected the ropes, expecting them to be rotting away. But they seemed to be sound. She could see some of them were newer, not as gray as the others. Some of the younger kids must have discovered the raft and fixed it up. They would be disappointed when it was gone the next time they came back.

After reassuring herself the raft was as river-worthy as it had ever been, and having grabbed a long stick to pole with, Nadie crawled onto it and untied the rope anchoring it to a tree on shore.

١

Nadie and Mouse had explored the river as far as they dared, but there was only so far they could go in a day and still get home in time for bed. While Nadie didn't have a set bedtime like Mouse, she had still gotten in major trouble the day they had been blasted with an unexpected spring storm and had been forced to shelter overnight to wait it out. While they had both returned home safe and unharmed, it had been Nadie who ended up being disciplined, while Mouse was just patted on the back and praised for taking care of himself. She had been confused as to why they were treated so differently. Nadie hadn't been allowed to go with Mouse again until well into the summer when the threat of squalls was past.

So they'd never been able to take the raft very far down the river, since they'd had to pull or portage it back and still leave enough time to walk home before Mouse's curfew. Pulling or carrying the raft was heavy, awkward work.

But today she didn't have to observe those rules. She could ride however far down the river she pleased. Or however far it was safe. Nadie didn't know how far she could get before running into rapids. She had to be careful if she didn't want to drown. Rafting so late in the fall, she would probably freeze in the cold waters before she drowned.

The river was lazy. She moved at a good pace, but it didn't rush like it did in the spring. The smaller rapids were easy to get through. There were a couple of bigger ones Nadie wasn't as sure of, so she poled over to the bank and played out the rope, letting the raft float down river by itself while she walked around the rapids on the land. Then she reeled it in, got back on, and continued on her way.

As the day wore on, it became comfortably warm. As long as she kept busy and stayed in the sun, she was warm enough without a coat. But winter was coming and Nadie hadn't packed properly for it. She would need to find a warm place to stay before too long.

❧

"Hey! Hey you, wake up! Hallo the raft!"

Nadie realized with a start that she had fallen asleep, lulled by the motion of the raft and the warm afternoon sun. She rubbed her eyes and looked around. There was someone standing on the shore waving to her. A woman. Nadie dug her pole into the river bed, pushing the raft closer to shore. Her hands were sore and blistered. She was weak after another day of no food and more physical exertion than she had had in months. When she got close enough, she threw the rope to the shore. The woman grabbed it and tried to slow Nadie and pull her in. She braced the rope around a couple of big rocks to stop the raft from pulling her into the water, and the raft's forward progress came to an abrupt halt, swinging into the shore. Nadie jumped off in the shallows and pulled the raft up onto the shore. She took the rope from the woman and tied it securely to a tree.

The woman was young. Close to Nadie in age, maybe just two or three years older. She had Indigenous features, her skin a shade darker than Nadie's own.

"Tân'si," Nadie greeted, a little awkward and formal, nodding her head.

"Aaniin," the strange girl replied, her face an unsmiling mask.

Nadie replayed it in her head, trying to remember her lessons about other nations. "Ojibwe?" she asked.

The girl nodded. "Yeah. What are you?"

"Nehiyaw. Cree."

"No Cree land near here. Where did you come from?"

Nadie glanced over at the river and made a small gesture toward it. "Upriver."

The Ojibwe girl stared up the river, shading her eyes against the sun, which was getting low in the sky. "How far?"

"I don't know. Just today."

"Where are you going?"

"Downriver." Nadie wiped her mouth with the back of her hand. "Do you have water?"

"There's water in the river," the girl said impatiently.

"Is it safe to drink?"

She pressed her lips together. "No."

"Do you have drinking water? I have none."

With a sigh, the young woman made a gesture for Nadie to follow and led her to a small camp just under the trees. She nudged a canteen with her toe. "That's boiled water. Help yourself."

Nadie's Grandfather would have given Nadie a licking if he had caught her being so disrespectful toward a guest at their fire. Hospitality was very important. He went out of his way to make sure a guest's every need was met, and that meant Nadie did too. Even to the point of giving away her own bed and clothing. Nadie crouched down and drank deeply from the canteen. Going all day without drinking water, even though it was cool and she was out in the water, had not been a good idea. Nadie cleared herself a little space on the ground and sat down.

"Why did you call me? Do you need help?"

It looked like the girl had set up a pretty comfortable camp. She didn't appear to need for anything.

"I haven't seen anyone for weeks. And I didn't know if you knew about the rapids."

"The rapids? No… where?"

The girl waved a hand downstream. "Not far. You can't really go any further than this. Wouldn't have wanted to hear you got drowned."

"Thanks." The girl didn't offer her any food, so Nadie dug into her bag and pulled out some jerky to chew on. "I'm Nadie. You?"

"Annie."

"Nice to meet you." Nadie nodded a greeting. "How long have you been here? You're not wintering here, are you?"

"Don't intend to," Annie said. "But it's getting colder. I need to get to a settlement, or at least a cabin." After due consideration, she sat herself down across from Nadie. "Everything is so far away from here."

"How did you get here?" Nadie asked, curious. "Have you been here for long?"

Though the camp was neat, the ground seemed worn, like Annie had been walking through it for weeks. How had she gotten stranded there, somewhere apparently so isolated? Trying not to stare or look too interested, Nadie analyzed what she could see, looking carefully for any sign Annie was not alone. Was there a man with her? Maybe waiting to see if Nadie had anything of value? It didn't make sense, a girl out there all by herself.

"Too long," Annie said. "What about you? You come all the way down here and you don't even know the river? Where the rapids are?"

Nadie was mentally criticizing the stranger when she herself was in similar circumstances. She had less equipment than Annie, was younger and less experienced, and didn't even know where she was, much less how to get to civilization. She could have drowned in the rapids without ever waking up if Annie hadn't called her.

"I had to get away," Nadie said lamely. "Things… haven't been so good, where I came from."

Annie snorted. "I guess not," she observed.

Nadie pictured herself. Waifishly thin, since she had stopped eating. Hair chopped off. Dirty and scraped up from hauling the raft around. Big ol' head injury, though hopefully Annie hadn't actually seen that. Nadie probably looked like she'd been on the run for weeks, instead of just that day.

"Things are tough in this country," Annie observed. "It makes the people tough too. No place for a little princess."

Nadie nodded. "You mind if I join your fire tonight? I've got to figure out what I'm going to do if I can't get any further down the river."

Annie regarded her for a minute, then nodded reluctantly.

❧

It was a strange and sullen evening. Nadie was used to camp-outs being cheerful affairs, with lots of good food, storytelling, and laughter. But neither of them was inclined toward talk. Nadie didn't want to talk about her heartbreak, her home, how she got there, or where she was headed. And she guessed Annie didn't either. Nadie's attempts at conversation were met with stony silence, or occasionally with a question fired back in her direction, or some sullen, sardonic observation.

As night fell and the temperature dropped, Nadie took it upon herself to light the fire. It was some time before Annie put some fish on to fry, grudgingly offering a portion to Nadie. They ate in silence and eventually Nadie spread out a ground sheet and her thin bedroll and lay down to sleep. It had been an exhausting day and, despite Annie's baleful stare, Nadie fell into a deep sleep.

CHAPTER FIFTEEN

When Nadie awoke, she lay still for a long time, listening. She didn't want to get up and disturb Annie. The other girl was grumpy enough without being awakened before she was ready. Nadie knew she was going to have to ask questions and insist on some answers if she was going to be able to continue her journey. And that meant she had to do her best to keep Annie in a good mood.

Eventually, though, Nadie's bladder couldn't wait any longer and she had to jump up and run into the bush to relieve herself. She went as quietly as she could and was glad she had slept with her shoes on so she didn't have to worry about stepping on rocks, pinecones, or worse.

She tiptoed back toward the campsite, still trying to be as quiet as possible in case she hadn't managed to waken Annie streaking for the trees. But when she got back to the fire pit, she didn't see Annie lying where she expected her to be. Annie must have had to get up as well, and gone into the trees in the other direction so they would both have their privacy.

Nadie went to roll up her bedroll and to flip over the ground sheet so it would dry. She was looking over the campsite as she tidied up, registering one point at a time.

Annie's sleeping bag was gone. She had already put it away. She must have gotten up earlier, and Nadie just hadn't heard her. Maybe she'd gone to catch some more fish for breakfast.

But the tarp that had formed Annie's tent shelter was gone too. Not just moved somewhere else to dry out or be repaired, but gone.

In fact, all of Annie's gear was gone.

No backpack.

No cooking implements.

No fishing lines.

Nothing.

Nadie stood there in disbelief, letting her bedroll fall back to the ground and begin to unwind again.

Why would Annie take off like that, in the night or the early morning? She had been using the campsite for days, maybe even weeks or months. Why would she suddenly abandon it? Because Nadie had come? She didn't feel safe with someone else knowing where she was? But Nadie knew it wasn't that. Annie had called out to her, had invited her into the campsite.

Her chest tight and stomach sick, Nadie walked to where she had tied the raft beside the river the afternoon before. It wasn't there. She looked up and down the bank. She might have misjudged exactly where she had left it. Like looking for Grandfather's truck in the wrong aisle in the parking lot at the grocery store. A different tree. A different outcropping of rocks. It was possible.

But it wasn't there. It was gone. Nadie walked back to her bedroll and rolled it back up tightly, securing it with a strap. She reached for her backpack, but it wasn't there. Nadie looked around for some sign of it.

Had Annie moved it out of the way while she was cleaning up?

It wasn't to be found.

Nadie folded up her groundsheet, even though it was damp. She needed to get moving quickly. Maybe she could catch up to

Annie. Annie couldn't have gotten that big of a head start. Maybe she would put ashore to eat breakfast. Or lunch. She would have to portage around the rapids. Even if Annie didn't have to carry the raft, she would still have to carry all of her gear. She was weighed down a lot more than Nadie had been.

Nadie started walking downstream. She tried just to focus on watching the waterway for any sign of Annie. Not thinking about what Annie had done, or why, or the predicament Nadie was in now. How was she going to get somewhere safe? Annie had been stuck there for days until Nadie had shown up with the raft. Now Nadie had no gear and no idea where to go. But she couldn't think about that. She just watched the river for any sign of Annie or the raft or any of the gear. If Annie didn't lash the gear down, she might lose some of it, and it would wash ashore.

The girl and the raft were long gone. The river ran way too fast for Nadie ever to keep up. It was like running down the highway trying to catch up to a car. Nadie tried not to think about it. Too much thinking and she would just get depressed. It wasn't hopeless. Annie would have to get out to go around the rapids, unless she was stupid enough to think she could just ride through them.

Nadie had been walking for an hour or more before she started to wonder if the rapids had just been a story to keep her from putting the raft back in the river after stopping to talk with Annie. Annie had needed an opportunity to get her hands on the raft herself while Nadie was sleeping. So she had said what was necessary to keep Nadie from riding any further down the river.

There were no rapids.

She didn't need to carry her gear by land to get around the rapids, because there weren't any. It was clear sailing.

❦

She stopped to rest when the sun was high in the sky. Nadie was still following the river, for lack of a better plan. She didn't want to think about what was going to happen to her now. She didn't even have clean water or food. Annie had taken all of Nadie's meager gear, leaving her with nothing.

Almost nothing.

Nadie took stock of what she did have. A tarp she had used for a ground sheet. Her sleeping roll, composed of several blankets. The clothes she was wearing, including shoes and a jacket. In her pockets, she had a knife and a couple of paper matchbooks, and the rest of the debris she normally carried about with her.

Not a lot, but she had been taught how to survive in the wilds. Grandfather could have survived with a knife and some matches. Maybe even with just a knife.

Sitting in the shade, Nadie picked up a stick and started loosening rocks in the riverbank. It wasn't high above the water level like it was in some areas she had come through. It was nice and low; but it was rocky. She pried rocks up with the stick before levering them up with her fingers and tossing them to the side. If she just used her fingers, they would be bleeding after ten minutes. She was tempted to use her knife, but she couldn't risk dulling or breaking the blade. She did use the knife to sharpen the stick, but she kept breaking the point off of the stick.

Nadie hoped by the time she dug down a few inches, she would get past the rocks and it would be easier going, but the rocks just got bigger. Harder to dig around. Harder to pry up. She was tempted to give up, but the hole was getting wetter. She pried out a couple more rocks, and then sat and watched the water seep in through the sand and clay into the bottom of her hole. Hopefully, Mother Earth had cleaned it well enough for Nadie to drink it without getting sick. She was still wearing the flannel shirt Nicole had helped her into. Nadie used her knife to cut the bottom few inches off of it and then used the resulting rag to soak up the water in the bottom of the hole.

It tasted like dirt, but it was wet and she was dehydrated. She sucked on the rag until she couldn't get any more moisture out of it, and then soaked up what had collected in the hole again in the meantime. She kept repeating the process until her stomach started to hurt and made sloshing noises when she moved. She didn't want to have to repeat the process again until she stopped for the night, so she drank all she could before moving on.

As she continued to follow the river throughout the day, she started to ponder on building another raft, or some other kind of boat. Annie's people, the Ojibwe, had made birch bark canoes. There was plenty of birch along the river. Nadie didn't know how to build a birch bark canoe, but she and Mouse had made the raft from saplings and store-bought rope, and Nadie knew how to make a sort of rope from the inner bark of the birch.

It had taken her and Mouse most of the summer to make the raft. How long would it take Nadie to make one out of deadfall branches and homemade rope?

Nadie had a working solution for water. She had the clothes she was wearing and her bedding. She was still pondering on the idea of making another raft. That still left the problem of food. It was too late in the year for berries. Even the old, dried ones had been eaten by the birds and the bears. She didn't have a fishhook. She didn't have anything to cook in.

It wouldn't be such a worry if she had been well when she left. A well-nourished person didn't have to worry about starving in two or three days. As long as they had water, they could keep going. But Nadie hadn't been eating much of anything since Luyu's death. Her body had already been consuming her fat stores, like a bear in the winter. Only she hadn't had much fat to start with. She hadn't been hungry since Luyu had died, but after being out in the fresh air for a couple of days, working her body hard, her appetite had come back full-force. Full-on hunger, with nothing to eat.

She knew it wasn't true there was nothing to eat. Just nothing she wanted to eat. She could really go for a box of mac and cheese. The wild food around her wasn't nearly as appetizing.

Nadie set to foraging before it started to get dark. She held her shirt out as a collecting basket and started to fill it. When she sat down to make her fire, she had a mound of mushrooms, roots from some of the plants growing beside the river, and white grubs. At first she had thought to skewer everything on a stick to roast over the fire, but they were all too small or too fragile. Instead, she made do with using some flat river rocks as her cooking pans. It wasn't long before everything was sizzling and popping in the fire. Nadie's stomach rumbled in anticipation.

It took a full day to figure out how to make rope efficiently. Even once she figured it out, it wasn't very fast work. Nadie was thankful for all of the hours she had spent on weaving; it had taught her how to sit quietly and work on a repetitive task for hours. The rope wasn't nearly as pleasant to look at as the blanket, but it was useful and gave Nadie a sense of accomplishment. Even if she weren't able to make a raft, the rope would still come in handy for other things. The outer birch bark she needed to remove to get to the inner fibers would be useful as well. She knew it could be used to make water vessels and other things she might need. Mostly, she thought she would use it on her raft.

When she got too tired of making rope, or her fingers too sore, she would take a break and scout around for more building materials. While there were lots of strong saplings that would have made a nicer-looking raft, she only had her pocket knife and didn't want to dull it unnecessarily. She collected plenty of deadfall of similar sizes, laying it all out. The raft she and Mouse had made had been big. Big enough for the two of them to lie down on comfortably. But her new raft didn't need to be that big. It only had to be big enough to support her standing or sitting. She didn't even need room for gear, thanks to Annie.

In all, it took four days to build a scrappy little raft that looked like it was ready to fall apart any moment. She didn't have enough rope to play it out in the water when she went around rapids, and that meant she would have to carry it if she got to impassible waters. It didn't look particularly safe. Grandfather would be horrified that she planned to ride the river on it. But it floated, and that meant Nadie could get down river, hopefully to some settlement where she could get proper food and water and a car ride to civilization. The nights were getting quite cold, her blankets coated with frost by morning. She wouldn't be able to survive much longer dressed and equipped as she was.

❧

Traveling down the river was so much faster than trying to cover the distance by foot. Within a few hours, she saw signs of other people. She wasn't about to get taken advantage of by another crook like Annie, so she chose her exit point carefully. She floated past several people who pointed or waved or tried to get her attention, until she came to a little family: a mother, father, and two small children. It was the little boy who saw her first. By the time she got close, he was jumping up and down, pointing and yelling excitedly. The father shaded his eyes but didn't signal to Nadie to come to shore. That suited her just fine. She didn't want to face another predator. Nadie poled to the side of the river and nodded at the children and mother, who greeted her as she pulled the raft ashore.

"Hi, there," she greeted, her voice rough from disuse. Her face felt hot and she didn't look at their faces.

"Are you an Indian?" the little boy demanded, jumping up and down excitedly. His mother tried to shush him.

"Yes. I'm Cree Indian. We call ourselves Nehiyaw." Nadie unstrapped her bedroll and put it down.

"Ne-hi-yaw." The boy attempted to repeat the word. "Wow! A real Indian!"

Nadie shrugged. "Do you have water?" she asked the mother.

"Uh, yes, a little…"

"I am very thirsty."

"Yes, of course. I'm sorry…"

Nadie didn't know what she was sorry for.

"We have Coke," the little boy offered. "Do you know what Coke is?"

His mother rolled her eyes and shrugged helplessly, giving up on trying to make him be polite.

"Yes," Nadie said. "I like Coke."

"Give her a Coke, Mom. She likes Coke!"

The father had walked over to join them. He had on tall fishing boots and didn't come all the way out of the water.

"That's quite the little craft," he said, looking over the raft. "I don't think I've ever seen anything quite like it."

"I had a better one, but someone stole it and all my gear."

He went closer to the raft, touching it and inspecting the handmade ropes. "You must be tired. How long have you been on your own?"

Nadie pressed her lips together and didn't answer. She didn't want any word of what had happened or where she had gone to get back to the reservation. And she didn't want to say anything else that this man might use to take advantage of her. There was no telling if he would turn on her like Annie had.

"We should break out the lunch," he told his wife. "We have enough to share."

She handed Nadie a can of Coke and, nodding to her husband, went back to the bright orange cooler to unpack their picnic lunch. Nadie's mouth watered as she watched them put out sandwiches, fruit, and chips. She sipped the Coke slowly so it would not make her sick.

"Thank you."

"How do you say 'thank you' in Indian?" the little boy demanded.

"Ay-hay."

"Ay-hay. Ay-hay for lunch, Mom. That means thank you!"

"Yes, Arty. I heard. You're welcome."

Nadie seated herself on the ground. There were only four camp chairs, two of them child-size. She didn't need a chair. The parents looked at each other awkwardly, but neither knew what to say.

"Come and get it," the mother said, putting the last of the dishes out. "We're delighted you could come and join us...?" she trailed off, waiting for Nadie to give her name.

"Thank you," Nadie acknowledged. She stood back up to fill a plate, careful not to take very much, and sat back down to eat.

The family dished up their plates and sat down.

"So, where did you come from?" the father asked. "You look like you've had quite a journey."

Nadie made a gesture up-river, offering nothing else.

"Where are you trying to get to?" the mother tried.

"Out of the bush," Nadie said. "Where are you folks going?"

They looked at each other, cautious. They didn't want to give her a ride.

"Winn-er-peg," Arty offered. "That's where my gramma is."

"Winnipeg," Nadie repeated. "That would be good."

Arty gave a little gasp. Nadie was worried he was going to end up choking on his food. "Mom, she could come with us! Can she ride with me in the back seat? There's room! She can ride with me and Candice."

The parents looked at each other, obviously reluctant to take in this rough-looking stranger. Nadie just looked down at her plate and said nothing. She nibbled at her food, even though she was starving. Arty continued to chatter, and the parents kept looking at each other, seemingly communicating by telepathy. The little girl was smaller than Arty. She was shy and mostly hid behind her parents. She didn't talk to Nadie like Arty. Her eyes were big and curious. She made Nadie think of Luyu.

When she was done eating, Nadie got to her feet. "Ay-hay. Thank you for your hospitality." She picked up her bedroll and headed toward the SUV she could see through the trees. She didn't ask for a ride, she just walked past the SUV to the road. She could hitch a ride from someone else if Arty's family were afraid of her.

She set out at a slow walk and a few minutes later, Arty's father jogged up behind her.

"We'll give you a ride to Winnipeg."

Nadie looked at his face. He still looked nervous about it. "I don't have a gun," she offered, lifting her shirt a couple of inches and turning so he could see she didn't have one tucked into her waistband. "I have a knife. You can take it if you'll give it back."

He made a face and to begin with, Nadie thought he was going to protest, to say he trusted her. But he finally nodded, looking down at the gravel road beneath their feet. Nadie was surprised. She hadn't expected him to take her up on it. He was smart to do so, of course. She could easily have held the knife at his or Arty's throat once they were in the truck. They couldn't have done anything to stop her.

Nadie wiggled her fingers into her pocket and worked out the pocket knife. She put it into the man's hand. "You have to give it back," she reminded him.

"I will."

She was trusting him to return it to her and not to do anything to threaten her. He was trusting that she didn't have another weapon. Nadie bit her lip and nodded.

"Come on back. We're not quite ready to go yet."

She followed him back past the SUV to their picnic spot. Nadie picked a spot under the trees. Lying down with the bedroll under her head as a pillow, she closed her eyes for a nap.

CHAPTER SIXTEEN

She hadn't realized how far away Winnipeg still was. It was dusky, night just falling, when they got to the city. To Nadie, the town near the reservation was big. She was always amazed at its sprawl when they arrived. All of the houses, so close together, the stores, the professional offices, even a few buildings that rose several floors above the ground. Mouse had called them skyscrapers when he was little, but she had seen pictures of skyscrapers in her library books and knew how big they really were, and she poked fun at him for it.

Even though she had seen pictures of skyscrapers, she had no idea how dwarfed she would be by them. They were unimaginably huge. Everybody in town could have lived in one building. Everybody in several towns. The streets bustled with traffic and, even though it was night, there were people on the sidewalks; individuals walking their dogs, couples arm-in-arm, even mothers getting off of buses pushing carriages.

"It's so beautiful!" Nadie breathed. "Look at all the lights!"

"Fairy lights," said the little girl. The first words she had spoken to Nadie. Nadie nodded, staring out the window in wonderment.

"Where do you want to go?" asked the father.

Nadie had no plan further than getting out of the reservation and into the real world. Now she was in the real world and had no idea how to function. Her stomach knotted. "Somewhere there are trees. Are there any trees here?"

He laughed. "Plenty. But I can't just drop you on your own somewhere. It's too dangerous. Don't you know anybody? What are you going to do?"

"No… I don't know."

"Do you have money? A job?"

Nadie didn't answer. She had nowhere to stay. No one to ask for help. What would he do? Turn her over to the police? Nadie knew from her books that the police could arrest someone just for not having a home. She thought harder, trying to dredge up enough details from the books she had read to sound like she knew what she was talking about.

"There's… a place downtown. Where one of my friends stayed…"

"Downtown?" the mother repeated, turning around in her seat to peer at Nadie through the dimness. "Do you mean some kind of emergency shelter?"

Nadie nodded.

The woman pursed her lips. "I don't think you'll be able to get into anywhere tonight. They'll be full up. The doors closed for the night."

"Well… that's where I'll go tomorrow. They'll help me out. They helped my friend."

"And tonight?" the father prompted.

"Like I said… just find me some trees. I'll camp out."

"It's been hours since we ate," the mother said. "You need supper. And you're not dressed warmly enough to be sleeping outside. It's below freezing. It's supposed to snow tomorrow and you don't even have a tent. You can't sleep outside."

She turned to her husband, dropping her voice low.

"We can't just abandon her somewhere. She has no idea what she's doing. She wouldn't last the night. Do you think she could sleep at your mother's? Just tonight? Then tomorrow we'll figure out what to do with her."

The man looked at Nadie in the rear-view mirror. Nadie looked away from him, out the window on the other side of the SUV. He swore under his breath. "How did we get ourselves into this? I can't take her into my mother's home. We don't know anything about this kid. She could have just murdered her family and run off, for all we know. She won't tell us her name, or where she came from. There's no way."

"Well, maybe..." Another nervous glance darted Nadie's direction. "Maybe some kind of compromise. We can at least feed her. What if she sleeps in your mother's back yard? She has trees. And then... we wouldn't be putting your mother or the children in danger. Not if she was outside."

"She could still break in and slit our throats while we sleep," he muttered. The words were more of a joke than they were harsh. But still a reminder that Nadie was an outsider, an unknown, and she could have ill intentions toward them.

They looked back at her in unison, as if dancing the type of ceremonial dance where everyone moved in the same way at the same time.

"Tell you what," the man said, raising his voice again. "You can come with us to Gramma's house—" There was a cheer from Arty that he was going to get to show 'his Indian' to his grandmother. "We'll have a bite to eat and then you can sleep out under the trees. We'll make sure you have enough blankets to keep you warm. Then tomorrow, we'll help you to connect with some emergency services; people who can help you to figure out what you are going to do."

Nadie nodded her agreement. "Sure. That sounds good. Ay-hay."

"Okay. That's settled, then."

Arty grabbed Nadie by the hand and pulled her up to his gramma's house, determined to show her off. Nadie was reluctant but tried to be a good sport about it. Gramma had red, shoulder-length hair and a pale complexion. Not very many wrinkles. She didn't look old enough to be the man's mother. Maybe he just looked older than he was. Gramma looked at Nadie with wide eyes, nodding at Arty's excited recounting of all that had happened from the time they saw Nadie floating down the river on the handmade raft.

"It sounds like you've all had an adventure," Gramma observed, looking from Arty to Nadie and giving her a good-humored smile.

"Yeah!" Arty exclaimed, and chattered on.

"Mom, I need to talk to you," the father said, trying to separate her and move her out of the living room.

"Dear—"

"I just need to talk to you. Please, for a minute."

He managed to get her out of the way where Nadie wouldn't be able to hear their conversation.

"Come on, come in!" Artie tugged on Nadie's hand.

Nadie didn't move from where she was. She was on the doormat just inside the door and she wasn't about to go any further. She gazed around at the room in awe. Never had she seen anything like it. A beige carpet that looked as soft as a kitten; heavy, ornate furniture; paintings on the wall; brightly lit lamps and display cases. It looked like a very expensive store display. One that Grandfather would have told her very sternly not to touch. There was not a speck of dust. Not one smudge or fingerprint. It was like a palace.

"I can't come in," Nadie protested, resisting Arty's pull. "No—I'm dirty—I can't!"

The mother was helping the little girl off with her coat and gave Nadie a reassuring smile. "It's okay. You're not going to hurt anything by coming in. Make yourself comfortable."

Nadie shook her head. She backed toward the door she had

just come in. "I'm going out to the yard. Where I'm going to sleep."

There were raised voices from the other room. Gramma obviously didn't like the idea of Nadie staying there and that sealed it for her. She wasn't going to stay where she wasn't welcome. Where she obviously didn't belong.

Gramma and the father came back into the living room in a rush. Gramma was in the lead. "No, don't go," she told Nadie. "Please, stay here. Let us help you out tonight. You're hungry. You're tired. You don't need to be out on the street trying to figure out a game plan tonight."

Nadie looked at her, confused.

Gramma shot a look over her shoulder at her son and took Nadie's hand. "Come with me. Let's get you into a hot shower so you can get cleaned up. How does that sound?"

"Like I died and went to heaven," Nadie admitted. "I'm covered in dirt and I'm sure I smell…"

"You smell like a campfire," Arty agreed.

"That's not all I smell like. I'm all sweaty."

"Sweat just means you've done a man's work," Arty declared, obviously echoing something he had heard before. Probably from his father, the way everyone laughed and glanced in the man's direction.

"Well, I've done that," Nadie agreed. "And a woman's work too."

"Come with me," Gramma invited. "We'll get you fixed up. Phil—" she looked at the mother. "If you'll take over in the kitchen until I get back; everything is started, you can see what needs to be done."

Nadie had never heard of a woman called Phil before. She went with Gramma up a wide staircase with on ornate handrail on the side. Everything in the house seemed like it had been made just for the house. And Nadie was sure most of the artwork and sculptures she saw were probably worth more than any of the trucks or houses on the reservation. She tried to think of what to say about it.

"Your house is very beautiful," she told Gramma. "It's like... a museum."

"Thank you. I'm glad you like it."

Maybe that was another reason the father wanted her to sleep outside. So she wouldn't steal anything from them. Nadie had read a lot of books from the library and knew the white man's views on possessions and ownership were a lot different from those of her band. For the band, the idea of ownership was much more... fluid. And for one person to have so much more than another was seen as unfair. Something that flew in the face of generosity. Nadie had no idea people actually lived like this, in such castles. She had thought it was the stuff of fairy tales.

"Here we go." Gramma led her down a hall and opened a wide, heavy wooden door. Nadie's jaw dropped open and she stared in amazement. She didn't even know what to call it. Certainly not a bathroom. The tub was more like the hot tub at the public swimming pool in the town. It was much more fancy, but that was the only thing Nadie could think of to compare it to. And there was what she could only assume was a shower, enclosed by glass set at varying angles and bigger than the whole bathroom in Nadie's house. There were two sinks, with silver gooseneck faucets and fancy cut-glass knobs. There were piles of fluffy, brilliant-white towels and cloths, like Gramma was expecting an army to come bathe.

"It's... wow..."

"Take as long as you need." Gramma studied her. "You're taller and skinnier than I am, but I think we can manage some clothes that will do."

"No, no," Nadie protested. "I don't want to take your clothes!"

"I have plenty. You need something. We'll wash what you've got on, but you need at least one change of clothing. Those look like they're going to fall apart."

Nadie hugged herself, looking down at the flannel shirt. It

wasn't that bad. It was dirty, but it was still sturdy, by no means threadbare. She had cut several inches off the bottom, though, and it was fraying.

"I just… don't want to put you out."

"Certainly not. Think nothing of it. Go ahead and get washed up. Put on a robe when you're done," she pointed to some snow-white robes hanging on hooks. "I'll have picked out some clothes by then and we can see what you like."

"Okay."

Gramma withdrew, pulling the door shut behind her. Nadie looked back and forth between the big tub and the shower. She wasn't sure which one to pick. She closed her eyes and thought. She had sat in the hot tub a few times at the pool. And she had had a couple of hot showers at Mouse's house.

She decided the hot tub would do a better job of refreshing her body, easing the muscle soreness and scrapes and bruises. So she went to the tub, and turned taps and pushed buttons until it was filling, the water almost too hot to stand. The water started to bubble and foam. It smelled perfumy. Nadie stripped off her dirty clothes, wincing at the shower of dirt that hit the white marble floor. She climbed into the big tub.

There were many significant looks and gestures exchanged over the dinner table as Nadie ate with the family. The children seemed unaware of the non-verbal communication going on between their parents and gramma, but Nadie was aware of every movement and glance. It wasn't, as she had first thought, that Gramma didn't want her to stay there. In fact, it was the opposite. Gramma was opposed to Nadie sleeping outside in the yard instead of in the house with everyone else. She didn't understand how a young girl like Nadie could be a threat to her. Or she believed that by opening up her home and being hospitable toward Nadie, Nadie would be too grateful to do anything to harm her. Either way, she did not want Nadie out in the yard; she wanted her in a bed inside.

After stuffing herself, Nadie helped to take the dirty dishes into the kitchen without being asked and, when she found herself alone in the room with Gramma, she spoke.

"I'm not going to sleep inside. I want to be under the stars. So don't be mad at him about it."

Gramma looked at her sideways. "You picked up on that, did you?"

Nadie raised her eyebrows and didn't say anything.

Gramma laughed. "Well, I don't approve. You can't tell me you sleep under the stars every night."

"No… but it's my first night in Winnipeg and I want to see the stars here."

"You won't be able to see very many. The streetlights block them out."

Nadie shrugged. "I'm going to get ready, okay? I'm tired."

"At least let me give you a sleeping bag. I put your blankets in the wash, but you need something warmer than that."

"Okay."

"I'll go get one."

Nadie went back to the dining room to collect more dishes. She stopped beside the father. "I need my knife back now. I'm going outside."

"Already?" Arty whined. "It's not bedtime yet!"

"Yes, it is," Arty's mother said. "You've had a long day. We ate supper late."

"Aww…"

"I need my knife," Nadie repeated, not letting them get distracted.

The man was reluctant. But he had promised to give it back. Nadie stood waiting. Eventually, he reached into his pocket and pulled it back out. "You're going out now? For the night?"

"Yes. I'll stay out there and not come back to kill you in your sleep."

His jaw dropped. Nadie reached over and pulled her knife out of his hand.

&.

The sleeping bag Gramma gave her was super soft and warm. Nadie had never felt anything like it. She also gave Nadie a backpack, which she had put Nadie's freshly laundered clothing into.

"Are you sure you're okay out here all night?"

"I haven't slept inside for a week," Nadie said. "And today I've had lots of food and water. I'll sleep well. It's very comfortable."

"Okay, then… I'll see you in the morning. I'll make you a good breakfast and then the kids will help you to find a shelter or a service that will help you to find a place where you can stay."

Nadie nodded. "Ay-hay. That's thank you. You have been very generous."

Gramma shook her head. "We've done no more than anyone else would. What kind of people would we be if we couldn't even help out a young girl on her own like you? I wish we could do more."

After a few more awkward moments, Gramma finally went inside to say goodnight to Arty.

Nadie lay still, staring up at the few stars she could see in the sky and keeping an eye on the house. A few times, she saw one of their shadows in a window, looking out at her, making sure she hadn't moved. She drifted off to sleep waiting for them to go to bed.

CHAPTER SEVENTEEN

When Nadie woke up, she could tell she had been asleep for a few hours. Her body had just been so exhausted that when she finally gave it sufficient food and water and a nice warm bed, there was no way she could stay awake.

The house was dark. Gramma had left a light on at the back door. Even though she had grudgingly agreed with her son to keep the door locked, she had told Nadie to ring the doorbell if she needed anything at all during the night.

Nadie wasn't going to ring the bell. She slid out of the sleeping bag and rolled it up as compactly as she could. She hesitated to take it at first. But thinking it through, she was sure Gramma would want her to keep it. And Nadie had left her blankets in the house, so it was a fair trade. Nadie crept out of the yard to the street and looked around. She didn't know anything about where she should go. Except that if she went downtown, there were emergency shelters. That sounded like a reasonable plan of action.

She could see the lights of the buildings downtown, so she knew what direction to go. But it looked like it was going to be a long walk. She started walking at a slow, steady pace.

Nadie heard an engine behind her and turned to look. It was a city transit bus. It was slowing, and Nadie realized she was coming up to a bus stop. She stopped and waited for the bus to pull up and open its doors. She stepped on.

"Fare?" the bus driver prompted, motioning to the box beside him.

Nadie looked at the list of ticket prices on the box. "Oh… I don't have any money. Do you… go downtown?"

"Yes. But you need to pay."

"I'm trying to get to an emergency shelter… I don't have any money. Someone stole my backpack and all my things."

She didn't tell him she hadn't had any money in her backpack to begin with. The driver looked pointedly at the backpack over Nadie's shoulder, saying nothing.

"Not this one. A lady gave me this one today. And the sleeping bag. But… no money."

He sighed heavily and closed the door, shutting out the cold night air. "Have a seat. But don't expect this to work again. Just because I'm a softie and there's no one else on the bus tonight, that doesn't mean you're going to get away with it again."

Nadie glanced around the bus. As he said, she was the only rider. She sat down on one of the seats close to the driver and watched out the window.

"You don't know where you're going?" the driver asked.

"I know there are places downtown."

"There are plenty of places downtown. Safe and otherwise. A young girl like you, you're not safe wandering around at this time of night."

Nadie shrugged. "I can take care of myself."

He shook his head.

"Do you know where the shelters are?" Nadie asked. That would be more helpful than him simply telling her she was doing the wrong thing. Telling her it wasn't safe was not the least bit helpful to her.

"I know where a couple of them are. But I don't stop at them. And they will be closed by now."

"I know. That's what they said. I'll go tomorrow morning."

"What will you do tonight?"

"Sleep. Walk. Wait."

"There's a lot of violent crime in Winnipeg. You don't come from around here, do you?"

"No."

"Where did you grow up?"

Nadie didn't bother to answer.

"All kinds of backwoods kids come to the city, thinking they can make it. They come to work, or party, or find some friend who ran away before them. I see dozens of them. It's a city full of runaways, not all of them kids. You need to go back home."

Nadie shook her head. "No. I can't."

"Even if things were bad at home, they can still be worse here."

Nadie stared out the window at the sparkling city lights. "It's so pretty."

"Don't be misled. It's not a fairy wonderland. Stay away from dark places."

She nodded. "Yeah. Except to sleep."

"To sleep too. Only sleep where it's bright and there's lots of people. Better yet, don't sleep."

Nadie didn't feel like sleeping anyway. She felt wide-awake, excited. She'd never been anywhere that felt so full of energy and excitement.

They traveled in relative silence. Every now and then, the bus driver pointed out a landmark he felt was important. A main street, a government building, a plaza where events were held. Then they were in the downtown. The big buildings rose up around Nadie, making her feel like she was in a canyon. Even though it was the middle of the night, there were people out. Young people dressed for partying. Drunks sleeping in doorways. Girls in clothing way too skimpy for the weather walking near the road, rubbing their arms in the chill air. Nadie turned her head, watching one with a silver top and mini skirt until she was out of sight.

"Are they prostitutes?" she asked.

He chuckled. "Mostly."

"I don't know how anyone could do that."

The bus driver looked at her for a minute, then back to the road. "Most of them didn't plan it that way. They made friends with the wrong people, or got addicted to something, or were kidnapped and forced into it. You don't come here planning to sell your body. That's what happens when you don't have a plan."

She heard the censure in his voice. She was one of those kids. One of those backwoods kids who came to the city without a plan, thinking she could make it. With no idea how to protect herself there and no plan of how to survive, she would just end up dead or walking the streets like one of those other girls.

"I'll figure it out," she muttered. "I just need a little time."

The bus driver had stopped at an intersection where there was no bus stop and let her out. He pointed down the street. "You go that way about three blocks and you'll find the mission. They can help you to find a shelter with space in the morning. Until then…" he pressed his lips together and shook his head. "You're going to have to stay out of trouble. Keep your eyes open. Stay around other people, but watch out for anyone who shows too much interest in you. It's… really not safe. This city eats kids like you up."

Nadie nodded and got off of the bus. "Thanks for your help. It would have been a long walk."

She was on her own again. No wise old bus driver to give her life tips. No gramma to see that she had the necessities of life and a comfortable place to sleep. No grandfather to get after her for being out too late and making him worry.

Nadie kept alert as she walked a few blocks to find the mission the bus driver had described. No one was going to sneak up on her in the night and catch her off guard. And she wasn't going to lose her backpack now that she had one again. She would be more careful. She would not trust anyone.

There were a lot of dark spots where street lights had burned out or been broken. Nadie tried to stay in the pools of light, her anxiety rising whenever she had to go half a block in the darkness. Most of the people she walked by ignored her. There were a couple who whistled or tried to call her over to them. Nadie pulled her jacket tighter around her and kept going.

It wasn't hard to find the mission. There was a much higher concentration of homeless people sleeping around the outside of the building. People who had not gotten there in time to find a place, she assumed. Arriving after it had filled up. Nadie felt sadness welling up in her as she looked over all of the men and women lying on the sidewalk, their clothes worn and dirty, thin blankets wrapped around some of them to keep out the cold. Most of them were Indigenous. Her own brothers and sisters. How could there be so many of her people without homes? And what were they going to do as the weather got colder?

Nadie was going to turn around and pace back the direction she had come, but there was a girl around her own age a little further down the block, standing near the street and lighting up a cigarette. The girl was watching Nadie's approach. Her features were Indigenous, but with very light skin. She had some blond streaks in her dark hair and was wearing a white winter jacket.

"Hey, noob."

Nadie frowned at this. "What?"

"Noob. You're a newbie. I haven't seen you here before."

"Oh. Yeah, I guess."

"Holly. You know, you gotta get here before five if you want to be able to get in."

Nadie nodded. "I heard. I thought maybe in the morning, they can help me figure out what to do."

"You a runaway?"

Nadie hesitated to answer. She didn't want to give too much

about herself away. She didn't know anything about Holly. Had no reason to trust her with information.

"Everybody's a runaway," Holly said, making a wide motion with her cigarette. "That doesn't matter. How long you been in the Peg?"

"The Peg?" Nadie echoed.

Holly laughed. "Winnipeg, Noob! I guess that answers my question."

"Oh. I get it."

"You straight off the reservation?"

Nadie didn't answer. She looked for a polite way to walk away from Holly. She didn't want anyone trying to find out her story or trying to take advantage of her ignorance of city life. Unable to think of anything polite to say, Nadie just turned around and paced back the way she had come. Holly fell into step beside her. Nadie glanced sideways at her, frowning.

"I'm not going to hurt you," Holly said. "We should stick together." She squeezed Nadie's arm with a friendly smile. "Girls gotta look after each other."

"Yeah."

Holly let go again. "You had anything to eat tonight? Hungry?"

"I ate good. Thanks."

"Yeah? Where'd you go? Not to a soup kitchen, if it was good!"

Nadie shrugged.

"You're pretty tight with your information there, aren't you? You think I'm a cop? I'm gonna turn you in?"

"No."

Holly laughed. "You've got an awful lot of learning to do if you're gonna stay alive in this town. First thing is, not to be out here after dark."

"You are."

"Yeah, but I got my crew out here, keeping an eye on things."

Nadie looked around carefully, looking for other kids their

age. There were a couple in sight, but none seemed to be looking Holly's direction or to be aware of her.

"You gotta have people looking out for you," Holly said. "That's the only way to make it out here. People who keep to themselves, loners, they don't last long."

Nadie nodded. It made sense. Being a part of a community always made a person stronger than standing alone. Holly took another drag on her cigarette and blew the smoke back out toward Nadie. Nadie wrinkled her nose, turning away. Pipe smoke was different. Pure tobacco or other medicine. The cigarette smoke was rank and made her choke.

"Sorry!" Holly laughed. "Maybe you want one?"

"No."

When Nadie turned around to pace the other direction again, Holly tugged on her sleeve. "Come this way. I'll show you around a bit."

"I dunno… I should stay around here…"

"Are you kidding me? You can't stay here all night." Her voice dropped down low. "People come here looking for kids like you. And I'm not talking just cops. That's how sisters disappear."

She pulled Nadie, and Nadie followed, uncertain. The bus driver had indicated she should stay put, but he wouldn't know if this was somewhere people trolled for young girls. Holly would know because she was from around there. She had people. She wasn't alone like Nadie.

"We won't go far. You can still come back here in the morning if you want to."

"Yeah, I do."

"We'll see. Maybe you'll change your mind."

They cut across a dark street and Nadie looked around quickly, worried about being ambushed. Holly patted her arm and pulled her closer.

"Don't worry, I'll take care of you, babe."

They were back out of the dark street, and Nadie breathed a sigh of relief. It was an exciting life, but maybe a little too exciting for her. She would have to confine her wandering to during the day, when all the creeps had gone to bed, or on to their day jobs, or wherever creeps hid when the sun came up.

Holly stopped to draw on her cigarette and look around. Nadie wondered just what she was looking for. Holly was like a hunter following some invisible signs Nadie couldn't see. Holly pointed her cigarette at a building with what looked like a restaurant and a club on the street level.

"Over there, that's a big drug-dealing location. You don't want the cops to see you around there. They'll have you arrested before you can say due process."

Nadie nodded. "Yeah, okay."

It made her itchy just standing there. What if a drug dealer was close by, watching them to see if they were going to buy? What if there were policemen in one of the dark cars that was parked along the street, just looking for someone to do something suspicious?

Holly observed her anxiety and nodded. "Best not to hang around here."

They moved on again. Another block down was a big, seedy-looking hotel. Holly put out her cigarette carefully and put it in her pocket.

"We're going in?" Nadie asked, surprised.

"Sure. This is my pad." Holly led the way.

Nadie followed. The hotel smelled smokey and stale. It smelled like body odor and unchanged diapers and other nasty smells Nadie didn't want to identify. Holly led the way to the stairs and started walking up.

"You gotta be quiet, hear?" she said in a low whisper. "We don't want people to hear us coming and going."

"What people?"

"Supervisors. It's CFS, right? We're all supposed to be in bed asleep."

Nadie frowned, concentrating on climbing the steep stairs. "Child Services?"

"Yeah."

"But this is a hotel."

"Sure. They don't have enough foster families and group homes, so they start putting us in hotels."

"In hotels with foster families?"

"No. In hotel rooms by ourselves. Supervisors are supposed to check in to keep track of us, but usually they just peek in, and if the light's off, they figure you're asleep and don't go in. Not that they can do anything about it if you take off! What are they going to do?"

Nadie thought back to the children taken from their families in the band. "But they're supposed to take care of you! Protect you!"

Holly laughed. "Yeah. Half the girls in the place are turning tricks. The other half are stoned out of their minds." She paused. "Of course… some of them are stoned and turning tricks!"

Nadie looked at her.

"Not me," Holly assured her. "I'm not part of that scene. Me and my crew, we look after each other, you know?"

Nadie's head was whirling. She followed Holly out into a corridor. Holly peeked around the corner first, looking up and down the hall before leaving the safety of the stairway. They crept quietly down the hall and to one of the rooms. Holly turned the handle and opened the door. It was dark inside, and there was a shape in the bed. Holly let the door shut and then turned on a forty-watt lamp. Nadie saw that the shape in the bed was just pillows and clothes. Holly sat on the edge of the bed and motioned for Nadie to sit beside her.

"The shelters are crowded and noisy," she said. "They're full of bugs and lice and people coughing their guts out all over the place. Sleeping on a broken cot there isn't much different than sleeping in an alley somewhere. Maybe worse, 'cause at least you can get some peace and quiet in an alley. Wouldn't you rather sleep here? Maybe it's not the best place, but you get a real bed and no one coughing germs all over you."

"But the shelter is safe."

"You'd be safe here."

Nadie looked toward the door. "You didn't need a key to get in."

"They leave it unlocked for the supervisors to get in."

Nadie had a sick feeling in her stomach. "Anyone could come in."

Holly studied Nadie with sharp eyes. "You're smarter than you look, aren't you? There's a chain. You can lock that if you want, but you'll have to get up to let the supervisor in if they're suspicious."

Nadie looked at the locks on the door. It wasn't a chain, exactly, but a long loop and knob that would allow the door to be opened only a few inches.

"It doesn't seem right. Why would they put kids in a place like this? Don't they care what happens to them?"

Holly gave an expressive shrug. "Why don't you sleep here tonight?" she said. "You can get a few more hours in; you look like you need it. Naive kid like you shouldn't be on the street by yourself. We gotta introduce you around, show you the ropes."

Nadie shook her head. But her body was telling her otherwise. The excitement had been sustaining her, keeping her awake, but sitting there on the bed in the dimly lit room, her eyes were starting to droop. The bed was soft and who knew where she was going to sleep the next day? A shelter cot was easier on the body than sleeping on the ground, but probably still not very comfortable.

"Come on," Holly pressed her toward the pillow. "You may as well get it while you can. Tomorrow, we can see if CFS will take you in, and you can get a bed here of your own."

"I don't know. What if they put me in a foster home?"

Holly blew out her breath with a laugh. "They won't do that. There's no room." She laughed again and patted Nadie on the shoulder. "Sleep on it. We'll talk in the morning."

She moved toward the door. Nadie was alarmed. "You're going out?"

"Gotta keep an eye out for any other greenies who might get themselves in trouble. It's a dangerous place out there." Holly stopped at the door. "You'll need to leave it unlocked in case a supervisor checks in. From the door, you look enough like me. But if you had to come up to them to unlock it, they'd know."

"But—"

"Ciao. See you in the morning."

Nadie lay down and closed her eyes, and tried to just sleep. Her body was so tired from the adventures of the last few days that she wanted to just drift right off. But she couldn't ignore the unlocked door. Anyone could come in. Not just the supervisor or another kid, but anybody off the street. There hadn't been any noticeable security in the hotel lobby. After so many dire warnings about violent crime, she couldn't put the anxiety out of her mind.

She got up and went to the curtained window, peeking out and looking down at the dark sidewalk. It looked even spookier and more dangerous than it had while she had been out there. The perspective made it seem even more remote and darker. The sky was not yet brightening. Still more time to sleep.

Nadie went to the bathroom and then returned to the bed to lie down. She shifted the pocketknife in her pocket that was wedged under her hip into a more comfortable position. Then she pulled it out. At least she had a way to defend herself if someone should come into the room. She opened the knife up and studied the blade. She always kept her knife in good condition. It was clean and sharp and there were no nicks in the steel.

She curled up on the bed, putting her hand under the pillow, clasping the knife. If a supervisor came in to check, they wouldn't be able to see the weapon in her hand, but if someone else came in, then she was ready to defend herself.

There was a baby crying down the hallway. Nadie wondered if it was a CFS baby. How many babies had they taken away, promising the baby was going to a better home, a safer place, only to be stashed in a hotel room because there were no beds and no families available? When they had talked about taking Luyu away, it had never occurred to Nadie they would put a child anywhere other than in a caring, capable foster family. Not as good as living at home with the family who loved you, but still somewhere safe and wholesome.

A siren screamed by outside. The lights flashed across Nadie's window and then were gone.

Where had Holly gone?

Nadie awoke to the sound of the door catch clicking and a soft squeak as the door swung open. She swallowed, tightening her grip on her knife, and strained her ears for footsteps. The hair rose on the back of her neck. Who was there? She didn't dare turn over to look. It might be a supervisor who would immediately recognize she wasn't Holly and then there would be all kinds of trouble. She couldn't do that to Holly and didn't want to get in any trouble herself. So she stayed frozen, breathing very slowly and evenly like she was still asleep, and listened for the rustle of clothing or footsteps across the carpet that would indicate the intruder was moving toward her.

There was another squeak and the soft click of the door being pulled shut and the catch engaging again. But was the intruder gone, a supervisor who had peeked in and moved on to the next room, or was the intruder now in the room with her, behind a closed door? Nadie's breath caught in her throat as she listened, straining with every fiber of her being. And still no sound.

Nadie stretched and made a noise as if still drowsy or moving in her sleep and turned slowly over onto her back. She opened her eyes just a crack so she could see the room and the open path to the doorway.

There was no one there. She was alone.

It must just have been a supervisor checking in. Nadie blew out her breath in relief. It was a long time before she was able to relax again.

CHAPTER EIGHTEEN

Nadie woke up with a start, her whole body convulsing in panic as hands were laid on her. She whipped the knife out before her eyes even finished opening, ready to defend herself against whomever had broken into the room.

"Ho! This one's not as green as you thought!" an unfamiliar voice exclaimed.

Nadie found herself looking at another Indigenous girl. This one big and broad, her face round and pockmarked. Her breath was vile. She jumped back out of the reach of Nadie's knife, laughing. Beyond her, Holly was watching. She gave a short laugh.

"Wake-up call, noob! Time to get up and at 'em, before the responsible adults figure out there's anything going on. You have a nice sleep?"

She hustled Nadie up, grabbing her arm to pull her out of the bed and pushing her toward the tiny bathroom.

"Pee and brush your hair and make yourself presentable. You got two minutes."

Nadie barely had time to think. Two minutes for what? She understood she had to leave before the supervisors saw her and realized Holly had been out at night when she was supposed to be asleep, but where was she going? To meet the people at the shelter?

Holly had wanted her to meet with CFS so she could get a hotel room of her own. Nadie had to admit it sounded like a pretty good deal, getting a hotel room all to yourself—private bathroom and TV included—without having to pay for it. What teenager wouldn't take up an offer like that?

She went to the bathroom, picked up the brush lying on the counter to get the knots out of her hair and smoothed it down with a little water. She poked through the makeup kit, wondering if that was what she was supposed to use to make herself 'presentable.' Without being sure what was going on, she brushed a little blush over her cheekbones and put on some lipstick.

"You done?" Holly hammered on the door, making her jump. "Come on, girl. Got to get moving."

Nadie opened the door.

Holly looked her over. "Not bad. By the way, you got a name, noob?"

She opened her mouth, then closed it again, considering.

Holly laughed. "No, huh? Well, let's call you…" she pursed her lips, looking Nadie up and down. "Tonya. How about that?"

The other girl spoke from behind Holly. "We'd better get her downstairs before roll call."

"I know, I know. Well, noob, this is Mitchell. She's going to take you downstairs and babysit you for a bit. Once they've finished room checks and breakfast, I'll come down and get you and we'll get you set up with CFS. Sound good?"

"I'm not sure I—"

"Doesn't really matter. Best you get signed up while there's still rooms available here. If you decide to ditch and go do something else, then fine. Just clear out. But you may as well get in while you can. It's the best placement in the city, you know."

Nadie opened her mouth. It was all spinning around in her head and she didn't like having to make a rushed decision. Mitchell motioned to her.

"Come on. Noob. Tonya. Whatever your name is. They'll be

here in about three minutes." She was checking the time on her cell phone.

"Okay, okay, I'm coming," Nadie agreed, and she followed the bigger girl out of the hotel room.

"Keep quiet," Mitchell muttered. "But put some hustle in it."

They hurried along the hall, to a different set of stairs from those Nadie had used the night before, and ducked into them. Mitchell stopped for a moment. She breathed out in a big puff of air. "Come on. Move it," she ordered, as if Nadie had been the one who suggested they stop. "Not safe to wait here."

They went down to the street level, out through a network of back corridors instead of the front lobby. They walked out of the alley and back around to the front of the building, where Mitchell lit up a cigarette. She made a gesture to offer it to Nadie.

"Oh, no, thanks."

"You got any food in that bag?"

"No. Sorry."

"Some people think to bring food when they're running away."

Nadie shook her head. "I didn't exactly plan to run away. And I did have food when I left… but it got stolen."

"Always someone hungrier," Mitchell said philosophically. "You gotta watch out for the hungry ones."

"Uh, yeah. I guess so," Nadie agreed.

Annie had been hungrier than Nadie. Annie had been out there for a long time already, and when she had seen her opportunity, she had taken it. Nadie didn't forgive the theft, but she understood it.

It was another twenty minutes or half hour before Holly appeared in front of them.

"All clear," she announced. "Now we can start the wheels turning. You ready?"

"Um, I guess… I don't really know what we're doing, though."

"Just let me do the talking. You're the naive noob; you don't need to know anything for this to work."

"Can I come?" Mitchell asked.

"Yeah, sure. You found her, didn't you?"

Nadie looked at the two girls in confusion. Mitchell looked blank for a minute, then she nodded.

"Yeah. I'm the one who found her," she said. "Last night."

"Give Mitchell your knife," Holly ordered.

"What?" Nadie put her hand over her pocket protectively.

"They're going to take it away if they see it. You'll get it back later."

Nadie looked at the two girls, thinking it through. Then she sighed and handed it over to the bigger girl.

"I take it you don't stay here?" she asked, indicating the hotel when she said 'here.'

"Nah. Aged out. You'd best figure out a trade before you turn eighteen, because when you do, they'll dump you on your ass. You'd better have somewhere to go."

Nadie nodded, filing the advice away for future reference.

"Moving," Holly encouraged, hustling Nadie and Mitchell along. Back into the hotel, back up the stairs, no censures to be quiet this time. Nadie had a tight, sick knot in her stomach. She barely understood what was going on. Holly led the way to a different hotel room. She knocked sharply on the door and then walked in. There were several adults seated around a table, talking and writing notes on their clipboards. They looked up as Nadie and Mitchell trailed Holly into the room.

"Holly… what's up?" one of the stern-looking women asked warily.

"Mrs. Prescott. Listen, do you think you could help out? You remember Mitchell, right?"

"Loretta," Prescott said, nodding at Mitchell. "Nice to see you again. How are things going?"

"Still lookin' for a job," Mitchell said. "Nobody wants to hire me. And I got kicked out of the Sally Anne shelter."

"We tried to explain you would have to follow their rules if you wanted to stay there."

Mitchell nodded, looking unhappy.

"And who is this?" The youngest of the women, a fresh-faced girl who barely looked old enough to be called an adult smiled at Nadie in a friendly way.

Holly nodded at Mitchell. "Mitchell met her last night. Out wandering by herself; she coulda got killed! Tonya's only fourteen. Got kicked out by her loser parents because they didn't like her boyfriend. Well, she doesn't want to live with him. She'd just end up in trouble that way, wouldn't she? She wants to finish school, but she can't do that if she's gotta make a living flipping burgers or turning tricks. Besides, he's still living with his parents. He's not gonna let himself get kicked to the curb."

Holly hadn't said she was going to make up a whole new history for Nadie. Nadie's head spun with all of the new details. She put her hand out to balance herself, touching Holly on the arm and stopping the flood of words.

"Well, hello Tonya." The only man in the room gave Nadie a reassuring smile that made her feel warm and comforted. "This must all be pretty overwhelming." He looked at the other social workers. "Why don't I take Tonya for an intake interview, see if I can get the whole story, and then we can get back together to discuss the best course of action?"

There were nods from the others, who immediately looked back at their notes, ready to go on with the meeting. The man smiled again.

"I'm Todd Swan, Tonya. We'll just grab a free room and have a little chat, huh?"

He indicated the door and they all started to head out.

"Oh, and Holly…?" Mrs. Prescott stopped them.

Holly looked around behind her to see what the social worker wanted.

"You know you are not to have anyone else up here on the floor. It's for everyone's safety."

"I just brought her to see you!"

"I'm not talking about now. I'm talking about a few minutes before head count."

"Oh." Holly looked down at the grungy carpet. "Yeah. Okay."

There was silence and then they shuffled out, all embarrassed at being discovered. Todd Swan led the way down the hallway and indicated a room. "We'll just use this one," he suggested.

Nadie started to follow him, then looked back at Holly and Mitchell. "Aren't you…?"

"He wants to talk to you alone, Tonya," Holly said. "Just answer his questions and he'll take care of everything."

Todd gave Nadie a reassuring smile and gestured for her to go into the room ahead of him.

After Nadie had answered Todd's questions, Todd told Nadie she could stay in the room that he had conducted the interview in. "I'll have to go through channels," he explained, "but I think everyone will agree we can't just leave you out on the streets. Our job is to protect youth like you."

"I don't know if…" Nadie trailed off, looking around the room.

Todd smiled knowingly and put his hand on her back. "You think maybe you could manage on your own. Maybe couch-surf at a friend's place or stay at an emergency shelter for a few days. Do you know Winnipeg has the highest murder rate in Canada? There's more violent crime here than anywhere else in the country." He almost sounded proud of the fact. "You need a safe place. These rooms fill up. Then we won't have any other options for emergency care. You ask your new friend Mitchell what it's like trying to make it without a safety net."

Nadie nodded, staring at the floor.

"Be glad you found us here."

He had given her a list of the rules she would have to follow, including keeping curfew and not leaving the building at night.

During the interview, he had questioned her in detail about her fictional parents and boyfriend. It didn't seem to be a problem that Nadie couldn't give him any ID. He said he could work around that in the system. He seemed far more interested in her relationship with her boyfriend. How old was he? How long had they been together? What was it her parents didn't like about him? Nadie shook her head and answered as few of his questions as possible. She didn't like having to lie. Especially when Holly had made up such a bizarre story.

The last thing he did before he left was to ask her about drugs and weapons.

"I don't have anything," Nadie said. "I don't do drugs."

"You don't mind if I perform a search of your bag, then."

Nadie looked at it. The only things in there were her clothes. The ones Gramma had washed for her. She shrugged. Todd searched it thoroughly. He even checked the pockets of her worn jeans before folding them neatly and putting them back in her bag.

"Your jacket?"

Nadie took it off and handed it to him. He again performed a thorough search.

"I need to check your pockets. I need to be sure you're not bringing any drugs or weapons into this hotel. This is a safe place."

Nadie froze. He approached her slowly, his movements non-threatening. Nadie stood with her hands up slightly, while he reached into her pockets, running his fingers around the inside to make sure she didn't have any pills. He patted her body down, checking anywhere she might have a weapon hidden.

"Okay, great." He gave her a big smile. "Hang out here while we get everything finalized. But make yourself at home. We'll want to set up some counseling for you, make sure you're registered for school, all that kind of thing. Just spend some time relaxing."

Nadie nodded wordlessly. He let himself out.

Nadie flipped shut the lock on the door. She went into the tiny bathroom and turned on the shower.

❧

Nadie wasn't sure where to go to meet up with the other girls. She went down the hall to Holly's room and knocked, but there was no answer. Nadie opened it and peeked in, but the small room was obviously empty. She went down the stairs and out through the lobby to the front sidewalk, looking up and down. There were a number of teenagers around. Smoking, talking, sitting on the sidewalk half-asleep. It was still fairly early; school hadn't started and there were still homeless people sleeping in various positions down the street.

"Who are you?"

Nadie looked to her left, at a boy who had spoken to her. He was tall, blond, one of the few who didn't appear to have any Indigenous blood in him. Nadie put him at sixteen or seventeen. "Oh… I'm new," she told him awkwardly.

"I can see that. When did you get here?"

"Uh… last night."

"They made an emergency apprehension last night?" he asked, frowning.

"No. I just… I just was going to the emergency shelter to see if they could help. And I met one of the girls here…"

"Holly."

"Yeah. So I just talked to CFS this morning… I don't know if I'm staying here yet…"

"They give you a room?"

"Uh-huh."

"Then you're staying." He thrust his hand out toward her. "Best."

Nadie stared at him.

"Noah Best. My name. Do you have one?"

"Oh. Uh." Nadie had to stop and think about it. "Tonya."

"Tonya. Holly pick that out? I thought we had a Tonya a few months ago."

Nadie shrugged. She didn't know anything about any other Tonya. The boy chuckled.

"Holly's around here somewhere. I saw her with that butch girl."

"Mitchell?"

"Yeah. Her." Best looked up and down the street. "You know, they probably went for coffee. I'll show you."

"Thanks."

Nadie fell in beside him, walking down the street in the direction she thought the emergency shelter was in. Nadie realized suddenly that she was trusting this boy to help her without knowing anything at all about him. He knew who Holly was and had offered to help, and she just assumed he was a trustworthy person. She was in an unfamiliar, dangerous place, and she didn't even have her pocket knife anymore.

Best looked back at her questioningly when she slowed. "It's just up here. What's wrong?"

Nadie dragged her feet. They were still on a busy street. There were plenty of people around if he tried to drag her into a car or a back alley. If she screamed, surely people would help.

"Come on!" He smiled, raising his eyebrows. He reached to take her by the arm, but when Nadie jerked back, he raised both hands in an 'I'm innocent' gesture. "I'm not going to hurt you, Tonya. Just helping out another kid getting screwed over by the system. Holly's probably down here," he pointed at the sign for a small, independent coffee shop half a block away. Not one of the big chains. "If you don't want me to come, then I won't."

Nadie looked at him and looked at the little cafe. By the looks of the sidewalk sign and how close the shops were together, it was a tiny place. She didn't particularly welcome the possibility of Best blocking the doorway behind her, boxing her in with Holly and Mitchell. Or maybe not even with Holly and Mitchell. There might be someone else in the little coffee shop. Someone who didn't have Nadie's welfare in mind. Best took a step back, seeing his answer in Nadie's eyes.

"Okay. Fine. I'll back off. You check and see if they are there. If they aren't, just come back to the hotel. We'll track them down. If they're not just getting coffee, maybe they headed over to the mall." He looked at a big gold watch on his wrist. "Maybe not the mall, the stores are not open yet."

Nadie shuffled past him, wary of being grabbed. He stayed back and left her alone. Nadie walked on by and headed for the coffee shop. She glanced back over her shoulder to ensure he was not following her. He headed back the way they had come, back to the hotel. Nadie checked out the little cafe before going in. It was small, as she had suspected. Only a few patrons inside. The smell of the coffee was deep and rich. Her stomach started to grumble about not being fed yet. Holly and Mitchell were standing at a counter talking, big disposable coffee cups in their hands. Nadie glanced around once more to be sure Best hadn't followed her and she wasn't walking right into an ambush and went in.

"She's back," Mitchell commented.

Holly turned around and saw Nadie. She gave a big smile. "There you are! Sorry we didn't tell you where we went. Didn't think we'd be long."

"That's okay. A blond boy pointed me in the right direction. Best."

"He's the best," Holly joked, letting out a sharp bark of laughter at her own joke. "So, how did it go? Todd give you a room?"

"Yeah. He said he still had to talk to the others about it, though."

"Aw, if you got a room, you're in. The rest is just formality." She looked Nadie over. "Already showered and ready to go?"

With no toiletries but the small shampoos on the counter at the hotel, Nadie didn't exactly feel ready to face anything else. She had finger-combed her hair but knew it wasn't sufficient. She still felt like a mess. And she was hungry.

"Go where?" she asked. "What else do I need to do?"

"We'll go over to the mission. They should be done clearing out the lice-carriers by now."

Holly indicated the door and they all started to head out.

"What are we going to the mission for? I've got a bed now, so I don't need to, do I?"

"You got a bed, but there's other stuff you're going to need. CFS is so backed up, they're not going to get you anything for weeks."

"Oh. Okay."

They were at the emergency shelter in a few minutes. There were a lot of people congregated on the sidewalk, talking to each other, laughing, some of them arguing. The homeless who had been sleeping on the sidewalk seemed to be gone, or they were part of the crowds of people standing around. Holly motioned for Mitchell to go ahead of her, and Mitchell barreled through the sea of homeless, pushing and elbowing her way through. Holly followed in her wake, ignoring the complaints of people who didn't appreciate being shoved out of the way. Nadie murmured apologies as she passed through. When they got up to the door, Holly reached back and pulled Nadie in front of her, so she was sandwiched between Mitchell and Holly with nowhere to go. Mitchell pressed on through the staff and homeless still lingering inside the building. They eventually reached a small office. A woman with long, straight, sandy colored hair was answering phones while she wrote down and filed information. Nadie wondered how she could keep it all straight in her head to do it at the same time.

The woman hung up the phone and looked at the three girls. "What can I do for you?" she asked pleasantly.

Holly spoke up. "This is Tonya. She got kicked out in the middle of the night last night. We got her a place to sleep, but she doesn't have nothing. Not even a toothbrush."

Nadie's face got hot. She looked down at the worn, red, patterned carpet.

"Hi, Tonya. I'm sorry to hear about your trouble," the woman said in a sincere voice. "Let's see what we can do for you, shall we?"

Nadie shrugged. "I don't want to be any trouble. I can make do."

"No, no. It's no trouble. That's what we're here for!" The woman stood up from her desk. "I'm Jennifer." She put her hand out to shake Nadie's, then she pushed all of her hair back over her shoulders so it was behind her. There was a slight sheen of sweat on her face. "Follow me."

She took them back out into the hall, which was slowly clearing.

"Let's move along, people. No congregating in the hallways. If you need counseling, set up an appointment."

People moved out of the way, most of them giving Jennifer a nod or smile. But there were a few angry scowls as well. Jennifer ignored or didn't see them and breezed by. They got to a locked door and Jennifer opened it with a key around her neck. It was a little supply room, stuffed floor to ceiling with shelves and cubbies full of various items. Jennifer grabbed a big plastic zip-top bag and handed it to Nadie.

"There's a hygiene kit for you. That should have all of the basics. Comb, toothbrush, deodorant, all the necessities. We'll just grab you a few other things while you're here. You've got a backpack? That's good. Put your kit in there." Nadie didn't have time to put the hygiene kit into her backpack before Jennifer plopped another bag into her hands. It contained an assortment of tampons, pads, condoms, a pregnancy test, and other items Nadie couldn't identify without reading the packages. Which she wasn't going to do just then. She shoved both bags into her backpack, her face burning with embarrassment. Holly was giggling at her. Jennifer had pulled out another zip-top bag, this one empty, and was swiftly adding granola bars, fruit bars, and other snack foods with long shelf-life to it. "Do you have any allergies? Diabetes?"

"No." Nadie's mouth was watering at the sight of the food. When Jennifer handed it to her, she didn't put it straight in her backpack, but took out one of the granola bars and tore open the wrapper.

Jennifer's eyebrows went up. "No breakfast?"

Nadie shook her head. "No."

Holly slapped a hand over her forehead. "Man, I'm sorry! You missed CFS breakfast because you weren't checked in yet and the mission breakfast because you were in your interview. Here we are, drinking our grande coffees in front of you, not offering you anything. You want some?" She held out her coffee cup toward Nadie. Nadie hesitated. She wouldn't normally say yes, but supper seemed like it had been a long, long time ago, and she could use the caffeine to steady her nerves. "Here," Holly wiped the mouth of the coffee cup with her shirt. "Go ahead."

Nadie accepted the cup and took a long drink of the hot coffee. It was fresh. Holly had loaded it up with sugar and cream, but it was still good. She handed it back to Holly, nodding.

"That's good. Thank you."

She continued to eat her granola bar, slower now that the edge of her hunger was dulled.

"What else do you need?" Jennifer asked, looking at the shelves. "We have postcards and stamps if you need to write anybody. Bus tickets, water bottles," she pulled a water bottle off the shelf and handed it to Nadie without waiting for an answer. "Bibles, laundry soap…"

"Bus tickets," Nadie said, and received a ten-pack of tickets.

"Get the laundry soap," Holly advised. "Works a lot better than shampoo if you have to wash your clothes in the sink. CFS isn't much help with washing machines. Can I get one of those too?"

Jennifer supplied each of them with a tiny bottle of laundry detergent. "Anything else?"

Nadie looked at Holly to see if there was anything important she was missing, then shook her head.

"No. That's really good. Ay-hay."

Jennifer smiled and nodded. She stepped out of the supply room and locked the door again. Her eyes lingered on Mitchell for a moment, then she looked at Nadie again. "So you've got some emergency supplies. You've got a place to sleep. You're with CFS, so they'll be helping with school registration and all that?"

Nadie looked at Holly and nodded. "Yeah. That's what they said."

"You'll probably find you need some kind of job as well. When you're ready to do that, I can direct you to the job bank and someone can show you how to search for something that meets your skill set. How about clothes?"

"I, uh… I have one change…"

"You're going to need more than that. Especially for school and work. Let's go back to my office."

The halls were clear now, only the office workers and volunteers getting everything squared away. No more homeless people blocking the way. Jennifer sat down at her desk. Opening a desk drawer, she poked through several boxes and pulled out a business card. She handed it across the table to Nadie.

"That is our clothing storefront. Don't worry about money, you just explain to them that we were helping you out here and referred you." Jennifer put her name and a sloppy initial on the back of the card. "They will help you pull together what you need. Don't let them forget about underwear and socks. They're not out front, so sometimes they forget. It's a thrift store; used clothing, but the underwear and socks in the back, they're new, still in their packages. So you don't need to worry…"

Holly leaned over Nadie's shoulder to look at the card. "Yeah, I know where that is. I can show you how to get there."

Nadie nodded and slid it into her pants pocket. "Okay. Thanks."

For the first time since she had met Holly, Nadie was starting to relax and feel more at ease. She had a place to sleep and eat and all of the other necessities she would need. It would be even better than home, where food had always been a question mark and there was no proper plumbing or electricity. She had her own room she wouldn't have to share with anyone, and her own bathroom too.

She was on her own, and she was going to survive.

Jennifer gave Nadie a reassuring smile. "I know how difficult this must be for you. I hope we helped a little."

"Yeah, you did. Thanks."

Holly gave Nadie a little nudge on the shoulder. "Time to go, girl. They got other work to do here."

Nadie followed Holly and Mitchell back out of the building.

"Sorry again about the food," Holly apologized. "You need anything else? I'll buy you a muffin."

"No, I'm okay now."

Holly met Nadie's eyes and held her gaze. "I'll buy you a muffin," she repeated. "And coffee."

Nadie wavered. "Well…" her stomach growled. "Maybe…"

"If you're hungry, you say yes," Holly said sternly. "Don't be wishy-washy with me."

Nadie nodded hesitantly. "Yes, then…"

"Right. Let's go get you some breakfast."

Much of the day was spent going from one place to another to get everything Holly decided Nadie would need. Nadie had never had so many new clothes. Holly gave her a few of her own cosmetics and told her to ask if she needed anything else. Nadie was still trying to get used to the idea she had her own room, all to herself. No more need to share it if Grandfather invited more people to stay with them. No need to run to the outhouse or to empty the camp toilet from the bathroom. She could have a hot shower whenever she wanted one. Twice a day, if she felt like it.

She was exhausted by afternoon and wanted to go back to her own bed for a nap. Holly shook her head.

"They expect us to be at school during the day. You don't want to remind them you're not. Better if they forget to register you altogether. I'm supposed to be at school too, and Mitchell…"

"I'm not with CFS anymore," Mitchell growled.

"Exactly. They don't like us hanging out with bad influences." Holly grinned so Mitchell would not take offense.

Mitchell rolled her eyes. Nadie rubbed her forehead and palmed her eyeballs, trying to soothe the aches away.

"I really need to get some rest."

"Not until tonight. Here." Holly dug into her pockets and, after a few minutes of sorting the contents out, she handed Nadie a few pills. "These will keep you awake. Give you a second wind."

Nadie looked at them uncertainly. "What are they?"

"Just caffeine. Like in your coffee. It will give you a bit of a push, sweep away the cobwebs. Give them a try."

Nadie gave in, washing a couple pills down with water from her mission water bottle. "I hope they work. I'm wiped."

"They will."

And they did. Within half an hour, Nadie was no longer tired. She was feeling energetic and cheerful and ready to take on a whole new day. Holly laughed at Nadie bouncing around on her toes.

"I'll introduce you to my crew," she said. "That will keep you busy for a while."

Nadie wasn't sure when Holly slept. She had been awake all night, as far as Nadie could tell, and all day, and was not showing any signs of wear.

Mitchell apparently was not part of Holly's 'crew,' and excused herself from any participation in the coming fun. "I gotta go make some money," she told Holly. "It was good seeing you again."

"Yeah, you too," Holly agreed. "I'll pay you for this job in a day or two when I get mine, all right?"

Mitchell nodded. "Good. Don't forget, I know where you live."

Holly chuckled. "Yeah, you do." She watched Mitchell's departure for a minute and then turned back to Nadie. "Okay, babe. You up for some fun?"

Nadie nodded. It had been a long time since she had done anything just for fun. Or since she had hung out with friends. She and Mouse were still friends and had kept up with each other. But all of Nadie's other friends from the reservation had dropped out of school and gone on to drink, have babies, or leave the reservation. She hadn't hung out with girlfriends for a long time.

Nadie looked around the dingy apartment. It turned out Holly's crew weren't all girls like Nadie had expected. She saw the tall blond boy, Best, who looked up from his conversation with an acne-covered Indigenous boy with barely any teeth and gave her a little wave. There were a couple of other boys, and some girls, apparently all Indigenous. Nadie's eyes lingered on one short, lithe girl who looked particularly Asian. She could have been Indigenous, but could also have passed for Polynesian or Chinese.

Holly rattled off everybody's names, but Nadie wasn't quick enough to catch them all.

"Is she joining up?" one of the girls asked, nodding to Nadie.

"CFS has given her a room," Holly said. "We'll see if she decides to stick around."

"It's pretty sweet," the girl told Nadie. "Having your own room and being independent and all."

"Is everyone here at the hotel?" Nadie asked, looking them over.

"No, not everyone… Everyone was there sometime, but not necessarily anymore."

Nadie frowned and nodded. She still got the feeling there was a lot going on she wasn't aware of. She kept trying to pick up all of the undercurrents. But these were kids who wouldn't trust easily. Why would they explain everything to a stranger they had only known a few minutes? It made sense they would be cautious around her. If they were all rule-breakers like Holly, there was a lot to keep secret.

"Well," said Best, "assuming she's not a nark, can we get some booze flowing here?"

There were cheers from the others and, in a few minutes, everyone seemed to have brought out one form of alcohol or another. After turning down drinks several times, Nadie finally accepted a can of beer. She obviously wasn't going to get any peace until she accepted their hospitality.

Their meeting place was an apartment owned by one of them, but Nadie wasn't sure which one. There was some broken-down furniture, but little else to indicate anyone actually lived there. Nadie sat on an uncomfortable couch sipping her beer and Best came over and perched on the arm of the couch beside her.

"So, what's your story, Tonya?" he asked. "What brings you to our little piece of heaven?"

Nadie looked at him and didn't answer.

"Spill," he persisted. "What's going to happen if you tell me something? You're going to turn into a pumpkin?" He tipped up his bottle and chugged down a few swallows.

"I don't know," Nadie shrugged. "I just had to get out of there. Everything was…" She shook her head, trying to put the thought into words. "Everything was falling apart. I felt like… if I didn't get out, I was gonna die."

"So you thought you'd come to the murder capital."

"Well… I didn't plan it that way. I might not stay here. Maybe I'll go west."

He laughed. "Don't bother. You don't think we've got a pretty sweet deal here?"

Nadie looked around at the other teens around them. At first, she had thought it sounded too good to be true. Now she was more convinced than ever that it was. They might be smiling and laughing, but that didn't mean they were happy. They were all there without families. Without tribes. They weren't meant to live alone. No one was, but especially not kids.

&

Nadie looked out the window at the darkening city. "When do we have to be back for supper?"

"Who needs supper?" Holly demanded. "Have another drink."

Nadie had already had enough to drink. She was getting queasy. Something solid would help to settle her stomach.

"Don't we have a curfew?" she persisted.

"Not until nine. And ten is the real cutoff."

Nadie shifted anxiously. "I'd like to go back for supper," she reiterated. "What time is it?"

"You're already too late for supper. Calm yourself."

Nadie watched Holly surreptitiously until she was deep in a conversation with the acne-faced boy, and then headed for the door of the apartment. She didn't have to stick around if she'd had enough. She was free to go wherever she liked. At least until curfew; if she was going to keep her bed with CFS.

"Hey!" Holly's yell cut across the conversations in the room and everybody stopped talking and turned around to see what was going on. "Where the hell do you think you're going, Tonya?"

"Back to my room," Nadie said, with a calmness she didn't feel. She took two more steps and was reaching for the door.

Holly was quick. Far quicker than anyone else in the room who was closer to Nadie. She had shoved her way through everyone that stood in her way and grabbed Nadie by the arm.

"You're not going anywhere, noob! I didn't give you permission to go."

"I don't need permission."

"You think you can just waltz in here, take advantage of me and my hospitality, and then take off without a word? I spent all last night and today getting you set up. You don't just walk away from me!"

It wasn't the proper way to honor Holly's hospitality, but Nadie was getting more and more uncomfortable with the situation.

"I'm sorry. I'm tired and I want to get back to my room. I appreciate everything—"

"You appreciate everything?" Holly's voice was hard. Her nose was inches from Nadie's. "You appreciate it? No, you don't! You're spitting in my face!"

"I just want to—"

Nadie didn't even see Holly's fist coming. It hit her square in the eye, driving her head back into the wall. There was a burst of light in Nadie's brain and pain flared in her face and the wound on the back of her head. Nadie was unable to restrain a cry. She put her hand up to her face,

The crew started chanting for a fight. Holly stood back from Nadie, both fists clenched, her eyes furious. Nadie stood there in disbelief.

"You can't fight?" Holly demanded. "Come on, noob, let's see what you've got!"

Nadie shook her head. "I don't want to fight you." Her voice shook.

Holly advanced and shoved Nadie's shoulder, goading her. "Put 'em up! It's time you learned. Let's see your mettle."

Nadie knew if she fought back, she was going to be beaten that much worse. Her only hope was that by refusing to fight, she would be able to de-escalate Holly's fury. Holly slapped her across the face, an open-handed crack that echoed through the watching room. She had hit the opposite side from the punch. Nadie's head spun. She fell against the wall, leaning on it to hold herself up.

There were a few cheers. But the chant for a fight had fallen away and most of the crew were quiet now.

"She's had enough, Holly," Best said.

"Who are you to tell me how to run my girls?" Holly

demanded, whirling around to face Best. "You think you got the right to tell me anything?"

He held up his hands. He was grinning, but his eyes were narrow, watching her warily. Holly left Nadie alone and flew at Best, landing several cracking blows before he managed to defend himself. Nadie watched with her mouth wide open, unable to move. The two of them exchanged a few more blows before the other teens pulled them apart. Then they went back to drinking and chatting as if nothing had happened, in spite of bleeding cuts and swelling bruises.

"Better watch your step," one of the girls said to Nadie as she stood there, watching the room. "Holly doesn't like any backtalk."

"Yeah," Nadie agreed faintly.

"There was a girl killed a few weeks ago, back behind the hotel. Beaten to death."

"Holly killed her?" Nadie's voice spiked up.

"Maybe Holly. Maybe she had someone else do it. But you don't want to cross her."

Nadie swallowed and nodded.

CHAPTER NINETEEN

Nadie fell into bed, physically and mentally exhausted. Her head whirled with all that had happened, good and bad. Leaving the reservation had seemed like the only thing for her to do, but she was starting to wonder if she had really left any of the bad stuff behind.

She and Holly had gotten lectures from the supervisors when they showed up just before ten o'clock, both with black eyes. Nadie had not had much to drink, so she was pretty steady on her feet, but Holly had gotten an earful about coming back to the hotel drunk.

"If you can't abide by the rules for this facility, we will have to consider alternatives," the social worker had said sternly.

Holly laughed in her face. "You think I don't know you don't have anywhere else to put us? You're lucky we come back here, instead of just running away."

"Holly…"

"Say my name all you like. Nothing is gonna change. I'm ready for bed and it's almost lights out; are you gonna let me go to bed or keep me up?"

So they'd been sent back to their rooms without any further discipline. Holly gave Nadie a cheery goodnight and went off to her room. Nadie went into her own, closed the inside lock, and crawled into bed.

Having missed supper because of the drinking party, she dug the emergency rations out of her backpack and ate a fruit bar before lying down and closing her eyes to sleep.

§

She had been sleeping for a few hours when she awoke to voices outside her door. Two men. She rolled over and watched the door, concerned.

The doorknob turned and the door cracked open just slightly. There were whispers. The door was pushed further open, and the security lock caught it and would allow it to open no further. One of the men swore. "It's locked."

"I thought they had to leave them unlocked."

"The handle is unlocked. It's the security latch."

The door banged against the lock a couple more times, as if the man was checking to make sure it was really locked. Then he knocked on the door, softly.

"Tonya. It's Todd Swan. Bed check."

"I'm here."

"Come open the door. They are not supposed to be locked."

Nadie slid out of bed and approached the door. "I'm here," she repeated, getting close enough to the gap in the door that he would be able to see her face.

"Unlock the door."

"No."

"We need to check on you."

"I'm right here. You can see that. I'm fine."

"Is there someone else in there with you? Is that why you won't open it?"

"No. I'm by myself."

"Unlock the door."

"No."

He said something quietly to the other man.

"Who's with you?" Nadie asked.

"Nobody. It's just me. We have to make sure everyone is safe."

"I'm fine."

With a sigh of exasperation, he pulled the door closed again. Nadie waited, listening. "Can't do anything about it," she heard Todd say. "Sorry."

There was a grumble from the other man and they moved down the hall to the next room. Nadie swallowed and tried to return her breathing to normal. She eventually returned to her bed, though she was unable to relax to go back to sleep.

It was an hour or two later she heard voices again, and the door again opened to the limits of the lock. Nadie waited for Todd to again call out to her to confirm she was in bed where she was supposed to be. Holly had warned that locking the door would make bed checks more cumbersome.

"She's got the lock on," Todd's voice pointed out. He was angry.

"Not my problem." The other voice was not a man this time, but a young woman. Holly.

"She's not supposed to lock the door."

"I didn't tell her to. She figured that out all by herself."

"Get her to take it off."

Holly's voice was tough. "The deal is I bring them to you. What happens after that ain't any of my business. I did my best to soften her up for you."

"You know—"

"I know you still owe me my cut. And if you try to squirm out of that one, I'm gonna start talking."

"You get a cut when it works out. This one hasn't worked out."

"You want to turn her out, that's your responsibility, not mine. I get the finder fee as soon as you get someone in a room."

"You watch yourself, Holly," Todd's voice was low and menacing. "I might just terminate our arrangement. I'll get someone else to help out. Like Mitchell."

"Mitchell?" Holly snorted. "She'll scare girls away, not bring them to you. Or else start setting up her own stable. Look, if you don't want my help, just say the word…"

There was silence while she waited for his answer.

"Okaaaay…" Holly sounded prepared to end their arrangement.

"Nothing has changed," Todd said quickly. "You'll get your money. I'm just not happy with the way this one is developing."

"You'll just have to keep working on her. She'll come around. Some of them just take a little extra finessing."

"At least talk to her tomorrow about not putting the lock on."

"That's gonna have to come from you. Why would I tell her not to protect herself?"

In the morning, Holly acted like nothing had happened. She didn't mention the party the night before or apologize for punching Nadie. She didn't mention the late night forays to Nadie's room and didn't suggest she should leave her door unlocked at night. She was bright-eyed for the morning headcount and grabbed herself a muffin from the assortment of breakfast foods provided. The muffins looked oily and sweet to Nadie, and she filled a bowl with cold cereal instead.

"Have a good sleep last night?" Holly asked.

Rather than confront her about her nocturnal activities, Nadie decided to lie. "Yeah. Really good. I don't think I woke up once."

"Good! You gotta get your sleep if you don't want to get sick." Holly took a big bite out of her muffin. "We'll see if we can't find you a way to make some money today."

Nadie looked at her sideways and made no comment. She might be a naive, backwoods kid, but even with her isolation on the reserve, she still had a pretty good idea by now of what Holly had in mind.

"I can check around on my own," she said. "I'll call the

number from the mission. They said they had jobs on their computers."

"Ah, noob. So naive. Those jobs are for adults. Even the ones that don't need a high school diploma, they still want grown-ups, not kids. When we want to earn a little cash, we gotta be more creative."

"Like what?" Nadie asked. Holly could say straight out what it was she had in mind.

"Well, I don't know where your skills are yet," Holly said cagily. "We'll take you out, see what you have an aptitude for."

At Nadie's stare, she expanded.

"I know some businesses that will hire kids under the table. You know, cash money, no taxes. Waitressing, sweeping floors, washing dishes, that kind of thing. Not easy to get into, though. Binning, panhandling, squeegeeing, anybody can do that. It's just the competition is a killer. You got any other ideas?"

Nadie shrugged uncomfortably. "I just... want a normal job."

"You're a kid. No one is gonna give you a regular job. They'll tell you to get a job, but they won't give you one."

"Nothing illegal," Nadie said. "I don't want to go to jail."

"Ah, they won't send you to jail your first time around. Look, you can do whatever you want. You can help little old ladies carry their groceries to their cars and hope they'll tip you more than a piece of peppermint gum for it. But if you want to make real money—you know, enough that you can eat and buy the things you need—you're going to have to be willing to stretch a little. Learn some new skills. Don't be scared you're gonna get busted."

"I can weave," Nadie offered.

Holly looked at her blankly.

"Textiles. Like a blanket," Nadie explained. "I made a really nice blanket."

"Well... good for you. But I don't think you're going to find much market for them in downtown Winnipeg. You can't make real money hawking crafts."

"Check over there for cans or bottles," Holly instructed, pointing to a garbage can on the other side of the food court.

Nadie was pretty sure Holly training her on 'binning'—turning in bottles for deposit refunds—was just another way to 'soften her up' for jobs that would bring in serious money. They'd only been at it for an hour, and Nadie's hands were so sticky and smelly, she didn't think any amount of soap was going to clean them up at the end of the day. Holly didn't actually touch any of the bottles, leaving the dirty work for Nadie.

There was a newspaper lying on one of the tables next to the garbage can, and Nadie glanced at it while she checked for bottles or cans. The words 'raft' and 'river' caught her eye. She took a quick look to make sure Holly wasn't watching her, and opened the paper up so she could see the picture and read the article. The picture was fuzzy, a couple of firemen in bright yellow uniforms were reaching over the side of a rescue boat to pick something up from out of the water.

The article indicated a young woman had drowned rafting down the river on a homemade raft. While the body was significantly battered, decomposed, and damaged by wildlife—Nadie supposed that meant eaten—she had been identified by the raft and her possessions as Nadie Laplante.

Nadie stared in stunned disbelief at the announcement of her own death. It had to be Annie. It served her right for stealing Nadie's raft and supplies and leaving Nadie to die in the wilderness.

"Newbie!" Holly snapped, punching Nadie in the shoulder. "Pay attention! I've been calling you. What's going on?"

Holly looked at the open newspaper, her eyes quickly scanning the headline and picture.

"Someone you know?"

"Knew." Nadie was dead. All of her family and friends now thought she had died. They were mourning her. Maybe even burying Annie's body now, thinking it was Nadie. They would not be looking for her or expecting her to come back. "I knew her a long time ago."

"Nothin' you can do for her now," Holly said briskly. "Let's pick up the pace. So far you're making about three bucks an hour. That's not going to support you even with CFS giving you a room."

&

After turning in the cans and bottles for the meager refund, half of which Holly took for herself, Nadie bought them both coffee and a danish at a nearby coffee shop. That depleted her funds to almost nothing. Holly watched her pocketing the little bit of change remaining. She shook her head.

"I told you, you can't make a living binning. Even once you manage to put on a little speed, you're lucky if you make enough for a mouse to live on."

"We could have gone back to the hotel for lunch. Then we wouldn't have to spend anything."

"You're gonna get tired of the CFS meals pretty quick. And you don't want to have to hang around there any more than necessary."

That was a change of tune over everyone insisting the hotel was the best living situation Nadie could hope for. She sighed, tired and confused.

Holly offered her a couple more caffeine pills. "Take another hit. We still got another stop to make." She led the way and Nadie followed, not really caring where they were going. The main streets surrounding the hotel were becoming more familiar now, but Holly led her beyond where she had been previously. She spoke to a lot of people on the street. It seemed like Holly knew everybody, and everybody knew her. They ended up in the alley behind a big brick building. Holly knocked sharply on the back door to one of the businesses.

"You stay here," she told Nadie. "Keep a lookout."

Nadie frowned at her. "A lookout for what?"

The door opened and Holly looked back over her shoulder as she went into the building. "Cops, what else?"

Nadie stood there staring at the closed door. Look out for cops? Exactly what was she supposed to do if any policemen appeared? Yodel? Nadie hadn't agreed to be a part of whatever illegal venture Holly had in mind. She looked around the narrow alley, considering leaving. She could find her way back to the hotel. But Nadie knew about Holly's temper and had been warned Holly would mess her up if crossed.

Nadie paced up and down the alley nervously. How long was Holly going to take to finish her business? Nadie's anxiety grew. Even if she did see something suspicious, something she needed to warn Holly about, she wasn't sure what she was supposed to do. Knock on the door? And tell them what? By the time she could get word to anyone, it would already have gone down.

Maybe Holly was just trying to keep her off-balance. She wanted to keep Nadie wound up. Maybe it was a test to make sure Nadie would be loyal to her protector and stay on guard even if Holly left her alone there for several hours.

Nadie walked to the end of the alley and looked out at the street. Everything seemed quiet. People walking around minding their own business. A few street vendors. Some homeless panhandling or sleeping.

As she stood there, she heard racing engines and stepped out of the alley to look further down the street. Two police cars with lights on but no sirens raced by on the adjoining street, the one in front of the building Holly had gone into. The engines quieted as the cars stopped.

Nadie stood there, frozen. Had they stopped in front of the business Holly was at? She tried to decide if she had time to run back to the door and knock on it, to raise the alarm somehow, but Nadie's feet wouldn't move. She was petrified, unable to make a decision. Another engine came around the corner behind Nadie, and the third cop car pulled into the alley. Because she was standing on the sidewalk just outside the alley, Nadie was not boxed in. They didn't pay any attention to her. Yet. Nadie took another couple of steps away from the alley and flattened herself against the wall, out of sight of the cops in the alley, leaning to support her shaking legs. She could hear shouts and a scuffle as someone tried to bolt out the back door. Holly? Nadie didn't dare look.

She swallowed and, as slowly and casually as she could, started to walk down the street. She looked down the cross street to see the police cars stopped in the middle of the road. There was also a police van she hadn't seen approach. It must have come from the opposite direction. She continued to walk past the spectacle. Her legs were shaking and her stride felt anything but normal. Everybody would be staring at her, knowing she was somehow involved in the bust that was going down.

❦

For a while, Nadie just walked in random directions. She didn't want to look like she was running away from the scene of the crime. If the cops who had pulled into the alley had seen her and put her together with whatever Holly's operation was, she didn't want them to be able to predict where she might be.

When she thought enough time had passed, Nadie headed back to the hotel. It took her a few minutes to get oriented the right direction, but then she started to recognize her surroundings and was able to get back to the building safely. A few of the CFS teens were outside the main doors, smoking and talking, an intense buzz. Several eyes flicked toward Nadie, then discounted her as anyone of importance or concern. She was just about to the doors when someone grabbed her arm.

Nadie reacted by reflex, trying to pull out of the grip and step back. But his fingers were like steel, and he didn't let her go. Nadie turned to see who it was and took in Best's shock of blond hair and steely stare.

"Let go!"

Instead, he pulled her closer, making her stumble. Nadie tried again to pull back, but he stared at her nose-to-nose and was unyielding.

"What are you doing here?"

"I live here," Nadie pointed out.

He shook her, his mouth tightening. "Don't get smart with me. You were with Holly."

"Yeah." The knot in Nadie's stomach tightened.

"What happened?"

"She… I don't know. She went in somewhere, but she left me outside. I don't know what was going on. She didn't tell me. Cops started showing up, and I left…"

"You ran?"

"I didn't run. I just walked. I didn't see any point staying around and getting in trouble!"

"Did you stick around long enough to see if they arrested her?"

"No."

He shook his head in disgust. He released her arm, giving her a little shove toward the door. "Go up to your room and stay there. That's where I expect to find you."

She wanted to protest that he wasn't her boss and she wasn't answerable to him, but she kept her mouth shut. Nadie didn't particularly feel like getting punched in the face again.

❧

It was Todd Swan who showed up at Nadie's room next, not Best as she expected. Nadie hadn't locked the door, but when she looked up and saw who had come in, she wished she had.

"The lost sheep returns," Todd commented. His voice was even, and he gave her a friendly smile. It was hard to reconcile the warm, reassuring social worker's manner to his voice and behavior in the middle of the night. She almost wondered if she had dreamed it or had a hallucination from drinking too much. Both he and Holly seemed perfectly normal after the late-night confrontation as if nothing had happened.

"Hi," Nadie said, her voice small.

"I hear you and Holly ran into some trouble today."

Nadie just looked at him. She had no idea how much of a hand he had in Holly's business. He obviously knew or was involved in some of her questionable activities, but how much? Nadie wasn't about to blab anything to him. Holly might only be gone for a day or two and, when she got back, Nadie didn't want to have to justify herself. She already had to explain her failure to warn Holly of the police's arrival. Best's reaction bore out Nadie's speculation; Holly was going to be upset about Nadie taking off when things got hot.

Todd sat down on the edge of the bed. It was the only place for either of them to sit down. Nadie was uneasy at his proximity.

"We understand how it can be hard to stay out of trouble sometimes," Todd sympathized. "You're down and out, on the brink of being homeless, and you're scared. You engage in risky activities because you don't know how else to face the future. The unknown."

Nadie nodded.

"Growing up around here," the supervisor went on, "you've seen trusted adults making bad decisions. Maybe breaking the law and not having to face any consequences." He studied her face, searching her eyes for confirmation or clues. "You may have learned to rely on drugs to make you feel better. Learned other ways to survive on the street."

Nadie looked down, away from his intense gaze.

"I've had an idea from the start that this story about your parents kicking you out was made up. I think you've been surviving on your own for a while, haven't you?"

Nadie chewed the inside of her cheek. Her head was pounding

and her breathing was too fast. She tried to envision something calm. A safe place. She was able to breathe a little more easily, imagining lying on the raft with Mouse, on the lazy river with the sun shining down on them.

"I wasn't with Holly," she said. "I was outside. She didn't want me in with her. I don't know anything about what was going on."

Todd's manner relaxed a little. "Well, I'm glad you weren't mixed up in… whatever she was up to."

"How did you hear about it? What was she arrested for? I don't know what's going on."

He made a motion as if to brush it away. "It's nothing. She'll be out before too long. I doubt if they have anything solid on her. Holly's pretty careful."

"What was she doing in there?"

"I think I'd better keep that to myself. As Holly's social worker, I have to keep things confidential between us."

They both sat in silence for another minute. Nadie swallowed.

"Well… thanks for checking in on me. I'm okay."

He recognized it as a dismissal. He put his hand on Nadie's thigh. "You can come to me if you need anything," he promised. "Anything at all."

She squirmed away from his grasp. Todd got up and headed for the door. He stopped as he opened it, looking back over his shoulder.

"Oh, and Tonya?"

"Uh-huh?"

"Leave your door unlocked tonight. It's against the rules I gave you. It could be a fire hazard."

Nadie nodded.

"We need to be able to access you—check in with you—during the night."

Nadie forced a smile, letting him think she understood and agreed. He gave her a friendly, sunny smile and walked out.

adie waited until after the ten o'clock head count, climbing into her bed and feigning sleep. She listened to people coming and going down the hall, talking or arguing in the other rooms, and to the babies crying as the supervisors tried to settle them for the night. Gradually, all of the noises calmed, and the rooms around her were silent.

Nadie got up and checked her pack. She couldn't fit all of her clothes in the backpack, but she made sure she had all of her other possessions. Toiletries, a few granola bars, her bus tickets, and what little change she had. It wasn't much, but it was more than she had when she arrived.

Nadie checked through her peep-hole for any supervisors in the hallway, then cracked the door open and looked up and down. She walked quickly and silently to the stairs and went down to the lobby. The hotel didn't seem to care about the kids coming and going all night. They didn't have any security to make sure they stayed in their rooms where they belonged. That was entirely up to CFS, and they did not have a guard on the ground floor either. Nadie stopped to look at the big bus routes map. It was a mess of colored lines and route numbers, and not being familiar with getting around the city, Nadie found it almost impossible to decipher. But she thought she had figured out the buses she needed to take.

With one more glance around the lobby for any adults who would keep her from leaving, Nadie headed for the doors. It was hard not to make a dash for it as if she was being chased. Just to walk calmly as if she had permission and didn't have any anxiety over her plan.

Once she reached the sidewalk outside, Nadie breathed a sigh of relief. It might not be safe for her to be out wandering the streets on her own at night, but she knew she wasn't safe staying there any longer. Between Holly getting out in a day or two and the pressure from Todd, she was going to lose all control of her life. She had to get out while she still could.

"Hey, where do you think you're going?"

Nadie whipped around and barely avoided being grabbed by one of the other teens, who had been hidden in an alcove out of sight of the lobby. Nadie danced back, staying out of reach.

"I'm going for a walk."

"Going for a walk?" the girl mocked. "You're not walking out here at night unless you're walking the stroll. Are you on the stroll?"

Nadie glanced around, making sure there was no one else sneaking up on her. "I can go where I want," she asserted and kept walking.

"Hey! Hey, you come back here! I'll send someone after you, you won't get a block!"

Nadie kept walking briskly away. The girl did not come after her. Nadie took a quick turn and looked back. Even if the girl wasn't supposed to leave her guard post, she could call someone on her phone to go after Nadie. Nadie needed to disappear before they could find her.

She slid into a back alley and waited for a few minutes, listening for footsteps or the sound of anyone looking for her. The street was quiet. She could hear the regular city noises, but no pursuit. She stayed where she was anyway, waiting. The minutes ticked by. She had gotten good at waiting when out hunting with Mouse. She could sit or stand quietly for an hour at a time.

Eventually, she decided to take the back alley, emerging on the other side of the hotel, the opposite direction to what they had seen her take. Eyes alert, she slunk through the lane and came out safely on the street. She took several more random streets and turns before trying to find a bus stop.

It was very late, or very early when Nadie got to the edge of the city. She stood at the last streetlight, her thumb out. Beyond the halo of light from the streetlight, it was pitch black.

Her anxiety should have been enough to keep her awake, but Nadie had been sleep-starved for so long, that even doing something so risky, she was dozing on her feet. She still had some of the caffeine pills that Holly had been giving her. She downed two of them, hoping they would keep her alert enough to get a safe ride and prevent her from falling asleep as soon as the vehicle started moving. She needed to stay aware of what was going on around her.

It wasn't long before a pick-up truck pulled over, and the window was cranked down. Nadie saw that the driver and passenger were both Indigenous men in their thirties or forties. The passenger looked her over and gave her a smile, several teeth missing from the wide grin.

"Hello, sister," he greeted. "Headed west?"

That much was obvious since Nadie was standing beside the westbound lanes.

"No, it's okay. You guys go ahead."

He drew down his brows, a squiggly wrinkle appearing over his nose. "Go ahead? You're hitching, we stopped to give you a ride. There's plenty of room; I'll move over."

Nadie shook her head. "No. Thanks. I changed my mind."

"We're not good enough to pick you up? You're waiting for some rich white dude?"

"No."

The driver was swearing and made sure that Nadie could hear the curses and the names he was calling her.

"You think any respectable man is going to stop to pick up a tramp like you?" the passenger demanded, his voice rising in anger.

Nadie took another step back from the car to ensure she was out of his reach if he decided to try to grab her and force her into the vehicle. If he got out of the car, she would run. Even if it meant abandoning her gear, she would get out of there.

"Sorry," she repeated.

The truck pulled away, spraying gravel while the passenger continued to yell at her and made a gesture out the window before pulling back into the flow of traffic.

Nadie breathed out. Her heart was pounding, and she was no longer tired.

❧

Eventually, a van pulled over beside her. Nadie peered through the glass. The driver was a woman. That was one point in her favor. Nadie opened the door and took a closer look at her.

"If you want a ride, climb in. If you don't, then shut the door."

The woman's voice had an odd quality to it. Not slurring or drunk. Just an odd pitch and clipped pronunciation. Nadie glanced at the back of the van and saw it had been turned into living quarters. A camper van. There were no other passengers.

"If you want a ride, climb in," the woman repeated.

Nadie considered for another moment, not letting herself be rushed. If she got into the wrong vehicle, she might never have the opportunity to correct her mistake. She and the other kids her age had all hitched to or from town at some point. Nadie was a pretty good judge of character. But she knew other girls who hadn't been so lucky.

"Yeah, thanks," she decided finally. She climbed into the van, putting her backpack on her lap.

"Seatbelt on."

Nadie pulled the door shut, and obediently put her seatbelt on before the woman would pull out.

"I'm Fay."

Nadie looked over at her and nodded.

"Tonya," she said, deciding to keep the alias Holly had saddled her with. Nadie Laplante was dead. She had started a new life as Tonya.

"Where are you headed?" Fay asked.

"West," Nadie hazarded.

"West how far?"

"Uh… Vancouver."

Fay glanced over at her, then back at the long, dark road ahead. "What's in Vancouver?"

"The ocean." Nadie had always dreamed of seeing the ocean someday. She loved the descriptions of the ocean or sea in the books she had read. She could just picture it. Enormous, the water blue or gray, tide lapping at her feet. The tang of salt in the air. She could practically taste it. But she had never figured she would actually make it that far.

"Well… if you want to stick with me, I can get you as far as Calgary. No ocean there. But I got people to see, and it's a nice enough place."

"Sure," Nadie agreed. "Calgary sounds good." She bounced her knees. The caffeine pills were working, making her heart beat extra times, and making her feel antsy and hyped up.

"You can have a nap," Fay said. "We have a long way to go."

"No, I'm good. How long?"

"We won't be there until tomorrow afternoon. And I'll prob-ably need to stop for a break myself, so it might be evening or later when we get there."

"Oh." Nadie looked out the window at the blackness of the night, regretting now that she had taken the pills. It would be hours before her brain settled down enough to get to sleep.

As she watched out the window, she started to be able to see the stars. With the lights of the city behind them and only occasional headlights, the stars were visible again. Not just a few, but a whole sparkling blanket of them.

Fay wasn't a big talker. She might make a comment or ask a question every few hours, and then lapse back into silence, thinking about Nadie's answer or whatever her own private thoughts were. As the sun rose behind them, Fay and the interior of the van became more visible. She was an older woman, maybe forty or fifty, it was hard to tell. She wore a baseball cap for the Winnipeg Jets, and there was a fringe of curly hair escaping here and there around the edges. She didn't wear any makeup. Her face was lined with fine wrinkles, especially around the eyes. She looked as if she did a lot of driving, baking in the sun. She wore blue jeans and a loose sweatshirt. When they got out at gas stations for a brief break or bite to eat, Fay pulled a heavy winter coat out of the back of the van and put it on.

The inside of the van was warm, making Nadie feel that much colder whenever they stopped and got out. It was definitely winter weather now. Without the shelter of trees or buildings, the wind that blew across the prairies was biting cold. Nadie's coat was not warm enough. Sleeping outside would be impossible within another week or two; even her warm new sleeping bag would not keep out the chill. That would mean a shelter. Nadie wouldn't be staying at a hotel or having anything to do with CFS again.

"Past Swift Current," Fay commented. "Next city isn't until Alberta."

The prairie seemed like it would never end. "Sounds good,"

Nadie said. She rubbed dry eyes. "So… you have family in Calgary?"

"I lived there a long time ago," Fay said, not answering the question directly. "It's been a long time since I spent any time there. A few hours, a day here and there. This is the first time I've gone back to spend any time."

"So, are you staying with someone?"

Fay shrugged and didn't answer.

❦

Winnipeg's size had overwhelmed Nadie. But it was nothing compared to Calgary. The city spread out in front of them, cars zipping by dangerously fast, and Nadie couldn't see where it ended. She could see the buildings downtown were even bigger than the ones in Winnipeg, and there were many more of them. A river wound through the city, in and out of sight. There were overpasses with multiple exit lanes that seemed to turn back in on themselves again. When they went over one of them, Nadie held onto the interior of the car, feeling like they were going to drive off the edge of a mountain. And there were real mountains. They seemed very close, and yet far away at the same time. Nadie knew it would be hours of mountain driving to reach Vancouver, if she went that far.

"Where to?" Fay asked. "Where do you want me to drop you off?"

"Anywhere," Nadie said. She'd have to figure out her way around sooner or later.

"No, not just anywhere," Fay argued. "Where are you going? Do you have someone to visit?"

"No. I'll just catch a bus, and figure out where to go. Downtown, I guess."

"You have money for the bus? You know the routes?"

"I have bus tickets."

"Where did you get bus tickets?"

"In Winnipeg."

"Calgary bus tickets? You can't use Winnipeg bus tickets here."

"Oh." Nadie thought she should have known that. She had only thought of the bus tickets in generic terms. If you had a ticket, you could ride a bus. She hadn't thought about the fact that different cities would use different tickets and not accept those from other cities. "Well, I have some change, too. They still accept cash here, right?"

"How much change?"

Nadie dug out all of the coins she could find from her pockets. Fay glanced over at the money, then back at the road. She shook her head. "That's not even enough for one ride."

"Oh."

Nadie could walk. It would take time, but she could get herself downtown and she could find her way around there. She'd have to find a shelter and a way to make some money like Holly had shown her.

"I'll take you downtown if that's where you want to go," Fay said.

"Are you sure?" Nadie looked at the big buildings. "It's a long way."

"I don't know how else you would get there."

"Thanks… that's really nice of you."

Fay had not insisted she couldn't let Nadie wander around the city at night. She didn't insist that Nadie had to come up with somewhere to stay or that she had to sleep in the van with her. It was a relief not to have someone tell her they knew better than she did. It was hard enough for her to figure out what to do, without someone else trying to act the part of a parent in her life. She was getting distinctly irritated with anyone who told her what she should be doing.

One thing that surprised her was how warm it was. Manitoba

and Saskatchewan had been getting pretty frigid, but in Calgary it was suddenly warm again, like it was only early fall. She could tell from the bare trees and the brown lawns that a hard frost had already hit, but it didn't feel like winter.

Nadie wandered for a while before finding a little treed park she liked the looks of. There were a few other homeless sleeping there, so the police obviously hadn't been by to roust them lately. Nadie had not slept at all in the van, even when Fay had pulled over to catch a few winks, and sleep was long overdue. Nadie picked a spot as far from foot traffic as she could without infringing on anyone else's space and unrolled her sleeping bag.

❧

Nadie awoke to someone pawing her. She opened her eyes to find an old man with shaggy whiskers, missing teeth, and breath so bad it could fell a deer going through the pockets of her coat. Nadie slapped his hands away and sat up.

"What do you think you're doing?" she shouted, furious.

He back-pedaled, putting his hands up defensively. "Just trying to wake you up. Cops will be by to get everyone on their way soon."

The sky was getting lighter. Nadie pulled her sleeping bag to her. He'd unzipped it to get access to her, she realized with revulsion.

"Stay away from me!" she ordered. "I've got a gun!"

He gave a leering smile. "No, you don't."

"I do too!" Nadie grabbed her backpack and toiletries spilled out the open top. He'd already been through her bag. "Get away from me or I'll call the cops!"

He was already backing away. "No need to get so mad. I was just trying to help you, waking you up before the police could. It's your funeral."

"Get away!"

He shambled off. Nadie slowed her breathing, focusing on the

197

in and out flow, trying to relax her bunched-up muscles. She swore under her breath.

Going through her bag and her pockets, it didn't look like he'd taken anything of importance. Her comb. The rest of her change. Her Winnipeg bus tickets lay on the ground and Nadie didn't bother to pick them up. She wasn't going back there again.

One thing the old guy was right about, though, and that was that she should move along before the police started to roust sleepers from the park. So late in the year, the sky didn't get light until people were heading off to their jobs, and she was lucky she hadn't already been kicked out of the park.

Nadie took the opposite direction from that of the man who had awakened her, and then followed behind another homeless person, a middle-aged woman, to see where she would go. Nadie kept her distance. She didn't want a conversation or confrontation; she just wanted breakfast. Hopefully, the woman wouldn't have money to buy her own coffee and wasn't the type who didn't eat until noon.

The woman turned into an alley and Nadie waited. She didn't want to get trapped in an isolated alley with anyone and suspected that the woman had only detoured to relieve herself. Two minutes later, her unknowing guide returned, smoothing out her clothing and verifying Nadie's suspicion.

She hated moving so slowly, but she couldn't very well race on ahead. There were other homeless starting to congregate and head in the same direction, and Nadie's heart started to beat a little faster. They had to be on the way to breakfast.

It was a big, new-looking concrete building. Nadie marveled, looking at it for a minute before following the other homeless people in. There must be a lot of homeless in Calgary for them to build such a structure.

She let herself be swept by the tide of people going in. The flow took her to a long room filled with tables and chairs and the hum of activity. It looked like most of the chairs were already taken. There were people around the edges of the room eating standing up. And some children sitting on the floor, chattering while they ate. Nadie got into line to get a plate. After a few minutes of being jostled from every side, she took her eggs, fruit, and muffin to an open space near an outside door that had been propped open for ventilation.

She ate her eggs, looking around at the crowd. The proportion of Indigenous faces was not nearly as high as it had been in Winnipeg. There, almost all of the faces at the shelters had been dark, and it had been a rare exception to see blond hair or blue eyes. In Calgary, it seemed like the majority were Caucasian. There were still Indigenous faces, but they were not nearly as pervasive as in Winnipeg.

Nadie wrapped her muffin in a napkin and tried to get it into her pocket without crushing it.

"You're not allowed to take food with you."

Nadie glanced around and saw the girl watching her. Pretty, wearing makeup and hoop earrings. Young, slim, Indigenous, wearing her black hair in two long braids that reminded Nadie fleetingly of Mouse's hair.

"What?"

"You're not supposed to take anything with you. Just eat what you can here."

Nadie finished tucking the muffin away. "Do they check?"

"If it's obvious or they see you putting something in your pockets." The girl pursed her lips and looked Nadie over. "I don't think anyone will notice."

"Good." Nadie nibbled at the fruit on her plate.

For a few minutes, they were both silent, each pretending not to be watching the other.

"I'm Charlotte," the girl introduced herself.

"Hi."

Charlotte laughed. "This is when you're supposed to tell me your name. I don't think I've seen you here before, have I?"

Nadie considered before answering. "Tonya," she said.

"And...?"

"And what?"

"Have you been in town for long?"

Nadie shrugged her shoulders and didn't fill Charlotte in. She didn't need another Holly taking Nadie under her wing and trying to run her life. The less Charlotte knew about how much of a newbie Nadie was, the better.

Charlotte studied Nadie, her eyes dancing. "I haven't seen you here before. So you must be new. From out of town, or did you just get kicked out?"

"I've been around."

"Well, you keep your cards pretty close to your chest, don't you?"

Nadie had another piece of apple. The room was beginning to empty, people hurrying off to work or school. Nadie didn't want to become conspicuous because she wasn't moving on. "I gotta go."

"You got somewhere to be?"

Nadie ran her fingers through her hair, untangling several snarls. "Do you have a comb I could borrow? Some bum stole mine..."

Charlotte giggled. "A bum stole your comb?"

"Don't know why, didn't look like he'd ever used one before. Maybe he didn't know what it was."

Charlotte laughed harder. "I've been rolled before, but never for my comb."

"Most valuable thing I owned." Nadie couldn't help smiling at Charlotte's boisterous laughs. She waited for Charlotte to settle down. "So...?"

"What?"

"Do you have a comb I could borrow?"

Charlotte scratched the back of her head. "Well… no…"

"You don't have one?" Nadie didn't believe it, looking at Charlotte's smooth, neat braids.

"You shouldn't share combs."

Nadie stared at her in confusion.

"Because of… you know… lice and stuff."

"You think I have lice?"

"No! No, but… you know… if you've been at a shelter lately, you could have picked something up and not even know it…"

"Or maybe you have lice and you're worried about spreading them." Not that Nadie thought she did. Charlotte's hair looked perfect.

"No!" Charlotte insisted. Then she laughed. "You're not so dumb, are you? I'll show you who to talk to here. They usually have that kind of thing."

Nadie waved her hand. "I can find out myself."

Charlotte frowned, all of the good humor melting off of her face. "I offered to help you. What's wrong with you?" Her tone, rather than being angry, was hurt.

Nadie felt guilty at the girl's genuine distress over being turned down. She struggled with how to explain. "I just want to do things myself. It's not you."

Charlotte was obviously not buying it.

"It's… well… I had a bad experience."

Charlotte looked hopeful at this. She shook her head slightly. "What happened?"

"Another girl was being really nice, helping me out. Showing me the ropes and helping me get the stuff I needed."

Charlotte nodded encouragingly.

Nadie didn't want to tell the whole story. But how could Charlotte understand how badly she'd been burned if Nadie didn't explain? "But it turned out… she was only acting that way to make me trust her and get me involved with… some stuff I didn't want to be doing… I could have got really hurt or messed up. Just about got arrested, just for being with her."

"Seriously?" Charlotte shook her head in disbelief. "That's cold! Who did that to you?"

"Not someone here." She didn't like giving away so much information about herself. "I left town to get away from her. It was the only way I could escape."

"Wow." Charlotte patted Nadie on the shoulder. "Poor you!" She apparently couldn't help herself, and put her arms around Nadie to give her a big hug. "That sucks!" She let go of Nadie. "How about if I just tell you how to get things here. No strings attached. You don't owe me nothing."

Nadie nodded, trying to maintain her composure. She wasn't used to people touching her and was a little overwhelmed by Charlotte's demonstrativeness.

They both returned their plates and left the building through the propped-open door, so they wouldn't have to push their way through the crowded room, and then headed back toward the main doors. Charlotte took a deep breath outside, embracing the fresh air.

"Are your winters always this warm?" Nadie asked.

Charlotte gave a little giggle. "No way. It gets pretty cold. Right now it's chinooking."

Nadie blinked. "Chinooking?"

"Don't tell me you haven't heard of chinooks before!"

"Uh… no…"

"Chinooks are one of the best things about Calgary weather! It's a warm wind that comes in over the mountains. Melts all the snow, lasts for a few days before going back to normal. The temperature can go up twenty degrees just like that. You wear a heavy coat in the morning, and it's shirt sleeves by the afternoon!"

"Cool," Nadie approved.

"No… warm!"

They both laughed.

adie was anxious fending for herself at the Step Up Center once Charlotte separated from her, but she was also glad not to have anyone with her. It was going to be a while before she trusted anyone who went out of their way to help her.

"You need to find somewhere to stay before it gets cold again," the volunteer who helped her advised. "Have you checked with any of the youth shelters?"

Nadie shook her head. "No. Not yet. Are there any downtown?"

"Oh, yes. Let me get you a list." She rifled through drawers and files, finally finding a slightly blurred photocopy for Nadie. "There are phone numbers and addresses and a little bit of information about their programs there. We do have a public use phone you can borrow to call them, save yourself some shoe leather. We have some spaces here too, but not a lot for youth. We don't like to mix teens and adults. It tends to lead to problems."

Nadie nodded.

"What else do you need? We have counselors here who can lend a listening ear and refer you to another program if there's something we can't address. Career and school advice. Family reconciliations. We have a lot of resources."

Nadie indicated the photocopied list and the comb in her hand. "No, this is good, thanks."

"What about addictions issues?" the woman pressed. "A lot of our Native clientele are struggling with addictions."

Nadie felt her face twist into a scowl. She tried to school herself, smoothing the expression away. "No, thank you."

"Okay. Well, come by again if you need anything. I hate to think of anyone out there in the cold, once the chinook is over. It's supposed to be a cold December."

Nadie nodded and quickly left the smothering volunteer behind. She couldn't put her finger on exactly what it was about the helpful volunteer that made her seem so patronizing and suffocating, but she couldn't wait to get away from her.

Once outside, Nadie took a deep breath and tried to decide upon a course of action. She did need to look into the youth shelters, and she should have accepted the offer of the public use phone. Without it, she was going to have to walk to the shelters. Even if she knew where to find a pay phone, she had no more change. She looked at the addresses and compared them to the street signs. The roads were lain out in a grid with numbered streets intersecting with numbered avenues. She picked the nearest youth shelter and struck out to find it.

Despite her best intentions, Nadie still got lost. She kept taking wrong turns and losing track of which way the numbers were going. She stopped where a small group of people were smoking in a huddle outside one of the countless office buildings.

"Excuse me?" She braved the foul cloud of smoke. "Can you help me with finding an address?"

A few of them glanced in her direction, but most of them studiously ignored her.

"Come on," Nadie protested. "Can't you help me out?"

"Get a job!" one of the women sneered.

Nadie was shocked. "I'm trying to find a youth shelter," she explained. "I need somewhere to live—"

"Why don't you go back where you came from, squaw?" one of the men asked.

Nadie stared at him with her mouth open.

"Go back to the reservation, we don't need another drunk Indian whore mucking up our streets."

One of the other men punched him on the arm but didn't say anything or make any apology to Nadie.

The other women stayed silent, looking wide-eyed at Nadie. The first one who had spoken made a little shooing gesture. "You heard him. We've got too many shiftless drunks already. Go get a job, or go back home. We don't want to have to support you, or deal with you, or look at your worthless face panhandling on the street every day."

Nadie turned and walked away from them, her eyes and her face burning. There was a lump in her throat. She was so humiliated and furious about it; she felt like her head would explode. She put her hand into her pocket to touch her knife. She could make them regret they had insulted her that way. She could make them hurt as badly as they had hurt her.

But she didn't turn back. She clutched the knife in her pocket, but she didn't take it out and open it up. She didn't threaten or cut anyone. She just kept walking, the fury practically steaming from her skin, until she was so lost and turned around she didn't know where she was. There was a bridge stretching out to an island in the middle of the river, and she walked across it and sat on a bench amid the trees.

She put her hands over her eyes and tried to contain the raging emotions.

She wasn't going to cry because of some ignorant white guy. He was the one who was worthless, not Nadie. He didn't care enough to educate himself about her culture or the problems her people faced. He was just ignorant. He and the woman too.

It was a long time before Nadie was able to pull herself back together. She hadn't had any lunch, but she wasn't hungry. She still had a muffin in her pocket, but she didn't want it. The winter sun was already low in the sky when she started walking again, looking at her addresses and trying to form a picture in her head of where everything was downtown. She was usually pretty good at getting around, at figuring out new places. Not that she'd been a lot of new places in her life.

The battle with her emotions and holding back the tears had left her exhausted. She had some caffeine pills left and took a couple to keep awake and alert. In a few more blocks, she started to perk up. The hurt feelings gradually washed away and she cheered up. Who cared what some ignorant jerk thought? He didn't know anything about her. Nadie wasn't looking for a hand-out. Just somewhere to sleep until she could get on her feet.

She looked down at the address on her paper and up at the building. She had expected a big, institutional building like the hotel or the Step Up Center, but the youth shelter was a house. It looked very old. But it was freshly painted and kept up. Nadie wasn't sure it was the right place and stood back on the sidewalk looking at it. She noticed a plaque beside the door with the name of the shelter on it. Butterflies in her stomach, she walked up the sidewalk. She knocked on the door and shifted her weight from one foot to the other, trying to relax. The worst that could happen was they wouldn't have space for her and she'd have to go somewhere else instead. That wouldn't be so awful. And if no one had any space open, the volunteer at the Step Up Center said they did have some openings. She'd go back there. There was no answer, and Nadie eyed the doorbell. On the reservation, no one used doorbells. Only outsiders. Anyone else would just walk in, calling out a greeting. Besides the cultural aspect, few had reliable electricity, there was no point in relying on doorbells. It seemed rude and intrusive to press the doorbell.

Nadie was just making up her mind to try it when the door opened, and there was a woman with a small dog on a leash, obviously about to go out.

"Oh, I didn't hear the bell. Did you ring?"

Nadie shrugged. "I was just going to."

The woman was older, maybe forty, but she seemed to be trying to look young and hip. She had a short, spiky hairstyle with the top dyed red. Not natural red, but circus-clown red. She had piercings down one ear and one through her nose. Under her unzipped jacket, Nadie could see a low-cut lacy top, skinny jeans, and high boots.

The woman scratched her head, looking at Nadie, then down at the dog. "I was just going to take Rolf out for a walk. I'm afraid he really can't wait. Would you like to walk with me?"

Nadie nodded. It would be easier to talk while walking out in the fresh air than being enclosed in some office space, having to talk face-to-face.

The woman nodded and stepped out the door, pulling it shut behind her. Then she led the way down the walk to the city sidewalk. She let the dog choose a direction, and they started off slowly. The dog had short legs and was easily distracted, so they didn't get anywhere fast.

"I'm Camilla. Cammy."

"Na—Tonya."

Camilla looked at her sideways and made no comment on the mid-stream switch. "Nice to meet you, Tonya. I take it you're looking for a place to stay."

"Yes. If you have any openings."

"Were you referred to us by someone? A social worker or anyone?"

"The Step Up Center, I guess. They gave me a list."

"Sure. So did you talk to them about your circumstances? Or just ask about youth programs?"

Nadie shrugged. "Just asked for youth shelters downtown."

"Why specifically downtown?" Camilla looked at her, a frown line between her brows.

"Just… that's where I am. I don't have money or a car to get around."

"I see." Cammy's tongue appeared as she played with a piercing, running the stud along her teeth, back and forth. "I'm going to be honest with you right off. We're a dry facility. Any sign of drugs or alcohol and you're kicked out."

Nadie nodded. "Okay. That's cool."

"What are you on?"

Nadie remembered the man calling her a drunk without knowing anything about her. Did everyone see her Nehiyaw features and assume she was an alcoholic? Anger bubbled at the back of her throat, and she strove to keep it out of her voice.

"I'm not on anything."

"Your eyes are dilated, and your speech is slow."

"I'm not on anything!" Nadie insisted. "Where would I get drugs or alcohol? I'm completely broke! What change I had, some bum stole while I was sleeping!"

"I've learned no money doesn't mean no drugs. People barter. Steal. Get free samples from friends or dealers who want to hook them. I can't let you into the home if I think you're an addict. It wouldn't be fair to give you a bed over someone else who really needed it, knowing you were not going to last more than a few days."

Nadie walked in silence.

"You don't want to come clean to me?" Cammy prompted.

"There's nothing to tell you. I haven't taken anything. I've barely even eaten today. All I had was a couple of caffeine pills, to help me stay awake."

Cammy's brows went up. "Caffeine pills, huh?"

"Those are legal! It's not like taking drugs."

"And where did those caffeine pills come from? You bought them at a pharmacy?"

Nadie shook her head. She watched the little dog sniff a tree on the boulevard and then raise its leg to tinkle. "I got them from a friend."

"And where did she get them?"

"I don't know. But they're just caffeine. I could go out and have a couple of cups of coffee. That's not illegal, is it?" Nadie's voice rose in anger. She bit her lip and stared down at her feet as they walked slowly on.

"What do they look like?"

Nadie looked at her. "Like pills."

"Little pink tablets?"

"No… They're red… bigger than an Aspirin."

They both watched the dog sniff all along the bottom of a hedge.

"I don't think your friend was giving you caffeine," Camilla said.

Nadie felt all of the blood go out of her face and limbs. She was suddenly very cold. The sweat on her skin felt sticky and clammy.

"Is this someone you trust?" Cammy asked.

"No. I came out here to get away from her."

"If you want to give the pills to me, I'll have them properly disposed of."

"I don't have any left."

Cammy ignored her assertion. "Don't flush them. That contaminates the water supply. We really don't want to be drinking meth in our water."

"Is that what you think it is?"

"I'd guess some kind of amphetamine. Meth is cheap and easy to produce, so that's what we see the most of."

Nadie rubbed her temples. She swore. "Why did I take it? She said it was safe. Why did I believe her?"

"Do you know what meth is?"

"I'm not just a stupid Indian."

"I didn't say you were. Do you know what it is?"

"It's what people take when they go to the city. And then they go to prison or die and never come back."

"Yes, that's true," Cammy admitted. "It's been pretty devastating to some populations."

The dog piddled against another tree. Nadie wondered how many times they were going to have to stop and wait for him.

"Did you really not know that was what you were taking?" Camilla asked.

"I wouldn't take meth."

"Even relying on caffeine to keep you awake, you have to know there's something going on with your body that needs to be addressed. You aren't getting enough sleep."

"Kinda hard to."

"We'll see what we can do about that! You're going to need to promise to stay clean if you're going to stay at the home. If we find any drugs or alcohol in your room, that's it. You don't get three strikes. It's a zero tolerance policy. No excuses."

"Okay. I'm not going to do anything like that."

Cammy nodded and sighed. "Well, this has been an interesting conversation," she said. "Rolf, let's go home! I'll go over the other rules and policies when we get back to the house. Why don't you tell me a little bit about yourself?"

"Like what?"

"Whatever you feel like sharing. Family, reason you're on your own, hobbies, whatever you're comfortable with."

Nadie thought about it. Since she had left, she felt like everybody just kept putting her into a box, without knowing anything about the person she was. Newbie. Indian. Runaway. Addict. All homeless people weren't the same. They were just as individual as anyone else.

She wasn't comfortable sharing her real name or where she came from. She was embarrassed about what had happened in

Winnipeg and didn't want to disclose it. But she wanted someone to know who she really was inside.

"I grew up on the reservation. My grandfather raised me. I was still in school before I left. I'm good with my hands. I just learned how to weave, and I'm really good at it."

"Weaving," Cammy repeated. "Very creative. Good for you."

"I made a blanket," Nadie told her. "For my—" She stopped. She didn't want to think about Luyu. "It turned out really well. I want to make more… someday."

"And you will. I promise. That must have been quite a big project."

Nadie nodded. "My friend helped to build the frame. The loom. They have big fancy ones that practically do the work for you, but I did it all by hand. It took a long time." She thought about the loss of the blanket after Luyu's death and worked hard not to sigh aloud.

"You have very sad eyes, Tonya."

Nadie shrugged, not sure what to say to that. They got back to the shelter and Nadie stopped, looking at the house. "Will you let me in? Even though…?"

"Come on in. We'll go over the rules and have a talk, and then we can decide together whether it is a good fit or not."

"But it's getting dark. If you decide I can't stay, it will be too late to find somewhere else for the night. Maybe I should just come back tomorrow." Nadie wasn't sure how she had let all of the daylight hours fly by. Had she really wasted all day and accomplished so little? She hadn't even collected a few bottles for pocket change. She had nothing but a comb to show for the day's efforts.

"Come in," Camilla repeated. "If it doesn't work out, the least I can do is give you something to eat and drive you over to the Step Up Center. They'll take you as an emergency placement for the night."

Nadie followed her into the house. It smelled like old cooking and antiseptic. There was a hum of activity; voices, music playing, a TV somewhere. Somebody was having what sounded like a heated argument, but Nadie couldn't make out the words.

Camilla rolled her eyes upward in the direction of the arguing voices. "It may not sound like a safe haven," she said, "but it is. Our kids fight and bicker like any kids do. And we encourage open and honest communication. It doesn't always make for a quiet, peaceful atmosphere."

Nadie nodded. She felt strangely at home. Things could get pretty noisy there too, with all of the people being constantly invited to stay. Everyone didn't always get along, especially once the drinking started. At least at the shelter, there would be no drinking. If there were, the violator would be thrown out.

"This way," Cammy invited, letting Rolf off the leash and leading Nadie to a small bedroom in the back that looked like it was being used as both a bedroom and an office. "Please ignore the mess." She handed Nadie a printed page. "Let's go over the rules."

They had covered what Nadie hoped was pretty much all they had to review when there was a tap at the door.

"Cammy, sorry to bother you, but Trent—"

Nadie turned around to look at the intruder, who immediately squealed and launched herself at Nadie.

"Tonya! That's so crazy! Are you moving in?"

Cammy looked at Charlotte, one eyebrow lifted. "I take it you two have met?"

"At breakfast this morning! Can she stay in my room, Cammy? We can fit a cot in there..."

"You know I have to be able to show that I have actual permanent beds for everyone. Your little hotel is already at maximum occupancy. She'll have to go in the blue room."

"Oh." Charlotte looked crestfallen. "Too bad."

"You guys can still visit all you like. Now, what about Trent?"

Charlotte looked blank.

"You came in here to tell me something about Trent," Cammy reminded.

"Oh! Yeah! Well, I guess he went back to his folks, and they called the police, and the police want confirmation he is registered here and under appropriate supervision, and all that. Can you talk?"

Cammy swore, and then covered her mouth. "I'm sorry, Tonya. Excuse my French. I do try to act like a grown-up around here. I don't know whether to blame Trent or his parents, but they mix about as well as oil and water. If they'd just listen to the professionals, things would go much more smoothly, but they have to keep picking at the sore spots..." She reached for her phone, pausing to look at Nadie. "Why don't you get Charlotte to give you the grand tour? If you have any concerns, you can let me know when you're done. I'm willing to have you stay with us if you follow the rules. Like we talked about. Okay?"

Nadie got up from where she'd been seated on the bed and headed out of the room. Charlotte gave her an impulsive squeeze around the shoulders.

"I'm so glad you came here! We're gonna have a great time." She made a few dance moves. "Party time!"

Nadie gave a little laugh. "There must be other girls here too."

"Sure, but none of them are as much fun as you're going to be. I can tell."

Nadie shook her head. She didn't consider herself a fun person. Not lately, anyway. She and Mouse used to have fun together. And she had had fun playing with Luyu. When she was younger, she loved it when Grandfather had taken her out on nature walks or whatever chores he had to do. Nadie had been fun back then. It seemed like a long, long time ago.

Charlotte gave her another squeeze, looking serious for a minute. Then she released Nadie. "Come on, I'll show you around."

The other kids reminded her a lot of the teens that had been staying at the hotel in Winnipeg. But the setting was a lot different. Bunk beds were packed four to a room and, with a couple of dressers to hold clothes and essentials, you could barely turn around in them. But the kids seemed satisfied with it. They ran into a couple of other adults as they made their rounds. There was definitely more of a supervisory presence than there was when each kid was sequestered in their own room at the hotel. There seemed to be more camaraderie. The youth couldn't help being in each other's way, but they seemed to take it in good humor. Other than the occasional yelling when someone snapped.

Charlotte poked her head into one of the boys' rooms. "And this is… looks like just Dylan is in right now. Hey, Dylan. This is Tonya. New girl."

Dylan was writing or drawing something in a binder, sitting on his bed against the wall with the binder braced on his knees. He looked at Tonya when she peeked through the door. "Oh, I see why you're all excited about her. Another Indian to keep you company."

Nadie's face got hot, but at least he hadn't insulted her like the other man had earlier in the day.

"Be nice, Dylan," Charlotte said with a put-on pout.

He scowled, shaking his head and looking down at his binder for a moment. "Why don't you grow up, Charlotte? You act like a six-year-old. Why don't you lose the pigtails and act your age?"

Charlotte grasped her braids protectively. "They're not pigtails. They're braids."

"Same difference. You're no Pippi Longstocking. It gets old."

Charlotte ran her fingers down one of the braids. "It's a spiritual thing," she said, her voice subdued. "You wouldn't understand it."

"She doesn't have pigtails," Dylan said, pointing to Nadie. "Are you saying she doesn't understand your spirit thing?"

Charlotte looked at Nadie, unsure what to say. Nadie's hair had started to grow out a bit but was still ragged and short. She touched it, a little embarrassed. "I cut it in mourning," she explained.

Charlotte's eyes got big and she patted Nadie on the arm. "I'm so sorry, Tonya. For your loss."

Dylan made a noise of disgust and looked down at his papers. "I don't believe in God or any of your voodoo spiritual stuff. When a person is dead, they're gone. They don't go somewhere else. You're never going to see them again. It's just over."

"It's really sad you feel that way," Charlotte said. "That must really hurt."

Dylan's expression didn't change. He continued to look down at his book, ignoring them completely now. Charlotte withdrew and Nadie went with her. Charlotte was right. It was sad. Nadie wasn't sure how much of the Nehiyaw spiritualism she believed, but she was sure of one thing. Luyu's spirit lived on. That spark couldn't be destroyed. Somewhere, Luyu still laughed and played. Nadie believed that for sure.

"Let's go back to my room. We can talk there until supper," Charlotte suggested.

"Sure."

They both sat on Charlotte's bed, the bottom bunk on the right-hand side of the room. Charlotte got out a little music player and offered Nadie one earbud to listen to. "You gotta hear this new song I found. It's got such a cool sound."

Nadie accepted it, and they each listened to one ear bud, heads close together.

"Who died?" Charlotte asked as they listened. "Someone really close, huh?"

Nadie gave a little shrug and a sigh. "Yeah."

"Your mom?" the other girl suggested. "My mom died when I was little."

"No. I'm not close to my mom. Didn't even recognize her when she came to visit."

"Oh yeah? That would be weird, huh? So who died?"

Nadie scratched at a hole in her jeans. "I don't really want to talk about it."

"Just tell me who. I won't tell anyone."

"A sister," Nadie told her finally. Tears prickled her eyes, and she tried to concentrate on the music. "Little girl I helped take care of. Luyu."

"Luyu," Charlotte repeated. "I'm really sorry."

"Yeah. I don't want to talk about it, though, okay?"

"What happened to her?" Charlotte completely ignored Nadie's plea. "Was she sick?"

"No!" Nadie got up, giving the earbud to Charlotte. "Where's the blue room? That's where Cammy said I was going to be sleeping."

"It's just across the hall." Nadie sniffled. "You're not going to sleep yet, though? We haven't even had supper!"

"I need to lie down."

Nadie went to the room across the hall. There was one other girl playing solitaire with a deck of cards on her bed. She glanced up at Nadie, but didn't say anything. They had been introduced, but Nadie didn't remember her name. Nadie looked at the other beds that were unoccupied. The other bottom bunk had no sheets or blankets on it, which Nadie assumed meant it was vacant and she could claim it. Without a word, she went over to it and lay face down. It wasn't particularly comfortable, with broken springs she could feel beneath the stained surface. But it wasn't any worse than her bed back home.

A pillow hit the back of Nadie's head and she turned her head, angry. The other girl had gone back to her solitaire game. The pillow had obviously come from her bed, leaving her with none. Nadie slowly tucked it under her head and closed her eyes.

"Thanks."

CHAPTER TWENTY-TWO

She didn't actually sleep. The caffeine or meth kept Nadie awake. But she was alone and safe, and away from all of the prying questions and rude comments, and the violence she had run away from in Manitoba. There was eventually a call for supper and Nadie went down with the other youth.

There was a big dining room table, but there wasn't enough room around it for everyone to sit down and eat. So it was set up buffet-style and everyone filled their plate and then sat down wherever they could in the dining room, kitchen, or living room. Nadie watched everyone to make sure she didn't break any rules or draw attention to herself. No one took their plates to their bedrooms, so she assumed that was against the rules.

"Not much appetite today, Tonya?" Cammy asked, looking at the meager portions on Nadie's plate.

Nadie wasn't even sure she could eat what she had taken. She didn't have any appetite for food. Cammy raised an eyebrow significantly. Nadie assumed that meant decreased appetite was another symptom of meth use. She sighed.

"Not today. Maybe after a good sleep."

Cammy nodded. "Come into my office after dinner."

"Uh-oh," one of the boys intoned. "First day and you're in trouble already!"

Nadie glanced at him. He was blond, with laughing eyes.

"You know she's not in trouble," Cammy said. "We just have some paperwork to complete."

&

In the morning, Nadie awoke to one of the other girls shaking her. Nadie couldn't even open her eyes, she was so tired. She groaned.

"Hey. Don't go back to sleep. Wake up." More shaking.

"No," Nadie insisted.

"If you don't get up now, there's no breakfast. Drag your butt out of bed."

"No. Tell 'er I'm sick."

"You're gonna be sorry. Lunch ain't until noon and it's only sandwiches."

Nadie groaned again, covering her head with her pillow. The other girl gave up and left her alone. But it didn't seem like she'd been gone for two minutes when Nadie felt someone sit on the bed beside her.

"Tonya?" It was Charlotte's voice this time, and a tentative hand on her back. "Are you okay? What's wrong?"

"Lemme alone," Nadie said. "Let me sleep."

"Sophie said you're sick. Is it your stomach? What's wrong?"

"My head. And I'm tired. Lemme alone."

"Your head. Do you want some Tylenol? I'll get you some."

Nadie considered. "Yes. Please."

"You just wait here. I'll be right back."

Nadie wasn't planning on going anywhere. She fell asleep while waiting for Charlotte to get back with the painkillers. She was having a weird dream about Mouse and Grandfather when Charlotte shook her awake again.

"Here, sit up for a second. Here are the pills." Charlotte put them into Nadie's hand. Nadie popped them into her mouth without opening her eyes. "And here's some water to wash them down."

Nadie felt the cool, wet glass in her hand and took several gulps of chlorine-laced tap water. Charlotte took the glass back from her. "There. Are you okay? Can you open your eyes?"

Nadie lay back down and curled up, pulling the blanket over her head. "No. Goin' to sleep."

Charlotte stayed there a few moments longer. Then she finally walked off, leaving Nadie alone.

❧

More dreams and disrupted sleep. Nadie couldn't believe how tired she was. Whenever she woke up, it was just to turn over and fall back asleep again. She couldn't raise her head or open her eyes to look at the clock or the position of the sun. She couldn't get up and rid herself of the dreams. It was like it was the middle of the night, and she couldn't understand why everyone else was up and around. People came and went from her room. Mostly, they left her alone, though some made comments about her being hung over or on drugs. Nadie didn't care. She just curled up in her warm cave and ignored them.

"Tonya. Tonya, wake up and talk to me for a minute."

It was Cammy this time. Nadie shifted.

"Mmm. What?"

"Here, can you sit up and open your eyes?"

"No."

"Are you sick? Nauseated?"

"No. Tired. Lemme sleep."

"Sounds like you're crashing from the amphetamines. It can be pretty brutal. Do you need anything?"

"No."

"You should drink. Keep hydrated."

Nadie just groaned at Cammy's interference, desperate to go back to sleep.

"I'll get you a glass of water."

She was gone and, in her dreams, Nadie drifted between planets and stars. When she got back, Cammy forced her to sit up part way so she'd be able to drink. Nadie took a few gulps of the water and handed it back blindly, still unable to open her eyes.

"Boy, it's really got a hold on you," Cammy observed. "You pay attention to how you feel now. That's how you're going to feel every time you take that stuff. And worse."

"I don't have any more."

"It's easy to get ahold of. You're going to crave more. Stay away from it."

"Uh-huh."

"How long have you been taking those pills?"

"Not long," Nadie lay back down. "Few pills… few days…"

"I hope that's true. If it is, you should be able to get over it fairly quickly. You won't be addicted too badly yet. But it's still going to be rough."

Nadie wasn't paying any attention. She was already drifting between planets again.

At some point, Charlotte came back in and asked, "Are you still sleeping?"

Which was stupid, because it should have been obvious to Charlotte that Nadie was. Charlotte offered further Tylenol tablets, and Nadie washed them down and went back to sleep. She wasn't sure whether it was still the same day or the next day when her body finally started to remember she was alive, and she was forced to get up and go to the bathroom and to stagger downstairs to forage for food.

"Ah, she lives!" Camille observed as Nadie descended the stairs.

Rolf, the little dog, ran up to Nadie barking furiously. She bent over and offered her hand. He stopped yapping and sniffed, then licked, her fingers.

"How are you feeling?"

"Uggh. Like something died in my mouth." Nadie smacked her lips in distaste. "Is there anything other than water to drink?"

"I've got a pot of coffee in the kitchen. It's an hour old now, but it shouldn't be too bad."

Nadie managed to make it to the kitchen. She followed her nose to the coffee maker and poured coffee into one of the chipped mugs lined up on a tray beside it. Cammy had followed her and watched her select a chair and sit down. Nadie took a sip of the coffee and put her elbows on the table, propping up her face.

"I don't think I've ever slept for so long."

"It's the drugs. And I'd say by the looks of you that you probably weren't taking care of yourself too well before that."

Nadie rubbed her forehead just above her eyebrows. "Do I look that bad?"

"Well... you don't look good."

"Yeah."

"Your body needs regular sleep and food. And no more pills. Right?"

"Right."

"Do you think your stomach can manage a snack? I'll pull something together for you."

"Yeah. Something little. Not really hungry, but... I feel empty."

She listened to Camille moving around the kitchen, softly clinking dishes. The woman put a plate down on the table in front of Nadie. She opened her eyes and looked at the sandwich.

"Thanks."

"That empty feeling may be more than just not having eaten for a while," Cammy said. "You want to tell me a little more about how you're feeling? Eating our emotions isn't the best way to deal with them."

"I'm eating the sandwich."

Cammy chuckled. "Yes. But you need to deal with whatever else you're going through as well. Do you want to talk about it?"

"No."

"It doesn't have to be with me. I can arrange a session with a psychologist. A professional."

Nadie shook her head and took another bite of the sandwich.

"I don't think you've been dealing with this, have you? Things are not going to get much better until you start examining your emotions and dealing with what you're feeling. You can't run away from yourself and you can't drug your feelings away. They're still going to be there, under the surface, as soon as you sober up again."

Nadie put the sandwich down and looked at Cammy. "I don't want to talk to anyone, okay?"

Cammy's face was serious. She nodded, accepting Nadie's answer, and didn't pursue it further.

"So, have you decided what you want to do? School? Find a job? You need to work on your plan."

"Not today. Just not feeling good." Nadie ran her fingers through her close-cropped hair. She felt the healing wound at the back of her head, remembering the stitches needed to be removed. She'd have to find the downtown clinic on the resource list the Step Up Center had given her. "Not school."

"School is important. You may regret that decision."

"Don't see the point anymore."

"We'll talk about it more when you're feeling better."

After a few minutes, Nadie pushed her plate away. She had gotten down half the sandwich and one bite out of the other half. She couldn't choke down any more. Cammy indicated the glass of water she had also set in front of Nadie.

"Drink too. Water is even more important than food."

Nadie sipped at her coffee instead. She needed the hit of caffeine. Although that made her think of the pills, and her naiveté in believing Holly when she said that they were just caffeine. She should have known Holly just wanted to use addiction to get control over her. It had been stupid to put so much trust in her.

Cammy was different. Nadie didn't get the same vibe off of her that she had gotten from Todd or Holly. She was pushy, but it didn't feel the same. Nadie didn't feel like she was being manipulated. Just guided and encouraged. Like Grandfather would do.

Her chest hurt when she thought about Grandfather and she tried to direct her thoughts in another direction. That Nadie was dead. She was Tonya now. No family. No roots. She could do what she wanted to and live her own life.

"I'm going to go lay back down," she told Cammy.

The older woman nodded. She looked remarkably motherly, despite her rebellious appearance.

"Okay. You get some more rest. Let me know if you need anything else."

Nadie nodded and went back to her bedroom. No one else was there. It felt very quiet. Lonely without the other girls. She had only been there for a day or two, and already missed the comings and goings of the other girls. The background noise of their conversation was comforting. It made her feel safe and not so alone.

Nadie was still tired, but her body and brain seemed to be slept-out and she couldn't get back to sleep again. She tossed and turned in bed for a while, waiting for sleep to come, but it didn't work. She sat on the edge of the bed, unable to sleep, but without any energy or desire to get up. Rubbing her eyes, she looked around the room.

She hadn't really paid much attention to her surroundings until then. The small closet and drawers were packed with clothing, though she could see one drawer sticking out slightly was empty and assumed that was for her to put her clothes into. The tops of the dressers were a mess of makeup, cheap jewelry, and other miscellany.

There was a bottle of nail polish remover, reminding her of the peach-scented polish remover Nicole had left behind when she retreated to the city. It hadn't worked as quickly as the gasoline, but it had provided her with some relief from the unabating emotional pain. Nadie already had a headache, and she knew she could no longer take the red pills that remained in her pockets. She couldn't let herself rely on them. A quick sniff of the nail polish remover, though... she didn't think she could get dependent on that. The stuff was so foul, she couldn't see herself ever using it unless she really needed it.

*

"Time for supper."

Charlotte shook Nadie awake.

"Cammy says you were up earlier and not to let you sleep through supper. So come on. Up you get."

Nadie groaned and sat up slowly, her head more painful than ever. A rag fell to the bed and Charlotte picked it up.

"You dropped..." She rubbed it between her fingers, frowning. Holding the rag up, Charlotte smelled the nail polish remover. "Whew. You doing your nails?" She looked down at Nadie's bare nails, frowning.

"Uh, not yet," Nadie attempted to take the rag back. "I still need to..."

Charlotte shook her head, an impish smile spreading across her face. "What are you doing on these kiddie drugs? I haven't sniffed since I was... hell... nine years old? You gotta come party with the grown-ups, babe!"

"I... wasn't..."

"The hell you weren't. Those nails haven't been painted in the last decade. No wonder you can't get out of bed. That stuff will kill you!" She sat down on the bed next to Nadie. She looked around the room and out in the hallway before proceeding in a low voice. "We'll go out tonight. After supper. Hit the town and have a little fun. Okay? Huffing alone in your room; that's no fun. I'll introduce you around and we'll just hang out."

"No…"

"Oh yeah!" Charlotte laughed. "After supper. No arguments!"

Nadie went with Charlotte, but only because she wanted to get out of the house. She had been sleeping so much; she needed some fresh air and company.

She had never been a partier on the reservation. Plenty of the kids would get together and drink. What else would they do while the responsible adults in their lives were drinking, doping, or beating on each other? The idea of the reservation actually being dry was laughable. But she had not usually joined in on the partying. She had Luyu to keep an eye on. And she was a loner. She didn't understand the draw of drinking yourself silly just to spend the evening with your friends.

But maybe it wasn't about being with your friends. Maybe it wasn't about having fun or getting drunk. Maybe it was about the pain, and the other teens had just worked out the solution of anesthetizing the pain with alcohol before Nadie had.

Charlotte was close enough to her size to share clothes and had a few vintage cocktail dresses she had managed to find at the Salvation Army or whatever other outreach programs she frequented. They both dressed, and Charlotte used a few well-placed pins to adjust the dress to Nadie's skinnier figure. Armed with a pair of shears and some bobby pins, Charlotte attempted to tidy Nadie's hair into something neat and sleek, but she frowned when considering the result.

"It will be better when it's grown out a bit more," she sighed. "That's the best I can do."

Eddie, one of the male supervisors, was outside the house smoking when Charlotte and Nadie went out.

"Doors are locked at ten o'clock," he warned them.

"We know," Charlotte shot back.

"What happens if we're later than ten o'clock?" Nadie asked.

"You find somewhere else to sleep," Charlotte said, shrugging. "Don't bother ringing the bell, because they won't let you in."

Nadie wasn't sure where she was going to sleep if she got locked out. In a skimpy cocktail dress with no backpack or sleeping bag? She obviously couldn't sleep out of doors and all of the emergency shelters would be locked up for the night. Nadie shivered, pulling her coat closer around her.

"Brr. It's getting cold."

"The things we suffer to look good," Charlotte said cheerfully.

Nadie was already regretting that she had let herself be dragged along. Charlotte must have seen it in her eyes, because before Nadie could open her mouth to suggest maybe they should go back and leave it for another night, Charlotte shook her head sternly.

"No. You're coming and you're going to have a good time."

Nadie closed her mouth again. Charlotte led the way, a few blocks away, to a club with flashing lights and music blaring from inside. Nadie was already limping. She was unused to the shoes she had borrowed from Charlotte. By the time they got there, she knew she was going to have blisters if the backs of her feet weren't already bleeding from the chafing. Charlotte put out a hand to steady her when she wobbled on the heels.

"You okay?"

Nadie nodded. Charlotte headed for the doors, bypassing the lineup outside. A bouncer blocked the way.

"Back of the line," he ordered. "No exceptions."

Nadie turned to go back, but Charlotte kept a hold on her and didn't let her retreat.

"We're special guests," she explained. "Private party."

He looked the two of them over, eyes doubtful. "The Rojas party?"

"Yeah," Charlotte nodded. "Now come on, it's cold and they're expecting us."

"You're later than the rest of the guests."

"Fashionably late." Charlotte gave him a breezy smile.

He looked like he would say no, then shrugged. He apparently had more to lose by turning away an invited guest than by accidentally letting in one or two girls earlier than if they'd waited in line like everyone else. He motioned to the door and let them through, despite the complaints coming from those who had waited in line.

The door closed behind them. Charlotte grabbed Nadie's hand to pull her toward the dance floor in the public area.

"Are we really here for a private party?" Nadie asked. Her stomach was tight. Had she run away from Holly, only to be presented as fresh meat for some rich guy's bachelor party? She pulled out of Charlotte's grip.

"No, that was just to get us in the doors!"

"What if he had double-checked?"

Charlotte smiled knowingly. "There hasn't been one time they've called a private party and asked 'are you waiting for two pretty young girls?' and turned me away. They always say yes."

"Oh. So we're not going in there." Nadie looked toward the private rooms off at the back of the building.

"With any luck, we will be by the end of the night."

At Nadie's expression, she smiled reassuringly. "Don't worry! It's a great way to get free drinks and have a little fun. Nothing's going to happen."

Nadie swallowed and nodded.

"Now let's dance and see who we can pick up! Just let loose, you're here for a good time."

Nadie's feet were too sore to do much on the dance floor. Charlotte took pity on her and let her sit down at a table to rest. Charlotte sat with her for a few minutes, then jumped up to dance with a guy who was giving her the eye, then was back again. She'd only been sitting for a few minutes when a tall, Latin-looking man in his twenties came over, giving Charlotte a big grin.

"Charlotte! Where have you been? Come to tear up the dance floor?"

"It's only a couple of days since I was here last," Charlotte laughed. "Where have you been?"

"I've been here. I guess we've just missed each other, then."

"I know I've missed you!" She stood up and accepted a kiss on each cheek. "Tonya, you'll be okay for a few minutes?"

"I'll be here."

"We won't be long," the man promised.

They danced through a few songs, and then returned to the table, laughing and talking over each other. Charlotte fell into her seat and let out a long breath. The man sat down with them as well.

"Tonya, this is Win. Win, my new best friend, Tonya."

"I thought we were best friends," Win said, affecting a sulk.

Nadie rolled her eyes over their continued lovey-dovey talk. "Hi."

"You don't dance, Tonya?"

"I borrowed Charlotte's shoes. They're killing my feet."

"Why don't you just kick them off?" he suggested. "Why be a party pooper?"

Nadie looked at Charlotte.

"Sure!" Charlotte exclaimed. "Why not? Nobody cares if you're wearing them or not."

"I always like heels on a girl," Win said. "But if it's the difference between dancing and just sitting around bored, then dance barefoot!"

"I'm not bored. There's lots to watch."

Win shook his head. "You have to get out there." He waved

down a waitress. "Drinks," he announced. "I'm buying. What do you want?"

Charlotte ordered a Long Island iced tea and Nadie thought that sounded like a safe bet and asked for the same.

"My favorite drink!" Charlotte exclaimed.

The waitress brought them back a beer and two iced teas. Nadie picked hers up and had a sip, and just about spat it back out again. She choked and swallowed and her eyes teared up at the corners. Charlotte took a sip of hers, eyes laughing.

"Are you all right?"

It was like no iced tea Nadie had ever had. There was, as far as she could tell, no tea in it at all, but plenty of very potent alcohol. She wiped at the tears leaking from her eyes and cleared her throat.

"It went down the wrong way."

"Burns, doesn't it? I hate it when that happens." Charlotte took another sip and Nadie followed suit, more careful this time and prepared for the bite of the alcohol.

"It's good," Nadie said, wiping her nose, which had also started to run.

"Have you ever had one before?" Win asked.

"I've had iced tea," Nadie said, and they all laughed.

Nadie let herself be talked into dancing. She left Charlotte's borrowed shoes under the table and went out on the dance floor. A couple of times with Charlotte, once with Win and then with a whole group of teens with wild haircuts and piercings. Nadie found herself smiling and having a fun time, not so self-conscious. The first couple of Long Island teas disappeared, and then a couple more. Nadie was feeling light-headed.

Charlotte grabbed her by the hand. "Come on… private party!"

"What?" Nadie resisted. "Who?"

"Come and meet them!"

Nadie followed uncertainly, still shoeless. She squeezed Charlotte's hand.

"Who is it? Do you know them?"

"Tonya. Come on. Just have fun. It doesn't matter. They're cool."

"But—"

"Just come, quit being such a stick in the mud!"

Nadie went along with her, still nervous about partying with people she'd never even met before. But a day ago, she hadn't known Charlotte, and Win seemed like a good enough guy. Charlotte pulled her into the private room. There were men and women; it obviously wasn't a bachelor party. Maybe a birthday party or some friends who got together every month. They were young people, in their twenties or early thirties. Everyone seemed to be having a good time.

"Here we are!" Charlotte announced loudly.

There was a murmur of greetings.

"Introduce everyone!"

Laughing, they went around the room, and Nadie didn't get any of the names. Her head whirled, trying to pin names to faces, but it just didn't work. She sat down in a nearby chair and looked around to get Charlotte to sit down next to her. But Charlotte was already on the other side of the room talking to a cute boy with his bangs in his eyes.

Nadie wasn't sure whether to get up and go join Charlotte or to stay where she was. It would probably be rude to butt in while Charlotte was making friends.

"What was your name?" asked the young man next to Nadie.

"Na—Tonya. It's Tonya. I didn't catch yours either..."

"Graham. So you know Charlotte?"

Nadie nodded. "Yeah, I guess. Do you know her?"

"Yeah, she's partied with us before. She comes here pretty often."

Nadie nodded.

"You don't have a drink," he observed and looked around for one.

"I've had a few already." Nadie wasn't sure whether she had had just the two Long Island iced teas, or whether there had been more.

"But that won't do," he said. He grabbed a bottle of beer from the table and passed it on to her.

Nadie accepted it, though she wasn't sure if she was actually going to drink it.

"How about food?" he asked. "Have you guys eaten? Anything else? You like coke?"

Nadie raised the beer. "I already got a drink."

He laughed. "No, not cola."

She suddenly realized he meant cocaine and her face got warm. "Oh—no. Thanks! I'm good."

"Today is payday, so if you want something…"

Nadie looked across the room to see what Charlotte was doing. She was laughing hysterically. Graham followed her gaze.

"Looks like Charlotte's already had something."

"Yeah, maybe."

Nadie caught a glimpse of Graham's watch. "Oh! What time is it?"

He looked at it. "It's still early. Eleven."

"Early? We were supposed to be back at ten!" Nadie got up to go talk to Charlotte and to figure out what they were going to do.

Graham motioned for Nadie to stay calm. "Charlotte never leaves that early. Don't worry."

"Where are we going to go? We can't go home until morning now!"

He smiled at her. "We'll go to an after-hours place. And then… we'll figure something out. A hotel, maybe."

Panic rose in Nadie's chest. Her heart started beating harder. Graham cocked his head at her, frowning.

"What's wrong?"

"No, I'm not going to a hotel."

"Why not?"

"I'm just not!"

Nadie hurried around the room to where Charlotte was.

"It's eleven o'clock! Charlotte, it's too late to go back to the shelter now! What are we going to do?"

"We're partying, Tonya. We're not going back tonight."

"I'm not going to a hotel with some guy! I thought we came to have a good time together, not to... hook up!"

Charlotte gave her a sideways hug. "What are you so worked up about, Tonya? You don't need to worry. I'll take care of you."

"I don't need to be taken care of! I don't want anyone setting me up or turning me out, or whatever you want to call it. I just wanted to get out of the house for a little while!"

"Come here. Sit down. Relax." Charlotte pushed Nadie into a chair. "Now just settle down. No one is going to do anything to hurt you."

Nadie fought tears. "What are we going to do, then?"

"Nobody is saying you've gotta hook up with anyone. If there isn't anyone you want to get together with, you can crash on a couch or something. Seriously. Just chill out."

"I'm not hooking up with anyone!"

"I said you don't have to."

Nadie's heart was still pounding. "I want... I want to... go back..."

"You know you can't. They won't open the door."

"But—"

Charlotte grabbed Nadie's shoulders, digging her thumbs and fingers in hard.

"Shush! No more arguing. Just calm down and quit being such a downer." She gave Nadie a shake. "Just have a good time. The night is still young."

"But—"

"If you can't have a good time, then at least shut up and stay out of the way!"

Nadie swallowed and nodded. "Okay."

What other choice did she have? She had nowhere else to go. None of the shelters would let her in. She couldn't sleep in the park dressed in a cocktail dress.

&a;

Nadie watched as Charlotte grew more and more drunk. Her movements were sloppy and her voice and laughter became increasingly shrill. One of the men pulled her down into his lap and she was too drunk to get back up again. Nadie watched anxiously, barely able to breathe.

"Maybe we should call it a night," Nadie said.

Charlotte paid no attention. Graham leaned toward Nadie.

"She's not done yet."

"She's completely wasted!"

"No, I've seen her a lot worse than this. A line of coke and she'll be back up on her feet again."

Nadie bit her lip. Was this what Nicole had been like when she had gone away to the city? Nadie could see a strong similarity in their personalities. She could picture Nicole in a room like this, or passed out in someone's living room, surrounded by drugs and booze and boys. Had anyone ever tried to help her? To get her out of that kind of life? How long had it taken for her to get herself straightened out? Nadie's entire sixteen years?

Still a bit light-headed herself, Nadie got up and went closer to Charlotte. She offered a hand. "I'll help you up."

Charlotte giggled. "I don't think I wanna get up," she slurred, snuggling up to the man. "I'm pretty comf'terble here."

"Let's get some coffee," Nadie suggested. "I think you've had a bit much to drink."

"Coffee this time of night? How am I going to sleep?"

Nadie frowned and looked for a response. Charlotte burst into peals of laughter.

"I'm not going to sleep, silly!"

"Charlotte… come on… this is… it's a bad scene…"

The man holding onto Charlotte sent Nadie a scowl. "A bad scene? What are you talking about? Everyone is having a good time. Except you. Maybe if you fixed yourself up a little, you could get a date of your own, and you wouldn't be trying to ruin everyone else's fun."

Nadie stood there with her mouth open. Her faced burned as she tried to think of a response.

Charlotte turned to look at the man's face, a little frown line between her eyebrows. "You be nice to my friend," she said in a pouty voice.

"Someone's gotta tell her. She could be cute if she put a little effort into it. Maybe if she was getting some, she wouldn't be so cranky."

She gave his face a playful slap. "I told you to be nice to Tonya."

He looked at Nadie. "If she'll stay out of my business, I'll stay out of hers."

Nadie wanted to explain that Charlotte had had too much to drink, and Nadie just wanted to protect her friend. She didn't want Charlotte to end up like her mother; pregnant by some stranger, messed up on booze and drugs, in no position to be a parent to anyone. Charlotte should be sleeping at the shelter, going to school to get her diploma, finding her career path.

"Go get a drink," Charlotte advised.

"Charlotte," Nadie grasped both of Charlotte's hands and gave her a little tug. "Let's get out of here. Let's just... why don't we go dance some more? I'm bored just sitting around here."

Charlotte's expression brightened at the suggestion. "More dancing?" She pulled one arm out of Nadie's grasp and put it around her partner's neck. "Let's go dance, Dev."

Dev gave Nadie an irritated look and shrugged. "You want to dance, we can dance," he agreed.

He stood up, picking Charlotte up to start with, and then letting her slide until her feet were on the floor, but he was still supporting her with an arm around her body. Charlotte made an attempt to walk, but it was a good thing she had someone steadying her.

Nadie led the way out of the private room, back out onto the dance floor. Graham followed her and made a little motion.

"You need a partner?"

Nadie nodded. "Thanks."

She wasn't really interested in dancing and she didn't put much thought or effort into it. Graham was competing for her attention, which was focused on Charlotte and Dev. They swayed to the music, pasted against each other. Charlotte's arms were around Dev, and Nadie could tell he was taking Charlotte's weight in his. They weren't moving in beat with the music, which was much faster than they were swaying. The music seemed only to be secondary to the long embrace on the dance floor.

"Tonya."

Nadie pulled her gaze back to Graham.

"Don't worry about Charlotte. She does okay."

Nadie shook her head. "She's going to get hurt."

"By Dev? He's not hurting her."

"But…" Nadie looked over at them.

"She's got a lot more experience than you do. She knows how to handle herself."

By the end of the song, though, Charlotte was limp in Dev's grasp. He bent over to scoop her up into his arms and carried her back toward the party room. One of the waiters saw and followed Dev, making inquiries. Dev waved him off.

"She's fine. No ambulance. She'll be back on her feet in a minute, just give me some space."

The waiter reluctantly backed off. He looked at Nadie and Graham, who were following the couple back to the private function room. His eyes were worried.

"We'll check and make sure she's okay," Graham assured the man and pressed something into his hand.

The waiter hesitated, giving Graham a long look, then he

nodded and moved on. Nadie clutched at Graham's arm as they followed Dev back to the room.

"I told you. She's had too much!"

"Shh. You'll get people upset."

"But—"

He shook his head at her, his lips pressed together. Back at the party, Dev laid Charlotte down on a couch. Nadie went over to check on her friend. The unconscious girl was breathing evenly. Her color was good. Dev squeezed himself to sit beside her on the couch and shook Charlotte's arm a couple of times. Too tentative; Charlotte didn't stir. Nadie tried to move in closer to check Charlotte's pulse and to make a better attempt at waking her up, but Graham held her back.

Dev pulled a strip of stretchy rubber or latex out of his pocket and tied it around Charlotte's arm. Nadie watched in confusion. Was that supposed to wake Charlotte up? It wasn't until Dev also pulled out a syringe that Nadie remembered the nurses at the clinic tying a tourniquet around Nadie's arm before giving her vaccinations. They said it made the vein pop up so it was easier to find.

"What's that?" Nadie demanded. "What are you giving her? You can't do that!"

Dev looked back at Nadie with a scowl of irritation. "Why don't you just butt out?"

"What is that? Are you a doctor?"

He smirked. "Yeah. A doctor." He turned back to Charlotte.

Nadie tried to pull out of Graham's grasp to stop Dev, but Graham tightened his grip and pulled her against him so she couldn't escape. Dev slid the needle smoothly into Charlotte's arm. He released the tourniquet, then drew the plunger on the syringe back, pulling blood into it. He pressed it down again slowly.

"You can't do that!" Nadie shouted, struggling to get over to him to stop him, even though it was already too late.

The buzz of conversation around her had ceased, and everybody was looking to see what was going on. Dev continued to push the plunger until the syringe was empty, then withdrew it. He put the safety cap back on the needle and slid it out of sight in a pocket. He rubbed the injection site, watching Charlotte's face.

Graham released Nadie and she elbowed him in the stomach, angry at his interference. She heard the thump and the whoosh of his exhaled breath, but he didn't hit back. Nadie hurried over to Charlotte's side and tried to shove Dev back out of the way. He resisted and pushed her away. Nadie was so skinny and so woozy from the alcohol that it wasn't hard for him to push her off balance. Nadie stumbled and fell ungracefully. The cocktail dress was not a good fit, and rode up on her, showing a lot more than she intended. Nadie pulled it down quickly and got up to her knees, where she could see Charlotte better and had more stability.

Charlotte was waking up. She stared at Nadie glassily for a few moments, then smiled. "Hey, cutie."

She pushed herself up onto her elbows, looking around. There was still very little conversation, everyone watching the drama unfold instead.

"Did I pass out?" Charlotte asked. She grabbed Dev's arm and used it to help pull herself up to a seated position. She let go of him and rubbed the injection site on her arm. "Mmm, good stuff," she murmured to Dev. "Got me feelin' good."

He reached out to embrace her. Nadie shoved him. She put a lot more force into it this time, angry at him for pushing her down. "Stay away from her!" Nadie growled.

She shoved him off the couch, forcing him to jump to his feet. He towered over her, face flushing red.

"You little—" He looked at Charlotte and choked back the rest of his attack. "You put your hands on me again and I'm gonna call the cops on you. Got it?"

She wasn't sure Dev would like the story she had to tell the police if he did. But she also didn't want to take the chance of being apprehended by the police or Child Services.

Nadie got clumsily to her feet, putting out a hand to steady herself. Dev was the closest one to her, and he reached out to her in a reflex. His hand lingered on her shoulder while they both looked at each other, unsure of how to react. Nadie pulled back slowly, compelling her legs to stay straight and strong, and keeping her head absolutely still and straight to prevent any further loss of balance.

Charlotte looked at Nadie and Dev, her eyes narrowing. "This one's mine, Tonya. Go find your own," she warned.

Nadie raised her brows, not daring to shake her head. "I don't want him," she declared. "He's just a big, fat jerk!"

"I see the look in your eyes." Charlotte got to her feet. In spite of having passed out only minutes before, she seemed steadier than Nadie. "You need to just back off. I didn't bring you along so you could steal my man."

"Charlotte! I swear I'm not interested. He's all yours!"

Charlotte didn't seem to be hearing anything Nadie said. She was stuck on the thought that Nadie was trying to steal Dev and wasn't going to be derailed. If anything, Nadie's words seemed to make her even more angry.

"Get the hell away from him!" Charlotte yelled. She shoved Nadie hard with both arms, throwing her to the floor for the second time in five minutes.

Before Nadie could straighten her dress or get to her feet, Charlotte was on top of her. Fists swinging, she went right for Nadie's face, landing punch after punch. It took Dev and Graham and another one of the men to pull Charlotte back. She clawed at Nadie's face, leaving burning hot stripes of pain on top of the aching bruises where Charlotte had hit her.

"Cool it, Char," Dev said in her ear. "You'll get us thrown out."

"Little slut is after my date!" Charlotte insisted as if she didn't even know who she was talking to. "I'm not letting her get her claws in him!"

"Nobody's got their claws in him," Dev soothed. "Come on. Let's dance some more. Work some of that energy off."

"Dance?" Charlotte echoed, distracted.

"Yeah. Come on. We'll go dance some more."

With another look at Nadie lying on the floor, Dev pulled Charlotte out of the room.

❧

Graham tried to help Nadie up. "Are you okay? Oh, man, she got you good, didn't she? Let me ask the bartender for some ice and we'll try to keep those bruises from swelling up."

Nadie didn't object, too dazed by the sudden turn of events to take it all in. Graham again tried to pull her up. He couldn't get her on her feet, but settled for getting her onto the couch Charlotte had vacated.

"There. Just relax there. Wait until I get back."

Wait to do what? Nadie lay there, her head spinning and face throbbing. One of the other party guests, a young woman, came over and sat on the edge of the couch.

"Are you okay? I'm so sorry that happened! There's not usually any trouble at our parties." She dabbed at Nadie's face with a tissue.

"What's she hitting me for?" Nadie asked. She heard the whine in her own voice. She sounded like a little kid. "I was trying to help her. I wasn't after her... boyfriend. I just wanted to help her!"

"It's not anything you did. It's just the drink and the drugs. Some people... turn mean when they're drunk."

Nadie remembered the encounter with Holly and nodded. Holly had acted like nothing had even happened the next day. Like she didn't even remember it. Would Charlotte be the same way? Nadie swallowed.

"Is Charlotte always like that when she drinks?"

The girl averted her eyes, shrugging. "I wouldn't know. I haven't seen a lot of her. Maybe once or twice. She gets... twitchy... but I haven't seen her hit anyone before."

239

Nadie moaned and brought a hand up to her head. The whole world was not only spinning, but rocking back and forth like a boat on the ocean. One of the bruises gave a big throb and the world dimmed. She wasn't aware of any passage of time, but then Graham was sitting there instead of the girl, gently pressing a cold cloth and an icepack over the side of her face. Nadie flinched at the contact and he gave a sympathetic wince.

"I'm sorry. It will help. Just give it a minute."

Nadie groaned again. She was starting to feel nauseated as well as dizzy and in pain. "I gotta get up."

"What? You can't get up, you need to rest and put some ice over that…"

"I'm gonna be sick, Graham."

He took a swift glance around and grabbed a wastepaper basket. "Okay. Here. Hang onto this, and we'll get you to the ladies." He helped her to get up and looked around to see who else could help. "Mary…?"

Mary was apparently the one who had been sitting with Nadie earlier. She took a look at Nadie's face and the wastepaper basket, and her eyes widened. "Uh-oh." She hurried to Nadie's other side and together, she and Graham helped Nadie toward the bathrooms. When they got there, Graham looked at Mary, gradually withdrawing his hold on Nadie.

"Have you got her? Are you okay?"

"Yeah, I think so."

Nadie didn't feel as secure without Graham balancing her on the other side, but with Mary's help, she managed to make it to the toilet before being sick. She heard Mary's heels click out of the bathroom, and could hear their low voices on the other side of the door, though she couldn't make out what they were saying.

Eventually, Nadie felt a little more clear-headed. She managed to make it to the sink to rinse her mouth and splash water on her face, then pushed open the bathroom door. Mary and Graham were still standing just down the corridor talking. Mary hurried over to take Nadie's arm.

"All better?" she inquired. "You're still pretty pale."

"She should lie down," Graham said. "With some ice on her face."

"Okay," Mary agreed. "Come on, let's get you settled."

Nadie was walking on her own, so they didn't grab her, but walked close by her side, waiting to dive in if she looked like she needed help. As they walked by the dance floor, Nadie saw Charlotte dancing with Dev. Unfortunately, Charlotte also saw Nadie and made a beeline toward her. Dev was hard pressed to catch up with her and tried to hold her back. Charlotte shook loose from his grip. Graham moved in to block her path, holding out his hands.

"Tonya's not doing anything to bother anyone," he told her. "She's just a bit sick to her stomach."

"We'll look after her," Mary added. "You go dance with Dev. We'll take care of everything."

"What's everyone's problem?" Charlotte demanded. "I want to see how my best bud is doing."

They all looked at each other, uncertain. Graham gave a little shrug and stepped back out of her way, but stayed close in case she attacked again.

Charlotte gave Nadie a hug. "Are you okay? I'm sorry, I don't know what I was thinking. I just freaked out a little."

Nadie held herself stiff in Charlotte's grip and didn't return the hug. She didn't even look at Dev, worried about triggering another paranoid attack from Charlotte. Charlotte let go of her after a minute.

"I am sorry," she insisted, tears in her eyes. "It just... I dunno. Something came over me. I know you weren't after Dev..."

Nadie still didn't look in Dev's direction. She wasn't taking any chances. Charlotte could go from sugar-sweet to dangerous in a second and she wasn't going to assume Charlotte's attitude reversal wouldn't switch tracks again.

She let Charlotte escort her back into the party room, and Charlotte fussed over her, making sure she lay down and put the ice on her face. Nadie closed her eyes and waited for the ice to calm the throbbing of her bruises. Her mind went to Nicole again. I hurt you. I hurt you bad, and they took you away. Charlotte appeared to be truly sorry, just as Nicole had, but she felt sorry too late to change anything.

Being sorry didn't change Nadie being hurt. It didn't make Nicole a mother or Charlotte a friend.

CHAPTER TWENTY-THREE

adie hoped to avoid Cammy or any of the supervisors
when she got in. She was quiet. She peeked in the
window of the door before entering to make sure no one was
around. But it was no use. She was halfway to her bedroom when
she heard Cammy behind her.

"Tonya?"

Nadie looked back over her shoulder. "Oh, hi." She kept
going, hoping Cammy would just leave her alone and let her go to
her room without an inquisition. No such luck. Cammy followed
her.

"We missed you at curfew last night," she said in a measured
tone.

Nadie lay down on her bed, facing away from Cammy. "Yeah,
I'm sorry about that. Lost track of time…"

"Turn over and look at me, please."

Nadie didn't obey immediately. She just lay there, still, waiting
for Cammy to either give up or press her further. Cammy did
neither. She stood there silently, waiting for Nadie to do what she
had been asked. Eventually, Nadie grew too uncomfortable with
the expectant silence and turned over again.

"Well." Cammy surveyed the cuts and bruises on her face. "What happened to you? And where is your new best friend?"

"Charlotte?"

"Yes. Charlotte. The two of you were together. Now you come home, looking like that. Where is she?"

"I don't know."

"You know a lot more than you're telling me. Did you get separated? Is that how you got hurt?"

"No. I mean, we didn't separate until… this morning."

"Does 'this morning' mean two o'clock or eight o'clock?"

Nadie swallowed. "More like… five o'clock."

"And where did Charlotte go at five o'clock?"

Nadie rubbed the center of her forehead, wishing she could rub away the headache. But considering the withdrawal, the alcohol she had consumed, and the beating, her headache wasn't likely to go away any time soon. She was probably lucky it wasn't worse than it was.

"It's not my business where Charlotte goes," she tried.

"Oh, it's not." Cammy leaned back against the frame of the door, staring at Nadie. "I assume that means she went off with a boy, or worse."

Nadie continued to rub her forehead, then looked at Cammy. "What do you mean or worse?"

"Just what I said. There are a lot of things that would be worse. She could be hurt or dead. Dealing drugs. Hooking. In jail, though that's probably not worse… depending on what she was there for."

Cammy waited for a few minutes for Nadie to reply, examining her fingernails.

"So does that mean she was with a boy?" Cammy surmised.

"None of my business."

"Maybe not. But it's mine."

Nadie didn't supply any information. Cammy sighed. "Do you need anything, Tonya? Your face is quite a mess."

"No. Thanks."

"Where did you get into a fight?"

"I'm tired," Nadie said. "Can I just go to sleep?"

"No. Sleeping is for night time. I'm thinking it's time to start assigning some chores. You've pretty much been sleeping since you got here."

"I don't feel good," Nadie protested. Chores? She could barely lift her head from the pillow.

"Up and at 'em, girl. I showed you the house rules, and that includes doing your fair share of chores."

"No… not really…?"

"Yes, really."

Scowling, Nadie forced herself to sit up. She held her face in her hands, barely able to hold her head up. Cammy waited, not giving in. Nadie steadied herself and walked toward Cammy.

"Okay… I'm up. What do you want me to do?"

"Let's start with laundry."

Nadie sighed. "Okay." Her hands were sore just thinking about it. Considering the number of people living in the house, there had to be a huge amount of laundry to do, even if people were supposed to do their own clothes themselves. She remembered from her talk with Cammy the first day that everybody was assigned days when they could wash their own clothes.

Cammy led her all the way down to the basement. She gestured at three full laundry baskets sitting waiting. "Sort them. Towels and bedding. You know how to use the machine?"

Nadie looked at the washer. It had a lot of buttons and controls on it. "Uh… no. We didn't have one like that."

"I'm sure it's all pretty much the same." Cammy ran quickly through the different settings and raised her eyebrows.

Nadie looked at her blankly. "Can you show me how? I… just one load…?"

Cammy cocked her head to the side, brows drawing down. "Are you seriously telling me you've never washed laundry before? You act like a girl who knows her way around the house."

"I've done laundry… but not in a machine."

"Not in a machine? Then how?"

Nadie made a scrubbing motion. "By hand."

"You did all of your laundry by hand?"

"Uh-huh." Nadie looked down at her bare feet, waiting for Cammy to laugh or make fun of her.

But Cammy didn't mock her. "All right, then. Let's do one together." She picked up one of the baskets and walked Nadie through the sorting process first. After they had gone through how much to put in the machine, and how much detergent, she showed Nadie the right settings for sheets and closed and started the machine.

"Get the rest sorted and then you'll need to listen for the machine to buzz, so you know when to put the next load in. Let me know when you're ready, and I'll show you the dryer. In between loads… you can work on dishes. Our dishwasher is broken. I assume you're experienced in washing dishes by hand as well?"

Nadie nodded. "Sure."

"I'll show you where everything goes."

Nadie followed Cammy up the stairs and was shown around the kitchen.

❧

It was late afternoon before Charlotte got home. Nadie stayed out of the way while Charlotte was lectured. Once finished with that, Charlotte came and found her. The girl was all smiles, just like always. No indication she was upset about the lecture or remembered their disagreements of the night before. She looked at Nadie scrubbing the tile of the counter backsplashes and laughed.

"How long have you been at it?"

"At the tile or at chores?"

"Chores."

"Since I got home," Nadie said, resting her aching arms. She sighed. "At nine."

"I coulda told you! Never come back early; you'll be slaving all day. You'll work until supper either way, so you'd best stay away as late as possible. I have maybe an hour of chores and you've had, like… eight."

"That's not fair!"

"You gotta be smart."

"But I didn't know about any of that."

"Which tiles have you done?" Charlotte asked, looking at the tiles. "I'll help you out before Cammy decides to assign me something in the dungeon."

"I already did the laundry."

Charlotte giggled. "Poor you."

"Actually, it was easy," Nadie said. "The machine does all the work. No scrubbing or wringing out or anything."

"Yeah," Charlotte gave her a sideways glance. "That's right."

They worked together in silence for a while.

"So where did you go today?" Charlotte asked Nadie.

"Nowhere… just kind of wandered around until it got light out. Went for breakfast. Came back here."

Charlotte rolled her eyes. "You must have been freezing! And those shoes already tore up your feet, what did you do?"

"Went barefoot most of the time. Once my feet were numb, it wasn't so bad…"

"You're crazy! Why didn't you just go with Graham? He was nice to you. You could have had a warm place to sleep."

"I told you, I'm not sleeping with a guy I've never met before."

Charlotte huffed and continued to scrub tiles. "Why not?"

"I don't want to get hurt. Or pregnant."

"That's not going to happen. I told you these guys are good guys. I've been with them before. They're not gonna beat you up and they'll use protection if you want."

Nadie shook her head.

"Do you have a boyfriend?" Charlotte demanded. "Is that why? You think you'd be cheating on him?"

Nadie thought about Mouse. "Not exactly."

"Oooh," Charlotte's eyes twinkled. "So there is a boy! Tell me about him."

A warm flush went up from Nadie's neck and all the way up to the top of her head. She scrubbed the grout between the tiles with great care.

"Name?" Charlotte prompted.

"Mouse."

"Mouse? Is that some kind of nickname?"

"Mouse Running in Dust."

"Oh, an Indian boy. And…?"

"And what?" Nadie scrubbed away.

"Did you two ever get together? Or are you admiring him from afar?"

"He's my best friend."

"Best friends who sleep together, or the kind who don't?"

Nadie frowned, scrubbing so hard that bristles were shedding from the brush. Her hands and arms ached from all of the chores.

"Well?" Charlotte prompted.

"Sometimes."

"Ah, I think we've found the problem! You're in love with this Mouse Run! That's why you won't hook up with a nice guy like Graham."

"No…"

"Uh-huh," Charlotte's tone broadcast disbelief.

"It isn't about Mouse. It's about…" Nadie struggled to put it into words. "Graham and those guys, they're not my people, Charlotte. I always planned to marry Nehiyaw, even if I left the reservation. White boys… they can't understand our ways."

"But you've left that behind." Charlotte stopped scrubbing and examined Nadie. "You ran away. So that's already off the table. You're not going to marry Mouse or another Cree boy. So why not have a little fun? Get to know some guys who aren't Indian."

Nadie shook her head. "I don't know."

After all of the work Nadie had done and the mostly-sleepless night previous, she should have slept like a baby. A baby who slept through the night. But Nadie was only asleep for an hour or so when she woke up, wide awake, restless, unable to get back to sleep. She tried both sides, front and back. She curled up and she stretched out. She flipped her pillow over. Pushed the blankets off and pulled them back on. It was no use, she couldn't get back to sleep.

Nadie got out of bed and went down the hall to the bathroom. She could get used to the modern plumbing at the shelter. It made for much nicer bathroom runs. She still felt wide awake and decided to try a nighttime snack and see whether that would help to settle her down.

Turning the corner into the kitchen, she gasped. Charlotte was coming the other way. They both froze and stared at each other for a minute, then started laughing. Nadie tried to keep as quiet as she could.

"You scared the crap outta me!" Charlotte whispered.

"Me too!" Nadie looked down at the cookies in Charlotte's hand. "Show me where those are."

They went into the kitchen together and Charlotte helped Nadie to raid the cookie jar. Then Charlotte took Nadie into the TV room and after checking carefully up and down the hall to make sure no adults were on patrol, they sat down together on the couch in front of the television. They turned it on with the volume way down low so it wouldn't wake anyone up. They munched on their cookies and strained to hear what was going on in the show.

Nadie snuggled her shoulder comfortably against Charlotte's. "This is nice. Way better than going out partying."

"You're what they call a stick in the mud."

"That's my middle name," Nadie deadpanned.

Charlotte turned to look at her for a moment before

discerning that it was a joke. She laughed. "I'll have to name one of my kids that."

Nadie caught one of Charlotte's bouncing braids and ran her thumb down it. "Do you sleep with it braided?"

"Yeah, sure. Doesn't get tangled that way. I brush them out and rebraid them in the morning."

"They're so beautiful." Nadie tickled Charlotte's face with the end. "They remind me of Mouse. He has such nice braids."

"What did he say about you running away?"

"I didn't tell him. I just kind of… left."

"You didn't say goodbye?"

"No."

"Why not?"

Nadie ran the braid across her face. "It was all just too much… and we sort of had a fight."

"Oh. Is he the one you're running away from?"

"No… not specifically…"

"Are we having a slumber party?" a voice questioned from the door.

Nadie and Charlotte both startled and whirled around to see who it was. Dylan stood in the doorway, smirking at them.

"Is it invitation-only, or can anyone join? Are we going to paint each other's nails and have a pillow fight?"

It was obvious from his tone he had no interest in actually joining them, only in irritating them.

"Get lost, Dylan," Charlotte growled.

"Get lost? What kind of an answer is that? You want me to go find Cammy, tell her you're up past curfew?"

"We're home. How much do you think she's going to care?"

"You're supposed to be in your beds."

"There's cookies in the kitchen," Nadie tempted Dylan.

He looked at her for a minute. He looked at Charlotte as if there were something else he wanted to say. Then he shrugged and walked away, headed toward the kitchen.

"Nice job," Charlotte said with a giggle.

"Guys are suckers for sweets."

❧

They eventually fell asleep there, leaning on each other. It was Eddie who discovered them there in the early morning before it was getting light.

"Oh, someone has been having a party!" he observed. "Up and at 'em, girls. Time to get up!"

Nadie blinked in the assault of the light Eddie flipped on. Charlotte groaned and swore at Eddie without opening her eyes.

"None of that. Get your butts moving. Clothes on, and meet me in the kitchen. I'll start you off with some chores."

"I need to sleep," Nadie protested. "I did chores all day yesterday. I'm so tired."

"Tough. You break curfew and we'll find more productive ways for you to spend your time."

"No… we didn't break curfew. We were home!"

"Curfew means you're in your bed," Charlotte intoned before Eddie could. She groaned. "Seriously, Eddie… it's too early. We'll start chores in a few hours. Teenagers need their sleep."

"Nope. You're up now. I expect you in the kitchen in fifteen minutes. There will be coffee."

Charlotte made no move to get up. Nadie nudged her. "Coffee," she repeated.

"It's gonna take a lot more than coffee to get me up."

"Let's go, ladies," Eddie encouraged. "The sooner you get moving, the sooner I'll stop harassing you."

Nadie shifted to get up and, not having anything to lean on, Charlotte was forced to sit up. Charlotte finally opened her eyes. "You are evil," she told Eddie.

"Move it along."

Both girls got up and moved like robots to their bedrooms to get dressed. When Nadie got into her bedroom, she looked at her bed. It looked so much more inviting than it had the previous

251

night when she hadn't been able to get settled back in. If she could just close her eyes for a couple more minutes…

It seemed like she had barely lain her head on the pillow when she was shaken awake again.

"You're done sleeping!" Eddie growled. "Get up."

"I'm so tired…"

"Of course you are. And you will continue to be until you learn to sleep at night instead of staying up. Move it."

"Just a few minutes…" Nadie slurred, trying to find the place her consciousness had been slipping into moments before.

A burst of cold water hit her face, making Nadie yelp and open her eyes in shock. Eddie was pointing a spray bottle at her.

"What the…?"

"Time to get up, Tonya. This could get worse."

"But I'm—"

Another spray hit her. Eyes open this time. Nadie closed her eyes and rubbed them. "You can't do that!"

"If the spray bottle doesn't work, I'll have to get ice cubes."

Just the thought made Nadie shiver. "I'm up. I'm up, I won't go back to sleep!"

He pointed the bottle at her again and Nadie flinched away. Eddie laughed. "Get dressed. I'll be back with the ice cubes if you're still in bed after I get Charlotte back up."

Nadie felt a bit better hearing that Charlotte had gone back to sleep too and would suffer the same treatment. She sat on the side of the bed rubbing her eyes, trying to get up enough energy to get her day clothes on. She laughed when she heard a string of curses coming from Charlotte's room.

"Get dressed," one of the other girls ordered from bed. "You're keeping the rest of us awake."

Nadie got up. She shut the door and clumsily stripped off her pajamas—a worn t-shirt and holey sweat pants. Her eyes kept trying to close even while she was pulling her clothes on. Eddie pounded on the door, making Nadie unbalance and just about fall down.

"You up, Tonya?"

"I'm just getting dressed."

"Kitchen in five minutes or I'll be back."

Nadie finished dressing, and then went to Charlotte's room. The door was shut. She opened the door and peeked her head in.

"I'm changing!" Charlotte squealed. But she wasn't getting dressed, she was sitting on the side of her bed, as Nadie had been doing a few minutes before, cradling her head in her hands.

Charlotte saw it was Nadie.

"Ready?" Nadie asked her.

"Not even close. Babe, it's gonna take more than a couple of cups of coffee to keep me awake today."

Nadie nodded, entering the room. "I know. Me too." She felt in her pocket. Despite her repeated insistence to Cammy that she didn't have any more of the pills from Holly, there were still a few more left. She put them in her palm and held them out toward Charlotte.

Charlotte's eyes darted to the sleeping figures in the other beds. She quickly plucked two from Nadie's hand. "Oh, you are a lifesaver! You can't have those around here, though. You know that, right? They do random searches, and if they find out…"

Nadie nodded. She moved to put the remaining pills back in her pocket. Charlotte eyed her. "You're not having any?"

"I'll try the coffee… maybe it will be enough."

Charlotte looked at the pills in her palm she had been about to swallow. "You trying to poison me or get me in trouble?"

"No… I just… I just got off of them. I don't want to go through that again."

Charlotte studied her, then nodded. She put the pills in her mouth. "Toss me some clothes."

Nadie looked around at the clothes on the floor and overflowing from the dresser drawers. Picking out a shirt and pants, she tossed them to Charlotte.

"I'll see you in the kitchen."

By the time Charlotte got to the kitchen, there was color in her cheeks again. Eddie surveyed the two of them.

"Okay. Fuel up. Coffee and something solid, because you're going to need the energy. I'm just going to my office to finish this list. I'll be back before you're done eating."

Nadie had almost finished her first mug already. She topped it off and blew on the surface of the coffee, trying to cool it down enough to drink it. The caffeine wasn't giving her nearly the lift she needed. Even standing there by the counter, her eyes were closing. Charlotte raised an eyebrow at her.

"I can't," Nadie said. "I'll get caught!"

"No, you won't. Don't be such a scaredy-cat."

"Cammy could tell the other day. From my eyes."

"We're going to be doing chores all day. No one is going to be looking at our eyes."

Nadie hesitated. She didn't want to have to go through withdrawal again, but she knew just one of those little pills would get her going, and keep her going most of the day. As long as she didn't take more than that, she should be okay. She wouldn't get addicted and there would be no withdrawal to speak of. The tiredness that would follow would just mean she could sleep the next night, instead of tossing and turning like she had the previous.

Nadie looked toward the kitchen door for any sign of Eddie, and then popped one of the pills in her mouth and chased it down with a gulp of coffee that burned all the way down.

CHAPTER TWENTY-FOUR

For the next few days, Nadie did a pretty good job of following the shelter's rules. She went to bed at ten and started to catch up on her sleep. It had been so long since she had kept a regular day/night schedule, her body was starved for sleep and she banked long hours. Some nights Charlotte went out, and others she stayed home and spent some time with Nadie and the other youth. The chore schedule was much lighter when Nadie kept curfew, less than she would have done at home.

Nadie resisted Cammy's attempts to persuade her to register for school, but she did discover the shelter's small library of used paperbacks and immersed herself in books like a desert wanderer finding a clear oasis pool. She read for hours on end, going through several paperbacks in a day.

"Hey, bookworm!"

Nadie marked her place with her finger and looked up. Charlotte stood in the doorway watching her.

"Time to put your books down and get some fresh air!"

Nadie stretched her muscles. She knew it was true, she should go out and get some sunshine. Grandfather always chided her when she binged on books, reminding her that she had to reconnect with Mother Earth and not lose herself all day in stories.

"Mmm. Where are you going?"

"Just to the mall. Do some window shopping."

"Maybe we could collect some bottles first," Nadie suggested. "Buy a cinnamon bun or something with the money."

Charlotte wrinkled her nose. She wasn't big on menial jobs. Nadie wasn't sure where Charlotte got her spending money and didn't want to know.

"Fine," Charlotte conceded. "You can pick some bottles and get a refund. But just for an hour. Then we shop."

"Okay." Nadie knew it was an inconvenience to have to run to the bottle depot, which was the opposite direction from the malls. "Thanks."

Charlotte nodded. She waited, fidgeting, while Nadie got on socks and shoes and her jacket and winter wear. It was getting pretty cold and binning wasn't warm work.

&

It was good to get into the warm mall after being outside for more than an hour. They were both rubbing their hands and stomping their feet when they got inside, trying to get warmed back up. Nadie was happy to have a few dollars in her pocket. Charlotte would probably end up springing for the cinnamon bun in the end so Nadie could save her money for what she wanted.

Charlotte hadn't told Nadie they were going to be meeting friends at the mall. She recognized one boy with a lip piercing she had seen Charlotte with before. Maybe dancing at the club; she wasn't sure. Charlotte ran through the names of the other kids too fast for Nadie to follow, as usual. They walked around aimlessly for a couple of hours; window shopping, horsing around, just enjoying each other's company.

"Let's go to the food fair," Charlotte suggested, after buying a silver necklace with green stones in it. "I need my fix."

Nadie was ready for something to eat too. And maybe a coffee. As they walked toward the food court, the boy with the lip piercing, whose name Nadie had now figured out was Cole, gave her a little nudge.

"You live with Charlotte?"

"Yeah. We're both at the same shelter."

"You from her tribe?"

"No… she's Ojibwe."

"So you two don't talk Indian to each other?"

Nadie shook her head, smiling slightly. "No."

He nodded. "Did you know her before you came here?"

"Uh-uh. I came from… further away."

"Oh. I see."

At the food court, they bought food at the various counters and snagged a few tables out in the middle of the seating area to eat together. As Nadie had expected, Charlotte bought the two of them a cinnamon bun to share, so all Nadie had to buy was her coffee. Nadie took a couple of bites of the rich confection, rolling her eyes.

"These are honestly the best. Even better than Beth's!"

Charlotte cut off a bite for herself. "Who's Beth?"

"Mouse's mother."

"Mouse?" Cole repeated. "What kind of a name is that? Who's Mouse?"

"A friend of mine," Nadie said. She rolled her eyes. "And it's his band name."

"Oooh." His cheeks flushed a little pink. "Sorry. Guess I should have figured that out. What about you? Do you have a name like that?"

Nadie shook her head. "My mom told my grandfather it meant wise. It's supposed to be a Nehiyaw name, but Grandfather said he doesn't think it really is."

"Nay-hih-yaw?"

"What you call Cree."

Cole nodded and took a big bite of his burger. He looked across the table at Charlotte and one of the other boys and snapped his fingers a couple of times to get their attention while he chewed. He swallowed strenuously.

"Hey, yeah, me too. Gimme… ten of crank."

Nadie looked and realized money and pills were being counted up and exchanged amongst the little group. She felt her eyes get wide as Cole exchanged his money for a small baggie of crystals.

"Do you think you should be doing that here?" she asked, looking around worriedly.

There were a few people watching what was going on, pretending they weren't, but sending quick glances over at them every few seconds.

"Relax," Cole said. "No one's busted us here yet!"

Charlotte slid a couple of pills across the table toward Nadie. "You shared with me, I share back with you."

"Oh, you don't have to… I don't need them…"

"You think I don't know you're out? And don't forget, I know how much you just got for bottles. You don't have the money to buy, and I know you're not bartering… yet."

"I'm fine," Nadie tried to push them back.

"Keep them!" Charlotte raised her hands, refusing to take them. "Hide them until you need them, if you don't want them right now. Next time you're out partying, you'll be glad for them."

Nadie glanced around, nervous of anyone seeing them on the table in front of her. It wouldn't hurt her to have a couple of pills around just in case she needed them. She had been able to avoid taking too many since arriving at the shelter and that gave her confidence. She knew she had the willpower to leave them alone on days when she didn't need them. She wasn't addicted and she didn't plan on getting hooked. She grabbed the two pills and shoved them into her pocket. Two wasn't enough to be harmful.

Charlotte nodded and went back to her negotiations with the other youths. Nadie squirmed in her seat, anxious at the drug deals being conducted right out in the open. But Cole and the others seemed confident they weren't going to get caught. Nadie hunched over, making herself small, and nibbled a couple more bites of the cinnamon bun. It stuck in her throat, the sweetness cloying. She had to swallow hard to get it down, then washed it down with a swallow of coffee, now lukewarm and bitter.

She glanced over at Charlotte again, worried. Charlotte shook her head. "She's such a baby," she said to one of the boys. "Scared of everything!"

"I am not," Nadie muttered. Not loud enough for them to actually hear her.

There was a loud tramping noise, and conversation was muted as everyone looked around to see what was going on. Nadie saw a wall of black-suited cops sweeping into the food court. Cole swore.

"Bust!" he warned.

Nadie and the others didn't believe it at first. The police were there for something else. Some other operation that didn't have anything to do with them. But within the next few seconds, they could see the cops were focused on them, advancing in their direction.

"Scatter!" Charlotte commanded, flying out of her seat and heading toward the hall that led past the bathrooms to an emergency exit, which would get her out to the parking lot. Nadie remained frozen on her feet, petrified by indecision. One at a time, the others peeled off, making a break for it. Nadie stood up. She could see Charlotte hadn't managed to escape. The hallway had been blocked by the police as well.

"Drop to the floor!"

Nadie turned to look at the cop who had closed in on her.

"On the floor!" he repeated, grabbing the back of her clothing and throwing her down.

Nadie tried to catch herself but didn't get her hands or knees down in time to break her fall. She reflexively tried to push herself back up and the cop kicked her back down.

"Stay down! Lace your hands behind your head!"

There was so much noise and confusion, Nadie was overloaded trying to process it all. Her brain seemed to be three beats behind everything else that was happening.

"Hands behind your head!"

He grabbed one of her hands and wrenched it behind her head, cracking the elbow painfully.

"Ow!" Nadie brought the other hand behind her head and obediently laced her fingers together. He started patting her down. Nadie flinched and jerked away at his touch, no matter how she tried to stay still. He thrust his hands into her pockets and turned them inside out, finding her knife, her change, and the two pills Charlotte had just given her.

"Those aren't mine," Nadie said, feeling sick. "Those are Charlotte's, I just took them because she wouldn't take them back. I didn't buy them!"

He didn't comment, putting them in a small bag so they wouldn't get lost. He continued to pat her down. Nadie squirmed at his touch. He grabbed each hand to pull it down to her back, popping her elbow again.

"Ow, you're hurting me!"

He clipped a pair of handcuffs over her wrists. When he released her, Nadie turned her head and looked around for the others. There were still people sitting and standing around the food fair, but all of the kids who had been seated with Nadie were on the floor like she was.

"I didn't buy any drugs," Nadie insisted.

He picked up the plastic bag and scribbled something on it. "What's your name?"

Nadie hesitated. He nudged her with his toe.

"Easy question. What's your name?"

"Uh—Tonya."

"Tonya what?"

"Tonya Nehiyaw." Nadie used the same last name she had given Cammy.

"Nee-hih… can you spell that?"

Nadie did. He wrote it in block letters on the bag.

"All right. On your feet."

He grabbed the inside of her upper arm and helped pull her up to her feet. He waved at one of the other police officers.

"Noelle, come check this one for me."

The policewoman came over.

"She was pretty squirmy when I was doing the pat-down. She could be trying to hide something."

"I'm not!" Nadie protested. "I just don't like him touching me."

"Stand still for me, then," the policewoman said. She started at the top of Nadie's head, working her way slowly down Nadie's body, including under her bra strap. She lifted up Nadie's shirt and checked her waistband. She went down Nadie's legs. "Take off your shoes."

Nadie obeyed, and the woman checked them. She put them back down and let Nadie put them back on. When Nadie looked back up at her, the policewoman was putting on a pair of blue gloves.

"Open your mouth."

Nadie did, and the cop put her fingers in Nadie's mouth, pulling her cheeks around and making her lift up her tongue and move it around. She nodded and stripped off the gloves.

"She's clean. If you're worried, do a strip-search at the station." She looked at the pocket knife, change, and two pills on the floor beside them, and gave a little grimace. "Yeah, I don't think you need to worry about this one."

The first cop nodded. "Thanks. Okay, Tonya. You're being detained for suspected possession of a controlled substance. Once we test these pills, we'll bring charges. You got a lawyer?"

"No."

"You want one?"

"I… I don't know. I told you, they're not mine. I don't even know what they are. They're not mine."

"They are in your possession, that's all that matters to me."

He escorted her out of the mall to where there was a line of police cars and vans parked waiting for them. He took her over to a van. Nadie thought there would be a big open area inside the van and she'd be able to talk to the other kids. But it turned out it was divided into individual little compartments with steel walls in between.

"You're going to be waiting in here for a little while," the policeman told her. "Just be calm and sit still."

She realized after he helped her in and closed the compartment door why he said that. It was as close as a coffin. There was no room to move or air flow. She tried to do what the policeman had said, just to be calm and sit still. She slowed her breathing and closed her eyes, pretending she was somewhere else. Maybe sitting in her room at night. Or outside in the woods, under the stars, with a campfire warming her feet.

She breathed in and out, in and out, even and regular.

Nadie was startled when the van started up its engine and pulled out, but glad to be on her way. She was getting sore sitting in the same position on the hard bench for so long. She could just hear noises outside the van, muffled enough not to be able to tell what was going on.

At the police station, a different policeman opened the compartment and helped her out, and took her in for booking.

"She have any ID?"

"Nothing on her. Gave her name to the arresting officer as Tonya Nehiyaw. See if she's in the system already."

The officer on the other side of the counter looked at the name on the evidence bag and typed it in.

"Nope. Where are you from, kid?" He looked at Nadie.

"Winnipeg."

"Never been booked in Alberta?"

"No. I've never been arrested ever."

"In foster care? Got a health care card?"

"No."

"Runaway?"

"No."

He looked at her for a moment, then looked back down at his computer. Nadie assumed he was checking descriptions in the missing persons database anyway. But he wouldn't find her there. Even if Grandfather had gone to town and filed a missing person report when she disappeared, the file would have been closed when Nadie Laplante was reported as drowned in the river.

The booking officer eventually shrugged. "I don't see her in here at all. You know your Social Insurance Number, Tonya?"

"No. Don't know if I have one."

He rolled his eyes. "Well, maybe the fingerprints will pop something. Let's get her entered."

Nothing showed up since her prints had never been entered in any system before. They completed the process, and Nadie was put into an interview room, where she had to wait again.

❧

Nadie had her head down on the table, tired from waiting. The door finally opened and a police officer came in and sat down across from her.

"Tonya Nehiyaw?" he asked, looking down at a computer printout.

"Yes."

"I am Constable Warner. You are being questioned in connection with methamphetamine discovered in your possession. Do you understand that?"

"They weren't mine," Nadie told him immediately. "They're my friend's. I just... she passed them to me and wouldn't take them back. I would have thrown it out, once I went past a garbage can..."

"You would have, would you?"

Nadie nodded. "I don't do drugs."

"Uh-huh. Never done anything?"

"N-no," Nadie's tongue betrayed her, stumbling slightly.

Warner tapped the piece of paper with the end of his pen. "That didn't sound certain."

"I haven't. I don't do drugs."

"Why would your friend give it to you, then?"

"I dunno. Maybe she wanted to get me hooked."

"Not something friends usually do…"

Nadie thought about Holly's manipulations. She was pretty sure Charlotte wasn't being manipulative the same way as Holly, but she also pressured Nadie to drink or take drugs when she didn't want to. Nadie thought it was just because Charlotte didn't want to drink alone, but she wasn't sure.

"Sometimes people pretend to be your friend… but they just want something from you," she said.

He lifted his eyebrows. "What do they want?"

"To get you addicted? Maybe they want you to depend on them… or to make you confused… vulnerable."

Warner leaned back, tipping his chair back on two legs. "Really. You think that's why your friend Charlotte gave you these pills?"

"I don't know. Maybe she was just trying to be nice."

"So you don't deny you had drugs in your possession when the bust was made."

Nadie hesitated.

"There were cameras on you kids while you were making your deals," Warner offered, his tone smug. "And on all of the arrests being made. We've got you dead to rights."

Nadie stared at him. "They said no one had ever been arrested making deals there before."

"Well, if they thought no one noticed or cared, they were wrong. There have been plenty of calls about drug deals being conducted right out in the open at the mall. That's why we were watching and set up the sting today."

"Oh."

"You hadn't been part of a deal there before?"

"No. I told you, I don't do that."

"How long have you been taking meth?"

"I don't. I'm not an addict. I don't look like one, do I?"

At least Nadie knew she hadn't had anything that day that would show up with dilated eyes or some other symptom. They could test her blood if they wanted to, she was clean.

"You can't tell a meth user until they're pretty advanced in their addiction. You're still taking pills, haven't moved on to smoking or mainlining yet. You're not going to have major signs."

"I'm not a user."

"What can you tell me about the other kids you were with?"

Nadie shrugged and shook her head. "I don't know any of them. Only Charlotte."

"Tell me about her."

"I don't know… I've only known her for a little while. I don't know anything about her taking drugs."

"You've never seen her take anything?"

"Just drinking… I saw a guy give her something… but she wasn't conscious. That wasn't her choice."

He looked up from his notes. "That's assault. One of the guys from the mall?"

"No. At a club."

"You've never seen her take pills like she gave you today?"

Nadie thought about Charlotte taking the pills Nadie gave her. It obviously wasn't something new to Charlotte. And Graham had talked about her doing coke and other drugs. She couldn't very well tell Warner she had given Charlotte drugs herself.

"When can I go home?"

"You're not going home," Warner said. "You're going to jail."

"But… all I had was two pills, and I told you those were Charlotte's…"

"It's still possession. And you were part of a larger trafficking operation. That carries pretty heavy penalties. Especially with minors involved and in an area where there were children around."

"I wasn't trafficking!"

"You'll get the chance to tell that to a judge. At some point."

Nadie put her elbows on the table and held her head. How could she get in trouble when she had been forced to accept the pills? It hadn't been her choice. It was Charlotte's fault.

"I haven't done anything wrong," she insisted. "I'm not an addict or a dealer. I was just there, I wasn't involved."

The door opened and someone else came into the room. Nadie rubbed her eyes, trying to wipe away the tears. Her nose was starting to run.

"The way you were drinking the other night?" a voice said. "You have a substance abuse problem, whether you want to admit it or not."

Nadie looked up. The other person who had entered the room was Cole. She frowned, trying to make sense of it.

"What?"

He sat down at the table with her, nodding a greeting to Warner.

"The other night at the club, with Charlotte. You were drinking pretty heavily."

"You weren't there." Or had he been? There had been a lot of people at the club. Nadie vaguely remembered dancing with a group of punk-looking kids. Had Cole been one of them?

"I'm not surprised you don't remember. You were pretty smashed."

"I didn't go there to drink. I thought I was ordering iced tea."

He laughed. "That's a good one. I'll have to remember that!"

"What..." Nadie looked from him to Warner. "What are you doing here? I thought you were arrested too."

"Tonya, I'm a police officer. I was undercover. Trying to break up this operation."

A wave of cold went over Nadie and settled in her stomach. She tried to remember all she had told him. How much had he seen at the club?

"You know I wasn't dealing," she asserted.

He leaned forward. "Here's what I can do for you, Tonya. I

think you're a victim of circumstance. But you did get caught in the middle of a drug trafficking ring and it was clear it wasn't the first time drugs passed hands between you and Charlotte. Things could go badly for you in a courtroom."

Nadie swallowed and waited for his offer.

"I think the most important thing is to get you dried out. Get you into an addictions program so you can kick the booze and the pills and get clean. If you will cooperate with us, I'll get you into a program. If you complete the program, the charges will go away."

"I'm not an addict!"

"I saw you at the club," he reminded her. "You were so wasted you could barely walk. You may be naive, but you're not clean and sober."

CHAPTER TWENTY-FIVE

Cole was the officer who took her to the rehab center. Nadie shifted anxiously and glanced sideways at him. It was impossible for her to see past the pierced, semi-punk, kid's face to the serious cop hidden beneath the mask. He played his role so well that even knowing it was a facade, she couldn't see past it.

"You okay?" Cole queried, glancing over at her.

Nadie swallowed and nodded. "Yeah. I'm fine."

"You must be nervous, huh?"

"Sorta. I don't want to be stuck in a place all surrounded by addicts and alcoholics. I'm not like that."

"Are you telling me you're not craving a drink or a fix right now?"

He was too close to being right. Nadie had just been thinking about how a drink, a pill, or even an inhalant would help calm her down and make it easier to go through with it.

"I'm not an addict," she repeated.

"You didn't answer my question."

Nadie continued to ignore it. "What's going to happen to Charlotte? Is she going to rehab too?"

"She's going to be incarcerated. Why, you'd rather go with her?"

"No. But… she didn't do anything that bad. I don't understand it."

"She's dealing drugs. What's not to understand?"

"Not that much. Just a few pills. And she's not pushing them; it's just people who wanted to buy in the first place. They'll go somewhere else if she's not there. She's not out trying to get kids hooked."

"First of all, what makes you so sure? And second, why would it matter? She's still dealing in a restricted substance. We have to stop the flow of drugs somehow."

Nadie looked out the window. She was struck again by how big the city was. They had been driving for half an hour, and there was no sign they were getting to the end of the city.

"What's this place like?"

"Sort of like a hospital. You're not locked in your room during the day. There are group sessions and individual counseling you're expected to participate in. I don't know how much time they spend on life skills or career planning, but you can expect some of that too."

"Career planning? I don't have any career."

"That's sort of the point. You need to have a plan when you get out. Not just hitting the streets and looking for another fix."

"What am I supposed to do? No one hires kids. Especially homeless Native kids." She threw him a glance. "Everyone thinks we're just drunks and junkies. Now they'll have proof."

"You think your prospects are any better if you still are a drunk and a junkie?"

He just didn't get it. Nadie was tired of being discriminated against. Being Nehiyaw didn't make her a drunk. Going out with a friend one night and having a bit too much to drink once didn't make her a drunk. But people like him would always assume she was. No one would give her a chance.

They pulled up in front of a building that looked like a

doctor's clinic or old people's home. Nadie's stomach was hurting and her chest was tight. She licked her dry lips, looking at the building, and then looking at Cole.

"This is it," Cole confirmed. "Ready?"

Nadie ground her teeth, but couldn't find any reason to object. It wasn't like she could persuade him to take her back to the shelter instead, just letting her off with a stern warning.

"Yeah. I'm ready."

He got out of the car and went around to her door to open it. Nadie was in handcuffs and felt conspicuous being escorted up the sidewalk into the treatment center. Her heart was pounding hard in her chest. Inside, there was a little reception area with a big desk in the center and two small tubular chairs off to the side. Cole walked Nadie up to the reception desk holding onto her arm. He showed the receptionist a badge and gave her the paperwork he had brought with him. Nadie looked at the heavy metal doors that separated the reception area from the rest of the center. Even though the reception area was in cheerful pastel tones and looked like it could be a doctor's or vet's office, it was obvious that once she went through those doors, she wasn't coming back out.

§

Nadie was shown to a waiting room where she was to sit down and wait for her intake interview. Nadie obediently settled herself into an uncomfortable plastic chair and the woman who had shown her in left. Nadie sat staring at the wall. There was a bulletin board covered with notices, inspirational quotes, and little motivational posters. She had read them all and the director's door still hadn't opened. The hall door opened and another girl walked in. Older than Nadie. Long, brown hair. Maybe Hispanic or part Indigenous. She looked at Nadie for a minute and sat down on the chair next to her.

"Intake?" she asked.

Nadie took a minute to process the inquiry, then nodded. "Yeah. You?"

The girl wore a blue uniform that made her look a little like a janitor at the library in town. She sighed; a long, tired sound. "Disciplinary."

"Oh." Nadie didn't like the sound of that. She didn't ask any further questions, afraid that would be offensive.

"Dr. Burton," the girl said, nodding toward the director's door. "We call him the human lie detector. You may as well tell him the truth, no matter how bad it is, because he'll always know if you're lying to him."

"Oh. Okay."

"Seriously. Don't even try."

Nadie nodded. The director's door opened and a man with a round, balding head and glasses showed a young man out. He looked at the two girls.

"Lorry?"

She rubbed her forehead, looking stressed. "Finkel sent me down."

He studied her for another long moment. His scrutiny made Nadie uncomfortable and she wasn't even the one being stared at. Lorry gazed down at the floor, getting red. Finally, the director nodded. He turned his gaze to Nadie.

"Come in, please, Miss Nehiyaw."

She followed him into the office and he shut the door. Nadie sat in the chair across from his desk. The room was bare and plain. He had some diplomas or certificates on the wall and a fake green plant on top of his long-drawered filing cabinet, and no other personal touches that she could see. The fake plant made Nadie miss the outdoors. Even though she had just arrived and didn't usually like to spend a lot of time outside. And even though it was winter and all of the leafy plants were dead or hibernating. She sighed and twisted her fingers together, trying to get settled in the uncomfortable surroundings.

"Welcome to our facility, Miss Nehiyaw. I hope you will

benefit from our programs. Now…" he spread several papers in front of him. Nadie couldn't read them from where she was, but assumed they were records of her arrest that the police had copied and sent over with Cole. Dr. Burton's eyes moved from one page to the next, reading and analyzing. "There isn't a lot of information here when you get right down to it," he said. "You were arrested for drug trafficking?"

"My friend gave me two pills. That's all I had. And I didn't ask for them or buy them, she just gave them to me and she wouldn't take them back when I tried to give them to her."

His eyes were intense. Even if Lorry hadn't warned Nadie about his unusual abilities, his gaze would have made her uncomfortable. It felt like they burned into her soul. Nadie looked down, avoiding looking at him. He didn't interrogate her any further on whether what she said was the truth. If Lorry was right about his abilities, then he knew she had told him the truth.

"Is that the first time you have had drugs in your possession?"

"Uh… no. But that doesn't make me a drug dealer."

"I didn't ask you if you were a drug dealer."

Nadie shrugged and continued to stare down at a knot hole on the desk in front of her.

"Have you taken drugs in the past?"

She couldn't help chewing on her nail. It was a long time since she had done that last. When she was a child, her nails were always bitten down to the quick, even bleeding. She had overcome the compulsive behavior by sheer willpower. But now she couldn't help herself. Nadie pulled her thumb away from her mouth and wound her fingers together to keep herself from biting them any more.

"Yes," she admitted.

He made a note on his scratch pad. His writing was too messy for Nadie to decode, especially upside-down and from that distance.

"Have you taken any today?"

"No."

"Have you taken anything today?"

"No."

His eyes bored into her. Nadie didn't even have to look up to know that he was doing it. She swallowed. She could feel his eyes. "A Tylenol. Couple cups of coffee. That's all. Unless you want to count the gooey cinnamon bun I was eating before they arrested me."

"Sometimes I wonder if those ought to be a controlled substance," Dr. Burton said, with a smile in his voice and a rumble of laughter. He patted his slightly rounded belly. "Once you start…"

"Yeah," Nadie agreed.

"No other pills today of any kind?"

"No."

"Alcohol? Mouthwash? Cough syrup? Anything with alcohol in it?"

"No. Nothing."

He wrote another note on his pad. Nadie wondered what he had seen in her face that he thought was worthy of a note. Did he think she was lying and had been drinking earlier in the day?

"How about inhalants?"

Nadie made a wide shrugging gesture that she intended for him to read as denial. But he didn't move on to the next question. Nadie glanced up at his face. His blue eyes, perfectly centered in his round glasses, stared steadily back at her. Nadie looked down again. She waited for him to either challenge her or move on. He picked up his pen and wrote something down and continued to wait. Nadie's chest hurt. Why couldn't he just move on?

"No," Nadie said. Her voice cracked like a teenage boy's. She cleared her throat and repeated it firmly. "No, nothing."

Dr. Burton took a deep breath in and let it out slowly, trickling the air in an exhalation that went on, and on, and on.

"I don't like to be lied to, Miss Nehiyaw. Tonya. Why don't we go back and try that one again? Have you used any inhalants today?"

"No… I mean… not on purpose. I mean… you use things all the time that smell and maybe make you light-headed. Nail polish. Markers. Cleaners…"

He wrote it down. "This is a difficult one for you."

"I'm not an addict."

"I didn't ask you that."

"I cleaned the whiteboard for Cammy today. With the cleaning fluid. And I wrote out the new schedule. With the markers."

"And did you get high?"

"Just light-headed." Cammy had come along part way through the job and cracked the window open. Nadie hadn't appreciated the gesture.

"And nail polish?" Dr. Burton looked down at Nadie's hands. Her nails were freshly painted a dark red she had borrowed from one of the other girls. "I find it interesting you don't wear any makeup or take care to look well-groomed, but you're wearing nail polish."

"I'm living in a shelter. I hardly have any clothes. Or makeup or anything else."

"But you have nail polish."

"I just borrowed it from one of the others. To make my nails look nice."

She caught herself before chewing on her thumbnail, forcing herself to put her hands back down, away from her face.

"And did you get high?"

"No."

"And tonight, when you decided to take the nail polish off again, would you get high on the acetone?"

Nadie rubbed the glossy nail polish with her thumb. There was a hard knot in her stomach. He was the human lie detector. He knew.

"Maybe."

He nodded and wrote a note to himself.

੪

After Dr. Burton was done with Nadie, he pressed a button on the underside of his desk, which called an attendant into his office. Nadie was shown to her new room.

It was a small, bare cell almost as small as the baby room. There was a bed and a tiny set of drawers in a side table and a rod to hang clothing on. No closet. Nowhere, she realized, that anything could be hidden.

"You are to stay here," the woman who had escorted her to her room advised. "Someone will come and get you when your counselor is ready for you."

"Isn't Dr. Burton my counselor?"

"No. He oversees all of the operations at the center. He doesn't have the time to do counseling as well. Your counselor will be Jeremy."

"Okay."

"Just take a break and stay in here. He'll come and get you when he's ready."

"Okay," Nadie repeated, a little more loudly.

The woman scowled at her. "Don't you raise your voice to me. I'm in charge here."

Exasperated, Nadie looked down at her hands and said nothing further, waiting for her escort to leave.

੪

Jeremy, Nadie was surprised to discover, was an Indigenous man who looked to be in his thirties. He looked tired.

"Tonya Nehiyaw?"

"Yes."

"Good. I'm Jeremy. Come with me and we'll get started."

Her papers had now apparently been given a home in a file jacket. She caught a glimpse of Dr. Burton's spiky handwriting on one of the pages as Jeremy perused it. The room he took her to was green. It housed only a wobbly table and four chairs. She sat in one and Jeremy sat down opposite her.

"Long day?" he asked her, stifling a yawn of his own.

"Yeah. Long and… stressful. Tiring. Weird."

"I'm sure it's been very unsettling. Why don't we start off with your questions? What do you want to know?"

"How long do I have to be here?"

"Our inpatient program is thirty days. After that, you're going to need outpatient counseling, some sort of support group like AA or NA, and long-term follow-up. An addiction takes more than a day or two to take root, and it takes longer to kick the habit permanently."

"Thirty days," Nadie repeated. That was the part she cared about. She knew she didn't need any of the other stuff. She wasn't an alcoholic or a drug addict. The inpatient period was all she cared about. "And after I'm done that, then the police wipe my record."

Jeremy nodded and folded his hands. "That's right. But you're still going to need continuing support if you're going to remain sober."

"I'm sober right now. I can stay that way."

"Good to hear it. Other questions?"

"The shelter… will they keep my room for me? They won't toss my stuff and make me start over, will they?"

She was painfully aware how little she had. It didn't seem fair that she kept losing everything.

"They'll be informed of your circumstances. You won't be the first kid they've had go into rehab."

"This program… do I have to believe in your god and everything?"

Jeremy raised his brows. "My god? No. You can believe whatever you want."

"Because I don't know if I believe any of that."

"We'll help you through it."

Nadie nodded.

"Any more questions?"

"No… not yet."

"Okay. We'll start you on step one tomorrow. For now, I just want to explore your addiction and who Tonya Nehiyaw really is."

Nadie shifted uncomfortably at that.

"Do you have something you want to tell me about yourself?"

Nadie opened her mouth to answer, and he held up a hand.

"Not about what you aren't. About what you are. Tell me about Tonya."

"I don't know. Nothing special."

"Everyone is something special. What makes you unique? What is it that makes you yourself?"

Nadie considered what to tell him.

There was a supper, but Nadie was so tired and stressed out from the day that she had no appetite. She could barely look at food without feeling sick. So when the nurse or aide came around to pick up Nadie's dishes, she found everything still full.

"You need to eat something," she growled, not taking the tray Nadie held out to her.

"I'm not hungry. I'll have something tomorrow."

"You need to eat this."

"No. I can't. Tomorrow I will. It looks really good," she offered. "I just don't feel well right now."

"Any symptoms need to be reported and logged. It's better if you just eat it and save us the time. I'm going to go around and collect the other trays and then I'll come back to you. Then you had better have eaten something."

Nadie looked down at the dinner again after the woman was gone. Normally she'd be happy with any food she didn't have to make herself. A warm meal she didn't have to slave over the stove for was something special. But the whipped potatoes, green peas, and nondescript meat and gravy looked fake. She couldn't explain it. They just looked unappetizing.

Nadie did what she used to do when she was a little girl. She pushed the food around so there was a big empty spot in the middle. She hid the peas under the potatoes so it looked like they were all gone. And she cut up the meat and heaped it into a pile and hid some under the potatoes so it would look like she'd eaten about half of the dinner. She took one bite of each thing, and she smeared a little gravy in the corner of her mouth and on the front of her shirt.

When the aide came around again, she looked down at the plate. "You still barely touched anything," she accused, not fooled by Nadie's creative rearrangement of the food. "Now I have to fill out an assessment form."

"I'm sorry… I'm just not hungry."

"Damn meth-heads," the woman muttered under her foul-smelling breath. She returned Nadie's tray to the rolling cart outside the door and retrieved a clipboard with a form on it. "Fill that out," she ordered, slapping the clipboard down over Nadie's knuckles.

"Ow!" Nadie jerked back and the clipboard went clattering to the floor.

"Pick it up."

Nadie gritted her teeth and picked it up. She looked over the long checklist of questions.

"Do I have to answer all of these?"

"Every single one. Don't miss any or they'll come down on me."

Nadie frowned and started working through the questions. It took a good half hour to fill it all out, all while the aide grumbled and breathed and muttered about how slow Nadie was and what a pain she was.

"You Indians are always so slow," she complained. "You can hardly even read, can you?"

"I'm grade ten," Nadie protested. "And I was the best reader in my class!"

The woman grunted and waited impatiently for the form. When Nadie handed it back, she glanced over it, then scribbled her name at the bottom.

"Tomorrow, you eat!"

"I will," Nadie agreed.

Even if it meant she threw up afterward, it would be more pleasant than having to deal with the dragon-breath woman and her form again.

Sleep did not come easily in the strange quarters, in spite of the exhausting day. Nadie was hyped up and anxious and couldn't find a way to settle down for sleep. There was obviously not going to be a night-cap at rehab.

There were unfamiliar noises. The ventilation system creaked and groaned like something alive. Even after her heavy metal door was closed, Nadie could still hear someone shouting and the muffled PA system. There were nurses and guards walking by the door, causing shadows to fall over the narrow observation window.

In the morning, she was not hungry but forced down more than half of her slimy porridge and toast. The girl who collected her breakfast tray was younger. She smiled pleasantly and picked up the leftovers without complaint. Nadie breathed a sigh of relief.

The day's work started with a group session. A counselor other than Jeremy led the discussion, introducing Nadie to the group and rattling off their names to her. She only caught his, which was Bryson.

"Today we are going to discuss feelings," Bryson said earnestly, looking around at them.

"There's a shocker," muttered one of the other inmates, which made Nadie laugh. Quietly, though, so no one would hear. The young man who had said it looked at Nadie, as if he could sense Nadie's laughter. He smiled at her conspiratorially.

"We take drugs to mask our pain," Byron said. "To suppress our feelings. To silence our fears. If we want to be able to overcome our addictions, we need to first deal with the feelings that we have been trying so desperately to hide from. Who would like to start?"

Everyone, including Nadie, was wearing the same blue scrubs as the girl that had sat in the director's waiting room with Nadie the day before. But they had all managed to make their own individual statements, small as they were. A different number of buttons done up. Collar up or down. Sleeves rolled up. Tucked or untucked.

There was a blond girl with very red lips sitting across from Nadie, and she took up the invitation to talk about the feelings she was trying to drown with alcohol. The victim of an aggravated sexual assault, she launched into a minute-by-minute explicit description of what had happened to her. Bryson tried several times to quietly interrupt and redirect her, without success. Nadie's face was getting hotter and hotter as she attempted to tune the words out. Finally, Bryson put his foot down.

"Tessa, stop!"

She stopped mid-word and looked at him.

"Tessa, you are still not discussing your feelings. You are telling what happened to you physically, but you are still not addressing how you feel about what happened to you. That's what I want to hear."

She looked at him for a long time, mouth open. She made several false starts and big tears started to roll down her cheeks. "I can't!" she wailed.

"What is it you're feeling right now? Sadness? Anger? Helplessness?"

She just shook her head and sobbed. Nadie looked across the circle at the traumatized woman. She looked so far away and alone. Nadie didn't want to walk across the circle. There was no empty chair near Tessa.

But she couldn't take it. She couldn't listen to Tessa cry like that and not feel compassion for her. Nadie got up and, dragging her chair all the way around the outside of the circle to the opposite side, she pushed it in beside Tessa's chair. The others shuffled their chairs around to even out the spacing. Nadie sat down and put her arm around Tessa. Tessa cried harder. Nadie pulled her close and rubbed her back, much like Nicole had rubbed Nadie's the evening before she had left to go back to the city. Tessa put her face against Nadie's shoulder and gradually her sobs started to slow down.

"Who else would like to share?" Bryson asked quietly.

No one volunteered.

"Clark?" the counselor prompted.

"I feel... isolated... alone..."

"Okay; good. Where do you think those feelings come from?"

"I don't have anybody." The boy named Clark looked at Nadie, cuddling Tessa close. "Nobody who cares about me."

"What about your mother? She cared enough to sign you into the program."

"That's not because she cares. That's just 'cause she wanted my sorry butt out of her house."

There were giggles around the circle. Bryson gave a small, tolerant smile.

"Tonya?"

Nadie looked around the circle before she realized all eyes were directed at her and remembered she was supposed to be Tonya.

"Ummm... yeah?"

"What feelings are you trying to deaden with drugs and alcohol?"

"I'm not an addict."

"That's not what we're here to discuss. We're here to discuss your behaviors. You drink. You do drugs. Why?"

Nadie shook her head. "I don't know. I don't know why."

CHAPTER TWENTY-SIX

There was a block of time scheduled for art therapy. Nadie looked around at the pencil crayons and paints without much interest. Drawing wasn't exactly her thing. She wandered around the room.

"Whatever strikes your fancy," said Poppy, the counselor in charge of the therapy. "If you're not drawn to anything, don't let that stop you. Just give something a try. You can give something else a go tomorrow. The important thing is to start."

Looking in the shelves of bins at the far end of the room, Nadie's heart quickened. She found a number of balls of yarn and string, some larger pieces of fabric, and some fabric scraps that would do for quilting or some kind of mosaic. She started pulling bins out for a better look.

"What did you find?" Poppy asked, darting in to help.

Nadie looked over the textiles. "I did weaving at school. I made a blanket."

"Well, you won't be able to do anything so big here, but you could make a cardboard loom and make some smaller pieces. Wall hangings or potholders. A baby doll blanket or rug, if you know a little girl who would like one." Poppy looked at her expectantly. She was a blond with long, fluffy hair and loose, flowing clothing.

She seemed like some sort of cross between a hippie and a fortune teller. Nadie supposed that was probably usual for artistic types.

"Or I could do crochet or knit," Nadie said. "I never got the hang of knitting, but crocheting isn't very hard."

"Sure," Poppy agreed. "Whatever strikes your fancy."

"Or I could quilt or stitch a mosaic," Nadie motioned to the brightly colored scraps of fabric.

"Yes. But we don't have a sewing machine, you'd have to do it by hand."

Nadie nodded. Poppy looked at her expectantly, but Nadie wasn't ready to make a decision yet. Her heart hurt when she looked at the various yarns and strings; but at the same time, she longed to pick them up and settle into a meditative rhythm of weaving, creating something beautiful.

"I'm not sure yet," Nadie said, trying to prod Poppy to give her some space.

Poppy got the message. "Okay, well give me a shout if you have any questions, I'll be close by…"

She went back to helping the residents who had been in the program longer than Nadie and who already had projects they had started on. Or those who just picked up the nearest drawing implements at random and started scribbling.

Nadie looked carefully over the materials and picked out a few yarns that worked well together. She would try a cardboard loom, as Poppy had said. That was how they had started in school before Nadie decided to build a full-size loom to make a blanket. But she wouldn't make a blanket and she wouldn't make something for a little girl. As she picked out her colors, she avoided anything red.

Nadie had been warned that the rehab program would include career counseling, but she hadn't anticipated anything so involved. First, there was testing. Hours and hours of testing over the first few days. Nadie dreamed of being able to go back to the youth

shelter to do chores all day instead of the psychoeducational testing. Her brain felt wrung out every day. It seemed like the only
time she could really find peace was when she was doing art therapy, mashed in between the testing, personal counseling, and
group counseling, which stretched her emotions to the limit. She
couldn't imagine what it must be like for those who were going
through withdrawals. When Nadie had experienced her post-meth
crash at the shelter, there was no way she could have managed any
of it. Even sober she could barely see straight at the end of
each day.

Finally, she was done the endless hours of tests and she sat
across the table from Jeremy as he paged through the thick report
that summarized the results.

"You were still going to school before you came here?" he
asked. "To Calgary, I mean?"

Nadie nodded. "Yeah."

"So up until, say, a couple of months ago?"

Time moved in a blur for Nadie, and she wasn't sure how
many weeks or months it had been since she had last sat in a class-
room with Running Deer and Mouse and the little children. "In
the fall," she said, to clarify.

He made a grimace and tapped the report with his pen.
"What were you doing at school? What grade level?"

"We had correspondence packages. Me and Mouse. Running
Deer didn't feel comfortable teaching high school."

"Running Deer. So you were going to school on the
reservation?"

Nadie nodded. Jeremy let out his breath in a long whistle of
air and leaned back his chair.

"Yeah. That makes sense," he acknowledged.

"Why?" Nadie asked, looking at the thick report. "What does
it say?"

He contemplated, looking through it again. "Your reading
level is almost grade level appropriate," he said. "You said you like
to read?"

"I love to read," Nadie said, nodding vigorously.

"But you probably didn't have a lot of reading material available on the reservation."

"No. But I borrowed books from the library in town whenever we went in. And the librarian didn't charge me fines because she knew I couldn't ever return them on time. I read just about everything in the library! Sometimes she special-ordered books from the city library just for me."

"That's probably why your reading level and comprehension are so much higher than the rest of your scores. How was your teacher with math?"

Nadie wrinkled her nose. "I didn't like the math in the correspondence book. The math we did before high school was a lot more interesting."

"Your grade level in math is about a four."

Nadie frowned. "What does that mean? Grade four?"

"Yes. You are able to do grade four math."

"But I'm in grade ten."

"And can you do grade ten math? Do you understand it?"

"Yes... a little bit... some of it..." Nadie trailed off. She and Mouse both struggled to understand anything in their packets for math. Running Deer was hopeless at explaining it. Mouse had given up and just copied the answers directly out of the back of the text. Nadie tried to do it without looking at the answers but rarely succeeded. She stared down at the table in the interview room.

"It's not your fault if you weren't taught," Jeremy reassured. "But before you're able to finish school, you're going to have to get some help in most areas. You have a lot of remedial work to do."

"I'm not going to school anymore. I'm done with that."

"You're old enough to drop out if you want to... but I wouldn't recommend it. A high-school diploma and the general knowledge that you would get go a long way to being able to get a good job. You don't want to just be a bum getting by panhandling or picking bottles, or with a minimum wage job that doesn't give you enough to live on."

"But if I went back to school, I'd be in grade four? With little kids?"

"No, you'd have to get some resource help. Get your skills upgraded."

Nadie had no idea what that meant. "But my reading is good. It's just my math...?"

"Your reading level is adequate. You might want to look at reading some of the classics, a little Shakespeare and Dickens, some harder material. It's a bit different than reading pulp novels. And the rest..."

"What else?"

"Science. Social studies. You're all over the place. You don't have a solid foundation."

"White man's subjects," Nadie pointed out. "Studying what's in a test-tube instead of outside your own door. And his history, not our stories."

Jeremy's nod conceded this. "But if you want to get along in the white man's world, get a diploma and a job, you need to know it. Have some understanding of it."

Nadie shook her head in frustration.

Jeremy straightened the papers. "For a good job, you need to be educated. I couldn't do this job without a university degree. And to get that, I needed to get a high school diploma and to do well on entrance exams. I did have to study a lot of stuff that wasn't relevant to social work. The next thing we're going to do is some vocational testing, see what careers would be a natural fit for you. Do you have ideas about what you want to do with your life? What you'd like to go into?"

Nadie shook her head. The future wasn't just unknown for her, it was a deep, dark, foreboding hole of nothingness. She couldn't see herself doing anything.

She thought about the kids she knew who had committed suicide. At least for them it was over. They didn't have to make any more decisions. They didn't have to choose a career or make something of themselves or choose between the white world and the Nehiyaw world. If she believed the Elders, they had moved on in their journey and were happy. If she didn't believe there was any more to their journey, then their pain had at least ended.

It seemed like the only real solution to the pain and uncertainty.

ઉ

When Nadie got out of her latest session with Jeremy, feeling tired, confused and bleak, she found Tessa waiting for her out in the hallway. Tessa gave her a smile of greeting and clamped onto her arm. Ever since that day in group, when Nadie had been the only one who tried to comfort her, Tessa had been attached to Nadie. Sometimes physically.

"Uh—hi," Nadie said. She had hoped for some time and space of her own to think. Or more likely, to take a nap and not have to sleep. Without any chemicals to help take her away from her troubles, there were few ways to escape during those blocks when she was not scheduled to be in some other therapy.

"Don't you just hate all the talk therapy?" Tessa demanded. "I don't know how it's supposed to help. Honestly, most of the counselors don't have a clue what it's like for us. Not many of them are like your Jeremy and have actually been addicted themselves."

Nadie glanced toward the closed door to make sure Jeremy wasn't coming out. "Jeremy was an addict?" she murmured. "I didn't know that. When?"

"You should ask him his story. He'd tell you. I don't know any details, just that he was an alcoholic before he became a counselor."

"I didn't know."

"And it's good they matched you with him," Tessa pointed out. "Because he's Indian too, so he can understand all of the cultural stuff. You know, how you grew up and your religion and everything."

Nadie shifted uncomfortably. She and Jeremy hadn't, in fact, discussed any of the 'cultural stuff' they might share. Since he hadn't said anything about growing up on a reservation, she assumed he had just been raised in the city, like everyone else. They really didn't have any more in common than dark skin and a few physical features.

"But there's no one here who can understand what I've been through," Tessa sighed.

Nadie glanced aside at her. "What?"

"You know," Tessa dropped her voice dramatically. "The rape."

"Oh. But that's pretty common, isn't it?"

"With addicts, you mean? I wasn't an addict when it happened."

"No, I just meant…" Nadie shrugged. "I thought it was something that happened… to a lot of girls."

Tessa frowned, a crease forming between her eyebrows. "No… more than it should, but… I don't think anyone else here…"

"People just don't talk about it," Nadie explained. "But everybody… well, most of the girls I know on the reservation… It's just something that happens. Especially when people get drunk. But other times too. Little girls." Nadie's voice cracked. She swallowed and gave a little shrug.

"That's not right," Tessa said.

"No. But… it happens."

"So you know what it's like." It was a statement, but with a little lift at the end of the sentence, like it was a question too.

Nadie started to walk down the hall. Pretty soon, Jeremy was going to be coming out of the meeting room, and she didn't really want him to hear any of the conversation. Tessa walked with her.

"Yes," Nadie said finally.

"When?"

"Grandfather always kept my door locked at night, so no one could bother me. We always had other people staying with us and

I guess he knew what could happen. But you can't stay locked up all the time, and things happened… in the house… on the way to school… in the woods…"

"I'm so sorry. You must have been really confused, and hurt."

Nadie tried to push the feelings aside. She didn't think about those things. There was no point in obsessing over bad things that happened. It was best to just put them behind you and forget about it. Bad feelings could rip the band apart. It was best to just forget about it and keep the peace.

"I'm okay," she said. "No permanent damage done."

The center buzzed with excitement over the arrival of a Christmas tree and decorations. Those who had privileges and wanted to were given the opportunity to help with the decorating. Nadie scanned the overcrowded tree for a space to put the next ornament.

"So, do you celebrate Christmas?" Clark asked.

At the silence, Nadie looked up to see who he was talking to. His eyes were on Nadie. Had he addressed her by name? She still wasn't used to responding to the name Tonya and had no idea whether he had called her name or not. Clark was looking awkward at Nadie's non-response. His eyes darted to the side, then down at the remaining ornaments.

"Sure," Nadie said, jumping in quickly. "Grandfather always cut down a big tree. Biggest one that would fit in the house. We decorated it with popcorn strings, and when Christmas was over he'd put it outside and the birds would all come to eat them."

"Did you exchange presents?" Tessa asked wistfully.

"Yeah, sure. We couldn't buy presents, but we'd give our old clothes and toys to the younger kids in the band or make something. Sometimes Grandfather gave me a present he had bought, something special."

"I don't know if my mom will bring me anything," Tessa said. "But she's going to come see me."

"Is that allowed?" Normally, they weren't allowed visitors in the inpatient program.

"For Christmas, yeah. They make an exception."

"Oh." Nadie nodded. "Okay."

Clark was looking at her. "You won't have any visitors?"

Nadie laughed. "No!"

He nodded, looking satisfied. "Me neither."

"Do you think we'll get presents from the staff?" Tessa asked.

Clark and Nadie looked at her.

"What's your deal with presents?" Clark demanded. "Christmas is for kids. You're not a kid anymore. Nobody's going to be giving us presents."

Tessa was crestfallen. "Yeah. I guess."

"We're lucky to have a roof over our heads this Christmas. So just quit going on about presents already."

Christmas morning, Nadie felt like a little kid.

She was all hyped up and excited and couldn't sleep, no matter how she tried to just stay calm and quiet. Her brain knew what day it was and wasn't going to be fooled.

Since it was a holiday, they didn't have any therapy scheduled. Wake-up came later than usual. Nadie went out to the common room where the tree was and waited for the others to come. She sat for a long time by herself, gazing at the over decorated tree, just enjoying the twinkle of the tiny lights.

A couple of the men had walked by without even looking at the tree, grumbling on their way to breakfast. Then Tessa finally dragged in, her face tired and gloomy.

"Hi, Tonya. Merry Christmas."

She collapsed on the couch next to Nadie, and rubbed her eyes.

"Merry Christmas!" Nadie tried to suppress her excitement.

Tessa blinked and looked at the tree, sighing. She blinked a couple more times, then frowned. She got up and went closer to the tree to squint at one of the little stars hanging from the branches.

"What...? Where did these come from?"

The stars were a tiny, woven pattern Nadie had created during her spare time, hiding them from everyone. A white star on a colored background. All different. Tessa examined one, turning it over to find a name on the back.

"These are... did you make these?"

Tessa moved on to look at the back of one of the other stars and then started to move from one to the next quickly, searching for her own name. She finally found it and took it off of the tree, going back over to Nadie.

"You made these? You made presents for everyone?"

Nadie nodded.

"That is so cool! I can't believe you did that!" Tessa started to wave at the others who were going past for breakfast. "Clark! Mary! You have to come see! Come see what Tonya did!"

Not everyone came, but after a few minutes, there was a small crowd buzzing around the tree to find their stars. Nadie sat back, smiling, pleased that the little gifts had made a difference.

Of course, Christmas was soon followed by New Year's Day, as it always was. As much as Nadie loved Christmas, she hated New Year's. An excuse to get completely plastered, New Year's Eve never turned out well. At the very least, there were hangovers and grumpy housemates to worry about in the morning. Some years there was violence, even a death or two on the reservation. Nadie dreaded it.

When she met with Jeremy, she wasn't expecting him to bring it up. But he did.

"You had a good Christmas?" he suggested with a smile. He was obviously aware of Nadie's gift to the other participants and how well it had gone over.

"Yeah," Nadie agreed. "It was really nice."

"I'm really impressed by your ingenuity and your generosity. There isn't normally any kind of gift exchange around here, and you really made it nice for the others."

She shrugged. "It was just a little gift. They didn't take long to make."

"It was something handmade, and from your heart. It doesn't get much better than that."

Nadie looked away, her face warming at his praise. Jeremy sighed and opened his folder.

"So, let's talk about how to make the new year successful too. What goals do you have for the next year?"

"You mean like New Year's resolutions? I don't have any. I don't do that."

"I don't mean like weight loss or going to the gym or anything like that. I mean... what do you want to do with your life? What things do you want to accomplish over the next year? This isn't about a habit you start on January first and abandon before February. This is about your life."

"I don't know. Get out of here, I guess."

Jeremy cleared his throat. "Yes, you'll be out of here. You will have put in your time so you won't have to worry about a criminal record. But what then? Do you leave here a better person? A healthier person? Or do you go right back to drinking and drugs?"

"I don't need to drink. I'll be fine."

"I don't think you're going to be fine if you won't even admit you have a problem," Jeremy pushed back.

"I have a lot of problems. Drinking isn't one of them. I'm not an alcoholic."

She didn't know how many times she had to repeat herself before he started to believe her. He probably never would. As far as he was concerned, everyone who came into the program was an addict of some sort. It didn't matter how much or how little they drank. Nadie had seen alcoholics. She wasn't one of them.

"Drinking has never caused you any problems?" Jeremy said. "No problems of any kind?"

"No."

"Or drugs."

"A headache, that's all. I don't take drugs."

"You have."

"A friend gave them to me and I didn't know. Just like with Charlotte. I didn't ask her for anything, she just gave them to me. And I didn't take any. I knew better."

Jeremy sat back in his seat and looked at her for a long time without saying anything.

"You're obfuscating. You have taken drugs. With full knowledge and intention."

Nadie looked away and didn't admit it. He didn't understand what it was like. She wasn't an addict just because she occasionally took a pill to help her get through the day.

"Let's circle back. What are your goals for the next year?"

Nadie didn't move or speak.

"You have a lot of things in your life that need to be worked out. A home. Work or school, probably both. Reconciling with your family. Dealing with any substance abuse issues you may have." He held up his hands to fend off any protest. "I'm just making suggestions. So what are your thoughts? You need to move forward. If you just let yourself stagnate, things are going to end up worse than they are now."

"I don't set New Year's resolutions," Nadie said firmly.

"I told you it doesn't have to be a New Year's resolution. It can be something you start working on in the spring. Or trying to get permanent housing before winter next year. Reconnecting with your family on your birthday. Or Mother's Day or Father's Day. I don't care about the timing. But you need to have a plan. You can't get out of here and just fall back into the same habits and into the same company as you were before you got here. You know where that will end up. And next time you won't end up here. You'll end up in prison. Or worse."

"Or worse?" Nadie echoed, her eyebrows crinkling as she thought about that.

"There are worse things than prison. You could end up turning tricks. Or dead."

Or even worse, she could end up back on the reservation.

CHAPTER TWENTY-SEVEN

The nights didn't seem to get any easier. Nadie had thought they would, in time. She'd get used to the noises of the building and to people coming and going. And then she'd be able to sleep. Just like when she was at home. She would go to bed at night and sleep and wake up in the morning. But her body seemed to have forgotten the rhythm. At night, she lay awake staring into the blackness, waiting for sleep to come. During the day she was tired, walking around in a daze, falling asleep during group or during presentations they were supposed to attend to learn about addictions. She just couldn't seem to get her body to work anymore.

Talking about the reservation and thinking about Luyu during the day made things worse. She needed to guard herself better and not think about those things. But when the night came, her heart ached for the home she had grown up in and for her little cousin who would never return. So many of her family and friends were gone now. Either run away to the city and to the white man's world, or dead. She envied them. It seemed so simple for them to leave or to die. Accidents, fights, suicides, illnesses. Death was rampant. But there Nadie was, lying in bed and thinking of how they had escaped the pain and left her to swim in it.

The bed was so uncomfortable. Sleeping on the ground outside was more comfortable than the broken-down bed. Frustrated, Nadie got up and threw the mattress off of the base and onto the floor. She lay back down on it. The floor was a definite improvement. Nadie ran her fingers along the bottom of the bed platform, unable to see it clearly, but picturing it in her mind with the information she got from her fingers. Thin metal straps, criss-crossing each other, leaving open squares in between. The distances between the straps seemed irregular. Perhaps some of them were missing. Broken after many years of wear. Some of the residents of the center were probably a lot bigger and heavier than Nadie and the supports had broken over time.

They were so thin and worn, they were almost knife-sharp. Nadie's finger slipped and she jolted at the pain. She'd cut herself. Probably no deeper than a paper cut, but it had startled her and stung like the dickens. Nadie put her finger in her mouth and sucked on it, tasting blood.

After the bleeding had stopped and her finger had stopped throbbing, Nadie fell into a deep sleep.

"Tonya. Tonya, wake up!"

Nadie awoke groggily as someone kicked at her mattress and shook her leg. The mattress took up the entire floor so no one could come in without stepping on it. Nadie rubbed her eyes and tried to focus on the man disrupting her sleep. It was Owen, one of the counselors, not Jeremy as she had initially thought, stupid with sleep.

The door was open and there were people bustling around in the hallway, so Nadie figured it must be daytime, in spite of her body thinking it was still the middle of the night. She must have slept through the wake-up bell.

"Okay." She cleared her throat. "I'm awake."

"What are you doing with your mattress on the floor?" Owen asked crankily. "It's a fire hazard. You can't have it down there."

"A fire hazard? How is it a fire hazard? I don't have any matches or cigarettes. It's not going to catch fire because it's on the floor."

"It blocks the way and would keep people from getting to you if there was a fire," Owen pointed out. "Come on." He kicked her leg instead of kicking the mattress this time. "Get up and put it back on the bed! Do you think I'm joking?"

Nadie drew her legs away from him, eyeing him warily. She got up as quickly as her tired body would allow and, wedged into the corner of the room, levered the mattress up and put it back on the bed frame where it belonged. She headed toward the door to shower and get ready.

"Happy?" she sneered at Owen.

She was irritated at being awakened from a sound sleep, but she shouldn't have mouthed off to him. His hand came up like lightning and he slapped her across the face. Nadie grabbed her burning cheek and stared at him. He shoved her, making her fall back into the wall.

"I'm happy now," Owen snapped. He watched to see if she was going to cause him any further trouble. "You'd better shape up, miss. You don't want to deal with me."

Nadie said nothing, staying where she was and waiting for him to leave. He continued to glare at her, then backed out of the doorway and left. Nadie took a few deep breaths and went to get a shower before breakfast was brought around.

❧

The next night, Nadie didn't wait long to move her mattress onto the floor so she would be able to sleep better. But just like every other night she had spent at the rehab center, she tossed and turned, unable to find sleep. She rubbed her eyes, holding back tears of frustration. It wasn't fair she had to go through all of the tedious therapy and over-programing during the day and still couldn't sleep at night.

She pulled the blankets to her. The room was chilly at night. She hated the scratchiness of the warm blanket and the smoothness of the sheets. She longed for the blanket she had made for Luyu. She'd be able to sleep if she had that.

Nadie pulled the blankets back off, banging into the bed frame beside her and letting out a groan. She wasn't an alcoholic, but a drink would certainly help her to be able to sleep. Or if they could give her a sleeping pill. Anything that might help. It was stupid that all kinds of pills were banned. They should be allowed if you really needed them. They could dispense medications so no one could abuse them.

If she could just get to sleep.

Nadie explored the underside of the bed with her fingers. They should fix the broken straps. In some places, there were obviously not just one, but several straps missing. She could put her whole arm through some of the holes. No wonder the bed felt so uncomfortable.

She should have known better than to let her arm touch the remaining metal straps as she demonstrated to herself just how big the holes were. Pain flared, making her jerk away and bang against the opposite side, ending up with cuts on both the front and the back of her forearm. Nadie carefully removed her arm from the hole. She rubbed the surface cuts, drawing her breath in between her teeth in a whistle. It was amazing how much a shallow cut could burn.

Gradually, the pain and restlessness was replaced by a new calm, a feeling of well-being. Rubbing her hand over the cuts didn't produce the same flare of pain, but a sort of warmth and comfort. Nadie hummed a lullaby she used to sing to Luyu, letting the feeling of calm carry her closer to sleep.

❧

Jeremy opened Nadie's file, getting thicker all the time, and paged through it.

"You're attending your group sessions, but not really participating in them," he observed.

"I participate."

"The point of group is to make connections with the others, to share your feelings and your journey. You can get help and give others help."

"I helped Tessa. And she sits with me every group session."

"And have you talked with her about your issues?"

"I don't have any issues." Nadie was tired and crabby, frustrated with the tedium day after day. "Look, you know why I'm here. Because a friend gave me two pills when the police were making a drug trafficking bust. I'm here to keep that off my record and not have to go to jail. But I'm not an addict. I'm not an alcoholic. I didn't even take the pills, I just put them in my pocket because she wouldn't take them back."

"Why don't you tell me about the first time you had alcohol?"

"I'm not an alcoholic."

He studied her. "Are you going to tell me you lived on a reservation and never saw alcohol?"

"Of course I saw alcohol."

"And you never tasted it?"

She didn't like the way he was trying to trap her. "I tasted it, but I'm not an alcoholic."

"Sometimes parents put alcohol in baby's bottles to help them sleep better."

Nadie shifted uncomfortably, remembering how strongly she'd been craving alcohol the night before when she couldn't sleep.

"I wouldn't know anything about that," she pointed out.

"You might have seen it done with other children. That would give you an idea."

They had done a lot of things to try to get Luyu to sleep. None of them had worked. The little girl just kept going until she fell asleep where she played, only to wake up again a couple of hours later, ready to go again.

"I wouldn't know," she repeated.

"Tell me about the first time you tasted it."

Nadie shook her head. "I don't know. I don't remember."

"Tell me about the earliest time you can remember."

Nadie closed her eyes briefly, searching her memories. For being a dry reservation, there had been an incredible amount of alcohol around. It was ubiquitous. Everyone had a batch of home-brew fermenting somewhere. Or a bottle of it from a friend. It was kept out of sight but was not hard to find when you were looking for it.

"I don't know. I remember... sneaking it at a friend's house. On a dare. Kids brought it to camp-outs. Floating down the river on a raft."

"So how old were you?"

"Nine, ten maybe. The earliest I can remember."

"So you've taken it on a dare and to pass time with your friends. What about drinking alone?"

"No... I never really did that."

He didn't say anything. Jeremy was almost as good as the human lie detector.

"Maybe a few times. But I don't really like to drink alone."

"Have you ever had so much to drink that you couldn't remember what had happened later?"

"Maybe, yeah." Nadie knew very well that the answer was yes. But she didn't like the way he was backing her into a corner. "But I have a pretty low tolerance. It affects me more than other people."

"Does it, or is that something you tell yourself to excuse any blackouts or other issues?"

She glared at him. "I'm not a liar."

"Sometimes we lie to ourselves so much that we think it is true."

"Can we talk about something else?"

"No. We're here to talk about your addiction. It's time you faced it head-on."

Nadie pressed her lips tightly together, resisting the urge to tell him yet again that she didn't have any addiction. He hadn't listened to her up until then. He wasn't going to believe it now.

"Have any of your friends ever told you that you drink too much?"

Nadie shook her head. "They drink more than I do," she said self-righteously. "They're always trying to get me to drink with them."

"Do they know you drink alone?"

Nadie shrugged. Jeremy tipped his chair back, considering her.

"Not all alcoholics drink constantly. Or even every day. You can have an alcohol problem and only drink on weekends. Or when you get stressed. It isn't how often you drink. It's why you drink, how it affects you, and how much you drink at a time."

Nadie hadn't ever heard that before. She frowned, thinking about it. She still didn't think she was a problem drinker. You could find problems with anyone's habits if you looked hard enough.

Nadie hadn't been scheduled to see Jeremy, so she was confused when Clarice, one of the grumpy aides, had informed her she had to go see him. Not only that, but Clarice had escorted Nadie to the meeting room he had been appointed and made sure she went in. Nadie had a heavy lump in her stomach, wondering what was going on.

Jeremy waited while she sat down. He looked at her for a minute without saying anything. He leaned forward. "Have you ever heard of intergenerational trauma?"

Nadie processed the question, trying to work her way through the words. She shook her head. "No."

And why was he asking?

"How about a soul wound?"

"Yeah, I've heard that." Nadie reached back into her memories to try to make sense of it. Grandfather had said Beth had a soul wound and that was why she had to go away to hospital sometimes. Nadie had heard it used for others in the band as well, from time to time. The medicine woman tried to help with herbs, and burning sweetgrass and cedar. Spending time in a sweat lodge or having a talking circle.

"Grandfather says the soul wound comes from residential schools," Nadie said. "But sometimes people who didn't go to residential school still get it too. But it comes from the schools." She frowned and shook her head. "I didn't really think it was a real thing. A sickness from the schools wouldn't spread to your children and grandchildren."

Jeremy nodded. He looked down at his papers, but Nadie could see he wasn't reading them, just staring. "That's where 'intergenerational' comes in. Our peoples were aware of it long before the white man and we called it the soul wound. Basically... what happened to our ancestors can hurt us. When the original people were killed and raped by the white explorers and the white government; when they gave the bands smallpox-infected blankets to wipe them out; when they put the children in residential schools and wouldn't let them speak their own language or worship their own gods and beat and starved and molested them; it caused a wounding in our peoples that has not been healed. Each generation still bears its mark."

Nadie had never heard him talk about the Indigenous peoples as if he were one of them before. She listened, spellbound.

"The scientists and behaviorists did not believe the soul wound existed until they started to see it in the children of Holocaust survivors. The children of the concentration camp victims showed signs of PTSD, even though they had been born after the war was over. They called it secondary traumatization. Then it also appeared in the grandchildren, so they called it intergenerational trauma."

"And that's what they have? Our brothers and sisters? They are sick because of what happened a hundred years ago?"

"And more than a hundred," Jeremy agreed. "Our grandfathers' grandfathers were never healed, and their wound was passed on to their children. One generation after another. And each generation had their own traumas too. The restrictions on reservations, new drugs, polluted lands and water, poverty… Is it any wonder our children are so hurt?"

Nadie sat back in her seat, shaking her head. It made sense to her. Just like when their school teachers had taught them about the history of their people or Grandfather told her their tribal stories and she felt the hurt that her people have suffered. It was like it had happened to her. She had experienced it. It wasn't a story to her, it was a memory deep within her soul. A wound so deep it was carried by generations upon generations of Nehiyaw.

"Why didn't anyone ever tell me this before?"

"Not a lot of people understand it. Your Grandfather tried to explain it to you."

"Yes… but I don't think he understood it either."

"It's hard to talk about it." He looked up from his papers, but he didn't look at Nadie's face. He looked up toward the ceiling. "It's hard for me to talk about it to you right now. A lot of people don't believe in it, even when you call it intergenerational trauma instead of a soul wound. I don't… I don't use a lot of my Indigenous background and knowledge in my work here. I use the methods they taught me in university. White man's methods. Sometimes they work for a while. But for a permanent solution… for real healing… I don't think those methods will work."

"For me, you mean?"

"For you. I think we both know that. Talking about what addiction is and how it is harmful to you doesn't heal your wound. It doesn't address the real problem. That started before you ever had your first drink."

Nadie nodded. Thinking about the wounds of the others in the band, her brain was running a catalog of the damage among her friends and family. Beth and Mouse. Grandfather. Nicole. Luyu. Poor little Luyu, the innocent victim of alcohol. Of the soul wound that led them all to numb their pain with booze.

"Show me your arms," Jeremy said.

"What?" Nadie focused in on him. All in a rush, she realized why she had been brought to see her counselor when she wasn't scheduled to. Why he was talking about the soul wound and how Nadie needed to heal.

"Please push up your sleeves and show me your arms."

Nadie swallowed. He waited.

"I will be forced to have you admitted to the hospital and examined there if I can't determine the extent of your injuries on my own."

Nadie's eyes prickled and her face was hot. Gulping back a sob, she gently pushed up her long sleeves and bared her forearms. Jeremy took one hand and examined the shallow cuts made at intervals around her forearm. They were scabbed over and she was sure he could tell they were not serious. No worse than paper cuts. There was certainly no need for a hospital visit. He released her hand and held onto her other one, studying the cuts on the other arm.

Jeremy let go and sat back again. "Is this the first time you've cut? Or has this happened before?"

"I used to cut when I was younger. But I stopped."

"Good for you. But now it's reared its head again."

Nadie nodded and waited for him to ask all of the logical questions. Why did you start again? What new stress is triggering you? Don't you want to stop?

But he said none of that. He seemed to be struggling with how to proceed.

"If you have intergenerational trauma—a soul wound—then that is what we need to treat. No matter what coping method you are using; drugs, alcohol, cutting..."

"So... how do you treat a soul wound? I don't need to go to the hospital..."

"No. We start with naming. Naming your sickness, and naming you."

"Like a naming ceremony for a baby?"

"Yes." He met her eyes. "It's a powerful medicine."

"You're not a medicine man."

"Of a sort, I am. I've studied under a medicine woman, and at university, and on my own. I bring the medicine from both cultures."

"You can't mix white man's medicine with tribal medicine."

"Actually, you can. Everything in the world is One. There is no white man's medicine and tribal medicine. There is only medicine. It all comes from the Great Spirit. And the Great Spirit gives us an invitation to use it to heal each other."

Nadie recognized the truth of the statement and didn't argue it further. She wasn't sure about the Great Spirit, but she was more comfortable with her Nehiyaw traditions than the white man's treatments.

"We need to make a gift to the spirits," she prompted Jeremy, as he seemed to be stymied with how to begin the naming ceremony.

He took a deep breath. "Tobacco, usually," he ventured.

Nadie nodded. He looked around as if someone else might have come into the room and be watching without him being aware.

"This could get me in quite a bit of trouble."

He got up and walked to the corner of the room, where he nudged the security camera around so it was no longer pointed at them. He opened up the window a couple of inches and pulled a few items out of his pocket before sitting back down. Nadie saw several plastic baggies with small amounts of herbs in them. He had a little disposable tinfoil ashtray and a lighter.

Jeremy pinched a few leaves of tobacco out of one bag and, holding it over the ashtray, used his lighter to burn it. There wasn't very much and he dropped it into the tray before it could burn his fingers. The tobacco went out quickly but made a good amount of smoke as it burned up. Jeremy held the tray up in offering, and then smudged Nadie, waving the smoke toward her.

Nadie looked at Jeremy for the next step. He was the medicine man.

"We offer a gift for the blessing of a name," Jeremy said, fumbling for the appropriate words. "First, to name the spirit of the sickness of this sister. We name it a soul wound, passed down from one generation to the next since the time of her grandfather's grandfather. And second, to name our sister, that the spirits will know her and she will be strong."

He looked at Nadie. She licked her dry lips. She tried to say 'Tonya Nehiyaw,' but the words stuck in her throat. Jeremy shook his head.

"Your real name."

How had he known? Nadie nodded slightly and took a breath. "Nadie Laplante. My name is Nadie Laplante."

"Nadie Laplante is how our sister will be known to the spirits. It is her true name and how she identifies herself to her spirit guide."

He lowered the little ash tray. After a moment of consideration, he put it on the windowsill by the open window, to allow the smoke an opportunity to clear. He looked at Nadie.

She felt at peace for the first time in a long time. She wasn't Tonya. She could stop being someone she wasn't. She was Nadie Laplante. It was a strong name and it was hers. And she knew the name of the pain deep inside her. So she could begin to heal instead of just carrying the hurt, or trying to bury it.

She felt drained. Ready to sleep for a week or two.

"Okay?" Jeremy asked.

Nadie nodded. "Yes. It's good medicine."

"Good. We'll continue, but not today. It will take time. Longer than you will have here. But we can start, and we'll try to find someone who can help you continue your journey when you are released."

They both stood up.

"I still want you to participate in the other therapies. Try to think of the group therapy as a talking circle. Take your turn. And Poppy said you are doing well in art therapy."

"That's the only part I like." Nadie couldn't hold back a little smile. "I am doing a weaving."

"Good. Take time to meditate and pray. Think about how we can start to heal your ancestors."

Nadie stopped with her hand on the doorknob. "How do I heal my ancestors? They're dead. Except for Grandfather. And Nicole."

"Their spirits are not dead. If your wound comes from them, then you can only heal yourself by first healing them."

Nadie puzzled over that. "Okay. I'll see you tomorrow, then."

"Goodbye, Nadie."

Nadie was a jumble of emotions as she returned to her room for quiet meditation time. She felt curiously light and energized, while at the same time confused, saddened, and exhausted. When she got to her little cell, she saw that they had removed the bed frame, leaving her only the mattress on the floor in its place. That was fine with her. The floor was more comfortable, more traditional, and they had removed the temptation to cut herself. For now. She knew the impulse would return; but if she could stay away from any temptingly sharp objects and focus on the medicine, she hoped to be able to avoid any further cutting. She had gotten over it once before; though, if she were to acknowledge the truth, part of the reason she had been able to give up cutting was that she had found that alcohol worked better.

Owen walked by and stopped to look at her. "Bed's gone, and we'd better not find any more blood on your sheets," he warned.

So he was the one who had reported her. She had wondered whether someone had seen her cuts in the shower, though she had taken great pains to avoid anyone getting close to her. But it had been blood on the sheets that had given her away.

"Stupid kid," Owen growled.

He seemed to be waiting for her to react, but Nadie didn't have the energy. She'd rather he was calling her a stupid kid than a stupid Indian.

"If there's one addiction I don't understand, it's cutting. That and anorexia. I could never give up eating."

He patted his belly and laughed, then walked away.

Nadie sat down on her mattress and crossed her legs, closing her eyes to think.

CHAPTER TWENTY-EIGHT

*N*adie greeted Jeremy nervously. He called her Nadie, as he always did now, honoring her real name and her naming ceremony.

"Did they say I could do it?" she asked.

Jeremy nodded, his lips curving up slightly in the corners. "It took some talking, I'll tell you. But in the end, they figured if you were supervised and it would get you further along in your healing, it would be worth a try."

She thought it would be rude to ask him if he'd brought everything she needed for the honoring the dead ceremony. So she waited.

"We're supposed to use the main auditorium. Better ventilation, I guess."

Nadie followed Jeremy's lead down to the small auditorium on the first floor. Everything was lain out waiting for her. She noted that the little baggies of sacred plants were lain out in the proper order of the medicine wheel. First she would cleanse the room by burning the sage, on the west quadrant of the medicine wheel. She would smudge both herself and Jeremy with the smoke. Then the cedar, on the north, to invoke the protection of the spirits. Then the sweetgrass braided and lying in the south to invite the spirits. Then she would pray to them, thanking them for all things.

"I'm nervous," she told Jeremy. "I've never done this by myself before."

"I'm here to help you if you need it. But this is your ceremony."

Nadie burned the first three plants and said her prayer of thanks. She looked at Jeremy, and he nodded, encouraging her to go on.

"I am here to honor my ancestors," Nadie told the spirits. "I am here to honor them for the suffering they endured and to heal the wounds to their souls."

She paused again while she gathered her thoughts. Then she began, naming all of the ancestors she could remember and acknowledging the others by their relationships to her. She told what she could remember of them from the stories Grandfather told, and what she had learned in her lessons at school. She praised them for their bravery and goodness, and all of the good traits they had passed down to her. She encouraged them to progress in their journeys and to be happy.

She had almost forgotten Jeremy was there. He had stayed very still and quiet, letting her commune with the spirits.

Nadie lit the tobacco from the east quadrant and held it out in offering to each of the four corners of the room. She prayed again, asking the spirits to guide her ancestors through the spirit world. Then she sang, a low mourning chant to start with, and then eventually a lighter song, a lullaby. She wasn't sure it was the right thing to do, but it felt right. She thought about Luyu and sent up an extra prayer for her.

She wasn't happy, but she felt like she could continue on her journey.

Nadie worked on her weaving, carefully working back and forth across the warp yarn. It was good meditation and she really needed the quiet, contemplative time. Discussions in group therapy had turned very heated. Although Nadie did her best to think of it as a talking circle, they didn't follow the rules of a circle and she always left feeling more anxious and disrupted than she had been in the beginning.

Nadie went over to the bins to choose the color for the central band of the pattern. She had previously picked out a deep blue, but every time she thought about working it in, she felt like it wasn't right.

Going through the bins, she came across a red yarn almost identical in color to the thread she had used for the background field of Luyu's blanket. She stopped, staring at it. It was eerie how similar in color it was.

"Oh, that's a beautiful color," Poppy said, looking over Nadie's shoulder.

Nadie startled slightly and turned to look at Poppy. Without thinking, her fingers had closed over the ball of yarn and she turned with it in her hands.

"I used this color before. For my cousin's blanket."

"I love it. It's so warm and rich. I think it's a great choice for your piece."

"I wasn't going to…" Nadie trailed off and walked back to the table where she had left the cardboard loom. "Do you think so? It's not too bright?"

"No. It's just right."

Nadie nodded, holding the yarn up to the weaving. It did fit. And unlike the blue, which she couldn't bring herself to start, her fingers itched to work the red into her pattern.

Bryson looked around the circle to make sure everyone was settled, looking each of them in the eye. He waited for their casual chatter to subside before beginning.

"Thanks for coming, everyone. We have a new admittee today; this is Celia. I'll get everyone to introduce themselves…"

They went quickly around the circle, giving their names, maybe smiling at the new patient and maybe not. The woman was older than Nadie, but she looked small and childlike, overwhelmed by all of the newness. Nadie remembered when she had arrived. Everyone had rattled off their names and she couldn't remember one. Now she knew everyone; not just their names, but the intimate details of all of their lives.

"Great. Let's get started. Does anyone have an experience they would like to share?"

He looked around. Nadie gave him a little nod. His eyebrows went up. "Excellent. Tonya is going to be leaving in a few days. We're glad to hear from her before that."

Nadie looked at a tile on the floor a few feet in front of her, not looking at any of the other patients.

"My name is Nadie." A murmur went around the circle. "I've been going by Tonya while I've been here, but my real name is Nadie. That's who I am and I'm not pretending to be someone else any longer."

She looked at Celia, so new and uncertain, perched on her chair like she would take flight if she were startled.

"I have… a problem. When I don't want to deal with life and with everything my people have gone through, I hide." She licked her lips and swallowed hard. "I hide behind drugs or alcohol or whatever it takes to numb the pain. I don't know if I'm an addict or not… but I have a problem."

She ventured a glance at the circle. They were all quiet, listening. There were a few nods of agreement or encouragement. No one interrupted or mocked her.

"I ran away from my life because it got to be too much for me. And because I was a coward. I should have stayed and tried harder, but I was just… so tired and fed up with it all. It didn't seem like anything would ever go right for me again."

She was silent and everyone waited to see whether she was done or would continue on. Nadie rubbed her forehead, the muscles so tight she was getting a headache.

"My baby cousin, my little sister I took care of… she drowned in a bucket of mash. I found her body… but I couldn't do anything for her. I didn't know how to go on. I didn't think I could." Nadie glanced at Bryson, but he made no attempt to cut her time short. His expression was drawn and sad. As if he'd been there to see Nadie pull Luyu out of the bucket. "I thought I might die on the river. And that would have been okay with me. In a way, I guess I did. Because the woman who stole all my things and my raft died. They buried her under my name and I haven't been Nadie since then."

"But now you are," Bryson said quietly.

Nadie nodded. "Being here has helped. I didn't think it would. But it has."

"I know it hasn't been easy for you," Bryson said. "But you've come a long way. I hope that will continue after you are gone."

Nadie nodded. "Yeah. Thanks."

૭ૐ

Tessa's release was before Nadie's. Nadie entered the room. Tessa had changed into street clothes and was packing away her belongings.

"Oh, hey," Tessa smiled and brushed her hair out of her face. "I guess this is it, huh? Time to say goodbye and hit the trail."

Nadie nodded. "You'll be okay?"

"I'll do my best. I've got all the numbers for the outpatient programs. Time to try sober living on the outside."

"Yeah."

"I'm sort of scared."

"I am too. I'll be out in a couple more days."

"Maybe we can get together, have coffee."

"Maybe. I brought this for you…" Nadie held out her weaving. It had turned out well; beautiful rich colors, an attractive pattern, a tight, even weave.

"For me?" Tessa's jaw dropped. "Really? But you spent so much time on it! Don't you want to keep it, or give it to someone else?"

"I can make another one. I don't know what you want to use it for. You can hang it on the wall, or you can use it as a hot pad for pots, or to keep a dish warm."

"It's lovely. I can't wait to get home and find a place for it." She gave Nadie an impulsive hug. "Thank you so much, Tonya—Nadie. Good luck to you, too."

"Thanks." Nadie returned the hug and wished she could just sneak away with Tessa and not have to wait the final couple of days. She didn't want to say goodbye to everyone and go through all of the final steps. She just wanted to go home without any further fanfare.

❧

Then it seemed like no time before she was getting to leave herself and felt the same pangs of fear Tessa had about leaving the protected environment and trying to make it on her own on the outside. She would again be exposed to drugs and alcohol and all of the other temptations the real world had to offer.

She would never have predicted in the initial days that she would have the hardest time saying goodbye to Jeremy. He wasn't allowed to hug her, but he shook her hand warmly, holding onto it longer and looking her in the eye.

"You keep working on healing," he encouraged. "You've made a good start, but it isn't done. Hundreds of years of damage can't be wiped away in a few days or weeks."

Nadie nodded. There was a lump in her throat and her eyes got hot. Jeremy released her hand and handed her a personalized list of resources she could access after she left. He shook his head at the list, scowling in dissatisfaction.

"More than these, you'll need to find a mentor or guide. A medicine woman, maybe. Someone who can help you with tribal medicine. There isn't anyone in our database…"

"Maybe you should start adding them to your list," Nadie suggested. "I'm not going to be the only Indian who needs a spiritual guide."

He nodded. "Yes… Well… I want to thank you, Nadie. You've helped me work on healing myself too." He smiled tentatively. "If you hadn't been so stubborn, I wouldn't have looked very closely at intergenerational trauma. Even though I was aware of it, I never thought it was so… relevant. That we needed to start working on healing our ancestors." He shrugged, embarrassed.

"Maybe your directors will let others use sacred plants and ceremonies now too."

"I think they will." Jeremy agreed. "We can't just keep ignoring what's bringing so many Indigenous peoples through our doors."

CHAPTER TWENTY-NINE

Nadie hesitated on the doorstep of the shelter. She was unsure whether she should knock like she was an outsider, or to just go in like she was a resident. She didn't know what she was anymore. She eventually decided to go in. Rolf barked his head off and ran up to her. Nadie let him smell her fingers, then scratched his ears. She found Cammy in her office.

"Tonya," Cammy said, not getting up to greet her. "Boy, has it been a month already? You're looking a lot better."

Nadie nodded. "Yeah… I'm feeling a lot better too…"

"Good for you. Glad to hear it. So, what can I do for you?"

"I wondered… if I could still stay here."

Cammy looked toward the door and then back at Nadie. "I told you the first day; no drugs or you're out."

"But…" Nadie looked for an argument. "I'm clean and sober now."

"We don't do three strikes. Zero tolerance."

"Oh. Okay…" There was a lump in Nadie's throat. She hadn't expected to be barred from going back to the shelter. She was back where she had started, with no home, trying to find someone to take her in.

"Your backpack is in the front closet. You can try the Step Up

Center. Or see if there's any space at other youth shelters. There might be some emergency spaces so you have somewhere to sleep. But things fill up when it gets cold and we've had minus forty temperatures while you were gone."

Nadie nodded. "Yeah. Okay."

"Sorry, Tonya. Take care of yourself." Cammy's voice held a tone of dismissal. She turned away.

"It's Nadie."

"What?" Cammy looked back at her, frowning.

"My name. It's not Tonya. It's Nadie."

Cammy's eyebrow lifted. "Okay… then goodbye, Nadie."

Nadie left the shelter to try to find a bed somewhere else.

It was a few days before Nadie ran into Charlotte. It was unexpected. She hadn't been looking for Charlotte, working under the assumption she was in jail. Nadie had filled her plate with breakfast at the Step Up Center and was looking around for a seat when she heard a squeal.

"Tonya!"

Nadie turned and saw Charlotte rushing toward her.

"Tonya, babe, how are you?" she demanded, giving Nadie an exuberant hug.

Nadie submitted to the hug for a second, then nudged Charlotte back, frowning. "What are you doing here? I thought you were in jail."

Charlotte laughed. "Never for more than a day! I'm 'awaiting trial,' but they don't keep you in the pokey the whole time. It's overcrowded enough already. And if you can get the trial delayed enough times, you never have to worry about getting convicted." She linked arms with Nadie and led her toward a table. "If things get too hot, I'll move on; take a different name and disappear. Maybe I'll go to Winnipeg!"

"Yeah… I wouldn't recommend it."

"So tell me how you're doing! You look good."

"I'm okay… other than needing a bed."

"I could help you with that," Charlotte suggested, giving Nadie a nudge and a wink.

They sat down at a table. Nadie looked around uncomfortably. Charlotte seemed completely at home with Nadie, but the feeling wasn't mutual.

Charlotte frowned at Nadie, sensing her reserve. "What's wrong?"

Nadie couldn't believe she had to tell Charlotte. "You got me arrested."

"I got you arrested? You got yourself arrested, girl. I don't take responsibility for that."

"You gave me those pills and that's what I got arrested for."

"A couple pills?" Charlotte scoffed. "It would never have held. They had surveillance cameras on everything; they knew you didn't pay for them. No one has time to prosecute for simple possession of two pills."

"They did arrest me. And they charged me with trafficking."

Charlotte dug into her eggs. "Would never have stuck," she declared. "You let them talk you into rehab." She chewed, studying Nadie. "And you're not even a junkie."

Nadie poked at her meal. She knew she had to eat and had become accustomed to having at least a small breakfast each day at rehab. But she felt anxious sitting with Charlotte, her stomach tightening into a big knot. Charlotte was probably right; they would never have convicted her of trafficking. But that didn't excuse Charlotte taking Nadie along for a drug deal or giving her drugs when she said no.

"You're still fresh from rehab," Charlotte said tolerantly. "It will take you a few days to acclimatize to the real world again. They brainwash you in those places."

They both ate in silence for a few minutes, thinking their own thoughts. Nadie thought about how like Nicole Charlotte was. How long was it going to take Charlotte to figure out she needed to turn her life around? She pretended to be happy all the time, but Nadie didn't believe it. Like Nicole, Charlotte was already scarred by her choices.

"Have you ever heard of a soul wound?"

Charlotte looked at her and made a wry face. "Don't try talking Cree medicine to me. I'm happy just the way I am. Any plants I smoke are going to be recreational."

"You would feel better if you made an offering to the spirits."

"Why don't you do it for me?" Charlotte suggested. "I'm not interested."

"But you believe your Ojibwe traditions, don't you?"

"Just the ones that are convenient for me."

Nadie ate, thinking about that.

"We gonna go out and celebrate your release?" Charlotte asked as she finished off her breakfast. Nadie's plate was still mostly full. She just couldn't choke the food down.

Nadie laid down her fork. "No. Thanks. I think I'd better stay away from partying…"

"Tonya Stick in the Mud. You're not seriously going to let this little thing put a damper on our fun, are you?"

"I want to stay sober. Deal with my problems another way."

"They've got you so brainwashed. There's no reason you can't have a little drink now and then. You've been away for a month, we gotta get together."

Nadie shook her head. "We're together now. We don't need to party to see each other."

Charlotte swore. "I don't need you telling me how I can or can't have fun. I've got nobody to tie me down and tell me what I gotta do. That's the way it's gonna stay."

Nadie shrugged.

Charlotte's eyes were dark and full of fury. "Why don't you just go back to the rez?"

Nadie didn't argue. Maybe she would go back to the reservation sometime. Not right away; it was too cold for travel. If she hitched, she might end up frozen like a statue next to the road until spring. But Nadie had discovered she'd never really left the reservation behind. She'd taken it all along with her. All that heavy baggage.

"You're stupid," Charlotte sneered. "You'll see. I bet you're back to abusing within two weeks."

"And you'll still be being abused."

Charlotte's mouth dropped open. "What? Nobody abuses me. I take care of myself. No one hurts me."

"Okay." Nadie got up to leave.

Charlotte stood up too. "What does that mean?" she demanded.

"It means okay. I guess I'll see you around," Nadie said. She turned away from Charlotte and walked away.

CHAPTER THIRTY

*L*iving on the street during Calgary winter wasn't easy. But it was better than Winnipeg. The chinook winds blew through every few weeks, eating up all of the snow and making Nadie think spring was coming. But then it would snow again. It didn't get below minus thirty once January was past, but it still was too cold to sleep outdoors and she was only able to get emergency beds, nothing permanent.

She diligently attended appointments with counselors, support groups, and job placement specialists, and didn't have too many setbacks. She saw Charlotte now and then and grew familiar with some of the other homeless she ran into repeatedly. Charlotte mostly ignored her, which was fine with Nadie. She got enough name-calling from strangers on the street simply for being Indigenous and homeless. She didn't need any more grief from Charlotte.

She spent a lot of hours at the public library, reading all kinds of books, even Dickens and Shakespeare like Jeremy had suggested. And it was a good place to go when you just needed somewhere quiet and warm. So that was her new hang-out.

Then it was finally spring. The night time temperatures barely dipped below freezing, and by afternoon, it was often shirt-sleeve weather. There were fewer people at the shelters. There were buds bursting on the trees and a green smell in the air. Nadie found herself craving green space. Mouse and Grandfather would have laughed at her. They were always trying to get her to put down her books and go outside. But now she was ready. She ventured west along the river as far as she could during the day before having to return downtown to the shelter. Eventually, she made the decision not to go back downtown. It was warm enough to sleep out of doors again.

Nadie soaked in the color and smell of the trees and the dirt. The river was high and fast with spring run-off from the mountains. Looking at the mountains, Nadie could see they were still capped with snow. Lots more water for the river. She realized she was walking west, which was the opposite direction from home. But she wasn't going home.

She was drawn to the trees and the river. There were too many people on the pathway; walking, running, biking, and blading. So she left the path and ventured into the trees. She kept going, looking for deeper and darker brush, until she could no longer see or hear anyone else. She listened to the birds and to the wind whispering through the new leaves, reaching out with her heart.

Mouse had said she was good at seeing things. Her naming ceremony and honoring the dead had strengthened her more than any of the other counseling or therapies. Maybe pursuing other spiritual experiences would help her heal further. Her cravings for relief from the pain were something she still battled daily and she wished she could progress far enough on her journey to leave them behind for good.

Mouse had said she should do a vision quest. Normally, it was something she would have asked the Elders for guidance on, but she was far from home and any of the Elders. She hadn't yet found a spiritual guide like Jeremy had recommended. It seemed like medicine men and women were few and far between in the city. She prayed instead for guidance from the spirits. Surrounded by Mother Earth, her heart was close to the spirit plane.

Nadie found a dry log and sat down. She slid her backpack off and rolled her shoulders. Reaching into the side pocket of her pack, Nadie pulled out the few spiritual tools she had been able to gather. A pipe she had found at the Salvation Army thrift store. It wasn't like the pipes the elders had, but it did the job. Pipe tobacco and sage had not been hard for her to beg from others. She didn't need much, just a couple of pinches. Cedar had been a little more difficult until the Step Up Center started mulching their trees with cedar chips. But she hadn't managed to find any source for sweetgrass. Nadie had been tempted to go back to the rehab center to ask Jeremy, but she wanted to be independent and do it on her own. And she didn't want to go back to the rehab center, even to see Jeremy.

Nadie wasn't sure of the proper protocol for a vision quest ceremony, so she burned the sacred plants in the same order and formula as for the ceremony honoring the dead. The smokes mingled in the air so she couldn't differentiate one from the other.

Then she sat, eyes closed, and just listened to the sounds around her. Once or twice, she could hear voices in the distance, but none of them came near. As the temperature started to fall, there was a train whistle and she could hear the rumble of the train wheels going over the tracks. When it was too cold to sit in shirt sleeves any longer, Nadie got out her sleeping bag and lay down. Once Nadie had been inside for a few minutes, she warmed up and was comfortable. They'd be wondering where she was at the Step Up Center. But they had enough other people to worry about; they wouldn't waste much time fussing about her.

When she woke up in the morning, her stomach was rumbling hungrily. She'd become accustomed to eating breakfast every morning and her body complained bitterly about her decision to fast. Nadie sat on the log, still wrapped up in her sleeping bag, and concentrated on her breathing and on the sounds around her. The spirits had a plan for her. A direction she was supposed to go. But she didn't know what it was. She needed to watch and to listen for their guidance.

It was difficult to do nothing but sit or stand and wait. The sun took its journey across the sky more slowly than ever. But she knew she was where she was supposed to be. This was where her heart had led her and she just needed to wait for her vision.

Evening came again, and she didn't sleep as comfortably as the previous night. She could feel the ground through her sleeping bag. She was hungry and thirsty, her lips chapped and peeling. The sleeping bag didn't seem to provide the same heat as it had the previous night. She shivered. Nadie breathed slowly and listened to the night sounds. If she focused, she could hear the river. The trains in the distance sounded mournful. Owls hooted occasionally and dogs or coyotes howled.

The third night, she couldn't sleep at all. Eventually, she got up and wandered down to the river, where she cupped water in her hands and wet her lips and face. She turned and tried to retrace her path but couldn't find the clearing again.

It was amazing how much she could see by the light of the stars and the full moon. She hiked through the trees, hoping the movement would warm her up. Even with the sleeping bag wrapped around her, Nadie couldn't seem to get warm.

An owl swooped down, so close Nadie could feel the wind from its wings. She watched in fascination as the ghostly shape alighted on the branch of a tree. The owl's head turned toward Nadie and it regarded her.

"Ôhô. Owl spirit," Nadie whispered. "Do you have a vision for me?"

Neither of them moved.

Nadie watched the owl closely, listening to the night sounds around them. There was another owl hooting in the distance. Leaves rustled in the wind or with the movement of other small animals. She opened her heart to all of them, waiting for guidance.

The owl bent over and bit at the branch it was standing on. Nadie wasn't sure if it was grooming its beak or had some other purpose. She stood like a statue watching the bird's movements.

There was the snap of a twig, and something fell at Nadie's feet. She bent down to see what it was, feeling where she had heard it land. Her touch was light and tentative, not really wanting to find a dead mouse or fresh owl pellet. But whatever the gift was, she would not refuse it. Her fingers found something dry and round.

Nadie picked up an acorn and studied it in the darkness. It was warm in her hand, radiating heat. She looked back at the owl and bowed her head slightly.

"Ay-hay, ôhô."

The owl took flight and vanished into the night with a whoosh of wings.

Nadie stood there for a long time, pondering on the visitation and the gift she had received. The small nut warmed her chilled hands. As the sky began to brighten and the stars dimmed, she carefully put the acorn into her pocket.

Going back down to the river, she drank until she was full.

Nadie knew what she was supposed to do.

CHAPTER THIRTY-ONE

*H*itchhiking back to Winnipeg had not been hard. But Nadie wasn't planning to stay in Winnipeg. It took longer to find a way to get back to the reservation. There was not a lot of traffic headed that way. Once she got to the town, Nadie wasn't sure what to do next. The only people who went out to the reservation were the Nehiyaw, and occasionally social workers or other government employees. There was no regular traffic.

Nadie sat on a bench in the little Centennial Park and looked at the green shoots poking out of the soil. She closed her eyes and said a little prayer to Mother Earth and the plant and animal spirits. She touched the acorn nestled warmly in her pocket, stroking the smooth surface. When she opened her eyes next, she knew what to do.

She walked to the police station and asked the uniformed woman sitting at the front desk to talk to Mac. The woman looked Nadie over, her eyes twinkling with curiosity.

"Mac is out right now. He may not be back for an hour or two. Would you like to set up a time to see him?"

Nadie looked around the small reception room. It didn't have many chairs, like a doctor's office waiting room, but there were a couple of hard plastic chairs against the wall in case someone needed to sit.

"I will wait here for him."

"He might be a couple of hours," the woman warned again.

"Yes. I will wait."

"Well… okay," she allowed.

Nadie went over to the chairs. She put down her backpack and she put down the heavy sports bag she had kept in a paid locker over the winter to avoid having to carry it with her. She sat and waited. It would probably have made sense to have gone to the library before the police station so she would have something to read while waiting. But she had felt compelled to go to the police station and had followed the urge. Sitting and waiting with nothing to do for a couple of hours was nothing, compared to three days of waiting for her vision.

It didn't take Mac two hours to get back. The policewoman kept looking anxiously at Nadie and had probably sent out several messages to track her boss down and have him return as soon as possible. Mac stepped in the front door and paused for a moment, blinking, for the time it took for his eyes to adjust from the bright sunlight outside to the artificial light inside the building. He looked at Nadie questioningly, but before she could say anything, his mouth dropped open and she knew he had placed her. It had been months, and he had only met her a couple of times, so she was impressed he had recognized her so quickly. She probably looked a lot different from when they had seen each other last. Her journey had taken her a long way.

"You are…" Mac trailed off.

"My name is Nadie Laplante." Nadie announced herself boldly so the spirits would know her. She didn't want there to be any confusion over who she really was. She stood up.

"But you were supposed to be… oh hell!" Mac's voice was filled with what Nadie figured was the realization of all of the trouble this was going to cause him. Burying the wrong person. Or burying the right person in the wrong place, under the wrong name. His whole investigation—the white man valued investigations—had produced the wrong results.

"Uh… yeah. I'm not dead," she confirmed.

"You knew?"

"I saw it in the paper."

"You didn't think to maybe give us a call and let us know the body had been misidentified?"

Nadie looked down at her feet. "I didn't want to be alive. I wanted Nadie to be gone. So I didn't say anything."

Mac looked at his receptionist. He motioned to Nadie to follow him to his office in the back.

"Please pull the Nadie Laplante file," he told the woman.

She nodded, eyebrows raised questioningly. Mac just shook his head in response.

In his office, Nadie again put her bags down and sat in the chair across the desk from Mac's. Where she'd sat while he'd asked her questions about Luyu and the social worker had made her accusations. Mac sat down and studied her grumpily for a moment.

"So, where have you been?" he asked. "And how have you been?"

"I went to Winnipeg and then to Calgary. Now I'm back."

"What made you change your mind? Homesick?"

"I had a vision."

"A vision of something on the reservation?"

"I can't explain it to you. I need to talk to the Elders about it."

"I see. Have you been back to the reservation yet?"

"No. I need to get a ride there."

"And that's why you came here?"

Nadie nodded.

The woman police officer came into Mac's office and put a file down in front of him. He made a motion dismissing her. He was silent for a few minutes as he looked through the contents of the files to refresh his memory of the case. He tipped his big office chair back, making it creak in protest.

"The young woman we found had your possessions with her," he said. "They were identified by your Grandfather."

Nadie felt heartsick for him. First losing Luyu and then losing Nadie, so close together. Looking at her possessions and confirming his granddaughter was dead would have been devastating to him. And the condition of the body… Nadie hoped he hadn't had to look at the body.

"She stole them from me. While I was sleeping."

"And your raft? Your friend told us you had taken your raft when you ran away."

Nadie nodded. "She stole that too. And I guess… she didn't know how to raft safely on the river."

"There's quite a bit of whitewater in the area where the body was found. She must have capsized."

"You have to portage around the whitewater. It wasn't one of those big air-filled rafts that stay up on top of the water."

"Even those won't make it through some of the rapids."

Nadie nodded.

"Do you know anything about her? Name? Where she came from?"

"Her name was Annie. That's what she said, anyway. She was Ojibwe. I don't know what happened, why she was out in the middle of the wilderness, all alone. She'd been there a long time. She didn't know how to get to where people were… until she saw my raft. She knew there were towns downriver."

"I'll see if there's anything that matches her description in missing persons."

Nadie waited. Mac sighed.

"I suppose you would like to see your family."

Nadie nodded. "If you know anyone who's going out that way anytime soon."

"Well, considering I have an accidental death investigation to reopen, I guess I'm going to have to, aren't I?"

Nadie suppressed a smile. She was happy he was going to take her back to the reservation, but she didn't want him to think that she thought a death was funny or that she was mocking him.

Mac gave a visible shudder. "I hope I'm not going to have to disinter the body. How are your people going to feel about a stranger's body in your burial ground? Will they be offended?"

Nadie considered it. "I don't think so... she was buried properly, and she is one of our people. It's not desecration. As long as her family doesn't want her moved..."

"If we ever find her family." Mac levered himself up from his chair and leaned his hands on the table. Looking over his desk, he picked up the investigation file and put on his black cap. He opened his drawer and pulled out an identification card on a lanyard he put around his neck.

Nadie looked at the card. "Native Liaison Officer?" she read aloud. She frowned. "That's new. Isn't a Native Liaison Officer usually... Native?"

Mac nodded and gave her a self-conscious smile. He led the way to his truck and they both got in before Mac spoke. "Whenever a Cree from the reservation leaves to get a college education, and trains to be a police officer, and goes back in his role as a police officer... he's shunned. He's considered a sell-out. Someone who wasn't really Cree inside."

He turned on his engine and put the police pick-up into drive while Nadie thought about that and had to admit to herself that it was true.

"Me, on the other hand, my roots are Polish, not Indian, and if I show an interest in the Native traditions and culture and show respect for the Elders in my investigations and dealings... then I'm not a sell-out, I'm a white man who is showing more respect than the average Joe Schmoe. I'm not ostracized like a Cree cop would be."

"Sort of backward," Nadie observed. "We're supposed to be self-governing, but we won't allow a Nehiyaw to do the job."

Mac nodded.

"It's a little weird they'd rather let me do it, but if that's what it takes… It's better to have a single point of contact."

Nadie watched out the window as they drove down the familiar highway.

Home.

She was going home.

She felt like she had been living on a strange planet, and now was finally coming back to the familiar. She touched the acorn in her pocket, breathing in a conscious rhythm to keep herself calm.

When they drove up the last little stretch to the gate that marked the beginning of the reservation, Nadie found she could barely breathe. This was it. She was home. With all of the happiness and sadness home entailed. But this time, it was a choice.

"To your Grandfather's house first?" Mac asked, glancing aside at her.

"Yes… if you would."

He nodded his agreement and drove over the rutted roads to pull into Grandfather's worn driveway.

Nadie was slow to get out, letting Mac climb out of the truck first. She wiped her sweaty hands on her pants and slowly climbed down.

Melinda had come to the door upon hearing the truck drive up and was watching Mac's approach warily. When her eyes moved to Nadie, she gasped and held onto the door frame.

"Father!" she croaked. "Father!"

The Nose came to the door. Horatio. He held Melinda to keep her on her feet. "Mel? What's wrong?" His eyes turned first to Mac, who was nearly to the door, and then to Nadie, further away. His mouth opened, and he swore. "Nadie?"

Mac got up to the door. The Nose tried to move Mel out of the doorway. "Let's sit back down, Mel."

Melinda refused to move. Nadie moved faster to greet her. She didn't want Melinda fainting in the doorway, and the sooner Nadie greeted her, the sooner she'd sit down.

"Mel. Tân'si. It's me."

"It's really you?" Mel asked as they embraced. She breathed in Nadie's ear. "Tân'si."

Her arms were shaking. When they released each other, Mel allowed herself to be escorted back into the house, where Horatio helped her to sit down on the couch. What had made her so frail? Was she sick? Had the Nose hurt her?

Grandfather came into the room, his feet dragging along the floor. "What's going on?"

None of them said anything. Grandfather looked around the room, frowning. He saw Mel and the Nose. And then Mac in his uniform. And finally, his eyes turned to Nadie.

"Tân'si, Nimosôm."

At first she feared he was going to have a heart attack and die right there on the spot. His eyes widened, he swayed, and his arms went out looking for support. His face took on a paleness like death, and he opened his mouth, gasping loudly. Nadie hurried to him and took him in her arms. "Nimosôm, it's me. It's Nadie. Please, it's okay. Say something!"

He didn't say anything but a burbled laugh, but he clutched at her, pulling her close to himself with much stronger arms than she had anticipated. "Nadie! Oh, Nadie, my baby!"

"I'm not a baby," Nadie protested, squirming in his tight grip. She managed to pull away from him slightly, though he was still holding onto her. "And... I'm not dead. I'm back, Grandfather. I'm sorry I ran away like that."

"Sorry! We thought you were dead!"

"I know. It was wrong of me. I ran away instead of dealing with my problems. But I promise I'll never do that again."

He squeezed her to him again. "You'd better not. It might just kill me next time."

A baby started to wail. Nadie froze and looked around at the faces of the others. "Who—?"

Mel patted her belly. It was not big and round, but Nadie remembered noticing Melinda's weight gain when she and Horatio had first moved into the house. That had been many months ago. Mel moved to get up.

"No, you sit. I'll get it," Nadie offered.

She went to the baby room and looked into the crib. The baby was very small and, judging by her face, only a few days old. Nadie assumed by the band around the baby's head that it was a baby girl. She carefully picked the swaddled infant up, and the baby stopped crying and stared up at her with shiny, very dark brown eyes.

"Tân'si, sister," Nadie whispered to her. "Welcome to the world."

She carried the bundle out to Mel and handed her over. Mel lifted up her shirt to nurse. Nadie looked at Mel's husband.

"She doesn't have your nose," she remarked.

Horatio laughed good-naturedly. "A good thing!"

"What is her name?"

Mel settled the baby nursing and looked up at Nadie. "Where is Joy," she answered.

"Where is Joy," Nadie repeated.

"Joy has been missing from our hearts," Grandfather said. He touched Nadie on the shoulder. "But now it returns."

The news that Nadie had returned spread through the band like wildfire. The band Elders were called together in council and Nadie presented herself to them to tell them about her vision quest and the direction she had received.

To her surprise, there were no reprimands for not being properly prepared for her vision quest or for questing when she was a girl.

"I have never known anyone who has pursued their vision past the point of death and returned to us," Chief Frank said, his eyes on Nadie.

Nadie refrained from pointing out she hadn't actually been dead. She knew he meant it in a spiritual way, the way they perceived it. They all knew she hadn't actually been dead.

"The owl has very strong spirit medicine," the medicine woman observed. "Especially for a woman. The spirit of the moon is very strong in it." She fingered the pipe in her hands. "Was the moon full at the time of your vision?"

Nadie nodded. "Yes, Medicine Woman."

"That is very strong medicine. Let us see the gift."

The acorn was passed around the circle, each person examining it; handling and feeling it, smelling it, shaking it to hear the nut inside. As it made its way through everyone's hands, Nadie explained the plan that had come to her after receiving the gift.

"Where is Mouse?" Nadie asked Grandfather. She had expected Mouse would be one of the first ones up to the house when he heard she was back. But he had not shown his face. Was he angry at her for running away? For losing the raft? Had he found a new friend, and was no longer interested in hanging around with her?

Grandfather sighed and stared off into the distance. "He wintered at the trapper's cabin. No one has seen much of him. He didn't want to talk to anyone."

"Is he okay?"

"After you died… I thought we were going to lose him. I'm not sure… if his mind is yet well."

Nadie's heart constricted at the news, hurting her chest. "Oh, Mouse… I have to go see him."

Grandfather shook his head. "It's too late today. You will need to wait until morning. I don't want you falling over a cliff in the dark."

"There is no cliff to fall over," Nadie pointed out. "I've walked in the dark before. I'll be fine. I have to go find him."

"My daughter," Grandfather said gravely, "we don't want to get you back just to lose you again. Mouse will wait one more day."

"No. I can't wait," Nadie said firmly.

She left him alone and went to her room to pack her backpack. She might be away for several days. The cabin was not close. Grandfather tried to stop her again before she left, but she was determined to go to Mouse.

The afternoon was drawing to a close, but Nadie paid no attention. She would survive a night hiking in the dark. If she got turned around or lost her way, she would stop and sleep until morning. Or at least wait. She had a feeling she wasn't going to be able to sleep until she had reconciled with Mouse. He was going to be very angry when he found out she had let him believe she was dead for months. It had been a cruel thing for her to put all of them through.

As Nadie walked, she realized she was going to walk right by the burial grounds. Past Luyu's grave. She needed to stop and honor her sister to make sure she was free to continue her journey in the afterlife. Nadie turned at the twin stones that marked the entrance to the burial grounds. She walked through the trees, remembering Luyu's death ceremony so she would be able to find the plot even if there was no kind of marker.

She wasn't expecting anyone else to be there, so she was startled when one of the dark shapes she thought was a rock or a bush moved. Nadie gasped and froze, straining her eyes to see who it was. The man was facing away from her. He was taller than she and very thin. He wore a traditional-style buckskin jacket with no fringes or decorations on the back. He wore his hair in two long braids.

Nadie stepped on a stick and his head turned slightly, alerted to her presence. Nadie saw his profile for an instant. His cheeks were cavernous and overgrown with a sparse, unkempt beard. He looked years older than when she had left.

"Mouse?"

He turned the rest of the way at her voice and stared at her.

"Nadie?"

He made no move to come to her, his eyes riveted on her. Nadie approached him.

"Mouse, it's me."

"You are a spirit."

"No." She was only a few feet away from him now and he must have been able to discern that she was real. "I am body and spirit. It's me, Mouse. I didn't die. I'm here."

"We buried you!" His voice was choked.

"You buried Annie, a girl who stole my supplies."

He reached out a tentative hand and touched her arm. Nadie closed her eyes. His touch was so light and it had been so long. She opened her eyes again and reached out both arms to embrace him. Still wide-eyed, not believing she wasn't a ghost, he reached out for her.

She was in his arms again. Mouse was warm and strong, but painfully thin. He was like a bear who hadn't eaten all winter. He must have suffered terribly up at the cabin. Mouse clutched her to him like a drowning man.

"Nadie," he whispered. "Nadie, it's impossible."

"I'm sorry. I should have come back. I should have told you. I was selfish to just run away and let everyone think I had died."

"Ehâ," he murmured. "Yes."

He pressed his face into her hair, nuzzling her and inhaling deeply. "You smell like white people."

Nadie giggled in relief that he wasn't angry with her. "I've been living with white people," she admitted. "It's not really surprising."

He rested his chin on her head, and turned, moving her with him, back in the direction he'd been facing previously.

"I brought you something," he said.

Nadie was confused. She looked down at the ground, at the small pile of stones, and realized they marked Nadie's grave. Annie's grave.

"We laid you close to Luyu," Mouse pointed out.

"Thank you… that's where I would want to be."

He let go of her and bent down to open a big canvas bag. It looked heavy. Untying the closure, he pulled out a bulky fur. He let it drape down from his arm, opening it up into a large blanket. Nadie felt a smile tugging at the corners of her mouth. She pulled the blanket away from him, holding it up and examining it front and back.

"It looks very warm," she said. The different pelts were stitched roughly together in a sort of a hodge-podge. He had been good for his word and provided a blanket big enough not only to keep her warm but the two of them together.

"It is. I tested it. Had to make sure it would do."

"Why did you still do it? If you thought I was dead, why bother?"

"I was going to leave it here." He looked down at the pile of rocks. "Spread it out on the ground, over your grave, and leave it here for you."

"To rot on the ground?"

"Someone else would probably take it. But it was my gift to you."

Nadie's face was warm. She wondered what his plan was for after that. Once he had honored his promise, what had he planned to do? She let go of the blanket with one hand and stroked one of his braids. "That was very sweet."

The lines on Mouse's face hardened. "It was our agreement," he pointed out. His voice was stern. "And what about your part of the bargain? You were supposed to spend the winter weaving a blanket for me." His chin tilted up and he looked down his nose at her.

Putting the fur down, Nadie shifted the heavy backpack off of her shoulders. She undid the buckle and the drawstring and pulled out a large, multicolored blanket. She put it into Mouse's hands.

"I didn't have our loom, so I had to come up with another way to make it." She showed him the individual squares. "I used a cardboard loom to make each square, and then in the end, I stitched all of the squares together. Like a blanket of crocheted granny squares. Except..." her face burned with embarrassment. "It doesn't look nice. I had to use whatever yarns I could find at the thrift store or unravel donated sweaters. So nothing matches. There's no pattern. Just a bunch of crazy squares."

Mouse held it up to his hollow cheek, feeling the texture. "It's very soft and tightly-woven. It will keep me warm."

"You have to come back to the reservation. It won't be warm enough for you in the cabin."

"It's spring. It's much warmer than it was."

"But you have to come back to the reservation."

He smiled. "I will."

CHAPTER THIRTY-TWO

It was late when Nadie got home, but Grandfather and the Nose and the Foxes and another young man she didn't know were all in the living room, drinking and conversing and passing the time. They all quieted for a moment when Nadie walked into the house and into the midst of their party.

"Nadie? Are you okay?" Grandfather asked immediately, concern in his face. "Did you lose your way?"

"No, I found my way," Nadie told him with a smile. She held up the fur for him to see.

"Ahh." Grandfather nodded. "Is that what he's been doing?"

Nadie nodded. She headed for her bedroom. She had been walking outside, so she had no problem seeing in the dimness of her room. Moonlight came in the window. Nadie walked over to her bed, frowning. She reached down and touched the blanket on the bed. Her blanket. The owl blanket she had made for Luyu. Nadie folded it carefully and put it to the side, spreading Mouse's fur over the bed instead. It draped long over both sides. She slid into bed and savored the feeling of being home again.

❦

In the morning, Nadie awoke to a baby crying. She was used to hearing babies crying at the Step Up Center so it took her a few minutes to fully awaken and realize she wasn't homeless anymore. She got up and padded over to the baby room, where little Where is Joy was crying. As she picked the baby up, Mel got to the doorway.

"Thank you, Nadie. I'll take Joy now."

Nadie handed the baby over to her. "She's so tiny and sweet."

"Yes," Mel agreed. She headed back to her room and Nadie returned to hers. She picked up the red owl blanket and took it into Mel's bedroom.

"Here. This is for Joy."

Mel looked up from the nursing infant and smiled. "That's your blanket, Nadie. I wanted you to have it back."

"And I am giving it to Joy. It is my gift. I have a new blanket from Mouse. I don't need this one."

Mel nodded to the bed, indicating that Nadie could put it down. "Where is Joy says ay-hay."

Nadie knelt down to hold it near the baby. "It has an owl on it," she told Joy. "Ôhô. The owl has strong medicine, especially for a girl. I hope it will keep you safe."

CHAPTER THIRTY-THREE

The school children were gathered in a semi-circle, chattering and laughing with each other. There were some whispers and glances toward Nadie that told her they were talking about her; maybe speculating about where she had been. Maybe talking about her reappearance after supposedly being buried.

They quieted when Running Deer called for their attention and watched raptly as the medicine woman chanted and burned the sacred plants, preparing for the ceremony. Then it was Nadie's turn. She cleared her throat and looked at Mouse. He nodded.

Nadie patted the trunk of the grandfather oak tree that had fallen when flooding had eroded the earth under its roots.

"This tree stood proudly in our community since before our grandfathers' grandfathers. My nimosôm remembers his grandfather talking about how he climbed and swung in its branches when he was a boy. It stood strong for many years. Birds made nests in it branches. Squirrels sheltered in its leaves. Just like the Nehiyaw, the grandfather oak stood strong and proud before the white man came to this land. But the same way the flood waters washed away the earth the oak was rooted in, the white man tried to take away our roots."

Nadie sat on the trunk of the huge tree, running her fingers over the rough bark.

"He took away our children, our language, and our traditions. He killed our people with violence, disease, and starvation. He took the virtue of our women. That wound to our soul has been carried from father to son for as long as this tree has stood." She looked over their faces. "It has wounded all of us."

They looked at each other, skeptical and curious.

"To heal ourselves, we must heal our ancestors. We have to reconnect with them and honor them. We have to start repairing what has been damaged."

She looked at the exposed roots of the fallen oak. She took the warm acorn from her pocket.

"This seed was given to me by ôhô, the owl. From this small acorn, we can grow another oak. One just as big as the one that has fallen. A tree our children and their children can climb and swing in, that the birds can build nests in and the squirrels can run along the branches. It is just one step to healing ourselves. A journey begins with the first step."

Each of the children took turns to dig the hole. Nadie placed the acorn, and then they filled it back in and watered it.

One thing was still needful and that was to properly speed Luyu on her journey. Nadie had been putting it off, but she couldn't delay any longer. She walked out to the burial ground and sat at the foot of Luyu's grave.

"Tân'si, sister," she whispered.

She went through the steps of honoring the dead, just as she had in rehab for her ancestors. But her heart was empty when it was time to say what she was grateful for and to share her memories of Luyu. She had come to let Luyu go, but she found she couldn't. She held the hurt close to her heart and refused to release it.

"We're thankful we knew her," a voice said softly.

Nadie turned her head slightly and saw Mouse. She wasn't sure how long he had been there, watching her. Long enough to know where she was in the ritual. She nodded her agreement. Mouse came over and sat beside her.

"All the times she made us laugh," Mouse elaborated. "Her lisp. Her pony undershirt."

Nadie tried to laugh, but a sob caught in her throat.

"Her energy and curiosity. Her wonder at the world."

Nadie's eyes burned. Mouse was silent for a few minutes.

"You haven't cried," he said finally. "You haven't shed a tear since she died."

"No," Nadie agreed.

"Her spirit doesn't ask you to be strong. She asks you to cry, and laugh, and let her go."

"I can't." Nadie's voice broke. She breathed, trying to regain control. How could she let her baby go?

"You can. This life was only the beginning of Luyu's journey. She still lives. It's time to let go."

One tear trailed down Nadie's cheek. Mouse pulled her over to lean on his shoulder and he put his arm around her, holding her tight. More tears came. Silently at first, and then with audible sobs. Then a heartbroken howl of pain.

Mouse started chanting, a low, mournful beat and, in the midst of her tears, Nadie tried to join her voice to his. It helped her to get control of her sobs but still to express her pain. They sat there for a long time, holding each other and singing songs of mourning. Then they were silent, each contemplating their own thoughts.

"She tore her clothes to shreds," Nadie said. She sniffled.

"Except her pony."

"I had to hold her down to get it off and wash it," Nadie said. "She put it back on while it was still wet, even though it made her shiver. After she crawled around the floor in it to hide from me, it was just as dirty as it was before I washed it!"

Mouse nodded, chuckling. "Remember the time she was missing and we had the whole band searching for her?"

"And you found her in the cupboard," Nadie recalled, smiling. "Tummy full of cookies and fast asleep."

"She never slept at night. I have no idea how she could fall asleep in the cupboard in the middle of the day."

Nadie caught the hand of Mouse's arm that was wrapped around her and kissed it softly.

"Ay-hay. Thank you for helping me."

He nodded.

Nadie sniffled. "I miss her."

"Me too."

Mouse picked up the tobacco and lit it. He offered it in each of the four directions, asking all of the spirits to help Luyu on her journey.

"Goodbye, Luyu. Continue on your path."

Nadie was looking through the school books she had brought home when she heard the voices and laughter that signaled to her that the other residents of the house had started drinking. She wiped her mouth with the back of her hand and tried to ignore the cravings that started in her middle. It had been a long day and she was tired. She missed Luyu; playing with her and putting her down for the night. Luyu had kept Nadie company when everyone else was drinking, and her absence left a hollow place in Nadie's center that begged to be filled up. But she had let Luyu continue on her journey. She had to be strong herself.

As the voices and laughter grew louder, Nadie left her room. She slipped along the hallway, trying to stay out of sight of the living room. She opened the door at the top of the cellar stairs.

Nadie hadn't been down there since finding Luyu. It wasn't somewhere she usually went anyway. She had been told that when her grandmother had been alive, there had been shelves lined with preserved fruits and vegetables and bins of hardy vegetables to get them through the winter. Now the space was empty and ugly. The bucket of mash still dominated the room. Nadie choked, nauseated, as she remembered Luyu's legs sticking out of the big bucket. The sour, yeasty smell of the mash filled the room and set off her cravings worse than ever. But at the same time, she felt sick at the remembrance of that day. Laughter wafted down from overhead. So many nights that started with laughter and convivial drinking ended with fights, threats, and violence.

Nadie walked over to the bucket. She looked down at the bucket and its murky, foamy contents. She put her foot on the rim and shoved it hard, tipping the bucket onto its side and spilling the contents out over the dirt floor.

"Nadie!" Grandfather was standing at the top of the stairs. He must have seen her flit by and wanted to make sure she was okay. But he was not pleased with the waste of his mash. He swore. "What do you think you're doing?"

Nadie turned to him, her face hot and muscles tight. "There will be no more brew in this house."

"Who are you to dictate that? This isn't your house."

"It is my home."

"But you don't own it. You don't make the rules."

"Do you own it?" Nadie challenged.

She made her way up the stairs toward her grandfather.

"It's my house," he said.

"The band owns the reservation land and houses, not you."

He looked at her and gave her an angry look. "I am the parent here. The parent makes the rules, not the child."

She walked past him and shut the cellar door.

"I have had my vision. I am an adult now. You are not behaving like a responsible adult, so I am."

"You don't have the right."

She met his eye. "Then I guess I'll be finding somewhere else to live."

"Nadie," his voice was gentler. "This is your home. This is where you belong."

"I won't live where there is alcohol in the house. This is supposed to be a dry reservation, so why does everyone ignore the drinking?"

Grandfather put his hands up. "I can't control what everyone else does."

She gave him a hard look. "No alcohol in the house. No more mash. No more home brew. There's a baby in the house—is Melinda in there drinking?"

He tried to meet her gaze but failed, dropping his eyes to the floor. Nadie waited a minute for him to give some sign, then headed down the hall back to her own room.

"All right," he said quietly. "No alcohol in the house. But people are going to blame you. They're not going to be happy."

"I can live with that."

He gazed at her. "You're so like your grandmother."

Nadie smiled. "I'm glad." They shared a contemplative moment. "What would Grandmother say about your pills?"

His smile disappeared. "I need my pills for pain. And to sleep. You don't know what it's like to be old and not able to go to sleep."

"I know what it's like not to be able to sleep without taking something," she countered. "And I know it's better to just have a restless night and let your soul heal."

"A lot of restless nights."

Nadie nodded. "A lot," she agreed.

Grandfather walked past her to his own room. Seeing the conversation was over, Nadie sighed and went to sit on her bed and look at her schoolwork again. She was feeling lighter, the cravings, having peaked, were now receding again. She was stronger than the alcohol.

She saw a movement out of the corner of her eye and looked up to see Grandfather standing in her doorway. She raised her eyebrows, waiting for him to continue the argument.

He walked in and handed her an orange bottle of pills. "You're stronger than I am. I'm going to need your help."

"We're both going to need help. Lots of it."

She saw his Adam's apple bob as he swallowed and nodded.

"It's okay to need help," Nadie told him. "And we're both going to get it."

Did you enjoy this book? Reviews and recommendations are vital to making a book successful.

Please leave a review at your favorite book store or review site and share it with your friends.

Don't miss the following bonus material:
Sign up for mailing list to get a free ebook
Read a sneak preview chapter
Other books by P.D. Workman
Learn more about the author

Sign up for my mailing list at pdworkman.com and get Gluten-Free Murder for free!

PREVIEW OF TATTOOED
TEARDROPS

CHAPTER ONE

(i)

TAMARA FRENCH HAS BEEN *a model inmate throughout her incarceration.*

Great reference. You could go far on that one. Tamara sat on an uncomfortable bench in the brightly-lit lobby waiting for her ride. It was strange being on the other side of the guard booth. She stared at the too-white sneakers that stuck out below her dark pant cuffs, wondering what kind of life she had to look forward to with that ringing endorsement. She jiggled her legs up and down, trying to resist picking her nails. Eventually, a tall, middle-aged woman with a bun came in and stood before her. Tamara stared at her boxy black shoes for a moment before reluctantly looking up at her.

"Tamara?" the woman said.

"Yeah."

"Ready to get out of here?"

"I guess."

"I expected a bit more enthusiasm," the social worker said with a hint of a smile in the corners of her lipsticked mouth.

"I'm sorta nervous," Tamara said.

"I guess that's understandable. Come on, let's go."

Tamara sat there for another moment, then finally stood and followed the woman out of the juvenile facility. She got in the car and buckled up, holding her bag tightly on her lap.

The social worker introduced herself, but Tamara paid no attention, completely forgetting her name the next minute. The woman attempted small talk a few times, but Tamara turned on the radio and stared out the window, freezing the social worker out. Eventually the woman got the message, and stopped trying to engage her.

(ii)

They pulled up in front of a brick house that was at least a hundred years old and needed some work. There had been an attempt made at landscaping, with some flowers and bushes bunched around the concrete steps leading up to the porch and the front door. There was peeling paint on the fence and mailbox post.

"Here we are," the social worker announced. "Let's go in."

Tamara unbuckled and got out slowly. The social worker took her in, knocking on the front door and entering without waiting for an answer.

"Hello, Marion, come on in," a woman's voice called from up above. "I'll be right down."

Tamara stood beside the social worker, waiting. She held her paper bag awkwardly at her side, wishing that she didn't have anything to hold onto. She made a show of examining the front hall and living room of the house, but in all honesty, she didn't care what it looked like. It wasn't prison. Her concern was not with the house, but what the foster parents were going to be like. The front room was fairly neat and presentable. No children's toys scattered about. A load of laundry neatly folded in the basket sitting on the couch. The TV shut behind the doors of an entertainment center so it would not be the central focus of the room.

The furnishings were nice, not thrift store or destroyed. There were footsteps on the stairs, and Tamara looked up for her first glimpse of her foster mother.

Mrs. Henson had a pleasant, round face. Blond hair that had been lightly styled in an attempt to hide that it was starting to thin. She didn't look more than forty. She was overweight, but not grossly. She just looked soft and comfortable. She was wearing a sweater and pants, and inconsequential gold jewelry. She didn't look anything like Mrs. Baker, but that was no guarantee.

"Hello!" her voice rang out cheerfully.

"Gerry, this is Tamara," Marion introduced as Mrs. Henson reached the bottom of the stairs. "Tamara, Mrs. Henson."

"Hey," Tamara muttered, without meeting her eyes. "Where do you want me?"

"Your bedroom is at the top of the stairs. First door on the right," Mrs. Henson offered. Tamara made the trek up the stairs. There was a dark wooden bannister, ornately carved. Not too scarred for being in a foster home. Tamara turned at the top of the stairs and opened the door to her right.

There was a bed and a crib, and Tamara stood there, her heart speeding up, wondering if she'd been sent to the wrong room. Surely they wouldn't have given her a room with a crib in it? She could almost see Julie's still form lying on the high mattress… Mrs. Henson was there a moment later, having said a quick good-bye to Marion. She breathed a little heavily after her trip back up the stairs.

"Go on in," Mrs. Henson encouraged. "We sometimes take teen moms, to help teach them how to take care of their babies. We don't have any right now, so you get this room. That way you don't have to share."

Tamara walked into the room. The walls were a light green, freshly painted, with a white board wainscoting all the way around it. There was a pull-down blind with gauzy green curtains around the window. Tamara tossed her bag onto the bed, where it sat looking pitiful and inadequate.

"The others will be getting home soon," Mrs. Henson offered. "I'll introduce you then."

"Yes, ma'am."

"I'm happy to have you join us, Tamara. I was very impressed with your file."

Sure. It was certain to be the last place she went that anyone was impressed with her prison record. She'd wowed them all at her parole hearing. There had been tears, and not all of them hers. So many of the inmates protested their innocence and refused to take responsibility or express remorse at their parole hearings. Tamara had been working on her performance for three years, and it was good. The board's vote was unanimous. Now she was free. But to what kind of life?

Mrs. Henson stirred, making Tamara jump, startled. They both looked at each other, not knowing what to say. Mrs. Henson smiled and nodded.

"Make yourself at home," she encouraged, motioning around the room.

Tamara nodded. Mrs. Henson backed off, and left her alone. Tamara stretched out on the freshly-made bed to wait. If there was one thing she was used to doing, it was waiting.

(iii)

There were no bells that rang to mark the passage of time and the transition from one activity to another. Instead, disconcertingly, it flowed along with small shifts and gradual transitions. Tamara heard the front door open and close several times, with voices reaching her ears even through the closed bedroom door. Mrs. Henson did most of the talking and others answered her questions or made comments during the pauses. Tamara couldn't tell what any of them were saying, just the tone of voice. They all seemed to be casual and relaxed.

There was a knock on Tamara's bedroom door, and before she could get up to answer it, Mrs. Henson poked her head in.

"We're going to get dinner going," she said. "Why don't you come down and help? Then you can meet everyone."

Tamara studied her for a moment, assessing her options. Was it a choice? Was there a consequence for not complying? She was so unused to making her own decisions that she wasn't sure what to do when faced with one.

"Come on," Mrs. Henson encouraged, motioning for Tamara to come.

Tamara got up slowly and followed her foster mother down the stairs and to the kitchen. She was suddenly confronted with a whole pack of new people to meet. All bigger and older than her. Tamara made an effort to unclench her fists and not look confrontational. This wasn't juvie. She didn't have to prove herself physically here.

It hadn't occurred to Tamara when she had met Mrs. Henson that the foster children would not all be white like her. But of course, she already knew the statistics. There were more non-white children in foster care, and very few non-white parents. So they couldn't pair black children with black parents. Tamara was intimidated by all of the dark faces looking back at her. She wasn't prejudiced, but juvie had taught her to be acutely aware of race relations, and how her white-faced, blond-haired presence could be aggravating to others. They would immediately judge her as stuck-up, privileged, and ignorant.

Tamara was fifteen, and not tall. There were only four other children, Tamara realized, not the mob that she had originally perceived them as. They were all bigger than her. Most of them taller than Mrs. Henson. Studying their faces, Tamara figured that they were seventeen or eighteen. One boy seemed even too old to be eighteen.

"Everyone," Mrs. Henson said, "this is Tamara, our new foster child. I know you'll all make her feel comfortable and help her get settled in."

They all nodded, smiled, and waved. Tamara nodded back.

"Hey."

Her voice was hoarse, the greeting barely audible. Tamara wasn't sure any of them had heard her. She nodded again and didn't repeat the greeting.

"Okay, are you ready?" Mrs. Henson asked with a wide smile. "This is Nita," a Hispanic girl with long hair and perfectly plucked eyebrows, "Deshawn," the darkest face, a girl with cornrows and a brilliant white smile, "Jason," black skin, close cropped black hair, probably eighteen, "and Harry." Harry seemed a particularly non-ethnic name for a boy who appeared to be some mixture of black, Hispanic, and native. He smiled nicely for her, but his resting face was serious, contemplative. He was the one that Tamara was sure must be older than eighteen. He should have already aged out of the system.

Tamara nodded again and swallowed. Now what? Was she supposed to repeat them back? Greet each one separately? Shake hands? Tamara just stood there, lost, then looked at Mrs. Henson for direction.

"Okay, let's get started on dinner," Mrs. Henson suggested. "Nita, why don't you show Tamara where the dishes are, and she can help you set the table…" She went on, but Tamara didn't hear the rest of the instructions she gave to the remaining kids. She had her instructions. Go with Nita and set the table. She made her way across the room to Nita, and Nita smiled at her.

"Welcome," she said in a low voice that was almost a whisper. "I hope you like it here."

Tamara nodded. "Yeah. Thanks."

"Well, come on. The dishes are in this cupboard here, and the glasses, and the cutlery." Nita indicated each location.

"How many…?" Tamara asked. She cleared her throat. "Is there a Mr. Henson? Or anyone else?"

"Yeah, Jesse will be home for dinner. That's Mr. Henson. So seven altogether."

Tamara counted out the plates and trucked them over to the table, where she put them down carefully. Her hands shook slightly as she set them down, and it was an effort not to let them clatter. There was a baby's high chair, pushed against the wall. Tamara looked away from it and continued with her work, breathing shallowly. Setting the table only took a couple of minutes, and then Mrs. Henson gave them various other small tasks until everything started coming together for the dinner. She looked at her watch.

"Thanks guys. Take a break for about twenty minutes. Then everything should be done cooking, Jesse will be home, and we'll eat."

The kids dispersed. Tamara headed back up to her bedroom. Deshawn stopped ahead of Tamara, blocking her way into her bedroom.

"Do you need anything?" she asked Tamara.

Tamara shook her head.

"Sometimes... people don't come here with very much," Deshawn said. "Missus buys up extra toothbrushes and all, and we all share clothes..." She glanced over Tamara's figure. "My pants won't do you much good, but if you want a shirt, some accessories..."

Tamara stood there and contemplated the idea. For three years, she had worn nothing but an orange prison jumpsuit. Social Services had provided her with two very basic changes of clothing for her release. T-shirt, pants, socks, underthings. One pair of white tennis shoes. It was more fashion than Tamara had access to in all her time in juvie, but she was aware that it was sorely inadequate for a teenager on the outside.

Deshawn made an encouraging motion.

"Come on. Let's see if there's anything you want to borrow," she said.

Tamara followed her to one of the other bedrooms.

"Nita and I share the room," Deshawn commented. Nita was not there; maybe she had gone to watch TV or something. The room was painted sky blue. There was a utilitarian set of bunk beds, a couple of dressers cluttered with scarves, jewelry, and books, and a closet that was jammed full. The knobs on either side of the open closet door had been pressed into use to hold more hangers full of clothes. "It's mostly thrift store," Deshawn said, "but you can find some pretty good stuff if you look hard enough. Sorry, it's sort of a mess. Come on. See what you like."

Tamara went to the closet and looked over the hangers full of brightly-colored clothing. It didn't appear that either Deshawn or Nita went for anything understated.

"If you want t-shirts, they're in the dresser," Deshawn pointed, "and just grab whatever you see that you like. Just bring it back or throw it in the laundry when you're done with it."

Tamara saw herself in the mirror mounted on the back of the closet door. There hadn't been any full-length mirrors at juvie. And the only mirrors that had been there were polished metal or plastic, and you could never really see your reflection very well. Tamara had grown up a lot in juvie. She wasn't the soft, shy little farm girl she had been when she went to the Bakers. They had changed her. And juvie had changed her. The years had not been particularly kind ones. But she had developed a figure now, and was going to have to learn how to dress it up, instead of simply shrouding it in a jumpsuit. She had tattoos and piercings that she hadn't had before her incarceration. Her hair was dull and lank, like everybody else's in juvie. Tamara wound one lock around her finger, staring at the stranger reflected in the mirror.

"Why don't we do something with your hair?" Deshawn suggested. "There's not much time, but if we blow-dry, we could be done before supper."

Tamara raked her fingers through her limp blonde hair, disgusted with it.

"Yeah. Could we?"

"Mmm-hmm," Deshawn agreed with emphasis. "We'll shampoo it in the bathroom, and use leave-in conditioner..." she led the way out into the hallway, still chattering away to herself what they would do. Tamara just followed.

Tamara knelt by the tub while Deshawn used the hand-held shower attachment to quickly wet her hair down. The warm water felt so good on Tamara's scalp, she wished she could get in for a full shower, and just luxuriate in it for hours. Three years of quick, cold showers. But Deshawn turned off the water way too soon, and applied a fruity shampoo with strong, capable fingers; working it in and then rinsing it back out. She handed Tamara a towel and while Tamara rubbed her hair, Deshawn rifled through the myriad toiletries lining the back of the counter, the medicine cabinet, and a couple of deep wicker baskets under the sink.

(iv)

"Girls! Dinner!" the impatient call came again from downstairs.

Deshawn poked her head out the door.

"Just one more minute," she called back. "We'll be right down!"

She returned her attention to Tamara.

"Okay, just sit still for one more minute, girl," she instructed.

Tamara sat frozen, while Deshawn wound sections of her hair around the fat curling iron, holding it and then releasing. There was no way that she was going to be done the whole thing in another minute. But Deshawn worked quickly, sure of herself.

"That will do it for now," she announced.

She laid the curling iron down on the counter and unplugged it from the wall. Standing Tamara up, Deshawn shuffled her over and turned her to face the mirror.

"Ta-da!"

Tamara looked with astonishment at the face in the mirror. She was amazed at what a big difference a hairstyle could make. She still didn't have on any make-up, hadn't changed her clothes or accessories, all she had done was let Deshawn clean and style her hair. Her image in the mirror was no longer so harsh and plain.

"You're gorgeous," Deshawn gushed. "You've got really good

363

color and proportions. We can have a lot of fun glamming you up. For now, this will do."

Standing behind Tamara, Deshawn used her fingers to wind and readjust a couple of curls. She lowered her head so that it was on the same level as Tamara's, and gave her a smile.

"What do you think?"

"It's… it's really pretty. Thanks," Tamara said. She cleared her throat, realizing that she was whispering. She had learned in juvie to use a strong, confident voice, not to be soft or timid. The Henson's home was so different in atmosphere, she felt like she was in a library or something. That she needed to be quiet to avoid upsetting the peace of the place.

"Come on, we've got to get down to dinner, or Missus will not be happy!"

Tamara followed Deshawn back downstairs and to the dining room table that she and Nita had set. It was now covered with serving dishes, and everyone was seated, waiting for them. All eyes turned to Tamara as she looked at the three empty chairs, trying to decide which one she should take.

"Tamara, doesn't that look lovely," Mrs. Henson complimented. "Here, sit down. These boys will eat everything before we even get a bite, if they have to wait much longer."

She gestured toward the empty chair nearest to her, and Tamara went over and sat down. Deshawn took what appeared to be her usual seat, beside Nita, which left one empty chair at the table of eight. Tamara looked for the first time at Mr. Henson. Slim, on the tall side. Handsome boyish face. Short-cropped curly red hair. He smiled at Tamara.

"Welcome, Tamara. I'm Jesse."

Tamara nodded, looking down at her empty plate. Her stomach tightened and it was suddenly hard to breathe. The only men that she had been around for three years had been guards, doctors, and administrators. The last man she had lived with before that… her foster father, Mr. Baker… that had been a bad scene. A very bad scene. Tamara swallowed. She tried to slow her breathing, but it just made her breath louder in her own ears. She was sure everyone would hear how loudly and quickly she was breathing.

"Dig in," Mrs. Henson said, and Harry and Jason acted like two Rottweilers just told to attack, diving into the serving dishes immediately. Conversation started up around the table, and rather than trying to follow any of it, Tamara just let it wash over her like white noise. She served up small portions of each of the dishes that passed her, and dutifully passed them on.

"So tell us about your last home, Tamara," Nita said. "Where did you come here from?"

Tamara looked at Mrs. Henson. The woman just smiled and gave her a small nod, and didn't jump in to help her out. If Tamara didn't want to answer questions, she was going to have to be assertive and speak up. The conversations around the table quieted as the others paused to listen for her answer. Tamara swallowed a very dry mouthful of potatoes. They stuck right in the middle of her chest.

"I wasn't at a home," she said finally, careful to keep her voice up, not to duck her head down. She was not vulnerable and had nothing to be ashamed of. She was strong and knew how to take care of herself. She had just as much right to be here as any of them. "I was in juvie."

There was an initial silence, and then conversations started back up again without further comment on Tamara's answer.

"Sorry," Nita said. "I didn't know."

"It's okay," Tamara said, shaking her head. "It's not a secret. That's where I was."

Nita nodded.

"Most of us have been in trouble at one time or another."

Tamara glanced around at their faces. None of them looked particularly troubled. They seemed happy and relaxed. At peace with themselves. Maybe they had been in trouble before, and maybe they hadn't. You couldn't always tell by looking at someone.

"Harry's probably spent the most time in juvie," Deshawn contributed, nodding to her brother. "How much time, Harry?"

"All together?" Harry questioned, laughing. "I don't know. Longest stint was two years. But I had plenty of shorter stays before that."

Tamara studied him more closely. He met her eyes and nodded.

"Harry's twenty," Mrs. Henson said without being asked. "So he's not officially a foster child anymore. But we told him he could stay on here while he does some more schooling and gets on his feet."

Tamara nodded, looking back down at her plate.

"That's really nice of you."

"It's to our benefit too. Harry contributes a lot to the family, and since he's working part-time, he's also paying a bit of rent to help keep us afloat. So it works both ways."

Tamara bit into some sort of casserole.

"I guess you'll learn about everyone's backgrounds gradually," Mrs. Henson said. "We try to be open with each other. Everybody's been through some pretty tough stuff. We don't judge. We just try to help."

"That's cool," Tamara said, pushing her dinner around on her plate. She wasn't hungry.

She watched everyone else chow down, and conversations flowed back away from her again. Tamara watched for the appropriate time to leave the table. There was no end-of-dinner bell anymore. She had to relearn all the social graces. How to judge the end of a conversation. When one could politely leave the dinner table. How long she could look at someone before they decided she was being too aggressive. It was like living in a foreign country. A dangerous foreign country.

"Not very hungry?" Mrs. Henson observed, as dinner conversation started to peter out.

Tamara looked down at her plate, still nearly full.

"No. I'm sorry… it's good… I just feel kind of… my stomach hurts."

"It's all right. It takes time to adjust. You can scrape it into the garbage. Nita can show you where. Everyone rinses their own plates and puts them in the dishwasher."

"Sure," Tamara agreed. She stood up, grabbing her plate, and Nita got up and led the way back into the kitchen, where they took care of their dishes. Tamara looked back at the dining table. "Do you want help with clean-up?" she asked Mrs. Henson. "Or would I be in the way?"

"Of course you can help. Usually, I'd probably tell you to go do your homework while I cleared, but you don't have any today, so why don't you and I clean up together?"

Tamara nodded, and she and Mrs. Henson bussed the serving dishes back to the kitchen, found lids for things, and put them into the fridge. Mrs. Henson turned the dishwasher on and wiped down the dining room table.

"You can watch some TV or take some 'down' time. In bed at nine, and lights out at ten."

"Okay," Tamara agreed.

She wandered around the house a bit, but wasn't comfortable sitting down with anybody else, and so she made her way back to her bedroom. As she approached, the door to the other girls' bedroom opened. Nita peeked out.

"Hey," she said. "You need anything? Do you have pajamas?"

Tamara shook her head.

"No," she admitted. "If I could borrow a t-shirt or something…"

"You bet. Come in."

Nita opened the door the rest of the way for her, and Tamara went in. Tamara looked down at Nita's feet, nails freshly painted and toes spread apart while they dried. Nita giggled and hobbled on her heels over to the dresser.

"You want to do yours?" she asked. She pulled out a handful of shirts and tossed them at Tamara.

"No. Thanks," Tamara said, fumbling with the shirts to see what her options were. "I'm going to hit the sack."

She found herself strangely unable to choose one of the shirts. There were three of them. They were all cute. Any one of them would work. All she had to do was decide which of the three she liked best. Nita was watching her, head cocked slightly.

"The blue one is a really good color for you," she suggested.

Not the blue one. Tamara looked at the other two. She didn't know which she wanted, but she had to decide before Nita made another suggestion. She had to make her own choice. Tamara tossed the blue one back to Nita, and with a knot in her stomach, tossed Nita the pink one too. Tamara looked down at the purple and blue patterned shirt in her hands.

"This one is good," she said.

She felt a little sick. Worried that she had made the wrong choice. How silly was that, to be worried that she had picked the wrong t-shirt to wear in the privacy of her own bedroom? But she was. She had an overwhelming feeling of dread.

"Have a good sleep," Nita said with a smile.

"Thanks."

Tamara went back to her room. She changed into the t-shirt, long enough to reach her mid-thighs. She lay down on the bed and stared at the ceiling. There would be no bell ringing to tell her when to go to sleep. Would her body know when it was time, without the bell? Would she be able to adjust to a new schedule? Not feeling the least bit tired, Tamara lay staring at the ceiling, twitching her foot and waiting for sleep.

CHAPTER TWO

(i)

TAMARA AWOKE. SHE WAS confused at first, disoriented by the sight of a bedroom around her instead of her familiar cell. Turning her head to look at the clock beside the bed, Tamara saw that it was five forty-five on the dot. The usual time for the reveille bell. Groaning, she rolled over and slid out of bed.

She didn't know what time the others usually arose, but she imagined there would probably be a bottleneck waiting for the shower. Moving as quietly as possible, Tamara tiptoed across the room and opened her door. She listened for any sounds of movement. There was a light on down the stairs, but it wasn't bright. It could just be a streetlight through a window, or a nightlight. The shower was not running, so Tamara darted into the bathroom, shut the door, and turned on the light. She started the shower running and stripped down. For the first time in three years, she stepped into a warm shower. The tantalizing sample of the night before when Deshawn had helped her wash her hair didn't even come close to the luxury of a hot, whole-body shower. Tamara took a deep breath. She could get used to this.

More out of habit than anything, Tamara very quickly soaped up and rinsed off. She forced herself to shut off the water again immediately. Even though she would have loved to have stayed in the shower for an hour, until the hot water ran out and people started banging on the door to tell her to get out, she knew she had to be considerate and leave some hot water for the others. With a family of seven, you couldn't be selfish and use it all yourself. Shivering, Tamara grabbed the closest towel and dried herself off. She realized with dismay that she hadn't brought in any clothes to change into. She only had the makeshift nightshirt she had just taken off. Tamara swallowed and steeled herself. She wrapped the worn towel around her body. It didn't cover much, and wasn't long enough to tuck it back into itself. So holding the towel with one hand, Tamara tucked her shirt under her elbow, and used the other hand to open the door.

Her room was conveniently right across the hall from the bathroom, so she only had to take three steps, and she was safe in her own room again. She heard the click of another door down the hall, and a minute later, the bathroom door closed and the water turned back on. Had whoever was in the shower now seen her in her dash from the bathroom? She hadn't dared to look for anyone. Tamara pulled on her sad little Social-Services-provided outfit and looked for a comb. She found one in the top drawer of the dresser, along with a few other necessities. As she carelessly pulled the comb through her hair to get it in order before it finished drying, Tamara's eyes sought out her reflection in the mirror over the dresser. Did she want a prison hairdo for the first day of school, or something nice, like Deshawn had done for her last night? But the curling iron was in the currently-occupied bathroom.

Trying to breathe calmly through her anxiety, Tamara crossed the hall to the bathroom door. The shower was still running. She knocked on the door and opened it up a couple of inches.

"Can I just get the curling iron?" she asked.

She didn't look toward the shower or the foggy mirror. She just kept her eyes down, waiting for a response.

"Sure, go ahead," a male voice answered. The voice was deep, probably Harry, but Tamara wasn't sure.

She opened the door far enough to rifle through the contents of the vanity and the baskets underneath, and found the curling iron, a brush, and some hairspray. Tamara retreated from the warm, misty bathroom and hurried back to her own room.

(ii)

Breakfast at juvie was served promptly at six and was over at six thirty, so by the time Tamara was finished styling her hair, she was starving. She went down to the kitchen to see what she could find to eat. Mr. Henson—Jesse—was eating a bowl of cereal on the kitchen island, reading through a newspaper. Tamara stopped short. He must have heard her footsteps on the stairs, though, because he looked up at her and smiled.

"Come on in, don't be shy," he invited.

Tamara approached cautiously, not getting too close. She knew foster dads. She'd dealt with a foster dad. But she'd learned how to protect herself in juvie. How to be careful and not leave herself open.

"You're an early riser," Jesse observed, dropping his eyes back down to his newspaper and taking another bite of cereal.

Tamara watched him for any change in attitude, any extra watchfulness. He glanced up again, then back down at his paper.

"There's juice in the fridge. Cereal and bread in the cupboard," he pointed. "Coffee's fresh."

"Thanks," Tamara said.

She kept an eye on him while she opened a couple of cupboards to locate the mugs, and poured herself a cup of coffee. Tamara inhaled the soothing aroma while she waited for it to cool down a bit. Perhaps Jesse could feel her gaze, because he looked up at her expectantly, eyebrows up. Tamara looked away.

"Sorry," she said. "I'm a bit dopey. Still getting the engine started."

He chuckled.

"Did you sleep well?"

"Well… okay, I guess. The bed is really comfy and everything. It's just…"

"Somewhere new," Jesse finished for her, nodding. "That's perfectly understandable. It will take a while before it feels natural. Like home."

"Yeah."

Tamara wondered if she would ever feel like this was home. She had been warned that parole wouldn't be easy. She knew inmates who had been back within a week of being released. Some had intended to follow the rules, and slipped. Some had never intended to follow any rules. She remembered when Mitchell had come back. Tamara had thought that she would make it. Mitchell was tough, one of the few who had managed to survive juvie without getting in with one of the gangs. She was strong-willed, and made it known that once she got out, she wasn't going to be back. She would do whatever it took to stay on the right side of the law and make a life for herself. A straight, honest life.

On her return, Mitchell's dark eyes were underscored by shadows. She looked almost haunted.

"I just couldn't do it," she told Tamara, as they both stood at the sinks in the restroom. "I felt so… exposed. I didn't belong out there."

She had held up a convenience store at knife point. With no mask. In full view of the security cameras. Not because she needed money, but because she wanted to go back. Back where she belonged.

Tamara sipped her coffee. She considered what else she might want for breakfast. Her stomach was still growling. She wasn't going to be able to make it to lunch on a cup of coffee. She was used to a full breakfast at juvie.

With another careful look at Jesse, she went over to the

cupboard that he had pointed out, and got herself Cheerios and a slice of bread, which she threw into the bright red toaster on the counter. She prepared the cereal and started to eat, leaning against the counter and waiting for the toast to pop.

"You can eat at the table," Jesse said. "You don't have to eat standing up just because I am."

Tamara didn't move. He didn't pursue it. She and Jesse continued to eat in silence. Mrs. Henson joined them as Tamara moved on to her toast, searching the fridge for some jam.

"You're up early," Mrs. Henson observed. "Couldn't sleep?"

Tamara nodded. She moved to the dining table as Mrs. Henson entered the kitchen, feeling crowded, anxious at both foster parents being in such close proximity. Mrs. Henson gave her a smile and got herself a cup of coffee. Tamara took a few quick bites of her toast and then laid the remainder down.

"Sorry, I took too much," she said. She dumped the toast in the garbage and slotted the plate away in the dishwasher. Then she retreated to her room.

As Tamara got upstairs, Deshawn was knocking on the bathroom door.

"Come on, Jason! Time's up! There's a line-up out here."

She smiled widely at Tamara as she waited for a response.

"Hey, girl," she greeted. "Go on in." She gestured toward her own bedroom. "Help yourself to whatever you need. Nita's awake, she's just playing possum."

Tamara hesitated.

"Go ahead," Deshawn pressed. "You going to go to school without putting your face on?"

Tamara had no experience with makeup, but she knew most of the other girls at school would probably be wearing it, and she didn't want to look any more different than she had to. So she nodded and went into the bedroom, tapping lightly on the door before she went in.

Nita didn't play possum, but propped herself up on her elbow, yawning.

"Mornin' sunshine."

"Hey. Deshawn said…"

"Yeah, of course. Help yourself to whatever you see. Except that orange scarf over there," Nita nodded at it. "That one's calling to me this morning."

"I'm kind of sick of wearing orange," Tamara said.

Nita snorted. "You don't say," she said with a giggle.

Tamara looked over the clutter of accessories on top of the dresser. She tried on a couple of necklaces before settling on one with a large, brassy sun-and-moon medal on it. She put in chunky earrings. She looked at the makeup and didn't know what to do with any of it.

"You want some help?" Nita offered.

Tamara hesitated, not wanting to owe Nita anything. She felt vulnerable letting anyone help her. Nita sat up and swung her feet over the side of the bed. She stretched and stood up.

"Why don't you sit?" she suggested, motioning to the chair in front of the small mirror and pile of makeup.

Tamara sat down. Nita started pawing through the makeup, sorting out what she wanted to use. Without further discussion, she started by applying some moisturizing cream. Then she brushed on some blush.

"Is everyone always so nice and perfect around here?" Tamara asked, watching Nita's actions in the mirror.

Nita laughed.

"We're far from perfect. We still have our fights and rough spots. But…" She paused while she moved onto selecting a shade of eye shadow. "We've all been there. Moving into a new home. Starting over again. Trying to figure out your place. First day of school. It works better if you're nice to newcomers rather than getting all territorial. A lot less grief."

"Oh."

As if to underscore her words about not being perfect, Deshawn pounded on the bathroom door, yelling at Jason again to quit being inconsiderate and get his bony butt out of the bathroom. Tamara and Nita laughed.

"And luckily, Deshawn and I both love having sisters to share with. Neither of us grew up with much family."

Tamara was going to nod, but thought better of moving while Nita worked on her.

"Me neither," she agreed.

"Yeah? Well, there you go. Now you've got two sisters who are going to love dressing you up and showing you how to do your makeup."

Tamara studied Nita's face in the mirror. Nita was beautiful. The lines of her face were almost perfect. Her smile was bright and even and could have been an advertisement for a dentist. There was the tiniest shift to the lines of her nose that made Tamara wonder if it had been broken at some point. Without thinking, Tamara touched the bump in her own nose. Nita stopped for a moment and pushed Tamara's hand away.

"Don't you worry about that," she said. "It's not obvious unless you're looking for it."

Tamara put her hand back down again. Nita handed her a tube of lipstick.

"I think you can do this part," she said.

Tamara screwed the lipstick out, and applied it to her lips. She looked at her face, at the overall effect of the makeup. It still looked like her. There was nothing too obvious or stark about the makeup. But her face was softened, more feminine. Framed by the silky blond waves, she could almost be pretty.

Nita was over at the closet, pushing clothes around. She was wearing a long Minnie Mouse nightshirt that reached her calves. She pulled out a couple of button-up shirts.

"Now how about one of these layered over your t-shirt?" she suggested. "I think that would be really cute."

Tamara took one of the shirts from her and pulled it on, then shook her head and took it back off.

"Not really my style," she said.

Nita shrugged.

"You want anything else? Don't be shy, just try on whatever you like."

Tamara joined Nita at the closet, and looked through the offerings. She pulled out a black jacket with silver hardware, and tried it on. Nita looked her over and nodded.

"You like it?" she asked.

"I think so."

"It's yours."

Tamara smoothed it with both hands and nodded, smiling shyly. "Thanks."

(iii)

Neither of the other two girls went to the school that Tamara would be attending, so she was on her own. Mrs. Henson offered to make the proper introductions at the school, but Tamara shook her head.

"Just drop me off," she said. "I can find the office and they'll give me what I need."

She didn't need to look like a little girl who couldn't manage to go to school on her own. She was strong. Mrs. Henson agreed. She drove slowly, pointing out landmarks that would help Tamara to find her way around the neighborhood in the future. Tamara stared out the window, not commenting, her stomach in a tight, sick knot. She was not looking forward to school. Of course she'd gone to all of her classes in juvie—not like she had been given a choice—but public school was not something she was looking forward to.

She checked in at the office, was given a locker, schedule, map, textbooks, and a number of covert looks. She was told who her guidance counselor was and invited to set up an appointment with him any time.

Tamara went to her morning classes, and at lunch went looking for the students' illicit smoking hangout. She had a few cigarettes left over from juvie, but getting her hands on more might be difficult. It didn't take long to find a small knot of students wreathed in smoke. Tamara nodded briefly and cupped her hand around a cigarette to light it. She drew the smoke into her lungs, the tension in her stomach subsiding slightly.

"Sucks being new," one girl offered.

Tamara nodded.

"Especially halfway through the year," she agreed.

"I'm Sybil." She had dyed black hair, a post through her lip and a piercing in her nose. Her makeup was stark, but not goth.

Some of the others offered their names.

"Hi. Tamara."

"You're staying with the Hensons?"

"Yeah." Tamara shifted her feet. "You know 'em?"

"They go through a lot of kids there. Some of them go to school. Some don't."

"Uh-huh."

Since Tamara was not yet sixteen, she didn't have a choice about school attendance yet. It was mandatory. Especially if she wanted to stay out of juvie. One of the boys, slim and pale and wearing a black leather jacket, looked her over curiously.

"So being with the Hensons, does that mean you've been in trouble?" he inquired.

Sybil rolled her eyes.

"Smooth, Jason," she objected. But that didn't stop her from listening with obvious interest for the answer.

Tamara blew out smoke in a thin, white stream. It was a question bound to be on everyone's mind.

"Yeah, I've been in trouble."

"What kind of trouble?"

"I just got out of juvie. Three years. Made parole." Word would get out one way or another. It might as well come from her and at least be accurate to start with. The more she tried to hide her past, the more the rumors would fly.

Jason whistled through his teeth.

"Wow. What for?"

"Murder," Tamara said flatly. No emotion in her voice or expression. Nothing that would show weakness or vulnerability.

"You're pulling my leg. Seriously?" he demanded.

Tamara shrugged. He could interpret the gesture as he liked.

"Who'd you kill?"

"None of your business."

"Some guy who asked too many questions," Sybil teased, and cracked up.

Tamara grinned at Sybil. Jason opened his mouth to ask another question.

"Shut up, Jason," Sybil snapped.

He closed his mouth and rolled his eyes. They continued to smoke. After a few minutes, Jason stepped on his cigarette butt and left. Sybil looked at Tamara.

"You want to walk?"

"Sure."

They walked in silence for a while. Tamara tried to make her cigarette last, not knowing how hard it would be for her to get another pack. In juvie, it was surprisingly easy. Here, she was going to have to get someone who was old enough to buy them for her, once she could get her hands on some money.

"News travels fast," Tamara observed.

"The grapevine is humming away," Sybil agreed. "Some of Henson's kids have made things... interesting around here, so when word gets out that they got someone new—well, the news travels."

"Great."

"Sorry. It'll die down again. Unless you're planning on making a splash."

"I'm not looking for attention."

Sybil nodded. They continued to walk and make small talk.

"So what was it like?" Sybil asked, and at Tamara's questioning look, elaborated. "In juvie."

"Not somewhere you'd like to be."

Sybil waited for more information, but Tamara shook her head and didn't enlighten her.

(iv)

The teacher walked up to Tamara while she was doing her classwork, and put a slip of yellow paper on her desk. Tamara looked down at it, and looked up at the teacher questioningly.

"You're wanted down at the office. That's your hall pass."

Tamara looked at it for a minute, and then closed her books and stacked them up. She picked up the yellow paper and headed out of the room and down the stairs. She got turned around a couple of times, but eventually found her way to the administrative office where she had started her day. She presented her yellow slip to the gray-haired woman at the reception desk.

"Yes. Tamara," the woman said, looking at the paper as if there was something wrong with it. "You are in conference room B."

Tamara looked around, and the receptionist pointed to a closed door behind her.

"Right there. Go on in."

Tamara wasn't sure what was going on. Was she in trouble for something already? Maybe someone had reported her for smoking. Or maybe it was something they always did at the end of the day when a student transferred mid-term. Checking up to make sure that everything had gone all right. That they had found all of their classes, hadn't had any trouble...

She put her hand on the doorknob. The receptionist had said to go right in, but she didn't feel right about it. Tamara knocked lightly on the door, and opened it, poking her head in. It was a small meeting room, four chairs around a small table. A tall black man sat in one with his long legs stretched out in front of him. He was dressed in a suit. His head was bald, maybe shaved. He smiled, but didn't show any teeth. The smile didn't reach his eyes. His face immediately fell back into a tired, grim look.

"Tamara," he greeted. "Come on in. Shut the door and have a seat."

Tamara obeyed, trying to analyze him. Not the principal. Maybe a counselor, if he'd been a cop in a previous life. He had the air of one of the guards in juvie. Not one of the day-to-day guards, but one of the supervisors or something. Higher up the food chain. More reserved, not as quick to pull out his baton or taser. Tamara sat down in the chair across from the man and waited.

"My name is Chad Collins," he introduced himself. "I'll be your parole officer."

"Oh." Tamara blew out her breath. Now it made sense. She wasn't in trouble. Not yet. This was her new shadow. The man who would be watching for her to fail. "Hi."

"I've read your file, and I think that you can make this transition successfully, if you put your mind to it."

Tamara nodded.

"It will be hard," he went on, "but you can choose to be a different person than you were before you went to juvie. Or while you were at juvie. It's a pivotal time for you. This is your chance to turn things around."

He rubbed his chin, looking down at the slim file in front of him.

"Okay," Tamara said.

"You don't want to be sent back for something stupid. It's important that you understand the terms of your parole."

Tamara nodded again.

"So what..." she started. She cleared her throat and tried to strengthen her wavering voice. "What are the rules?"

He pulled a single sheet out of the file and placed it in front of Tamara.

"Okay, let's go over it." Pointing to the top line, he started out. "I will tell you when and where our meetings are, and you'll be there. On time. Every time. You're living with the Hensons, and you're not allowed to move anywhere else without my say so. You have a nine o'clock curfew. No matter what, you're home by nine o'clock every night. Right?"

"Yes, sir," Tamara agreed.

"No weapons, no alcohol, no drugs. Not on your person, not in your room, not anywhere near you. You don't associate with anyone carrying weapons, alcohol, or drugs. You'll submit to random drug testing. Whenever I say. On the spot. You are not allowed to be around anyone who has been convicted of a felony."

"What if…"

"No one. No 'what ifs'. It doesn't matter if you knew them in juvie, before juvie, or met them since. No criminal associations."

"Okay." Tamara nodded.

"You're not allowed to be around young children. No one under six. And you'll attend mandatory counseling at least weekly."

"Yes, sir," Tamara said. "What kind of counseling?"

"Something to help to ease the transition, give you the skills that you need to stay clean outside of juvie. Anger and stress management. Addictions counseling, if you need it. Anything that I or your therapist decide that you need."

Tamara nodded and swallowed.

"Okay."

"Do you have any questions?"

"No, sir."

"What are you going to do if you think of questions? If you're not sure about something?"

She continued to stare at the paper in front of her.

"I guess I call you," she said.

"That's right." He pointed to his contact details at the bottom of the page. "Do you have a cell phone yet?"

"No."

"When you get one, you put me on your number one speed dial. I'm the person you call if you have any questions."

"Yes, sir."

"What if you slip up and break a rule, what do you do?" he demanded.

Tamara picked at the skin around her nails, hiding them under the table.

"Fix it," she suggested. "Don't do it again."

"The first thing you do is call me. You report yourself. 'Mr. Collins, someone offered me a beer and I was stupid enough to drink it.' 'Mr. Collins, I was ten minutes late for curfew.' 'Mr. Collins, a friend from juvie called me up, but I hung up on her.' Any violation, no matter how big or small. You call me. Got it?"

"Yes, sir."

"Things will be much worse if I hear it from someone else, or it shows up in a drug test or something. Tell me, and you might not get sent back to juvie."

"Okay."

Tamara had an overwhelming desire to bite her nails, and it was only with a huge exercise of will that she was able to keep her hands in her lap, hidden, away from her face, still picking at the cuticles.

"What if you have some other kind of problem?" he questioned.

Tamara looked up at his face, the slight flare of his nostrils and curl of his lip.

"Call you?" she suggested.

He nodded.

"Now you're getting it," he agreed.

Tamara mirrored his nod. Neither one of them said anything for a while, and Tamara eventually looked back up at Collins again, wondering what else she was in for.

"How was your first day?" he asked.

Tamara relaxed a little in her seat, letting out a pent-up breath.

"Okay. Not bad. The Hensons all seem really nice."

"They're a good family," Collins agreed. "They've dealt with a lot of tough cases. Everything is pretty calm there now, and I'm hoping that you won't make things too difficult for them. Give them a bit of a rest."

"I don't plan on getting in any trouble."

"Good. But it can be harder than you would think. These things are rarely planned. But temptations show up, catch you at a weak moment. You feel loyal to a friend or family member and think nobody will know, nobody will get hurt."

"I don't do drugs," Tamara said. "Or drink. I never even had a cigarette before juvie."

He studied her, eyes narrowed slightly. Tamara felt the need to defend herself further. She might not care what the kids at school or the Hensons thought, but she thought her parole officer ought to know what kind of a person she was.

"I'm not a troublemaker," she said. "You look at my juvie file. Or my school records before... before it happened. I never got in any kind of trouble. Ever."

Collins rubbed his chin, his dark eyes boring into her.

"You have admitted to the murders more than once. In court and to the parole board."

"Yes."

"What does *that* say about you?"

Tamara stared back down at the paper again. She picked at her cuticles under the table.

"It was a bad situation," she said. "I was trapped, and hurt, and the hormones... made me so foggy and emotional. I didn't know what to do. I know it doesn't make sense when you say it like that, but I was so... confused."

There was silence from Collins at first.

"This time," he said finally, "you have someone to talk to. You're not alone."

Tamara looked at him again. His voice was low, almost gentle.

"Call me," he said, tapping the piece of paper with the eraser end of his pencil. "For any reason."

"Okay. Thanks."

Tamara nodded. She felt very teary and emotional all of a

sudden, and she didn't like it. She couldn't let her guard down. Couldn't make herself vulnerable. Collins' lips pressed together in a thin line for a moment, then the look vanished. Collins unfolded himself from the chair, towering over her. Tamara scrambled to get to her feet. He offered his hand, and Tamara shook it, feeling a bit awkward.

"Call me tomorrow before curfew," he instructed.

Tamara nodded.

He was still holding her hand, and looked down at it. Tamara saw that her fingers were bleeding around the nails, and pulled her hand out of his grasp, hiding it behind her back.

"I'm not the enemy, Tamara," Collins said. He sighed. "I'll get you in to see the therapist as soon as possible. Transition and stress management. You'll go."

"Yes, sir."

"Talk to you tomorrow, then."

Tamara nodded, and he left the room. The door swung shut behind him, clicking softly into place. Tamara put her hands over her face and tried to calm and compose herself. She was tough. She could manage it. She'd show Chad Collins that she wasn't like any of his other parolees. He didn't know her. She could make it.

Tattooed Teardrops, Book #1 of the Tamara's Teardrops series by P.D. Workman can be purchased at pdworkman.com

ABOUT THE AUTHOR

Award-winning and USA Today bestselling author P.D. (Pamela) Workman writes riveting mystery/suspense and young adult books dealing with mental illness, addiction, abuse, and other real-life issues. For as long as she can remember, the blank page has held an incredible allure and from a very young age she was trying to write her own books.

Workman wrote her first complete novel at the age of twelve and continued to write as a hobby for many years. She started publishing in 2013. She has won several literary awards from Library Services for Youth in Custody for her young adult fiction. She currently has over 70 published titles and can be found at pdworkman.com.

Born and raised in Alberta, Workman has been married for over 25 years and has one son.

Please visit P.D. Workman at pdworkman.com to see what else she is working on, to join her mailing list, and to link to her social networks.

If you enjoyed this book, please take the time to recommend it to other purchasers with a review or star rating and share it with your friends!

facebook.com/pdworkmanauthor

twitter.com/pdworkmanauthor

instagram.com/pdworkmanauthor

amazon.com/author/pdworkman

bookbub.com/authors/p-d-workman

goodreads.com/pdworkman

linkedin.com/in/pdworkman

pinterest.com/pdworkmanauthor

youtube.com/pdworkman